D1176334

# SING FOR US

# SING FOR US

STEVEN WISE

LAKE UNION
PUBLISHING

This is a work of fiction. Names, characters, organizations, places, events, and incidents are either products of the author's imagination or are used fictitiously.

Text copyright © 2015 Steven Wise

All rights reserved.

No part of this book may be reproduced, or stored in a retrieval system, or transmitted in any form or by any means, electronic, mechanical, photocopying, recording, or otherwise, without express written permission of the publisher.

Published by Lake Union Publishing, Seattle

www.apub.com

Amazon, the Amazon logo, and Lake Union Publishing are trademarks of Amazon.com, Inc., or its affiliates.

ISBN-13: 9781477829912
ISBN-10: 1477829911

Cover design by Mumtaz Mustafa

Library of Congress Control Number: 2014921616

Printed in the United States of America

*In honor of Phoebe Pember, who, for a time, in a place called Chimborazo, held at bay the Angel of Death.*

# PROLOGUE

*Sunset, October 28, 1864—Boydton Plank Road, Petersburg, Virginia*

The old man drove the wagon over a rise on the rutted road for which men had just died. He squinted against the slanting rays of sunlight and tipped down his hat. In his right coat pocket he carried two small squares of cloth, knowing he would soon have need of them. Clusters of dark objects ahead first appeared to the old man as scattered cordwood, and somewhere in his chest he allowed the worthless hope to grow— maybe this time, just this once, they would be chunks of wood rather than men. He listened to the rumbling wheels beneath him as they mingled with those of the wagons trailing behind, heard it as an old song, a rueful chorus that would not fade away. The evening air was listless and still, without energy to clear the acrid smoke that lingered like a high, thin fog. The old man felt the childish wish slip from his chest, saw clearly the shapes of men, strewn randomly in the colorless grass of late autumn. It was always the same—some men were already a part of the earth, needed only to be straightened a bit and lowered a couple of feet. It was for the others that the old man came. He came for the men who writhed in the grass and uttered sounds that were the stuff of nightmares.

He pulled back on the reins as he guided the wagon off the road and into the grass. The gray mare halted, tossed her head from side to side, uneasy with the smell of blood and the guttural cries. Other helpers shuffled forward and began to sort through the quick and the dead. The old man sat rigidly on his wagon seat, stared at the mare's ears, assigned to himself the task of counting the number of times that they twitched. Sometimes, as he waited for his loads, he would attempt to identify shapes in the mottled coat of the horse, as he had with nighttime clouds in childhood when the moon was bright and clear, filled with offerings for the imagination. He did not consider his inattention to the necessary work uncaring; he had in truth once cared so much that he would wake in the long hours past midnight on a sweat-stained mattress, see again the grim sum of it all. But no more. There had been too many wagonloads, too many screams of agony.

He felt the slight movement of the wagon bed as the first soldier was laid on the hard wood and half dragged to the rear of the bed just behind his seat. The soldier's cries were muffled, shoved against the back of his teeth, but the old man knew that very soon other men whose pain was greater would be loaded, and that as the wagon bumped over the uneven road, they would all release their cries. He reached into his pocket, located the cloth squares, and put them into his mouth until they were moist. With his fingertips, he rolled them into small wads and stuffed them securely into his ears. The long ears of the mare twitched again, and the old man said to himself, "That's six."

Thirty feet from the wagon, a wiry little man squatted beside a wounded soldier, his ear held close to the gaping mouth. With a single shake of his head, the wiry man looked at his heavyset companion, who knelt on the opposite side of the fallen soldier. The bigger man's features were contorted thoughtfully, as if he were contemplating a move on a checkerboard. He pushed up the short brim of his hat and asked, "He's a goner, huh?"

"Closer to the next life than this'n, Lester. Ain't no use wastin' space."

Both men stood and began to walk toward a soldier with a wild, black beard whose back rested against the trunk of a hickory tree. He made no sound, following the approach of the two men with steady dark eyes. His left hand rested atop a revolver in his lap. His right hand grasped the belt he had tied just above the stub of his right leg.

The wiry man lowered himself to his haunches, studied the white bone, the oozing flesh. "Damn them cannonballs. Got you clean, didn't it?"

"Saw it comin' . . . looked lazy, bouncin' along. Fooled me. Thought I had a second or so."

"You ready to go to the wagon?"

"Ain't lookin' forward to it, but I reckon I oughter."

The two men wiggled their arms under him and carried him to the wagon bed. They sat him down on the only remaining space, near the sideboard. Whimpers and moans arose from the wagon bed, and the two men did not wish to tarry. The wiry man slapped the side of the wagon. "You got a load, old pard."

The old man stared straight ahead, unmoving. The wiry man walked to the side of the seat, tapped him on the leg. The old man jumped and looked down. "Said you got a load," the wiry man repeated. "Move 'em out."

With a sudden lurch, the wagon moved forward and made a tight turn back onto the road. A cacophony of agony arose from the bed, growing louder as the wagon rolled away. The two men turned quickly and walked in the opposite direction until the doleful sounds had faded into the dusk. They stopped beside three bodies arranged shoulder to shoulder, unable to just walk past.

The big man glanced down at the still forms. "Reckon they might be the lucky ones, considerin' where them boys in the wagons are headed."

"Ain't so sure, Lester. They're headed to Chimborazo."

# CHAPTER ONE

*Five days later—Chimborazo Hospital, Richmond, Virginia*

The tip of the man's tongue darted from his mouth into the thicket of black beard, probing deeply into the stained corners where he hoped to locate a reminder of the juicy plug he had been working on when the solid-shot cannonball neatly snipped off his right leg just below the knee. The memory of the instant in which he was flipped upside down in a pink mist was a fuzzy blur, mysteriously recorded on the insides of his eyelids, and the man was careful to blink quickly. Now, with the passing of each minute, he became increasingly irritated at the lack of a necessity as simple as tobacco in the famous Chimborazo Hospital, in the very capital of the Confederacy, no less.

Crump turned back to the man in the bed next to his—the man with two leg stumps hidden beneath the clinging wet bandages—and picked up where he'd left off. "A man with one stump-leg's got a chance to make a life for hisself, I reckon. That is if'n he's got a decent trade to ply."

The man's solemn features betrayed no acknowledgement of the voice reaching across the narrow aisle separating the two low beds.

"I'm more'n a tolerable farrier, if'n I do say so myself. Reckon I can get me a good peg leg and still deal with the horses after the war, make a go of it." He glanced sidelong at the void under the other man's bandages. "Well, least you got good, low stumps. They might fix you somethin' like feet—good hickory squares with little wheels maybe, huh? Reckon they could do somethin' like that."

The words came softly, without rancor, the weariness palpable: "From what I have witnessed, sir, there will not be enough horses left alive in the South to afford you opportunity to ply your trade."

The black beard did not move for several seconds, then twitched three times in rapid succession. "Well, no sirree, I don't believe that for a minute. The blue boys ain't gonna kill all of us, and they ain't gonna kill all the horses neither, no sirree."

"What is your name, sir?"

"Rector Crump it is, Sergeant Rector Crump. Come up with General Henry Heth's division, fine boys all. I give up this leg holdin' the Boydton Plank Road with them boys. Not far from here, matter of fact. You?"

"Pollard. Granville Pollard."

Crump waited for the unit identification and rank, but after a clumsy silence of several seconds, realized that he would be forced to inquire. "Well . . . who was it you fought with, Pollard? And I don't believe you said your rank neither."

Pollard allowed the weight of his head to press full force into the pillow propped at the base of his neck, accepted the prickle of the straw poking through the coarse cloth. Despite the chill seeping through the plank wall behind him, the sheen of perspiration on his brow matted the sandy locks of hair, and he reached up and slowly pushed aside the moisture and the tangle. The weariness and the pain were opposite forces in his brain, and he concentrated on the weariness, willing it to grow and envelop the pain for a time, but Crump snorted impatiently, breaking his concentration. Pollard spoke in what he perceived to be a strong voice, but it was little more than a strained whisper.

"I suspect most of the men I fought with are dead, or praying to be. And since my war is finished . . . I am of no rank."

"I cain't abide such talk, Pollard. I don't 'spect my war will be over till they toss dirt on my dead ass. What's more, if'n I can talk 'em into a cavalry assignment, I mean to carry on from horseback."

Crump nodded in satisfaction at the sound of his statement. The fact that Pollard did not respond to it was of no concern. He would take up the matter with him again after he had time to recuperate a bit. The man had just lost his feet to a sawbones who likely was little more than a glorified butcher, probably in a barn or a cold tent at the edge of the battlefield. Yes, he would be granted rest for now. One day soon he would return to his senses and talk like a decent Confederate soldier.

Crump rolled away from the sleeping man and faced the dying man sprawled on the bed to his left. He had not moved more than a few inches during the last two days. The skin of his forehead was little more than white paper, and Crump had the eerie feeling that if he stared at the skin long enough, he would see the little spidery lines like those on the skulls he had studied on the battlefield. The matron and the toddling soldier-nurses had done their best to comfort the boy— Crump figured him for maybe twenty—but now even the attentive matron had evidently decided to waste no more time with him.

He shifted his weight away from the sorry sight, looked about the room that had become his temporary home. The ward was about thirty feet wide and sixty feet long, and housed, by Crump's rough count, forty patients. The matron claimed that there were one hundred and fifty of the ward buildings comprising Chimborazo. He huffed a little laugh; the hospital ward was, like its inhabitants, a sorry sight—plank walls and a ceiling constructed of inferior lumber, as was the floor. Crump had spied two nearby holes in the floor large enough for the rats to squeeze through. The matron and his fellow patients assured him after the first night that all efforts to plug the rat holes would prove futile. A chill passed up his spine with the thought; the rats were a menace beyond sound reason, and though he chastised himself at least once a day, he could not shake his fear of the bold creatures that ventured out with the darkness. Soon, the lamps would be turned very low and the rats would come; it was a fact of Rector Crump's temporary life.

Two hours later, musical sounds drifted toward Crump, who blinked hard against the twilight and attempted to sort reality from dreams. The sounds were not from his dreams, but from Pollard's. Crump turned his head and squinted at the dim profile, studied the small twitches that accompanied each note of a melody that Crump could not identify. There were no words sung, just the haunting, beautiful melody, hummed low and sweet by the dreaming soldier, and Crump hoped that the music of his footless companion would last a very long time, hoped that it would grow loud enough to cover the sound of the rat scratching in the corner of the room.

A slender woman stood in the shadows, listening to the melody rise from the tortured man whose name she did not know. She had heard his music the previous night, after the delirious man was clumsily carried to his bed from the rickety wagon that had been pressed into service as an ambulance. Letha Bartlett had dressed more stumps than she cared to remember—hundreds of oozing, ragged reminders of arms and legs—but none so poorly fashioned as the two she tended last night. She shuddered involuntarily at the memory, amazed that she was yet capable of such a reaction in a room with floors bearing the bloodstains of three-and-one-half years of war.

She moved closer to his bed, blocking out the snores and groans of the other men in her ward. It had come as a surprise when, only an hour before, she thought she heard the man murmuring replies to Sergeant Crump's yammering, but he had lapsed back into unconsciousness before she could work her way down to them. Two more silent steps placed her near the foot of his bed now. She folded her arms, pulling the shawl tightly around her as she studied his face in the faint light. The features were more interesting than handsome. No doubt the lines of his face were once rounded and well formed, but now the cheekbones rode high and too close to the skin. His nose was short and straight, pointing to a full moustache that drooped at the ends and covered most of his upper lip. He wore his hair unusually short, trimmed behind his ears and without sideburns. She put his age at more than twenty years but less than twenty-five, and somewhere inside her the fact that she was thirty-two flitted past like an irritating insect, too quickly gone to trifle with.

The heavy moustache rose and fell with the passing of each soft tenor note. It was a melody Letha Bartlett had never before heard, and this was a great puzzlement to the woman whose love for music was as much a part of her as lacy gowns and the aroma of azaleas on cottony spring air. The notes grew faint and a shudder passed through his thin body, rippling down from his shoulders and into his legs. Letha reached down and tucked the covers closer to his body. Within a month they would all need thicker covers, for then the wind would come from the northwest and whine through the cracks in the walls, poking like icy fingers.

A low voice came from behind her, three beds down the row, and she turned toward the sound. "I'm needin' a drink of water, ma'am; could you fetch me one?"

Before she could answer, Nathan Fisher pushed up from his bed on the opposite side of the aisle. "Ma'am, I'll tend to him so's you can make sure the new one's all right."

Letha smiled at the boy, shook her head. "No, Nathan. It's kind of you to offer, but the new patient is asleep. I'll get the water."

She quickly returned with a cup of water and gathered the pillow behind the man's head, gently holding him up while he sipped. Satisfied, he drew the back of his hand across his lips. "Much obliged."

"Not at all, sir. Are you warm enough?"

"Reckon I am. But from the looks of these here walls, I hope I ain't layin' here come winter."

She remembered his leg wound—a rifle ball had passed through his calf muscle, the bone untouched—and she knew that he would not remain in Chimborazo until winter, knew that he would again sleep on the cold ground with his unit. "I should think you would enjoy your small comforts here for now, sir. Take a day at a time."

The man rolled his head away from her, pulled the blanket to his chin. "That's sound advice."

Letha walked to the side of Nathan Fisher's bed, smiled down at him. "You're getting frisky, Nathan. That is a good sign."

"Yes, ma'am, I can fairly fly on the crutches now."

"Well, let's not fly too fast just yet. The surgeons want to make sure the bone has completely mended before you get really active."

"I know, but I can't soldier no more. Might as well help a little around here."

"It is appreciated, Nathan, rest assured. Just don't overdo, all right?"

"All right." He nodded in the direction of Pollard's bed. "That new one can sure hum a tune, can't he?"

"Indeed."

She reached down and patted his shoulder, then walked to the kitchen. There, a barefoot soldier sat slumped in a chair, his chin resting on his chest. Letha smiled at the sight of the male ward nurse and laughed a tiny, mirthless laugh under her breath—the slightly wounded tending the severely wounded, but it could be no other way. A common annoyance was the fact that about the time the makeshift nurses learned to be of real use, they were declared fit for duty and sent back to the field. Letha pulled a chair from the small table and plopped down, resting her hands in her lap. The weariness caught up with her, tugged at her shoulders and arms like powerful invisible hands.

She looked down the long aisle between the rows of beds, focused on the murky spot that hid the winsome face of Nathan Fisher. Letha was certain that the boy who claimed to be eighteen was actually closer to sixteen, if that. Some of the older soldiers would from time to time tease him about the "peach fuzz" that lined his cheek and jawline. His features were delicate, nearly feminine—great, hazel eyes deep-set under full dark brows that matched his wavy hair, and straight nose, perfectly formed above a smallish mouth that seemed always to seek the curvature of a smile. For Letha, he was the personification of the son who should have known her nurture, the son who should have been given to her and the fine husband who had succumbed to the wet rattle in his chest eight years past. But Nathan was in truth much more than a surrogate son to her, and she was happy to share him. He was a son to the older soldiers, a little brother to others, and simply a brother to the other youngsters. Sooner or later, and almost always sooner, the others came to like him a great deal—love him, really—though Letha knew that they would never openly admit such a thing. So be it. Let them love him in silence.

He was a gift from God, Letha felt certain, at least one human treasure saved from the death angel. That he now lived, nearly fully recovered, was a miracle of escape from the knife and saw. He had taken a piece of shrapnel high on the thigh, near his hip, the jagged piece of steel breaking his femur before coming to rest just under the skin. The field surgeon who first tended him was preparing to attempt the risky amputation despite the location of the wound, so sure was he that the operation was the boy's only hope of life. But Nathan Fisher told Letha of another surgeon who arrived on the scene, even as the assistants held the boy down on the crude operating table. Nathan remembered only three things about the man—his blood-covered hands and forearms, dirty red and huge; the long black beard that grew wild and high on his cheeks; and the words of Nathan's salvation. He knew that he would always remember the words that growled from the middle of the fierce beard: "No, boys, a higher power than ours will decide this one. Lay him aside."

And now, eight months later, the broken bone had somehow slipped together and a ligature had lapped itself over the once-separated parts. The healing was not without price; the outward growth of the mending band had shortened the length of the wounded leg by a full two inches. When she allowed the thought to penetrate her brain, the vision pained Letha: Someday, after the crutches, young Nathan would walk with the horribly rolling gait of a crippled old man. But if he himself had seen this sad specter looming in his future, no one could know, for he was unremittingly cheerful, uncomplaining, and helpful to his fellows. A jewel saved from the rubble of war.

Letha looked away from his bed, closed her eyes, and in the silence felt no remorse as she contemplated the relative worth of human beings.

# CHAPTER TWO

The world returned to Granville Pollard in muted shades of morning gray, and with the gray came the pain. It was as if his feet were yet a part of him, laid side by side on an anvil and methodically rapped with a blacksmith's hammer in perfect time with the beats of his heart. He clenched his teeth, blinked slowly at the human form hovering above him until the form became the fuzzy image of a woman with something cradled in her hands.

"Wake slowly, sir. We are never in a hurry to wake here."

She knelt beside the bed and held a tin cup near his head, allowing the aroma of the warm liquid to waft upward. "I have some fine broth for you." She nodded knowingly. "It is laced with a good ration of spirits for your pain, I might add."

Pollard turned his head and strained to focus on her face. Despite the pain, or perhaps because of it—he could not be certain—he hoped that her features would be a match for the soothing tone of her voice. Hair the color of chestnuts was pulled into a functional bun atop her head, but enough airy strands escaped to frame her features. For Pollard, it was a face made for an oval frame—wide-set green eyes and little more than a hint of a nose, lips full and nearly pouting, even now as they formed a careful smile. Her slender neck disappeared into the high white collar of a pink dress that seemed at once ill-suited to the dreary environs and yet a perfect adornment for the woman.

"Thank you," he said, attempting to raise his head from the pillow.

The warm touch of her hand at the base of his neck was marvelous, stunning, and Pollard nearly recoiled from it, so foreign was the memory of feminine flesh—Lucy's flesh, soft and scented and white in the Charleston moonlight that spilled onto the veranda. And with the memory of her flesh came the lilting voice—teasing, pleading, toying with him as well as with the revelers surrounding them. *"Oh, sing for us now, Granville. Sing us the song you wrote just for me. Oh, sing . . . sing now . . ."*

"Are you all right, sir?"

He blinked at her, allowed the lovely face to replace the memory. "I . . . I am sorry, ma'am." He nodded toward the cup. The dark hot liquid was awful and wonderful, a welcome fire descending to his belly.

"My name is Letha Bartlett. I am the matron of this ward."

Pollard posed the question with his eyes before he spoke. "Matron?"

"My duties are fairly diverse. I—"

Rector Crump's voice rolled toward them. "That means she totes everything from soup bowls to piss pots, Pollard. And sometimes there ain't much difference twixt the two." Crump laughed, deep and from his belly.

Letha shook her head, but did not appear offended as she looked at Pollard's neighbor. "Sergeant Crump is not given to delicate observations. Are you, Sergeant Crump?"

"No'm, it ain't my nature." He laughed again, a little wheeze curling up at the end. "I was mostly just teasin' though."

"Mostly? I'll take that much as a compliment to my soup, anyway."

Crump nodded, the slit of a smile parting his beard.

Letha held the cup for Pollard as he sipped again, and then she set it on the box that served for a table. She slipped her hand into the pocket of her dress and retrieved a small cloth-wrapped object and deftly tossed it onto Crump's chest before his hands could close around it. He looked at her quizzically for a moment before unwrapping his gift.

"I'm told it is at least average-quality tobacco," she said.

"Jerusalem! And to think for five days that I thought you was a mere woman. And here you prove to be a pure angel from on high!" He jammed the plug into the corner of his mouth, closed his eyes, and bit off a chew.

"Just one thing, Sergeant. We have enough messes to deal with around here, and . . ."

Crump raised a hand to silence her, eyes still closed. "If'n you ever see juice on anything 'cept my lips or beard, you feel free to cut a length off'n my good leg and beat me with it."

Letha shook her head again and smiled down at Pollard. "Well, sir. I know your last name, may I have the first?"

"Granville," Crump said wetly. "And he ain't much of a talker."

She shot a glance at him. "Sergeant Crump, the source of that tobacco could slip my memory."

Crump rolled his head toward her, opened his eyes. "I now fall silent, ma'am."

She looked back at Pollard, noticing the color that had returned to his face. "I'm pleased to meet you, Granville Pollard."

"Likewise," he said, looking up into her face, his smile feeble.

The morning sounds of the ward were subdued—the clinks of utensils on metal plates, the slow shuffles of the nurses and helpers as they tended the men, snippets of quiet conversation up and down the rows—muted sounds at the edge of war. Pollard heard them for the first time, could not reconcile the housed mutterings of bedded soldiers with the recent dissonance of the battlefield, could not appreciate the nearness of a beautiful woman, the touch of her hand. He lowered his gaze, a few inches at a time.

She wanted very much to mention the lovely humming, but swallowed her question and said instead, "We will all do our best to help you recover, Mr. Pollard. It is a long road, but many have traveled it."

He looked down at the flat bed cover, remembered how, as a child, he pretended his toes were the peaks of little white mountains and that he was omniscient, placing the mountains where he pleased. "I have seen many men travel roads without shoes, ma'am . . . but not without feet."

He dismissed her with the closing of his eyes, the turning away of his head.

Letha watched as Assistant Surgeon Avery Crawford peeled away the stained linen bandage that fell from the wounded man's side like layers of a rotten onion. He lowered himself to one knee and sniffed the wound, his nostrils flaring, and then he probed around the puffy edges of the entry hole of the rifle ball. The soldier flinched but said nothing, continued to stare at the ceiling.

Crawford patted him on the rib cage. "Roll on your side."

The surgeon removed the remainder of the bandage, repeated the sniffing and probing at the site of the exit hole, just above the man's buttock. It was a good wound, as wounds go. The ball had missed both kidney and intestines; absent the growth of gangrene, the man stood a reasonable chance at full recovery. Crawford used the edge of the bed for leverage, pushed up.

The soldier rolled his head toward Crawford. "How's it lookin', sir? Am I gonna do all right?"

Crawford nodded before he spoke, passed a hand over thinning gray hair. He was three years and hundreds of deathbeds beyond making definitive predictions to the wounded. "For now it appears to be a tolerable wound. I think you stand a fair chance of returning to your unit within three weeks or so."

The surgeon motioned to the barefoot male nurse to take some of the bandages from the basin cradled in Letha's arms. "Bind him back up, Henry."

Letha sorted through the stacks, attempting to locate the least soiled. There was not a bandage in the basin that had not been used a dozen times on various parts of many patients. Letha and her helpers had washed the strips of cloth with the scraps of soap remaining, but the soap was all but gone now, and she knew there would be precious little coming.

"They all look the same to me, ma'am."

"I suppose you're correct, Henry, but it makes me feel better to try." She extended a loosely wound strip, four inches in width. "Here."

She watched with Crawford as the nurse began to unwind the bandage. Crawford glanced down at the man's feet. "Henry, have you no shoes whatsoever?"

Henry looked down, raised and then lowered his grimy toes. "Well, sir, I was of a mind to save 'em till the bad of winter."

Crawford nodded in resignation, turned and began his stoop-shouldered shuffle toward the next bed. He paused at its foot, looked down at the blanket-covered figure upon it. Only the man's head protruded, features expressionless, blank eyes seeing nothing. Crawford stood motionless, his hands folded neatly in front of his body, as if paying respects in a funeral parlor. Letha had often discreetly studied the surgeon's profile and did so again. His body took the form of a six-foot comma, the greatest degree of the bend starting at his waist and arching forward to the top of his head. A month before, he had, for reasons unknown to Letha, commented on his posture. "I feel as though I have been walking into a strong wind for the past three years." He had said no more, turned from her and walked away. She could not remember ever having been caught staring at him, though in fact she possibly could have allowed her gaze to linger too long. No, she had assured herself, his comment was not born of an indiscretion—by her or anyone else. It was as if, in a darkly insightful moment, the weary man had seen himself as others saw him—bent beyond his years from the constant tending to men stretched on low beds or the ground.

He wore a full dark brown beard that stood in stark contrast to the wispy gray that swept behind his ears and to his collar. His nose was prominent—nearly Roman, in Letha's judgment—though his mouth was small, hidden by the whiskers, and seemed hardly to move when he spoke. During the thirty months they had worked together, Letha had never heard him raise his voice above a conversational tone, even at times when other voices rose out of control. He nodded his head twice in benediction over the dying man, then resumed his walk.

When he approached Nathan Fisher's bed, Crawford's beard creased with a smile as the boy rose on one elbow and lifted his other hand in a respectful greeting.

"Well, how is young Private Fisher getting on?"

"Near about dandy, sir, I reckon."

Crawford knelt. "Let's have a look, shall we?"

The surgeon examined the thick scar covering the wound, then held the boy's upper leg with both hands and tested the movement in several directions. He was disappointed with the outward growth of the healing bone, but it was a small price to pay for life itself, and a bipedal life at that. Crawford motioned toward the hip brace lying at the foot of the bed.

"Mrs. Bartlett's creation continues to be of aid, I trust."

"Yes, sir," he beamed, then glanced at Letha. "I can handle the crutches mighty fine now with it on."

She allowed a modest spurt of pride to well up in her chest. Though guided in the final phase of construction by Crawford, the idea for the brace was Letha's. After locating dozens of sheets of coarse brown paper, she pasted them together and baked them around the stovepipe in the kitchen. She correctly judged that the diameter of the pipe was a close match for Nathan's hip, and the boy soon began to enjoy the added support when he used his crutches. His already lofty opinion of Letha's healing powers rose to a near-embarrassing level, and more than once she had reminded him that it was little more than a curved section of homemade pasteboard, and that far greater aids awaited him in the months and years to come.

Crawford said, "You still need to exercise some judgment, but I believe you may now move about freely and continue to build your strength."

"Yes, sir. That's my plan."

Crawford stood, nodded a final time, shuffled across the aisle, and looked down at the wide face of Rector Crump.

"Sergeant—Crump, isn't it?"

"It is, sir."

Crawford pulled up the covers, loosened the bandages covering the puffy red stump, then tucked them back into place. "Things appear to be in order down here, Sergeant. Besides the pain, are you doing all right?"

Crump nodded and tongued the wad of tobacco deeply into his cheek. "Always suspected a shot-off leg would hurt some. The rations are a might scanty, but so long as this fine lady keeps me in a decent chaw, I figure to get better real soon. Be on horseback chasin' Yanks in a couple weeks."

Crawford snorted a laugh. "Well, I won't be the one standing in your way." He nodded toward the pair of crutches leaning against the wall. "You need to get up and around some now. Your stump will pound, but you need the exercise."

Crump glanced down the aisle separating the closely spaced beds, then raised a hand toward Henry, the nurse, who stood obediently behind Crawford. "Might be a good thing for this sturdy boy to guard my bad side till I get the hang of them things. If'n I was to topple, the damage to others could be consider'ble."

"I think Henry can manage that, Sergeant."

Letha stole a glance at Pollard's face as she and Crawford turned toward his bed. His eyes were half open, his head turned away from them. Crawford walked to the far side of the bed, lined himself up directly with Pollard's line of sight. The surgeon had no wish to again inspect the shoddy work performed on the stumps. Clearly, they would require the attention of the chief surgeon, Dr. James McCaw. If anyone could tidy up such a mess, it would be him. They had already spoken about the matter, and Crawford hoped that McCaw could find time and energy to tend to the wounded man before another day passed— another day during which he feared the growth of the foul monster gangrene. Crawford surmised that the man had lain on the battlefield for two or three days before someone found him and managed to get him to the makeshift field hospital and the piece of butchery that befell him.

Crawford spoke softly, not knowing if he was heard. "I have spoken with Dr. McCaw about your case and he will soon tend you, sir."

Pollard's opened his eyes slowly, allowed the silence to grow for several seconds before responding. "What, sir, remains to be tended?"

"I am not satisfied with the condition of your wounds. Better repairs must be made to ensure your proper healing."

Pollard focused on Crawford's eyes, held them as he spoke. "I doubt that I could survive another chopping that I could feel."

"No, no, I did not mean that. Just clean up the stumps, lessen the likelihood of . . . later trouble."

"Gangrene, you mean?"

"Yes." Crawford paused, then asked, "How long before you were found?"

Pollard moved his head upward, stared beyond the wood ceiling, did not know if he was willing to go back to it. He drew a jagged breath, swallowed against the queasiness sneaking up from his belly. "Somehow the fighting pushed a handful of us down toward a little ravine, all tangles and brush, and we could not fight our way back. They cut us off, fired down on us from high ground. It was essentially an execution. I had just finished reloading and had cocked the hammer when a ball smashed my right ankle. The force spun me down and as I struck the ground, my own weapon discharged into my left ankle." He shook his head, dredged up the rest of it. "I remember parts of two nights. Remember trying to scream, then growing too weak to scream. It was sometime during the next day when I was found."

Crawford raised a hand, kneaded the furrowed skin above his tangled eyebrows. "The thing now is for you to regain your strength. We will start by merely propping you higher, a bit each day, and getting some food in you. Mrs. Bartlett and her aides do a marvelous job, despite our meager stores."

Pollard looked at Letha for only a moment, nodded politely. "I am sure."

Crawford and Letha were two paces down the aisle when Crump's voice chased after them. "Perk him up, Doc. He sings a fine tune in fitful sleep and I want to hear him sing when he's awake."

Pollard jerked his head toward Crump and the sudden movement made him dizzy, caused him to close his eyes and sink his head into the pillow. Crawford's voice came at him from a long tunnel at first, then rose to a normal tone. ". . . yes . . . would be . . . something for all of us to look forward to."

Pollard carefully rotated his head away from Crump, waited for the silence to grow and chase them all away.

# CHAPTER THREE

Letha placed the three-inch square of cornbread beside the two short strips of greasy bacon. A large spoonful of greens completed the meal in the shallow tin plate. The sight of the bacon was displeasing to Letha; she preferred it nearly crispy, slipped alongside a couple of nice hen's eggs, fried hard, and a lovely dollop of apple butter for her biscuits. But such a plate was now just a strong memory, and she had long ago instructed the cook to take the bacon from the pan before it shriveled to absurd proportions. One day soon, she feared, there would be no bacon at all.

With the help of an orderly and Henry trudging behind her, Letha carried the final six plates to the end of the row of men. It was not happenstance that Letha walked toward Pollard's bed. Rector Crump had already pushed himself to a sitting position, his gaze fixed on the plates in Letha's hands. She extended her right hand and he eagerly accepted the little meal and began to eat immediately. Two weeks had passed since his arrival, and he no longer teased Letha about the meager portions. Crump was a large man and he now spent all of his waking hours in varying degrees of hunger, which had become a matter of grave concern for him. Crump's levity would never again be directed toward either the food or the woman who strove mightily to stretch the dwindling supply to its limits.

Letha turned to Pollard and handed him his plate. He had first smiled at her two days before, and although it was a nearly unrecognizable thin-lipped effort, it was real, and she returned it warmly. She looked for the smile as their eyes met, decided that it had grown yet another fraction.

"Good morning, Mr. Pollard."

"And to you, ma'am."

She folded her hands in front of her apron, glanced at the floor for a moment before looking back at him. "I'll be back in a bit . . . with a favor to ask of you."

Before Pollard had a chance to react, she turned toward Crump, who was already licking the bottom of his plate. He did so carefully, methodically, and without shame, savoring the last of the moisture from the greens, the tiny crumbs of cornbread clinging to the film of bacon grease.

"If promises from the supply people hold true, Sergeant Crump, we will do a little better next week."

Crump placed the plate on the edge of his bed, looked up at her. "Ain't no need to 'pologize for somethin' you cain't control."

Letha nodded as she picked up the plate and then walked quickly down the aisle.

"That's a damn fine little woman," Crump said. "If'n I didn't have one waitin' down home, I allow that I might ask her to marry me."

Pollard chewed thoughtfully on a bite of the rubbery bacon, concentrated on the thin meat strip rather than the fat. "Perhaps she has someone waiting at home as well."

Crump shook his head. "Naw. Henry says she was widowed a few years back. Her man got the consumption and his lungs frayed, he says."

Pollard made no reply, bit off a corner of the cornbread square, wondered what favor Letha would ask of him. Probably having to do with music, he decided. She had already dropped a couple of casual hints, but he had ignored her.

"Got yourself a woman somewhere, Pollard?" Crump asked.

The image came to Pollard in a fiery rush—auburn ringlets framing the white beauty of her face, full lips in an open smile, and then her lilac smell enveloping him. *"Sing, Granville . . . oh, sing for me . . ."*

"No."

Crump glanced sidelong at Pollard as the soft word hung in the close air. "Which kinda 'no' is that, Pollard? 'No,' there never was, or 'No,' there was, but ain't no more?" Crump paused for a moment. "Sounded like the last kinda 'no' to me."

Pollard laid the plate in his lap, rested his hands beside his legs. "Sergeant Crump, you have in me a captive audience, shall we say. And sometimes you—"

Crump knifed a hand through the air, cut him off. "You're right, altogether right, Pollard. I can be an irritatin' turd at times, Lord knows. But I was really tryin' to help here."

Pollard sighed. "How so, Sergeant Crump?"

"Well, I know you must be worried about your gone feet, and how your people will take it. Mind you, I've had a week longer than you to chew on such thinkin'. And any fool could hear the kinda 'no' you squeaked out there."

Pollard rolled his head tiredly on the pillow, lifted the fingers on one hand.

"Now, wait, dang it," Crump continued. "Hear me out. If'n I was sent home lookin' like a gunnysack with nothin' but a head, my Nelda would take me back with open arms. Good women are as strong as a mule's hind quarters 'bout things like that, I tell you."

Pollard had written the letter four days ago, spilled out the truth with pencil lead on coarse white paper, wrote words that he fervently hoped would sustain her, renew her love for Granville Pollard—musician and fallen soldier in her cause. Granville Pollard—whole man in spirit, if not body. Perhaps Crump, the crude philosopher, was correct. It would be wrong to jump to a sad conclusion in a place already filled with sadness.

Pollard turned his head toward Crump, who pilfered a guilty glance before looking away. "Sergeant Crump, I hope your reasoning is sound."

"Wife or sweetheart?"

"Sweetheart."

"What do they call her?"

"Down in Charleston they call her Lucy."

Pollard watched from the corner of his eye as Letha, followed closely by Henry, walked down the aisle toward him. She folded her hands at her waist, looked down at Pollard. "Now for that favor, sir."

Pollard nodded slightly, made no attempt to mask his quizzical expression.

"Henry and I would be honored if you would allow us to assist you on your first upright exercise." She paused, waited for the silent recoil that she knew would come. "Someday—fairly soon, I should think—Major Crawford will fashion your prostheses. In preparation for your legs to once again bear weight, it would serve you well if you began to move about in the upright position." She cocked her head to one side in a final query.

Pollard drew a quick breath, pushed back at the growing apprehension. "I'm not sure how you . . ."

Letha quickly stepped forward, motioned Henry to the opposite side of the bed. She discreetly looked away as Henry and Pollard lowered the blanket and arranged his bed clothing.

"All right, ma'am," Henry said.

She turned back and assisted Henry in positioning Pollard's legs over one side of the bed, then sat down beside him. "We'll rest here for a bit, until you're ready."

Though Pollard felt the dull pounding begin in his stumps and hoped that it would not increase, the thought of being lifted to his full height was suddenly very appealing. He waited for only a few seconds before nodding.

"I am a good deal stronger than I appear, Mr. Pollard," Letha said. "Put your arms on our shoulders, and we will brace ours behind your back as we lift you. Easy does it. Here we go."

With Pollard's stumps gliding a few inches above the floor between them, Letha and Henry took careful half steps until they reached the center of the aisle, then inched their strides longer as they moved forward. Letha glanced at Nathan Fisher, smiled as the boy reached for his hip brace and crutches and scrambled to the side of his bed. His voice sang down the long rows.

"Got Mr. Pollard up for the first time, boys! Don't let's let him walk alone." He fell in step behind Pollard, then stopped after a couple of steps and looked back over his shoulder at Crump. "Come on, Sergeant Crump, you need the practice."

Crump threw back his head. "Ha! I reckon you're right, boy." He swung his legs over the side of his bed, planted his foot on the floor, and pulled himself up on the crutches. "Damned if'n I've ever been in a crutchin' parade before."

Nathan laughed and moved to the foot of another bed. "Come on, John, I ain't seen you up in two days. Come on now."

By the time Pollard and his helpers reached the end of the aisle, six men trailed after them, the uneven rhythm of the crutches tapping loudly on the wooden floor.

Crump's voice boomed forward, a great wind chasing after Pollard. "Pollard, I'll swear, but a little tune would go mighty good with this here parade!"

Pollard fought the growing weakness in his arms and shoulders, concentrated on the lovely firmness locked into his right side, the spurts of exhilaration that passed through him. "Soon, Sergeant Crump. It will soon be time for a song."

For a moment, Pollard thought he might be imagining soprano humming, light and airy in his right ear, but the beautiful notes were Letha's. It was the melody to a song he knew well, a song called "When This Cruel War is Over."

Pollard listened closely as the moan of the wind around the corner of the building changed to a higher pitch, nearly musical despite its eeriness. Crump snored unevenly in fitful sleep, as did a dozen other of their comrades scattered up the rows. Pollard moved his head a couple of inches, aligned his vision so that the bright star peered through the crack in the roof like the faraway eye of God. He turned away from the star, squinted through the murky light down the long row, and saw Letha kneeling beside a bed, tending to one of the men, working with a bandage that covered most of his head. Pollard hoped the tireless woman would work her way toward him, so that he could thank her for reminding him of the grand feeling of uprightness, of seeing the world from six feet instead of two, of feeling like man.

She walked silently down the aisle, carefully avoiding making the slightest tap on the hard wood with her shoes, pausing for a moment alongside each bed, looking, listening, assuring herself that she had done what she could. When she neared his bed, Pollard raised his hand in greeting and spoke softly, just above a whisper as he motioned toward the foot of his bed. "Do you have a moment, ma'am?"

Letha nodded, sat down carefully on the edge of the bed. The tone of her voice was level with his, the beautiful lilt of the South full in it. "Yes, Mr. Pollard, but with a condition."

"And that would be?"

"That you would call me Letha."

He smiled. "Only when the ward sleeps?"

She raised her hands from her lap, opened her fingers like the petals of a flower. "Whenever you wish."

"So be it—with a condition."

"And that would be?"

"That you call me Granville whenever you wish."

"The bargain is struck."

"Good, good." He paused, sought her eyes. "I wish to thank you for this morning, for pushing me up from this bed. The self-pity was . . . taking hold, I suppose one could say."

"It was my duty, but also my pleasure, Granville. I have seen self-pity kill in this place as surely as the rifle ball. More than two years ago, I vowed that I would never again watch it fester without putting up a fight." She looked away, down the rows. "It is one way I can be a soldier with the rest of you."

"Indeed," he said and waited for her to turn back toward him. "Do you ever rest?"

"Yes, but I do not seem to require a great deal. I have access to a boarding house a few blocks away, but I usually prefer to take my rest in my quarters beside the kitchen. I have a bed there." She laughed softly. "Beside the whiskey barrel, and not by accident I might add, though I do not partake myself."

"I would imagine that would be a rather popular destination."

"Oh my, yes. I could tell you tales."

He laughed with her. "I am sure."

She tilted her head to one side. "You are not from the deep South, that is apparent, yet your speech hints at it from time to time. It puzzles and intrigues me."

"My speech pattern is something of a mongrel. My family is from Pennsylvania—Pittsburgh, to be exact. My father is a man of means, owns a foundry—perfectly appropriate, given that he is as much iron as flesh." He lifted a hand toward the bed to his left. "May well have fashioned the cannon that fired the ball through Crump's leg." He drew a long breath, shook his head against the pillow. "I spent the first eighteen years of my life there, and mostly blissful years they were, despite my father's . . . iron. The gift of music came early to me—I have no memory of life without it—and early on, he wished to send me to Charleston to study with a master musician, to find out how gifted I really was. But I resisted, actually begged him not to send me, and I succeeded until I was eighteen. And then he essentially shamed me into going. Told me of all those chest-puffing attributes that I must claim by virtue of my proud bloodline. The pride is his, not my mother's nor mine. My voice is hers alone." He rolled his head again and laughed mirthlessly. "And now I know he wishes that I had never entered the land of enchantment, never met a Southern woman. He will never forgive me. He said as much in the only letter he wrote me after I declared my intentions of joining the Confederacy. Mother wrote me two years ago—a painful, half-hearted thing it was—and I have heard no more from them or my three sisters."

"Surely you will write to them now, let them know of your wounds."

"I have drafted a letter that I suppose I will send."

"Oh, please send it, Granville, I urge you. Time changes us all."

"You do not know my father, but I know that I should, for Mother and my sisters, especially my baby sister, Catherine."

He stopped suddenly, surprised by the torrent of words, and felt a tiny sting of embarrassment. "I apologize. I am not quite sure where that came from."

"Any apology in order would be mine. It was I who probed into your past."

Pollard softened the word he then spoke, careful to cleanse it of any resentment, for there was none. "Why?"

She allowed the silence to grow. Was not afraid of it; in fact, she welcomed it. The next words would be chosen carefully; there would be no denigration of the other patients. All were worthy of her utmost concern, including the illiterate, the crude, the unlovely—she managed to bond with them all in some fashion. Each had shed his blood.

"I cannot help but become interested in all of you, each in your own way, but I must admit that it is a special pleasure to talk with someone of your background—your attention to language, your manner."

"The music?"

"That goes without saying."

"And yet you've only heard me humming feverishly, most surely in a nightmare."

"It was enough for now."

He waved his hand. "Enough of me. Tell me how a woman of culture came to labor in a place like this."

"I too come from a family of wealth, in Charlotte. My father owned a great deal of productive land, as did his father before him. I was the belle of many balls, married the man I was intended to marry, was well on my way to being a grand lady of the South." She waved her hand in theatrical fashion. "Ah, but the vicissitudes of life. A long struggle with tuberculosis took my husband a year before the outbreak of the war, and I moved back to be with my family. My father arranged for himself a colonelcy, which led him to the front of his troops at a bridge over a creek called Antietam. There, we were told in a splendidly written letter, he died gallantly. His gallantry meant little to Mother, only his loss. She may recover in time, though I doubt it."

She shook her head, had not meant to touch the subject of her mother, to deal with what Letha considered a personal failure in her attempts to restore the woman's spirit. "We seemed to do each other no good, for lack of a better way of putting it. Mother and daughter, double widows . . . too much pathos in a closed space. Doomed to fail." She lifted both hands. "As to how I came to call Chimborazo home, I must risk sounding self-important, but so be it."

"My acquaintance with no less than Mrs. George W. Randolph, wife of the Confederate secretary of war, brought me the offer to serve as matron here. I considered it for only two days before agreeing to serve, actually being naive enough to believe that I would be accepted here, if not with open arms, at least quietly. Oh my, what a silly notion. I was quickly put in my place in this world of men. I have fought my little battles with the small fry—assistant surgeons, contract surgeons of pitiful ability, supply officers—their numbers seem legion. And were it not for Dr. McCaw, whom I consider a saint on Earth, I would still be peering down the aisle from the doorway, afraid to set foot among the wounded. But his word is law around here, and he gave me a chance to prove myself." She looked directly into Pollard's eyes. "And I have."

"Indeed you have."

"Ma'am." The call came from a bed near the front of the ward, a quiet urgency to it that Letha recognized immediately, though Pollard did not.

Letha stood, glanced down the aisle, then looked back at Pollard. "I have never made a personal request of a patient until now."

"You need only ask."

"A song for tomorrow."

"Done."

He watched as she walked away, and could not hear the sound of her shoes.

# CHAPTER FOUR

An hour after breakfast, Rector Crump listened as the frail man in the next bed died. Crump had heard death come many times, heard the labored, wet rattle go silent, but never in a quiet place, and never without the smell of smoke in his nostrils. It was expected on the battlefield, as much a part of the landscape as scorched grass and bloody mud and trees pockmarked from rifle balls and shrapnel. But this death was different. He could not walk away with a curse and a promise for the Yanks on his lips, could not trust his sturdy legs under him as he marched away, feeling like an avenging angel. So it was that Crump studied the new corpse for several minutes, lost in captive thoughts, before he summoned Letha Bartlett.

"Ma'am, you need to come down here."

She walked quickly to the foot of Crump's bed, glanced at Pollard, then looked at Crump. "What is it, Sergeant?"

He did not look as he pointed to the bed next to the wall. "This'n here's done met his maker."

Letha knelt beside the man's bed, placed two fingers over his carotid artery, then reached down and flipped the covers back from the feet. Before she stood, she rolled the corpse to its back, squared the head on the pillow, and folded the hands. From her pocket she took a darning needle threaded with yarn and sewed together the toes of the socks. Then she pulled the blanket over the body and neatly tucked it in at the edges, so that when she was finished there was an immediate orderliness to the corpse, the semblance of honorable death.

Pollard watched, enraptured with Letha's economy of motion, the precise manner in which she rendered the death protocol. He wondered how many times she had performed the solemn ritual, knew that he would never ask. He too had witnessed death many times, and now the wild azaleas burning in the Wilderness crept toward him, their smoky beauty yet again threatening to fill his brain with the horrible scene, and only when he pushed his stumps against his bed and summoned the pain did the memory fade away.

Letha turned away from the deathbed and spoke to all those nearby who witnessed her actions. "His name was James Treadway, his age twenty-four, and his home was Alabama. May God rest his soul."

She took three steps, stopped in front of Pollard's bed, and said, "My request has changed slightly. May I pick out a hymn for you to sing after we have carried him away?"

"It would be my honor."

Within minutes, Henry and another male nurse, followed closely by Avery Crawford, walked up the aisle bearing the body on a stretcher. Some of the men sat on the sides of their beds, others only able to push higher on their pillows, and a few stood. One by one, as the little procession passed, they offered good-byes—a quiet word or two, the raising of a hand, a slow salute—and then James Treadway's body was gone.

Five minutes later, Letha walked down the aisle with a small brown hymnal in her hand, and when she reached Pollard's bed, she extended the open book to him. He looked down at the two pages, then back to Letha.

"Which one?"

"'Rock of Ages, Cleft for Me.'"

Pollard softly closed the hymnal and laid it on the side of his bed. He pushed himself higher against his pillow, filled his lungs with air, began to sing.

> Rock of ages, cleft for me, let me hide myself in thee;
> let the water and the blood, from thy wounded side
> which flowed . . .

The tenor voice was strong and vibrant, far more beautiful than Letha had imagined it would be, the words and syllables perfectly formed, the notes carried in stately three-four time. It was a voice like none other she had ever heard, and she had heard soloists of the highest quality and accompanists no less skilled in concert halls with grand acoustics. Pollard sang with chin uplifted, gaze fixed at a point beyond the far wall of the building.

When he had completed the first two verses, he stopped, and the sound of the last word sung lingered in the air like the note of a trumpet. He turned his head toward Letha and said, "Would you join me in the last verse?"

She was taken aback for a moment, struggled with an uneven breath. "If—if you wish."

Pollard smiled, then lifted his right hand in a timing motion and nodded once as a signal to begin.

> While I draw this fleeting breath, when mine eyes
> shall close in death,
> when I rise to worlds unknown, and behold thee on
> thy throne . . .

Crump sat motionless on his bed, mouth agape, as the two voices blended in harmony. It was a sound so beautiful that it was almost frightening, and he allowed that perhaps there did exist beings called angels, and that if in fact they did fly above the earth, they would sing like this from their high places.

"Good God a'mighty," he whispered to himself. "Good God a'miiiighty."

Rock of Ages, cleft for me, let me hide myself in thee.

Letha and Pollard held each other's gaze as the final note faded away, and both knew that something had passed between them, something airy and free. It was Letha who looked down first, suddenly aware of the many eyes trained on her. Crump stared unabashedly, as did the man to Pollard's right, holding himself up on one elbow. Letha turned her head carefully and saw Nathan Fisher leaning on his crutches two steps behind her, his features awash with emotion. Beyond him, on both sides of the aisle, men appeared as statues, frozen images on their beds, as if painted on a canvas. In the doorway at the end of aisle, Henry stood beside Avery Crawford, each peering with owl eyes, each with a hand on the frame.

Pollard saw her growing discomfort, and though part of him desired to prolong the spell, to remain a part of it for a very long time, he knew that he could not. "Thank you," he said, making certain that his voice carried far down the aisle. "I have never sung a duet with a finer partner."

Letha nodded to Pollard, then turned away and began walking up the aisle. She had taken only three steps when Nathan stopped her with an outstretched hand. She grasped his fingers with her own, squeezed gently. Nathan slowly shook his head. "I didn't know you could do that."

"Neither did I, Nathan."

She slipped her fingers free and resumed her walk. The sound of the first clap came from behind her, and she knew that it was Nathan. Immediately, the applause grew to a steady ripple, and when she passed through the doorway, the sound filled her ears.

Within seconds, silence again claimed the room. Crump could not will his eyes away from Pollard, who looked straight ahead, his face expressionless. Crump furrowed his brow, rolled the wad of tobacco in his cheek. He sought diligently for words to offer a proper compliment to the man who sang with a voice from the clouds, but he knew that whatever he said would be insufficient. Rector Crump did not know that many proud words.

Finally, he said, "Be damn near worth dyin' just to get sung over like that."

Two days passed and no one in the ward had mentioned the duet sung in James Treadway's memory. The lack of adequate food was nearing crisis levels, and the attention of the soldiers could not long be diverted, even by wondrous singing, from their growling stomachs. Letha and the steward collected every morsel available and stretched it with all of the imagination and skill they had acquired over the course of the war. Pans of cornbread were meticulously measured with lengths of string before being cut, bacon strips were halved and sometimes quartered, coffee was weakened to little more than dark water, and still they all harbored the unspoken fear that the worst was yet to come. If Union forces ever seized control of the railroad lines into Richmond, the end would come quickly. Just three days before, during a skirmish on the outskirts of the city, a small but determined Union force had succeeded in cutting the rail tracks, stranding the incoming wounded. When word of the skirmish reached Crump, he muttered a curse; three days to a severely wounded man was an eternity in pain.

Crump, more than anyone else except Nathan Fisher, longed to hear more singing, but he restrained himself, passing only idle conversation with both Pollard and Letha. This was due mainly to the fact that he neither saw nor overheard anything other than the normal routine pass between the two singers. Given the slightest opening, Crump would have pounced on the opportunity to suggest more music, albeit something on the lighter side. Henry and Letha took Pollard on two or three "footless" walks each day, and invariably the man's spirits rose for an hour or two after he was returned to his bed. It was following one of these walks that Crump managed to engage him in conversation, although Crump did most of the talking. Then, after Pollard had settled back into life on the bed, the conversational window closed.

From time to time, Crump watched from the corner of his eye as Pollard penciled the string of musical notes above and below the lines he had drawn on the coarse paper Letha had brought him, raising his head every few moments in what Crump knew to be silent hums. But the big man knew nothing of the strange markings; they were silent and irritatingly mysterious things, as were most words on a printed page for that matter, so he dreamed of food. He closed his eyes and remembered the wonderful brown look of fat hens roasting on the spit, remembered the aroma of beefsteak sizzling on a metal pan, the great fluffy biscuits with which he sopped the thick juices, could almost feel them in his fingers. But it always turned into self-torture; he knew that he must find other diversions. So it was that Sergeant Rector Crump—a fallen, ravenously hungry soldier—wondered how much longer he would have to tolerate Pollard's withholding of the greatest pleasure he had enjoyed since coming to Chimborazo.

He would later come to count as a great blessing the arrival of the man with no tongue as his new neighbor, the man who filled James Treadway's bed.

. . .

The long, curved shadow of Avery Crawford passed in front of Letha and Henry before the man himself entered the ward through the kitchen door. A gust of chill air ushered him into the small, dimly lit room, and he closed the door behind him and removed his hat and coat. Letha reached for the hat and coat and as he thanked her, and the cumbrous, sweet odor of whiskey filled her nostrils. On his hands she saw the dried blood, detected the slight tremor in the right hand. It was only nine o'clock, but Assistant Surgeon Avery Crawford was already deep into the horror of the arriving rail cars.

He slumped into a chair, locked his fingers in a tight knot at his waist. "How many empty beds have we in this ward?"

"Only two," Letha answered.

"They won't be for long. We've sorted through them all now . . . laid out the dead, which numbered twenty-one. The litter bearers are working this way. The night will be long." Eyes hollow and dark found Letha. "Might Henry draw me a small ration from the whiskey barrel?"

The request was a formality. Technically, the dispensing of whiskey was one of the assigned duties of the matron, but she could hardly deny an assistant surgeon—especially one who was about to begin labors that would possibly stretch until dawn. Still, he always asked; it was the proper thing to do.

"As you wish, sir," she said, nodding at Henry.

Henry returned with a tin cup half full of whiskey. With both hands extended, Crawford received it, his tongue peeking through tight lips. He stood, walked to the stove so that he could feel the heat radiate toward him, warm him from the outside as the fiery liquid warmed from the inside.

Letha said, "Henry, find what bandages you can and heat some water. I need a breath of cold air to stir me up."

He nodded, turned, and walked away. Letha glanced at Crawford, who carefully cradled the precious cup in both hands. For some, the whiskey served to bolster spirits, if only for a time, and though she did not entirely approve, she understood, neither condemned nor judged. Only once, when she came upon a drunken contract surgeon setting the wrong leg of a groaning man, did she lash out. Even then, there was no real indignation, only sorrow for the wounded man and anger tempered with pity for the chastised surgeon.

For Letha, the cold air sufficed, and she was thankful that winter was drawing near. In summer, the stifling heat, dank and thick from the ocean, held the odors of the wards close to the earth, and the flies swarmed—a relentless legion from which there was no refuge. Only now, deep into November, had the pestilence abated to a tolerable degree. So the cold winds cleansed the place, at least to a degree, and in their chill, Letha revived herself.

She closed the door behind her and walked several brisk paces. The clatter of horse hooves, wagon wheels, shouted orders, and groans carried to her, the lights from lanterns blinking like giant fireflies as they disappeared then quickly reappeared from behind the dark shapes of buildings and wagons. She allowed the cold to penetrate her body, fill her to the point of discomfort before she turned and saw the forlorn figure shuffling toward her.

He walked with an unsteady, tilted gait, some strides of normal length interspersed with choppy little steps, almost childlike. For a moment, Letha stood motionless, mesmerized by the strange sight, for as he drew within the thin light cast from the kitchen window, his head came into view. It was wrapped with a ragged and filthy assortment of rags, intertwined with no pattern, the loose ends flapping in the wind. Only a slit for his eyes and a tuft of hair poking from the top identified the head as human. Ten feet from Letha, he reached out with both hands, and she rushed to meet him, positioned one of his arms around her shoulders as she clasped her right arm behind his back. Without a word spoken, she guided him toward the door.

Letha stopped at the door and kicked the toe of her shoe against the wood. After three loud raps, Henry jerked the door open. "God a'mighty, ma'am, where'd you find that one?"

"That hardly matters, Henry. Help me get this man to a chair."

Together, they managed to seat the man at a small table near the door to her quarters. Letha retrieved a nearby lamp and positioned it on the corner as Crawford walked to meet them. He eyed the gruesome wad of bandages encasing the man's head, spoke softly to him. "May I proceed, sir?"

The man nodded, wrapped his fingers around the edge of the table for support, as if to signal his acquiescence to the coming ordeal.

Letha took the heated pan of water from Henry and set it between Crawford and the wounded man. She dropped a small chunk of Castile soap into the water and began to soak two soft sponges. Crawford found the end of one of the strips near the top of the soldier's head and carefully unwound it and tossed it onto the floor.

"Where is your wound, sir?"

The man pointed to his mouth, replaced his hand on the table exactly as it was before. Crawford located another end and repeated the unwinding process. After four more strips, the man's eyes and nose were uncovered and he blinked wearily, continued to look straight ahead. As Crawford began to peel away the next rag, he nodded to Letha. With a damp sponge, she moistened the dried blood until Crawford was able to pull away the bandage. The process was repeated until only the final piece of cloth covering his mouth remained. Letha soaked a fresh sponge and worked her way from one cheek to the other. When Crawford removed the bandage, she recoiled involuntarily before quickly recovering her composure.

"He has taken two balls sideways through the mouth, not an inch apart," Crawford said.

The lips, slightly parted, were hideously swollen, protruding like two greasy strips of red meat. From the opening seeped thickened blood and matter, and as Letha raised the sponge to his lips, she saw the first of the squirming maggots, white against the dark backdrop. The putrid odor claimed the air. Letha automatically sealed off her nose, began to breathe through her mouth.

Crawford placed one hand behind the soldier's head and with his other hand supported the man's chest. "I want you to lean forward until your lips are in the water, then cleanse your mouth. Just draw up a little water at a time and release it. Ready?"

With a nod, he lowered his head and sucked some of the soapy water into his mouth, then raised his head slightly and released the contents back into the cloudy water. With muffled, tinny sounds, the tooth fragments settled to the bottom of the shallow metal pan.

"Again," said Crawford. He looked up at Henry. "Fresh water, Henry."

Henry quickly replaced the fouled pan with a clean one.

"Again," Crawford ordered.

When the man finished and raised his head, Letha dabbed at his mouth with a clean sponge as Crawford began his inspection. He held the lamp close to his work, poking and probing with his forefinger and thumb as the man sat stoically, unmoving and silent. With quick tugs, he jerked free the two remaining front teeth that dangled loosely and tossed them into the pan. When he finished, Crawford set the lamp down, passed a hand through his stringy hair, looked into the man's eyes.

"You will be all right now, I suspect. You have the maggots to thank for the condition of your wounds, especially the remains of your tongue. They were the equivalent of hundreds of tiny scalpels." He paused, shook his head, marveled at the salutary entanglement of a man and lowly creatures. "We have whiskey for the pain and this fine lady will provide you nourishment through a quill for a time, and after that, chop your food so fine that all you will have to do is swallow."

Before Crawford could turn to walk away, the man's hand shot up from the table, mimicking the motions of writing. Henry saw what he was doing and located a scrap of paper and a pencil. The man's fingers slowly curled around the pencil and he began to write in large block letters.

## MY TONG HOW BAD AND TEEHT

Crawford sniffed and said, "Your tongue was severed; it is mostly gone. You have three jaw teeth remaining, two bottom and one top . . . unfortunately, on opposite sides. They are loose, but I believe that they will firm back up."

## WILL I TALK AGIN

"Perhaps in time, after a fashion. Let's not worry with that for now."

The man nodded, laid the pencil on the paper as Crawford walked away. Letha moved to his side, picked up the pencil, and put it back into his hand.

"My name is Mrs. Bartlett and this is Henry." She nodded toward the hulking figure beside her. "We would like to know your name, sir."

He looked up at her for a moment, then back to the paper.

## CLOYD ANDERSON AM THRSTY WANT TO LAY DOWN

"We have a place for you, Mr. Anderson. Let's help him down there now, Henry."

Before they helped him to his feet, Letha picked up a sponge and cleaned his mouth once again. "After we get you settled in, I will bring you some water and a quill."

"Which bed?" Henry asked.

"The end, on the left."

When they reached the bed, Letha helped remove Anderson's coat and tattered shoes, spoke a final assurance to him, then left as Henry began guiding him into bed. Two minutes later, Henry padded up the aisle and rejoined Letha in the kitchen. He poked around aimlessly for a couple of minutes, then turned toward her, waited for her to notice him.

"What is it, Henry?"

"Well—no disrespect, ma'am, you understand—but I was a-wonderin' why in the world you'd put a man with a shot-off tongue next to Sergeant Crump, seein' as how there was another empty bed across the way."

Letha lifted her head, cocked it to the side. "Because I think it might be mutually beneficial."

Henry sniffed needlessly. "I'd sure rather have the empty bed if it was me."

"But it's not you, is it?"

He locked eyes with her for a frozen moment. "No, it ain't, sure enough." He turned and walked away.

# CHAPTER FIVE

Rector Crump had said nothing during the time Letha and Henry assisted Cloyd Anderson in settling into bed. Even in the poor light, Crump could see that something was terribly wrong with the new man's face. As soon as he lay down on the straw mattress, his eyes closed and long sighs leaked from his mouth, but there was no rhythm to them and Crump concluded that he was awake. A shadow from the aisle crossed his vision and he turned his head away from the man, saw Letha holding a cup in each hand.

She placed one cup on the upturned box, and then sat on the edge of Anderson's bed, waited for him to open his eyes. "I have some water for you, and some broth as well."

Crump watched as she held the quill to the swollen lips. The man appeared to draw the water slowly, but he did not stop until the cup was empty. He nodded in thanks to Letha, pointed to the other cup. Again, slowly and steadily, he emptied the cup of broth. Letha said, "Very good, Mr. Anderson. Get some rest now. I'll have some soup for you in the morning."

She hooked a forefinger through the handle of each cup and stood. With a look at Crump, she said, "Sergeant Crump, your new neighbor is Cloyd Anderson. He has a serious mouth and tongue injury and is unable to talk for now."

"That'd make him about the equal of my other neighbor."

Letha glanced at Pollard. Pollard shook his head and said, "There is a time for talking and a time for contemplation, Sergeant Crump. For now, I require more of the latter."

"Well, I surely wouldn't want to mess with your requirements." Crump reached for his crutches. "Think I'll one-leg it over to sit a spell with young Fisher. He's more of a talker than a contemplater."

Letha stepped aside as Crump made his way past her. Pollard looked past Crump's empty bed at Anderson, who had already fallen asleep, his chest rising and falling with long breaths.

"How bad is his injury?"

Letha moved to the edge of Pollard's bed, sat down. "Among the most gruesome wounds I have seen—two balls through the mouth took out his teeth and most of his tongue. The Yankees cut the rail three days ago, so the wound had festered for at least that long." She paused, arched her eyebrows. "But the surgeon said that the maggots had done their work. Except for his speech, he should recover quickly."

"Ah, the maggot brigade. Friends of the wounded."

"The vagaries of war are strange indeed, Granville."

He nodded and asked, "May we talk later?"

Letha wondered why he bothered to ask the question; their night conversations had become a pleasurable routine. "Yes, the ward is full. We have no new arrivals to tend to. In a couple of hours, all right?"

"I look forward to it."


Pollard watched her as she walked up the aisle toward him, dark dress melding with the shadows, only the white flesh of her face captured by low lamplight. She paused at Fisher's bed, glanced down at the sleeping boy in motherly fashion, then moved to Pollard's bed and settled comfortably on the edge, near his waist.

"Has Mr. Anderson been resting well?"

"Not a sound."

"Good."

They allowed the silence to gather around them, shut out the low mutterings of the ward. It was something that each had learned early on about the other—this willingness to embrace silence. Letha studied Pollard's features openly, knew that it caused him no unease. For a week now, he had taken a keen interest in his grooming. His hair and moustache were always combed, his face and hands well scrubbed, the washing of his shirt and trousers requested every two days. Letha surmised that he was a man accustomed to being looked at, perhaps even stared at.

He turned his head, studied her features, and said, "I have been thinking about our duet."

"And I also."

"Did you believe me when I said that I had never sung with a finer partner?"

"No, but I still take it as a sweet compliment."

"One thing you must know about me is that I am not given to hyperbole. It was true."

Letha looked away, thankful for the dimness of the light as she felt the warm blush fill her cheeks. She adjusted her position on the bed, folded her hands in her lap. The words formed in her brain and she listened to them carefully, unsure if she was willing to accept the vulnerability that would come with their utterance.

Before she could decide, Pollard spoke again, his voice a whisper. "It was true."

"I . . . I must tell you that the hymn was one of the most wonderful moments of my life."

"And mine."

This assurance should have uplifted her, reinforced the grand compliment, but Letha felt immediate unease, and though for an instant part of her denied the reason, she could not banish the thought as she wished. It was possible, even probable, that what sounded like growing affection for her was only notes on a page well sung, nothing more than harmonious sounds, lovely though they were. It was probably true that if she were sixty years old, with slabs of fat draping her bones and curly black whiskers jutting from her chin, he would have said the same thing—if only the old fat woman could sing well.

"What is it?" he asked.

"Oh . . . nothing, Granville. I apologize for doubting you, that's all."

"Well, your apology is accepted." He reached out, absently patted the back of her hand.

"What will you do with your music after the war?"

He grew silent, instantly dark, and Letha regretted the question until he cleared his face, forced a little laugh. "Ah, you have struck on the growing question, Letha."

"I am sorry. I didn't intend to be meddlesome."

"No, no, not at all. Perhaps it would help to air it out, hear it spoken out loud." He pushed his head back on the pillow. "It will all be sorted out very soon when I receive a letter from my fiancée."

Letha knew of the lovely Lucy down in Charleston; word of the woman had drifted her way in snippets of conversation between Crump and Fisher. Despite the fact that Letha had dealt with the knowledge, shelved it as best she could, Pollard's mention of the woman touched her like the point of a knife.

"Her family was instrumental in seeing that my talents were given proper notice by all the correct people. My star was rising. And then"— he swung a hand toward his stumps—"the great alteration to Granville Pollard.

"The night I left for my unit was oh so grand—toasts and folly with Lincoln and boasts of a quick and stunning victory over the

Yankees. I am quite sure that Lucy and her family believed that my comrades and I would march north, shoot a few Yankees without so much as perspiring, and pick back up with our marvelous lives. I knew better, knew of the industrial might of the North. Was actually a part of it. But I marched gallantly away just the same." He paused, drew a cleansing breath. "I can see myself now from a clearer perspective." He gestured again at his stumps. "I marched away for her, more like an infatuated fool than a gallant soldier off to fight for a cause that even then was shrouded in mystery."

As if she were riding in a buggy pulled by trotting horses, the crossroad rushed toward Letha, but she knew which way she must turn, had decided even before Pollard stopped speaking. She straightened her back, composed herself, spoke in a soothing voice that masked her mixed emotions. "Surely your fiancée will realize that your career has not been affected. But, more than that, she will know that you are still *you*."

Pollard glanced down at his legs, stroked his moustache with a thumb and forefinger, and nodded. "That should not be too much to expect, should it?"

"Certainly not."

He looked up at her. "It is something of a relief to hear a woman's opinion on that, I must say. Thank you. So much."

She stood, said, "You're welcome," then smoothed her dress. "I have a few more things to attend to, and I am a bit weary, so . . ."

Pollard smiled. "An angel of mercy who tends wounds of the heart as well as the body. I admire you greatly."

She attempted a smile, but did not know if it formed properly. "It is a good thing that I have Sergeant Crump to balance you out, otherwise my head might swell. Goodnight."

. . .

With his hip brace firmly in place, Nathan Fisher wielded his crutches with the abandon of youth as he returned from his lap around the building. There had been no rain for over a week and the ground was firm, so Crawford had granted the boy's request to "get some decent air inside me." As he neared his bed, he saw Crump beckon to him with a hand motion.

"Come on over here, young pup. We got us a new neighbor."

Nathan crutched his way to the space between Crump and the new man, who was sitting on the edge of his bed penciling busily on a piece of paper. The paper was pressed on a smooth plank laid across his thighs, and Nathan noticed that the heavy block printing covered most of the paper. Crump motioned for Nathan to come closer, then waited until the new man stopped writing and looked up.

"Cloyd, this here is Nathan Fisher, a good boy."

The man laid the plank aside and stood, extending his right hand. Nathan leaned his weight on his right armpit and shook his hand. The swollen lips and seeping wounds on both sides of his face were not a distraction to Nathan, now a veteran of many months in the viewing of wounds. The new man was older than Pollard, but not by many years. Nathan painted a quick portrait of the man's face sans the wounds and judged that it was once a pleasant face. His green eyes were bright and inquisitive, showing no trace of pain or anxiety. His sandy hair was unruly, falling down on his forehead nearly to his eyebrows.

"Pleased to know you," Nathan said.

Anderson nodded, attempting to form the semblance of a smile as he first pointed to his own chest and then back to Nathan.

"Damnedest thing, what happened to Cloyd," Crump said. "Caught two balls through the mouth and gave 'bout all his teeth and tongue to the Cause, he did."

"Sorry to hear that," Nathan said quietly.

The man nodded a silent thank you, then sat back down.

Crump said, "He writes with a fair hand, pup, and I told him I'd serve as his mouthpiece." Crump tossed a glance toward Pollard. "Seein' as how I don't exercise my voice as much as I should."

To Crump's surprise, Pollard pushed himself up in his bed and swung his legs over the side so that he faced the three men. "If you are indeed his spokesman, Sergeant Crump, you would do well to introduce his last name as well as his first."

Crump narrowed his eyes at Pollard. "Thought I did."

"You did not."

Crump gestured grandly toward Pollard. "Well, then, let's see here. Private Cloyd Anderson, of the great state of Alabam', would you care to meet Granville Pollard, a soldier of unknown rank from an unknown land who speaks little and sings, like I've been tellin' you, more'n tolerable, but contemplates a lot." He paused, raised his chin majestically. "Will that do?"

"Quite nicely, Sergeant," Pollard said as he extended his hand toward Anderson.

Anderson popped to his feet and walked to shake hands with Pollard, who said, "I am pleased to make your acquaintance, sir."

Anderson tapped his chest and pointed a finger at Pollard. He looked back at Crump, cocked his head in a question. He pointed to his own mouth, then to Pollard as he made rippling up and down motions with his fingers and bobbed his head rhythmically. Crump did not understand his query.

"He sings like nothin' you ever heard before," Nathan said, reverently.

"Like a pure angel," Crump added, catching on.

Anderson spun on his heel, walked quickly to the ragged coat hanging on the wall peg. From a pocket, he pulled out a harmonica and wiped it slowly across the sleeve of his shirt as he made his way back to his bed. He picked up the pencil and began to write. When he was finished, he tapped the words and handed the paper to Crump.

"Says when his mouth gets better, he'll play while you sing, Pollard."

"I look forward to it, Mr. Anderson," Pollard said.

Crump looked at Nathan and then they both looked at Pollard, as if to assure themselves of what they had just heard.

"You promise?" Nathan asked.

"I promise, Nathan."

"Well, I'll be damned and soaked to the hocks in mud," said Crump. He addressed Anderson, but continued to look at Pollard. "Cloyd, I don't mean to hurt your feelin's, but from the looks of them lips, it might be a spell before we get to hear Pollard sing again. I might already be gone a-chasin' the Yanks on horseback." He paused, rearranged his chew of tobacco. "And that'd be a pity."

Pollard looked down and smiled inwardly, wondering for a moment how it was that he had come to feel such affection for the earthy man who possessed not the slightest trace of social grace. The answer came with the acrid smell of the battlefield, suddenly as clear in his nostrils as that horrible day in May when the screaming men and the wild azaleas together burned alive. The battlefield had melded them all together, changed them forever with hot rushes of agony—Crump and the boy and the tongueless soldier and the burning men and himself. And Letha, she too had been changed forever by the battlefields she had never trod. He waited as the solace sunk into his breast, accepted it as a gift from an unknowable source.

"I have a tune picked out just for you, Sergeant Crump. We shall all sing it this afternoon."

Anderson picked up his pencil and wrote several blocky words, then walked to Pollard and handed him the paper.

*MY TONG IS MOST GONE CAN I PLAY GOOD WHEN IT BETTER*

Pollard said, "It will not be exactly the same, but you will play well again."

Word about Pollard's promise to sing quickly spread through the ward. Once the realization sunk in for Crump, he trumpeted the happy news up and down the rows, thumping along steadily on his crutches, making sure that everyone was aware of the appointed time—"right after dinner vittles."

A half hour after the plates were cleared away, Crump sat on the edge of his bed, resisting the temptation to stare at Pollard, who was penciling notes and words on a piece of paper. By his own estimation, Crump had succeeded admirably in his effort not to pester, but his patience was fragmenting. He suddenly realized that his tobacco chew had dwindled to a mere speck and he swallowed it, swished his tongue from cheek to cheek. He began to tap his sock-covered foot on the floor, softly at first and then with increasing vigor. Pollard ignored him for a full minute as the tapping grew louder, but finally raised his head, a bemused look on his face.

"Are you thinking of a tune, Sergeant, or just attempting to further weaken the floor?"

"Ha! No, I wouldn't do nothin' to hurt the only thing between me and the rats." He shook his head. "I sleep bad enough as it is, just thinkin' about them lousy devils down there."

"That surprises me. I would have thought a rugged fellow such as yourself would pay no attention to small varmints."

Crump hung his head for a moment. "I know it ain't a natural thing, but I cain't help it." He narrowed his eyes at Pollard. "Some of 'em ain't so small."

"That's true enough, but—"

Crump cut him off. "Down here on the floor in my haversack is the prettiest little Colt Navy .36-caliber revolver you ever saw, loaded and ready for the fray. And if'n I was to spot one perched on my bed"—he cocked his head thoughtfully—"well, I figure I could get overcome and have to splatter him. Course, I'd be sure that my line of fire was clear of you boys."

Pollard searched the man's eyes, saw that there was no jest in them. "That's something of a comfort, I suppose—you being sure of your line of fire and all—but I imagine that if the rest of us took a vote, we would prefer that you just shoo the creature away."

"Pollard, I know what's reasonable as well as you, but I'm just sayin' that I might be overcome."

Pollard shook his head and opened his mouth to speak, but Crump again cut him off with a sweeping wave of his hand. "Damn it, Pollard, I don't want to talk about rats! I want to get on with the singin'." He pointed to the paper in Pollard's lap. "You a-workin' on our song there?"

Pollard shook his head. "No, not this one." He folded the paper in half, laid it aside. "You might have heard the one I'm thinking about. It's called 'Jine the Cavalry.'"

"Ha! They say old Jeb Stuart hisself thought that one up. I know a few of the words."

"Well then, gather all who care to join us."

Crump snatched his crutches, bounced up from his bed. "Cloyd, Nathan, you pup," he shouted. "Get the boys. It's time!"

Within two minutes, the space around and behind Pollard's and Crump's beds was filled with half of the ward, many of whom leaned on crutches. Pollard glanced from man to man, then back to Crump, who had reclaimed his seat on the edge of his bed.

"Sergeant Crump desires to join the cavalry one day soon. Let's sing 'Jine the Cavalry' for him. I know two verses; some of you may know the others."

He lifted his chin and filled his lungs with air, then began to sing.

> We're the boys who crossed the Potomicum,
> crossed the Potomicum, crossed the Potomicum!
> We're the boys who crossed the Potomicum,
> bully boys, hey! Bully boys, ho!

Pollard stopped, having not heard a single note from the onlookers. Wide eyes stared straight at him. One of the men on crutches, wearing a forage cap cocked at a jaunty angle, said, "I myself would not care to mess up your voice with mine."

A consenting murmur rippled through the loose half circle, punctuated with bobbing heads. Pollard said to them, "You boys must understand that I would very much enjoy blending my voice with yours." He began again, singing softly, urging with his eyes. He first heard the deep, chesty rumble of Crump's bass, then the high tenor of Nathan Fisher, tentative and halting. After the first line, others joined in, and finally the man in the forage cap added his voice. Pollard homed in on it—a decent baritone—and nodded to the man, who began to smile as he sang. They sang the two verses Pollard knew, but paused for only moment before a voice began another verse, and Pollard listened as the six or seven men who knew the words carried on without him. The man who began the new verse ended it with a loud "Again!" and Pollard and the others joined back in.

No one knew another verse, so they sang all three again, louder and with more spirit. When they finished, someone shouted, "'The Bonnie White Flag,'" and they began anew.

> The sword into the scabbard, the musket on the wall,
> the cannon from its blazing throat no more shall hurl
> the ball;
> from wives and babes and sweethearts no longer will

we roam,
for every gallant soldier boy shall seek his cherished
home.

Letha stood in the doorway to the kitchen and listened to the voices, now free from self-consciousness. Ten feet down the row to her right, a soldier clad in dingy long underwear rose unsteadily, began to shuffle toward the singers. She walked quickly to his side, clasped arms with him, and together they walked to the edge of the half circle. She knew the words, had hummed the tune on many occasions, and she softly lifted her voice with the men.

Our battle banners furled away no more shall greet
the eye,
nor beat of angry drums be heard, nor bugle's hostile
cry.

Pollard identified her voice before he was able to see her, turning his head to the sound, finding her eyes. He smiled at her as he sang, shut out the other voices from his ears, heard only hers. Several of the men nearest to her turned their heads toward her.

The blade no more be raised aloft in conflict fierce
and wild,
the bomb shall roll across the sward, the plaything of
a child.

Pollard raised his hand, waited for all the voices to fade into silence. He gestured toward Letha. "I believe that I have just heard a soprano among us."

With Pollard, the men looked to the edge of the gathering, with those nearest her backing a step away, leaving her and the pale-faced man locked side by side. He coughed from deep within his thin chest, the moist rattle portending the death that Letha knew would visit him before winter had gone, and she despised the sound as she held him tightly, waited for the paroxysm to run its course.

"Let's make a place for Charles, shall we?" she said.

The men near the foot of Pollard's bed moved back and allowed Letha to guide the man to the empty space. After she had settled him in, she walked back to the edge of the group. Before Pollard could speak again, Cloyd Anderson nudged his way forward and handed him a scrap of paper. Pollard looked up at him, but Anderson's eyes were locked on Letha. The note had been quickly scribbled, but its intent clear.

## YOU AN HER PLES BY YURSELFS

Pollard was amazed that Anderson had been able to identify the quality of her voice from his position behind Crump. Even with his own trained ear, Pollard had not picked her out that easily, for she had not sung to be noticed.

"Mr. Anderson has made a request that you join me in a duet. Do you know the last verse?" Pollard said.

"Yes, if it is agreeable to the boys."

Crump spoke up. "There ain't no fools among us."

Pollard extended his hand, touched Letha's fingers as she stepped to his side, then released them. "Ready now," he said, and they began in perfect time.

> The plow into the furrow then, the fields shall wave
> with grain,
> and smiling children to their schools all gladly go
> again.
> The church invites its grateful throng, and man's rude

striving cease,
while all across our noble land shall glow the light of
peace.

They held the final note until their voices faded into silence. The man with the forage cap now held it in his hands, his head slightly bowed. He watched as Letha leaned forward to help Charles to his feet and began to lead him back up the aisle. His fingers crept around the edges of the cap as he sought words to express his feelings.

"Like God loosed a brace of angels to sing for us down here."

Other men murmured their agreement, but it was Nathan Fisher who spoke the benediction. "Could be he did."

# CHAPTER SIX

Henry the soldier-nurse began to wear his shoes regularly during the second week of December. The first time he pulled them on he was surprised at the looseness of the fit. He had taken them from a Yankee corpse left on the battlefield the previous July, after having inspected the footwear on several bodies for quality and size. He knew that several pounds had sloughed from his body since coming to Chimborazo—the fit of his clothing told him as much—but the realization that even his feet had shrunk was a bothersome thought, and seemed to cause his belly to growl with hunger at ever-increasing intervals. Chimborazo had become a place of hunger, and although the knowledge that he would rejoin his unit in two days was a looming cloud, there was one bright exception—the boys in the field knew much about foraging for food.

Henry stood, hands dangling useless at his sides, awaiting instructions from Crawford, who was busy poking his forefinger into the foot wound of a soldier whom everyone called Hound. The man, whose real name was Lyle Patterson, was so nicknamed for his practice of bragging on the skill and tenacity of his coon hounds back in the mountains of North Carolina. Henry could not recall ever hearing

Patterson utter a word about any subject other than his foot wound or coon hunting.

The wound was of the curious sort. Patterson had taken either a ball or a piece of shrapnel to the instep of his left foot, leaving a gaping hole. Over the course of several weeks, the wound had sloughed away around the edges, leaving an ugly mass of flesh in the form of an island protruding from the center. The surgeons were reluctant to remove the lump for fear that it might be attached to the nerves of the foot, and had simply decided on a course of watchful waiting. And now, as if by magic, the lump had vanished overnight, the once grisly wound trimmed and leaking only minute amounts of blood.

Crawford finished his inspection and wiped his finger on the leg of his trousers. He motioned for Henry to wash the wound with the Castile soap and water. "I've never seen anything quite like this," Crawford said as he backed a step away.

"I'll swar if I ever felt a blamed thing the whole night long," Patterson said, looking up at Crawford from under wild bushy eyebrows. "What'cha reckon took place?"

"It was a rat, possibly accompanied by a friend, though I suspect only one, and he performed the surgery."

The dark eyes widened. "Jehoshaphat! A blamed rat done that?"

"Indeed. Scampered right up there and did what we were afraid to do."

"He didn't mess nothin' up, chewin' that knot away?"

"To the contrary, sir, I think that you stand a good chance to heal now."

"Jerusalem and Jehoshaphat!" Patterson flopped back on his pillow, cackling with glee, the thought of running with his hounds through the mountain forest filling his brain. Crawford turned and walked slowly up the aisle, with Henry trailing after him, wet cloths in both hands.

Across the aisle from Patterson, Nathan Fisher and Crump looked up from the card game spread over part of Crump's bed.

Crump reached down and drew a card from the stack, positioned it in his hand. "What you soundin' like a dyin' hen about over there, Hound?"

Patterson lowered the volume of his laughter and curled his leg toward his body so that he could closely study the handiwork. "Old Slim and Little Jennie better limber up their runnin' legs, for we's gonna run them mountains when I get back. And a blamed *rat* done it!"

Crump froze in place for a moment, then slowly laid his cards down on the blanket. He looked across the aisle at Patterson. "What sort of craziness you spoutin' over there, man?"

"Taint no craziness 'bout it. You can ask the sawbones yourself. A rat clumb up with me here last night and et my knot away."

Crump and Nathan reached for their crutches and made their way to Patterson's bed. Patterson pointed proudly to the clean wound. "What'cha think a that?"

Nathan leaned forward for a close inspection. "Slick as a whistle, sure enough." He took a sidelong glance at Crump. The big man's fear of rats was now well known throughout much of the ward.

Crump ignored the question and the comment, refused to look directly at the silly grin pasted on Patterson's face. He turned away, banged his way back to his bed and sat down. Pollard's empty bed added to his irritation; Crump very much desired to talk about something besides rats or hounds, and the man of music and learning was often able to fill his mind with pleasant thoughts. But he was off on a jaunt with the pretty matron, who, with Crawford's assistance, had fashioned a crude wooden prosthesis that allowed him to bear some of his weight on the better of his stumps. With a crutch supporting his right side and Letha locked to his left, Pollard was making clear headway at rejoining the upright world. Crump waited impatiently as the man and woman slowly clumped their way back down the aisle.

When they neared Patterson's bed, the rejoicing man called out to them. "Come lookee here, won'tcha. I been cured by a blamed rat!"

"Yes, Major Crawford told us of the good news a few moments ago, Mr. Patterson. Quite remarkable indeed," Letha said.

Patterson began to cackle again, softly and contentedly, his face inches from the cleaned wound. Nathan fell in step behind Letha and Pollard, stopping at his own bed; the card game was clearly finished.

Letha knelt, removed the wooden tube from Pollard's leg, and laid it under the bed. "Well, a good stroll it was. You gentlemen will excuse me; chores await."

Pollard settled comfortably against the propped pillow, felt Crump's troubled eyes peeking over the black beard. Pollard spread apart his hands, released them into his lap. "It does not mean that they get in everyone's bed, Sergeant."

Crump tilted his head. "Reckon not?"

"Certainly not. It was an open, bleeding wound, barely bandaged the last time I saw it. The rat merely followed its nose."

Crump glanced at the stocking covering his stump, found relief in the knowledge that the wound had not bled in a very long time. "That does make some sense, sure 'nuff."

"Yes, it certainly does." Pollard pointed a finger at Crump's haversack. "I trust that the sidearm will remain in there?"

"Should."

"Only 'should,' Sergeant?"

"One of the devils might get mixed up, jump the wrong dern bed. Cain't never tell about a thing like that."

"You are an obstinate man, Sergeant Crump."

"I take it that ain't a good thing to be, by your reckonin'?"

"Not in this case."

"Well, I am what I am, Pollard."

"Indeed."

With a forceful breath, Crump shoved the last of the rat thoughts away and looked at the two card hands lying face down. "Pup, you just gonna lay over there dreamin' about the fillies back home, or you gonna let me teach you to play cards like a real soldier?"

Nathan popped up from his bed, reached for his brace and crutches. "If I remember right, I was the one ahead."

"Just cause I let'cha, pup. We gonna get serious now. 'Fore I'm through with you, you'll be scratchin' your head and contemplatin' like Pollard does."

Pollard smiled.

Private Brady Ayden stood beside Henry in the corner of the kitchen, watching the nurse's fingers deftly wind the frayed bandage into a roll. Within the hour, Brady would become the new ward nurse, and the knowledge caused him neither anxiety nor contentment. It was simply the latest twist in a life that had for Brady become a gigantic unsolvable puzzle—a life that he believed God Himself had created for His own lofty entertainment. That the entertainment included such things as a man's entrails hanging from a tree branch in the form of a perfect "B"—a sight that had so mesmerized Brady that he had to be shamed away by no less than three of his friends—seemed no longer to matter a great deal. During the strange lifetime that now stretched from Shiloh to this place called Chimborazo, Brady Ayden doubted all things he once considered foundational. So now, three weeks after the chunk of humming metal had passed low on his forehead and gouged away his eyebrows along with a thin finger of flesh, Brady listened absently as the low drawl of his mentor expounded on the mysteries of rolling a bandage.

"They's usually one end bigger than t'other," Henry said. "And they like for you to start windin' the little end first so's the big end unwinds first when they cover up some mess on one of the boys."

Henry studied Brady's eyes for signs of understanding. One of the eyes wandered high and to the right, as if it had discovered a separate world of its own to view, and Henry yielded to the temptation of following it for a moment but was soon lost and returned his focus to the eye that seemed to look in his general direction. "That make sense to you?"

Brady nodded, flopped his hands away from his trousers. The angry scar replacing his eyebrows would mark him for life, but as the markings of war went, it was not among the more terrible identifications Henry had studied. A week's worth of brown stubble bristled along Brady's jaw line. It was a face of maybe twenty years, maybe thirty—it was difficult to know after they had been marked—that Henry had seen in a hundred variations at one time or another, and he knew that this one would soon fade from memory. Brady wore the remains of a buttonless, gray waist-length jacket, though the color was barely identifiable. The collar was missing, as if gnawed off by some large, dull-toothed creature. His trousers were a patchwork of browns and grays, whose tattered cuffs stopped three inches above the tops of shoes that did not match.

Henry waited a respectable time for a reply before continuing. "Anyhow, most of what you need to do they'll just tell you straight out. The matron's a real nice lady, ain't the least bit bothered by any grade of mess. The surgeon around here most is Major Crawford. Ain't a bad sort neither, 'cept he's dippin' in the whiskey barrel a mite often, you ask me."

Henry risked a little laugh, but Brady's expression did not change. Henry forgot which eye to look at for an instant, hoped that Brady did not notice. "Ain't much more to tell you, I reckon. I s'pect you ain't used to eatin' much. All the wards the same, huh?"

Brady nodded.

"There's some good boys in there," Henry said, motioning toward the rows of beds. "One of 'em can sing like nothin' you ever heard. And

Miz Bartlett, the matron, she can sing like an angel too." He shook his head. "You ought to hear 'em together."

Brady finally turned his head toward Henry, and for a moment Henry thought the man desired to say something, but the flicker in his good eye disappeared, if it ever existed at all.

Henry cocked his head. "Well, it's a good thing talkin' ain't a requirement for this here job." He paused, rubbed his nose. "Don't have much to say, do you?"

Just how he could be so absolutely certain, Henry could not fathom, but he knew that Brady entered into the separate world of the wandering eye when he finally said, "Did once. Don't no more."

Henry shambled down the aisle toward the beds at the end of the row, following the tentative sound of Cloyd Anderson blowing on his harmonica. Cloyd's lips were now clearly of the human variety, but one of the ball holes in his right cheek still leaked air when he blew too hard. So the notes were not full, but Henry judged that soon they would be worthy of a man's full attention. Pollard was busy, his tongue poked thoughtfully inside his cheek, no doubt drawing the little black grasshopper marks on his lined page, and Henry wondered if Cloyd's blowing was a hindrance. Crump and the boy sat on Crump's bed, cards fanned expertly in the hands of each player, and from the look of the older man's eyes, the boy was getting the best of it.

Henry came to a halt near the foot of Pollard's bed and stood motionless until all four of the men ceased their activity and looked at him. He reached up and pulled off his cap, held it with both hands in front of his thighs. He addressed them all, but looked at Pollard as he spoke.

"Goin' back to the boys out there now. Come to say so long."

He shuffled his feet, looked at the floor for a moment. "Feller named Brady's gonna take my place. He ain't got much to say, but he'll do what you tell him to."

Crump spoke first. "You get back out there, Henry; 'member there ain't no shame in findin' thick trees and big rocks to shoot from."

Henry nodded at Crump, then saw Cloyd hold up a hand in a farewell gesture. Nathan said, "Thanks for helping out, Henry. You take care now, hear?"

"I will."

Henry looked back at Pollard. "It was mighty nice hearin' you sing."

"Thank you very much. I am happy you enjoyed it." Pollard smiled from under his droopy moustache. "Don't try to win the war all by yourself, Henry."

"Don't plan to."

Henry turned slowly and walked back up the aisle, and each of the men left behind wondered if they were watching the walk of the doomed.

"I'll be derned if'n I can remember that boy's last name," Crump said.

"I never heard him say, best I remember," Nathan said. "He was just Henry."

Letha wrapped two squares of cornbread in a sheet of paper, each cut in half and filled with short strips of fried bacon. Henry was already shaking his head as she approached him, the wondrous gift extended toward him.

"No, ma'am, I ought not take that. Them hurt ones layin' in there hungry and all."

Letha lifted his right hand and placed the food in his palm, closed his fingers around it. "Henry, I do not remember a single instance when you argued with me about anything, do you?"

"No, ma'am."

She smiled at him, caused him to look away. "Well, sir, do not start now."

"It's mighty kind of you."

"Not at all. You are a soldier again and it is my honor to feed you, meager though it is."

"I'm mighty glad I got to hear you sing, ma'am. I told Mr. Pollard the same."

Letha studied the face that was once round and boyish and open; now it was longer, cheek and jawbones well defined. She peeked past the brown eyes, probed for signs of sadness or fear that she might attempt to rid him of before he departed. But the eyes were not burdened, so far as she could tell, and she patted his hand.

"It is good that you have at least a few happy memories to take with you from here."

He turned toward the door, stopped after he opened it, and said, "Things get too pressin' on me out there, I'll remember the singin'." Then he was gone.

Letha looked at the closed door for several seconds. Something was missing from the conversation, some small but irritating void hanging in the air. A busy hour passed before it dawned on her that she could not recall Henry's last name.

# CHAPTER SEVEN

The letter from Lucy Penders arrived buried in a motley assortment of envelopes delivered to Letha Bartlett's quarters by a runny-nosed man in a long frock coat and a wide-brimmed hat too large for his head. Letha fought the impulse to reach out and tilt the hat back so that the top of the man's ears would not protrude sideways, but it was apparent that the ears served as hanging pegs for the hat. She accepted the string-bound bundle and, with a nod of her head, dismissed the deliveryman, who snorted wetly against the back of his hand as he turned to leave.

Letha took the letters to her table, loosened the string, and began to sift through them. The handwriting ranged from crude block lettering to elegant cursive script, and it was the beauty of such a hand that attracted Letha's attention even before the flowing strokes that formed "Pvt. Granville Pollard" were seared into her brain. "The great answer," she whispered to herself—the inky markings on a piece of paper that represented a clearly defined fork in the road of life. Within minutes, the markings would send Granville Pollard down one of two paths. *They will also send you, Letha, they will also send you,* she thought. The thud of her heartbeat rose in her ears, and she registered not a hint of guilt for coveting Granville Pollard, for hoping that Lucy from

Charleston had proven unworthy and undeserving of his affection. *Is it not love, Letha? Why will you not say "love"?*

To calm her heart, Letha set about arranging the nine envelopes in the exact order that Brady Ayden would deliver them—down the left side of the aisle and then back up the right. Despite her concerted efforts to interest the spiritless man in learning the identities of the patients, she knew that he would have to call out most, if not all, of the names. But this too was good exercise—the simple utterance of words—for Letha considered Brady no less a patient than any of the bandaged men resting on beds. His real wounds were hidden in a place that she had not yet been able to identify. Now, in these leaden moments, she felt a peculiar thankfulness for Brady's needs. The fork in the road had appeared too suddenly, had popped up in front of her as she innocently walked around a blind curve. She would concentrate on Brady as best she could, attempt to draw his spirit from its hiding place, but the fork loomed.

He stood in the doorway to the storeroom, looking in her general direction, but she was unsure of the separate aim of the two eyes.

"Mr. Ayden, we have mail to deliver. Would you care to assist me?"

Brady shuffled to the table, closed his fingers around the neatly stacked envelopes.

"Let's see if you are able to match some of the faces with names. I will be right behind you. What do you say to that?"

Brady studied the name on the top envelope, did not look at Letha as he slowly shook his head. Letha said, "Cummings. Third bed on the left. Off we go."

She followed a couple of paces behind him, watched as he placed the envelope in the eagerly extended hand. "Much obliged," Cummings said, nodding his head at Letha rather than Brady. The reluctant postman took a halting step forward before turning to Letha, the next envelope pinched between his thumb and forefinger.

Letha shook her head, said softly, "No, sir. If you do not remember, you will have to call out the names."

Brady made an unintelligible sound in which Letha could not clearly identify irritation, though it was likely the case. But for now, it did not matter; ten steps ahead, she saw Pollard's reclining figure, then his face as it turned to look up the aisle. The sound of her heartbeat began to sneak back into her ears. In just a few moments, after Brady Ayden stammered out three more names, Pollard's envelope would be on top, and she would look at him—would *have* to look at him. She would make certain that Granville Pollard knew that he did not face the fork in the road alone.

She felt her feet move forward, heard Brady's faraway voice compete with the swishing in her ears, accepted the terrible risk in what she was about to do. The contents of the letter be damned. Without uttering a single word, without so much as parting her lips, she was going to tell Granville Pollard that she loved him unconditionally and without a hint of pity.

"Gran . . . vil . . . Po . . lerd."

Pollard reached out a hand, unable to utter a thank you.

For an instant, the dingy gray of Brady's jacket filled Letha's vision, then, like a soggy rain cloud pushed by the wind, it drifted away. She stood at the foot of Pollard's bed, saw the muscles of his jaw tighten as he fingered the envelope, watched as the tension grew in his frame, as if strong hands inside him were compressing a great spring. Slowly, the jaw muscles relaxed and the spring decompressed, allowing the vulnerability to leak from his features. To Letha, he suddenly seemed much more a boy than a man, almost like Nathan—open-faced and with eyes asking questions that could not easily be spoken. She stood silently, unyielding, allowed her presence to become a part of the moment. From behind her, Brady's voice spoke the name of Nathan Fisher, and it was then that Pollard looked up at her.

He said, "Well, the time has come."

He waited for her to respond, say something soothing, encouraging, as she always did. But she said nothing, only looked into his eyes, held them until he comprehended what she was doing. Stunned, Pollard looked down at the envelope, ran his fingers over the lettering, scratched furiously through the great inventory of words in his head. But the effort was futile, and he knew that even if he could suspend time and sort through each of them, he would never find the right words to acknowledge Letha's unspoken pledge.

When he looked up, Letha had already turned away and had almost caught up to Brady Ayden.

Pollard's mind reeled with the weight of it all. He should have seen what was happening, should not have been so selfishly lost in himself that he allowed this good woman—this angel of a woman—to—

*To what, Pollard? To love you?*

It was unmistakable—the yielding in her eyes, the flinging away of all consequences without knowing the contents of the letter.

*Dear God, Pollard, what have you done?*

Suddenly the weight of the envelope registered in his fingers, pressed against them like a square of lead, and he released it into his lap. He struggled to control his breathing, to slow the rise and fall of his chest. Only moments before he had rested in a peaceful and controlled scene, yet now it had become something strangely akin to battle— fear and doubt and confusion and dread of the unknown, all tangled together with the roaring in his ears. Only battle's horrific sights and the smells were missing.

He closed his eyes, pushed his hands into the straw mattress as if bracing himself against an oncoming charge of blue-clad troops. Slowly, he withdrew into a compartment in his brain, closed the door behind him. He had been there before; the white haven had served him well on many occasions. Beyond the door was snow, clean and cold, and he reached down with little mittened hands and scooped up tiny handfuls and tossed them into the air. The melodious laughter of his mother chased after him, sailed past him on the winter wind like a song, and he threw up his arms to encircle them, so beautiful were the notes.

The child plowed on through the snow toward the great circle of the frozen pond, the song of laughter sweeping him along until he stood on the high bank where brown tufts of grass poked from the whiteness. It was always here that his mother knelt behind him, her breath warm in his ear as she whispered her love for him. The child heard his name spoken, but something was wrong. It was his last name, and the voice was not his mother's.

"Pollard, you aw'right?"

Pollard opened his eyes and turned his head toward the sound and blinked Rector Crump into focus. "What—what did you say?"

"Had me worried there for a bit, Pollard. Didn't look like you could get your air."

"Yes. Well, I'm better now."

Crump glanced at the envelope in Pollard's lap; he had no doubt about the sender. He replayed the scene just past when Letha Bartlett stood far too long after the delivery of the letter. Before he had studied her face, Crump wrongly assumed that she was without clear purpose in her staring, even being a trifle rude. But the very thought of the matron being impolite caused him to further search her features, and it was then that he knew Nathan Fisher was correct. Crump had nearly scolded the boy when he first mentioned that there were sparks between the singers, but now he was glad that he had not. The only detail Rector Crump was unsure of was whether there were two sparks or just one.

"Ain't you goin' to look at your letter?"

Pollard cursed the fact that he could not rise on two good legs and discreetly retire to a solitary place. The knowledge of his incredible dependence on others struck him like a fist in the stomach. He had never dwelt on the fact before now; like most of the others, he was a severely wounded soldier, and dependence was a fact of life, not a choice. But now, with the confusing thoughts churning about in his head, he stifled a great urge to scream at Crump, to scream at all of them, though he knew he had no right.

It was then that Rector Crump did something that caused Pollard to feel a shame that would be a part of him for a very long time, for Pollard had always considered the underestimation of virtue in another to be a sin. "Cloyd," Crump said, "why don't you grab that music maker of yourn and come with me and the pup for a stroll around the lovely grounds of Chimborazo."

Pollard did not look up as the three men prepared to leave.

Crump continued. "Cloyd, I been thinkin' on it, and it seems to me that you could hold your thumb over that leak hole in your cheek. You ever think about tryin' that?"

Pollard listened as the crutches banged up the aisle, but still he did not look up. When the sound of Crump's deep voice faded from the ward, he slid his forefinger under the flap of the envelope and broke the seal. With the first glance he knew that it was not a lengthy letter, and when he pulled out a single page the dread began to creep forward on cat's paws. Without yet focusing upon the words, Pollard pinched his thumbs and forefingers along the folds until the page was flat. Then he looked down at the familiar script.

Dear Granville,
It was with the heaviest of hearts that I learned of your tragic loss on the glorious field of battle. Oh, how this war has proven to be cruel beyond our gravest imaginings. Who could have ever believed that it would extend through years—through years, Granville? Through a thousand days and nights, and with each dark night the minute changing of each life . . .

*No, Lucy; please do not say 'changing' like that.*
*Do not say that you have changed.*

. . . until now the sum of those nights causes me to wonder if my sanity holds. Oh, Granville, it is all so unfair, so terribly unfair. How else can one say it?

*Say what, Lucy? Oh, God, say what?*

You should take comfort in your great sacrifice for the Cause we hold so dear. I am certain that it will hold you . . .

*No, no . . . hold us, Lucy.*

. . . in good stead in the years ahead, and bolster you as you put your life back together. Oh, Granville, how different everything is here, how very different everything is now that war has ravaged our land.

*How different you are now, Granville. Poor cripple; wretched footless man.*

I take my only solace from your gallantry in battle and in your noble understanding of the way in which life will never be the same for any of us.

*It was too much to ask. Pollard, you fool. What would she do? Pull you through the streets of Charleston in a little wagon? Scoot you onto the dance floor on your stumps?*

I shall always remember . . . good times . . . wonderful . . .

Songs . . . about . . . the sound of . . . oh such . . .

. . . marvelous . . . tenor . . .

. . . shall always . . .   hold dear . . .

. . . part . . . always . . .   held . . .

. . . heart . . .

Pollard closed his eyes tightly, listened to the sound of the crumpling paper as his fingers drew it into his palm. Other sounds came to him—quiet groaning from somewhere in his chest—and he turned to face the emptiness of Crump's bed, did not care if anyone heard them.

Letha stood in the doorway to the kitchen, thankful for the strong wood frame that now bore most of her weight. For a moment, after she saw him curl into a pitiful ball and turn away, she thought her legs were failing her, and had it not been for the doorway, she might have sunk to the floor. She steadied herself still, not yet trusting her legs. Brady Ayden was walking slowly up the aisle, a huge tangle of bloody bandages in his hands. She drew a quick breath and managed only to turn sideways as he brushed past her, the wet, putrid odor from the bandages trailing in his wake. From outside the building, the faint notes from Cloyd Anderson's harmonica floated toward her—a brief respite from the turmoil in her mind—but she quickly shut them out.

Letha willed her legs to carry her to the chair beside the little table. She stared at the stained wood of the tabletop, clasped her hands together, fingers interlaced. The burning in her throat was like a tiny bed of hot coals, and she swallowed against it, could not put it out. She closed her eyes, replayed the scene, but nothing had changed. The finality of it all struck her like a blow to the stomach. If the knowledge of her newly offered love had meant anything at all, if there had been only the tiniest of latent spark in his own heart, then he could not have reacted like a wounded animal. Dear God, why had her love not provided at least the semblance of a balm to his soul . . . something, anything?

The weariness pressed down on her, the kind that sometimes came in the small hours past midnight—hours burdened with visions of torn flesh and hollow-eyed men too proud to beg for more food. Hours filled with the restless murmur of the soon dead, quietly begging their way into the next life with hoarse, demented whispers. And with the weariness came guilt; her desire had been granted—Lucy from Charleston had proven unworthy. From inside her head, a sensible voice attempted to soothe her, assure her that the feelings of guilt were unreasonable. The fateful decision had been made by Lucy long before the desire had grown full in Letha's breast. But the sensible voice was unconvincing and soon faded away.

The scuffing of Brady Ayden's shoes shook Letha from her grim reverie. The sound grew louder until she knew that he stood only a step beyond her left shoulder. After several seconds of silence, he sniffed quietly in announcement of his presence. The urge to leave the building suddenly overwhelmed Letha, and she pushed away from the table and rose to her feet. She waited until she was certain of her strength and then brushed past Brady as she dashed toward the door.

For long moments, Brady Ayden tiptoed around the old place in his brain where his feelings once lived, peering into the dimly lit room through thin curtains as he wondered if he truly cared that the matron was distressed. He thought for a moment that he did, and the light seemed to glow brighter. But he was not certain why he had walked to her side, and now that she had rushed away, he surmised that he should have maintained his proper distance. It was but a minor confusion in the midst of the Great Confusion, and it brought him no anxiety; it was the way life was now. He sniffed again, wiped his nose on his sleeve. Soon the light behind the thin curtain grew dimmer, and then it was gone.

Letha walked briskly away from the building only to be faced with another building. It was like drifting in a muddy sea filled with rectangular drab-looking boats, each equally homely, and fitted with little square portals shut tightly against the wind. Crawford had informed her that there were now, according to Dr. McCaw's accounting, one hundred and forty-eight ward buildings. She looked down, picked her way over the remaining patches of dead grass as she avoided the muddiest places. Letha walked for only a hundred yards before she found herself hemmed in by a perimeter of deep mud and buildings. She halted, suddenly aware of the chill, and folded her arms tightly against her bosom. She laughed coldly at herself. She could walk halfway to Atlanta and still be unable to shake the sight of Granville Pollard curling into a fetal ball.

Ten paces distant, two huge rats, screeching like earthbound demons, fought at the base of a ragged mound of soiled bandages. Each of the combatants had laid claim to opposite ends of the same blood-soaked strip of linen. Finally they struggled into the mound, and it was the eerie sight of the bandages moving that spun the woman around. She began to retrace her steps until the sound of Cloyd Anderson's harmonica reached her. The notes were reasonably cohesive, though she could not identify a song, or even a piece of one. She saw them now, Crump and young Nathan Fisher seated on the same rickety box, and Anderson propped against the wall of the building as he moved the harmonica back and forth between his hands. Nathan saw her first at a distance and raised a hand in greeting as she neared, attempting to mask his surprise. It was very strange for her to be outside and wandering about. Crump quickly followed with a little wave of his hand, his wild eyebrows pushing up quizzical furrows on his brow. Anderson allowed the notes to fade softly away and smiled at her as if to apologize for his diminished skills.

Letha stopped a few paces from the men and said too softly, "Please don't stop, Mr. Anderson. I could use a tune just now, although I don't recognize that one."

Cloyd shook his head as he made a writing motion with his hand.

"Didn't bring his paper and pencil along," said Crump.

"Oh, I am sorry. You can write it for me later, back inside."

Cloyd shook his head vigorously, poked himself in the chest with one hand as the other drew the harmonica across his lips.

"Says it's his tune," Crump interpreted.

"Oh my," said Letha, attempting a smile that would not form correctly, "I am doubly impressed now. Please play on."

Cloyd positioned the instrument between his lips as his right thumb covered the unhealed cheek wound, and then he began to play. It was not a jaunty tune, but there was a quiet happiness to it, and Letha lowered her head and followed the melody. Crump and Nathan exchanged knowing, sidelong glances before training their eyes on Letha. The redness in her eyes and the tone of her voice told them that things had not gone well after the letter reading. For now at least, there was simply nothing either of them could do for the woman and they accepted the fact, would wait for another opportunity. They hoped that Cloyd could soothe her now, if but a little, with his music.

Letha did not raise her head for the several minutes Cloyd played, and when he played the final note, she knew that she would be able to hum it to herself, alone in her quarters, when the hours past midnight came. She raised her head and nodded her thanks to Cloyd.

"Well done, sir."

She looked at Crump and Nathan, comfortable with the likelihood that they all knew how the pieces of the puzzle had come together. She had never been skilled at hiding her feelings, though it was never her words that betrayed her heart, and she was certain that neither man had ever heard a word about this one-sided love. But they had watched, could not help but watch, in the compressed life that they all led. They could not help but see the pathetic drama played out, tucked away in the little wooden boat as it drifted on the sea of Chimborazo. Crump and Nathan were doing their best at putting on normal faces, but the effort was obvious. Letha loved them for it and quickly put an end to their misery.

"Gentlemen," she said, and turned and walked away.

Crump waited until she was out of sight, then said, "It does pain me to see her sorrowful."

Nathan nodded, looked at the place where she had stood. "I think Cloyd might've helped some."

"Yep," Crump said. "It was a purdy tune, Cloyd." The breeze freshened, curled around the corner of the building, and pushed against Crump's beard. "Let's go on back in there 'fore I catch a cold in this dern stump. Don't plan on givin' no more hide to the Cause if'n I can help it."

# CHAPTER EIGHT

Crump whittled laboriously in the first suitable light of dawn, the shavings from the figurine gathering slowly on his trousers. He paused, turned the carving in a careful circle, wondered if it would ever take on the likeness of the fine stallion pictured in his head. Probably not, he decided, tossing the knife and the wooden horse on his bed. He looked closely at his hands—wide across the knuckles and thick-fingered—and realized that he could not remember when he last had actually trained his eyes on them. They were hands well tailored for sturdy craftsmanship, better suited for hammering out horseshoes than for delicate whittling. Before the war, Rector Crump had believed that there were but two categories of men who trod the Earth—the sturdy and the delicate. Oh, there were exceptions, to be sure, but not enough to constitute a separate category. Just a sprinkling of men along the way who seemed to combine the sturdy with the delicate, and in truth Crump had believed that, even with the exceptions, one trait or the other was dominant, and would sooner or later swallow the weaker characteristic.

But the war had shaken the men in his neat categories the way his wife shook pieces of chicken in a flour sack, so that when she took them out they were all uniformly coated in white. Crump's men of war were coated in grays and blues and browns and all hues in between, and they were coated in blood both new and old, and sootlike grime that flowing streams could not wash away, ending in little half moons of black under their fingernails. He could no longer sort out the categories, had long since quit the silly effort. He had seen boys younger than Nathan Fisher—boys who should have been snuggled between their parents on stormy nights—club with rifle butts the mottled gray brain tissue from sturdy men until it lay on the cold ground, leaking tiny clouds of steam. He had seen tall, broad-shouldered men with the strength of four such boys whimper at the sight of the advancing enemy and drop to their knees, ignoring the pistol-pointed threats of summary execution by their superiors.

War changed everything; it was brutally simple, yet profound and extraordinarily confusing. Rector Crump knew that he would for the remainder of his days tussle with the leavings of war, but he was not yet willing to confide in anyone the curious darkening shadow of doubt in his warrior's mind—the thought that one day soon the only concept that would retain meaning was love, and especially the love of his wife and sons. The shadow had first appeared the night before as he lay in his bed, pondering the pitiful sight of Pollard curled on his side, covers drawn about his chin. Three days had passed since the letter reading and it appeared to Crump that his neighbor might soon enter the twilight that caused men to cease the struggle to survive. Here lay a man whose ankle bones had been splintered, and whose feet had been hacked off by weary men, but a man who again had risen up to face life in smiles and song. Yet now he lay, still and silent, felled even more grievously than before by the loss of love.

Crump rubbed his hands together, looked now at Pollard's quilt-covered back, believed that he himself could well represent the grieving man's only hope for rebirth. For the most part, Letha had avoided the end of the row, relegating the duties she normally performed to the runaway-eyed nurse with the snotty nose. Nathan Fisher, as much as he desired to help, was but a pup, and would not invade Pollard's closed world. And Cloyd Anderson could hardly write notes to a man who would not open his eyes. No, the duty had fallen squarely to him.

"Pollard?" Crump waited several seconds before continuing. "Pollard, I know you ain't asleep. I can tell it from your breathin'."

Crump reached under his pillow and retrieved a ragged plug of tobacco, bit off the corner and shoved it back into storage. "I's a-wonderin' . . . since you're fixin' to die, if I could have them music papers you was workin' on." Crump glanced at the papers lying in a tidy stack on the upturned box. "The preacher's wife down home can make sense of such music things. Might even be able to play 'em on the pianner. Hope she wouldn't try and sing 'em, for she screeches wors'n a hoarse mule in a tin shed."

Crump rolled the tobacco back and forth in his mouth, allowing the juice to pool under his tongue before he swallowed, savored the bittersweet bite of it on his throat. "I got you figured for 'bout two more weeks, so's you don't have to make up your mind right now. 'Course, if'n I don't ever hear another peep outta you, I'm just gonna take 'em, you understand?" He paused, swallowed again. "I'd always figured I'd be a tellin' my grandbabies one day 'bout how I fought in the big war and donated a leg and all that . . ." His voice trailed away slowly until the silence had gathered enough to make a sound of its own. "But that ain't what I'm gonna tell 'em, Pollard. I'm gonna tell 'em that one time I heard a man and a woman sing back then like airy angels. A good man and a good woman. Then I'm gonna teach 'em to hum the tune on your paper—I'll know it by then. Then I'll tell 'em that one day the man decided to curl up like a bug in winter and die. And bein' younguns and all, they'll ask me why he would do such a thing. And I'll say that he got some real bad news one day, but that won't satisfy 'em. Younguns bein' the curious critters they are, they'll keep after me 'bout why a man would up and die from bad news. But

I ain't gonna make excuses for you. I'm just gonna tell 'em that you warn't the man I thought you were." Crump stood.

When Crump was halfway up the aisle, Pollard opened his eyes and stared at the lumbering hulk until it disappeared through the doorway.

With the tip of his tongue poking from the corner of his mouth, Hound Patterson pinched a small glob from the sliver of bacon fat saved from supper and rubbed it carefully along the thin wire just above the fish hook. Nathan Fisher sat on the edge of Patterson's bed, his mouth half open in what Hound perceived as a grin.

"Ain't you never seen a man bait a hook, boy?"

"Not with bacon fat."

Hound began to thread the sliver of fat over the point of the hook, looping it back and forth until it was packed tightly over the length of the hook. "Well, to tell you the strict truth, it's a first for me too. 'Course there ain't no fishin' holes round here, just rat holes."

Nathan shook his head. "Mrs. Bartlett says it's a waste of time to try and kill 'em. Says if you kill one, there's two a-waitin' to take his place."

"Well, I hope the good matron's right as rain, boy, 'cause I aim to get me some meat between my teeth."

Nathan squinted, unable to wipe the pained look from his face. Hound chuckled. "You've et squirrel, and duck, and coon, and possum, ain't you, boy?"

Nathan nodded. "Yeah, but—"

"'But' my ass, youngun. Ain't no 'but' to it. I bet you close your eyes and take a bite outta a nice roasted rat, you'd not spit it out. 'Specially around this here starvin' barracks." He shook his head. "No sirree, reckon you wouldn't."

"You've had 'em before, huh?"

Hound hesitated for an instant and considered telling a small lie, but chose not to. "Strict truth is, I ain't. But I've talked to boys that've cooked 'em up and they swear they ain't much worse than a bad-cooked duck, or a possum that ain't been caught alive and fed out proper."

"How they say to do it?"

"Well, you skin 'im and gut 'im and wash 'im out some, then tack 'im all stretched out on a board and grease 'im good with bacon fat, and then jist roast 'im over a hot fire like you would a canvas-back duck."

The mention of squirrels had set Nathan's mouth to watering, and he imagined himself peering over his mother's shoulder as she fried a young one in her heavy black skillet, the morsels hissing softly in the deep grease. "Reckon if I saw one all done like that, it might be tolerable."

Hound held up the baited hook, twirled it in front of his face as he made a final inspection. "Yep, that'll do."

"Where you gonna drop it?"

Hound pointed to a jagged three-inch hole in the floor near the base of the wall. "I been hearin' 'em down there for three nights now." He paused, cocked his head to the side. "The one that carved the mess off'n my bad foot might be down there, though I surely hope not." He cackled. "We need all the sober surgeons around here we can get."

Nathan's brow furrowed. "What's that mean?"

"Old Crawford. Since my foot's better, I been slippin' down to the whiskey barrel some at night, pretendin' like I'm goin' out to piss or get some air, and he ain't never far away from it."

A black look seized the boy's face, and the transformation stunned Hound to his core. Nathan gave his head a sharp shake as he fought to fend off the creeping demon. "He don't ever seem drunk to me," he said in a ragged, hopeful whisper.

"Good drunks don't never seem drunk, boy."

83

The demon was at his shoulder then, aging the boy ten hard years in an instant. "Well, I reckon that makes my daddy a bad drunk then."

"Hmm. Well, I hate it's that way for you, boy."

"Was."

"Dead?"

"Hope so."

Hound waved his free hand, desired to hear no more. He wanted the real Nathan back, not this bleak, angry imposter. "Anyway, when they turn the lamps down," Hound said, hopeful that Nathan would return, "I'm gonna tie this line to my bed leg and start to fishin'."

Nathan reached for his brace and crutch, then turned and walked away.

The rat swallowed the hook and commenced its death throes an hour past midnight. Although five other men, including the fisher of rats himself, were closer to the hole than Pollard, it was only he who lay awake and listened to the long struggle. At first Pollard believed it to be no more than a disagreement between two of the creatures; it was a common occurrence under the floor. But soon he realized that the terrible squeal came from a single rat that was in agony, and he placed his hands over his ears for a full minute. When he removed his hands the squeals had taken on a different pitch and were louder than before. Pollard heard the heavy body thrashing about, wondered what strange fate had befallen the rat that now struggled so mightily for his life. Mesmerized, his hands slid down from the sides of his face and he focused on the sounds. Pollard had heard many human squeals on the fields of slaughter, all stored in some dark fold of his brain, and he dug them out, compared them to the rat squeal. For what Pollard reckoned to be five more minutes, the rat clung tenaciously to life, and then, with a final thrash of his body, death claimed it.

. . .

Rector Crump was aware that someone was staring at him even though his eyes were tightly shut. It was a phenomenon that he had experienced several times during his life, and it amazed him as much now as the first time. Just a boy, he had wandered away from the house and fallen blissfully asleep in the corncrib, and while sleep was giving way to consciousness, he sensed a mysterious transfer of energy into his brain before he looked up into the long, stern face of his father. So it was now in the silence of early morning; someone's energy sought him, looked at him with probing eyes.

"Why should it be, Sergeant Crump," Pollard said, "that the rat clings to life more tenaciously than we men?"

Crump attempted to blink, felt his matted eyelids unwillingly separate. He blinked forcefully, and then again, before Pollard's haggard features came into focus. Crump replayed the question in his mind, and when he'd satisfied himself that it was not part of a dream, he answered, hoarse and low. "I'll be damned. You ain't saw fit to let out a peep for three days, and you up and ask somethin' like that."

"It is a fair question. You will be pleased to learn that I heard one of your little enemies perish last night beneath the floor."

Crump squinted. "Immortal God, Pollard, but you're a curious sort."

"Be that as it may, you have not answered my question."

"Don't reckon it'd come as a big surprise if'n I told you I hadn't thought on it before now."

"No, but you can humor me and ponder it now, can't you?"

Crump rolled onto his back, stared at the ceiling. That the man talked at all was a sign of progress, albeit difficult to measure given the course of the conversation. Perhaps he had slipped into a delirium—Crump had heard sick men utter many foolish things—but he did not sound as if he was losing his mind. He sounded just like he always had—like some brainy, book-learned professor, spilling things from his head that bewildered men who thought on lower planes. Crump decided to consider the question, strange though it was.

"To start with, Pollard, I don't go along with what you're claimin'."

"Ah, but you didn't hear this rat fight death."

"I've heard critters die slow before. And men."

"And men, yes, on the killing fields. So have I. But I heard more whimpers and screams and pleas than I did struggles against death. Many pleas *for* death, as a matter of fact."

"But a man's got sense to know he's a goner; a critter don't. Man's got sense to want to pass on to the next life."

"Heaven's bright shore, Sergeant. Do you believe in the sweet paradise in the heavens?"

"Yes, sir, I do that, but I don't claim to know particulars."

Pollard sighed, the air slowly leaking from his thin chest. "I must confess a bit of confusion about that just now."

"Ain't nothin' to be confused about. You either believe it or you don't."

"But—understand, I'm not trying to provoke you—but what if you believe fervently in it, and yet it does not exist?"

Crump shook his head, did not look at Pollard. "Pollard, there's just some things a man knows, down inside. Just knows."

"Then why is it that God would allow you to know, and not me?"

Crump felt agitation prickle the back of his neck, like haircut trimmings wedged under his collar. "Maybe it's just because you're too infernal smart for your own good, Pollard. Not everything in the world needs pickin' apart and studyin' like—like one of your music papers."

"I didn't mean to—"

Crump pushed up from his pillow, swung his good leg over the side of the bed. "And I'll tell you another thing too, Pollard. When the cannon ball took my leg, it didn't take none of my heart with it." He groped for his crutches, jammed his foot into his shoe. "Wish't I could say the same for you."

He stood, tottered a moment as he gained his balance, then looked down at Pollard. "And while I'm tellin' things, I'll tell you this here, too." He cocked his head to one side, rolled his eyes back at Pollard. "If your gal wouldn't stand by you in your predicament, she warn't worth much a'tall to start with."

Nathan Fisher peered over Hound's shoulder at the roasting carcass of the rat, sprawled over the board to which it was nailed. From a distance of ten feet, Letha and one of her cooks watched the curious proceedings. The helper, a shrunken black woman of sixty, nibbled steadily at her lower lip, pausing every few moments to mutter inaudibly as she shook her scarf-clad head. Letha had reluctantly granted permission for the cooking chore to take place in the kitchen, with the understanding that the skinning and preparation was to be completed outside the building and that the carcass would not come into contact with her stove. Hound had allowed that the open fire door would do quite nicely, but he was no longer certain that the arrangements were suitable.

"Good God and Jehoshaphat! I ain't sure but what my hands ain't gonna get done and tender before this here meat does." He shifted the board to his other hand, glanced over his shoulder and beamed again at what he saw there: Nathan, the bright lad, returned to them. "Boy, you want a bite of this feller, you're gonna have to help me cook 'im."

"This dern leg won't let me squat down there like that, Hound. And anyways, you can have it all to yourself."

"I forgot about that, boy. Sorry."

Hound withdrew the cooking board and inspected the meat. "I reckon that's good enough. The board's soon gonna catch afire anyhow."

Hound stood and smiled broadly, looked at the two women. "I thank you kindly, ladies. Now we'll be off to the yard for the picnic."

Letha raised a hand. "Mr. Patterson, you may take some utensils if you like."

"No, ma'am, I take my wild game with fingers and fangs. Don't waste none thataway."

With his free hand he tipped his cap and limped toward the door. "Come along, boy. The day'll soon come when you're fightin' me for that fishin' hole yonder."

As soon as the door closed behind them, the cook crinkled her nose. "I'll declare, Miz Bartlett, but that don't rightly seem decent to me."

"Bess, there are many things that once were not decent, but now are acceptable. These men are hungry. How may we deny them meat—using the term loosely?"

The woman shook her head. "Never ought to a came to this."

"No, it shouldn't have, Bess." She paused, wondered if Nathan would eat the thing. "But it has." She put her arm around the old woman's waist, pulled her close. "We've seen some sights in this place, haven't we?"

"That we has, Miz Bartlett. That we has."

# CHAPTER NINE

Six days before Christmas, Rector Crump learned that he would soon lose more of his leg. The burning itch had bothered him for several days, but he had paid little attention to it, assuming that it was yet another phase of the healing process. But now Avery Crawford stooped over the exposed stump, his nose only inches above the discolored wound. He raised his head, avoiding Crump's gaze, and dug two fingers into the deep folds of flesh above his eyebrows. Letha stood beside him, the old bandages balled loosely in the metal pan that she held.

"Well, let's hear it," Crump said.

"These things seem to have no rhyme nor reason, Sergeant Crump. Simply no rhyme nor reason."

"Are you tellin' me it's rotten?"

Crawford moistened his lips and then pursed them before answering. "There is, without doubt, a gangrenous infection in your wound, sir."

Pollard rolled his head to the side, drawn by the ugly word that hung in the air and blotted out the other words of Crawford's pronouncement. Without moving his head, he looked at Crump. The big man's shoulders slumped visibly, and for an instant Pollard saw fear spread across the wide face like a thin coating of grime, and then it vanished with the blinking of his eyes.

"Reckon that means I'm gonna have to donate more of this leg to the Cause?"

Crawford nodded. "It would be foolish to wait long. Mrs. Bartlett will increase your rations so that you can build up some strength over the next few days."

"Ain't no need for much of that," Crump said. "I'd just as soon get on with it. I'm plenty strong enough."

"I insist on two days at least."

Crump patted his thigh. "How much more off?"

"Midthigh, hopefully. Some stump will remain."

No one spoke for several seconds. The conversation had spilled beyond Crump's bed, and both Cloyd Anderson and Nathan listened intently from the edge of their beds. Nathan's eyes were locked on Crawford and saw the telltale signs of the whiskey barrel—unsteady hands, fidgeting like great bony spiders, and the tongue that swept hungrily over his lips after each utterance. Pollard stole a quick glance in Letha's direction, careful not to look directly at her. Letha's fingers began to fidget around the edges of the pan, and she decided to break the silence.

"Sergeant Crump is a man of high spirit, and I for one am not worried about the outcome of this."

"I 'preciate you sayin' that, ma'am," Crump said.

"Well then, we're settled here," Crawford said. "I leave you in good hands, Sergeant." He turned slowly and trudged up the aisle.

Letha moved closer to Crump, touched his shoulder in a final reassurance. "It appears that you will have to put up with even more of my cooking, Sergeant." She smiled. "Are you up to the task?"

"That I am, ma'am."

She turned quickly and followed Crawford up the aisle. Crump looked first to his left at Cloyd, then across the aisle at Nathan, and finally to his right at Pollard. He was looking at Pollard when he said, "Well, boys, ain't no need to worry 'bout me. Long as they don't cut the heart out of me, I'll be all right."

An hour after the lamps were turned down, Crump rolled onto his right side and studied the murky silhouette of Pollard's head, satisfying himself that the man was not asleep. "Pollard?"

"Yes."

"You awake enough to talk?"

"Yes."

"I won't bother you long, but somethin's been weighin' on me since Crawford found the rot in my stump."

Pollard turned his face toward Crump. "What is it, Sergeant?"

"Well, 'fore I get to that, why don't you just call me Crump." He paused, did not like the sound of what he was about to say, but knew it as truth. "I don't much feel like a sergeant no more."

"Certainly. Plain Crump it is, then."

"Well, what I need to say is . . . aw, dammit, these here leg cuttins' don't always work out. Truth is, I ain't near as strong as I claim to be, and who knows but what I might give up the ghost after they're done with me."

"I doubt that."

"I 'preciate that, Pollard, I surely do, but just the same. If'n it don't work out, I don't want no bad feelin's between us to go unmended. I said some hard things toward you. Reckon I stepped across the line some, and it really ain't like me to do that about a man's private affairs, but I hauled off and did it anyhow."

He waited for a moment, gave Pollard time to say something if he desired, but he remained silent and motionless. "I, uh, just want you to know that I did it 'cause I think a lot of you. I didn't do it outta hatefulness."

"I know that."

"Well, that's good. Real good, Pollard, 'cause I'm not a hateful man." He whispered a mirthless laugh. "Truth is, down deep, I don't think I really even hate the Yanks, and I have kilt some of 'em. If'n one lay wounded and asked me for water, I'd give it to him."

"I'm sure you would."

A minute of silence passed between them before Crump spoke again. "No hard feelin's then, about me spoutin' off at you?"

"None whatsoever, my friend."

*My friend.* Crump allowed the words to sink into his brain, felt the pride lift his chest a bit. It was as if he had received a new title, bestowed by a man who would not bestow such titles haphazardly.

After a silence, Crump heard himself say, "Pollard, I don't mind tellin' you that I'm a mite scared by this leg choppin'."

"That's understandable. Anyone would be."

With his left hand Crump reached across his chest and under the pillow, located his chew of tobacco. He bit off a small chunk and replaced the plug. "I'd feel some better if'n Crawford warn't so deep in the whiskey barrel."

"Were I in your place, I would ask Letha if Dr. McCaw would perform the surgery. From what she has told me, they seem to have a mutual respect."

"But he's the head man in this whole hospital."

"True, but he also continues to do some surgeries. He repaired my wounds."

"You don't say?"

"It's true, I assure you."

"I 'spect she would put in a word for me at that, wouldn't she?"

"I would wager that she already has."

For the second time, Crump's chest puffed out with a proud breath. "Reckon, sure enough?"

"You can ask her, just to be certain."

"She's somethin', that woman."

"Yes . . . an extraordinary woman."

Crump's brain processed Pollard's last words and the inflection of his voice, which was little more than a whisper. "I'll tell you one thing, Pollard. If'n I didn't already have a fine woman of my own, I'd be tempted to smother you with your pillow one night."

"Huh. I doubt that would be necessary."

"For such a man of learnin' and all, Pollard, even the likes of me could teach you a thing or two about womenfolk." With a final low growl of exasperation, Crump rolled onto his left side, swallowed the remains of his tobacco, and closed his eyes.

Avery Crawford led the small procession back from the surgery unit, followed by Letha as she guided the front of the gurney bearing a groggy Rector Crump. Brady Ayden walked behind the gurney, although he had no earthly idea why; the matron and another attendant from surgery were doing all the work. The men near the end of the aisle watched and listened as the rumbling of the wobbly wheels on the wood floor grew louder. Letha carefully positioned the low gurney beside Crump's bed and then took her place directly behind Crump's head.

Crawford walked to Crump's right side, tugged at the corners of the loose dressing covering the stump, then said, "Let's proceed."

The surgery attendant, a sloped-shouldered, powerful-looking man with an expressionless face, stood opposite Crawford. Crawford nodded. Simultaneously, Letha, Crawford, and the attendant worked their hands and arms under Crump's body.

Crawford looked at Brady Ayden. "When we lift him clear, you pull the gurney out and move it into the aisle. Quickly." Crawford glanced quickly at each in turn. "On the count of three."

With a slight groan from Crump, the task was completed, after which Crawford again adjusted the wound dressing to his liking. "Mrs. Bartlett, the sooner he is able to take some nourishment, the better."

"Certainly, Major. I will see to it."

Crawford looked down at Crump through bloodshot eyes. "It went well in my estimation. Dr. McCaw is a masterful surgeon. However, it is out of our hands now." He turned slowly and walked away, followed by the attendant and Brady Ayden.

Letha made a quick circle around the bed, fussing with the bed clothing and Crump's covers. Satisfied, she stepped back, crossed her arms over her bosom, and looked down at Crump's ashen face. Nathan Fisher made his way to stand beside her, and she acknowledged him with a quick smile. From the corner of her eye, she saw Cloyd Anderson approach, a scrap of paper extended from his fingers. She turned to him, took the note.

## WHIN CAN WE TALK TO HIM?

"I suspect it will be another hour or two, Mr. Anderson. The chloroform will take some time to wear off, and then his head is likely to ache for a while longer."

Cloyd nodded, took a step backward. Nathan hopped a few feet closer to Crump's face, then looked back to Letha. "I don't like the way his face looks . . . all drained out, sorta."

"It is to be expected, Nathan. Major surgery is quite an ordeal for a man already weakened by a wound. I hope to get some color back into his face very soon."

Nathan said, "He's gonna get my bacon for as long as he needs it, so you might as well put it on his plate to start with. I'll go to eatin' rat meat with Hound if I need to."

A slight shudder passed through Letha's body. The thought of Lyle Patterson eating a rat was far less than pleasant, but the extension to Nathan Fisher, a mere boy who should be at home eating the golden fried chicken from his mother's pan—that was absolutely unacceptable.

"Nathan, I don't think—"

Nathan quickly looked up at her with flashing eyes that did not appear boyish. "No disrespect, ma'am, but I mean that. You can do it in the kitchen, or I'll do it out here and maybe make him feel bad. Either way, it gets done."

Cloyd stepped forward, nodding vigorously, his right forefinger tapping steadily against his chest.

"Well, I—" Letha said.

Pollard's voice rescued her. "May I make a respectful suggestion?"

Letha shrugged off the discomfort of hearing him address her, looked at him, and said, "Certainly."

"With my ration included, that makes three total, and if you halve each of them, he should have ample extras, and still allow us each a bit." He glanced at Nathan and Cloyd. "But if he should require all of mine, I, like Nathan and Cloyd, will gladly give it all."

Letha stood motionless for a moment, then looked up at the ceiling, collected her swirling thoughts, and said, "As you wish, gentlemen. I am sure that Sergeant Crump would do the same for you. It is indeed an honor to know men such as you."

Rector Crump dreamed of wild horses on a vast, windswept plain, the thunder of their hoof beats loud in his head, like rolling drums. They were running sidelong past him, led by a magnificent white stallion whose mane trailed halfway down his back. Suddenly, the stallion veered toward Crump, and as if by some mysterious command, the herd slowed its pace and fell a respectful distance behind the leader as he drew near. The great white horse, black eyes trained directly on Crump, pranced closer and closer until he was only a pace away, and Crump could feel the heat radiating from the muscular body, smell the sweat that shimmered in the sun. With an unshod hoof the size of a plate, the beast pawed at the dusty ground, and Crump knew that he offered himself to be mounted. The mesmerizing black eyes held him, beckoned Crump to enter the wilderness of which the animal was lord and king, beckoned the frail human to be one with him and feel the might of his back under him, feel the wind tear at his hair and beard as they streaked toward the sun. Then Crump looked down at the empty space below the stump of his right leg. Strangely, he was able to stand in perfect balance on his left leg and it was only when he attempted to hop toward the horse that he fell to the ground. The stallion reared up on his hind legs and pawed the air above Crump, and for an instant, he believed that the horse would trample him in his misery as he lay helpless in the thick dust. But the white stallion spun away and raced back to his herd, leaving billows of dust to be caught by the wind. It was when Crump realized that he would never experience the exhilaration of the wild ride that he moaned pitifully. When the sound of the moan subsided in his ears, other sounds replaced it—the murmur of voices nearby and the clumping of crutches on a wood floor—and Crump knew that the pounding in his head was not hoof beats, but pain. The throbbing in his head kept perfect cadence with that in his stump, and he knew that he would not be allowed to escape the world of pain on the broad back of the grand stallion.

He blinked against the splotchy patches of light overhead, and two forms appeared at his bedside. As if from a treetop, a voice spoke his name in the form of a question. "Sergeant Crump?"

He blinked harder, felt his cheeks rise forcibly with the effort. Again the soft, masculine voice called his name, but from closer now, and Crump traced the voice to the form nearest his bed.

"It's me, Nathan. Can you hear me?"

Crump swallowed dryly, the sides of his throat like opposing pieces of sandpaper. "I can hear you, pup." He rolled his head a couple of inches, identified Cloyd Anderson as the other man standing over him. "I'm mighty dry, boys."

Nathan said, "Miz Bartlett said you'd be thirsty."

Cloyd had already reached down and picked up the cup of water waiting on the nightstand. He knelt and lifted Crump's head so that he could drink. Crump took several sips from the cup before Cloyd lowered his head back to the pillow.

"They told us that the operation went well, Crump," Pollard said.

Crump turned his head, focused on Pollard. The fingers of his right hand crept spiderlike until they reached into the void beginning high on his thigh. "Appears so."

Detecting the note of sorrow in the raspy whisper, Pollard said, "Ah, but my friend, they stopped far short of your heart, did they not?"

The low rumble of laughter rose from Crump's chest in a single huff. "You're damn right they did, Pollard. Way short."

Pollard smiled, glanced at Nathan and Cloyd, who smiled in relief with him. "Letha informs us that the latest supply trains have brought bacon, so you need to get your appetite back very soon, all right?"

"What time is it?"

"About ten in the morning."

"Don't think I'll be ready for a while. Seems to be a little feller workin' on the inside of my head with a fair-sized hammer."

"That will pass," said Pollard. "We won't bother you any longer for now. There will be time for talking later."

Crump closed his eyes, heard Nathan and Cloyd shuffle quietly away. He moved his head by fractions of inches until he located the position that offered the least pain. Without warning, the memory drifted toward him, the scene taking shape in his brain as if skillfully painted by an artist working with great speed. At the time it happened, years before, it was one of the moments that were given as gifts, but the memory came darkly now, not as a gift, and Crump sought to shield himself, hoped that Pollard could come to his aid.

"Pollard?"

"Yes."

"Why do things come back to people?"

"Come back? How do you mean?"

"From years ago. Little things that stick in your mind that were good . . . but now ain't."

"Who can say, Crump. I believe the human mind to be an awesome mystery."

Crump wanted to raise his head and rest it on his hand and elbow, but decided the price would be too great. He would have to talk with his head sunk into the pillow like some white-haired old man. "Somethin' came back to me that I wisht hadn't."

"What was it?"

"Long time ago, maybe eight or ten year, I come out of a general store down home and saw the purdiest little girl I ever saw in my life. She was standin' off to the side of the door, waitin' on her momma. The sun caught her hair and it was all long and curled. Red as fire, it was. She was dressed up like a little doll. Had the face of a little angel. Her momma'd just bought her a cinnamon stick and when she saw me lookin' at her, she held it up and smiled." He paused, swallowed. "Then she broke off a little piece and ate it, and before she was done nibblin' that one up, she broke another'n off. I musta watched her break off a half dozen pieces 'fore I got to feelin' silly about standin' there for so long. It was such a purdy thing to watch then."

Pollard knew what Crump would say next, but he remained silent, let him spill it out. Crump said, "I'm damned if'n it don't remind me of the way my leg's disappearin', Pollard."

"I don't know why things like that come back, Crump. Perhaps you can hang onto the memory of the child and in time let the cinnamon stick go."

"Hope so."

"You will."

"Hope I ain't gonna lose my sense, have crazy things start to worryin' me a lot. I've always been scared to death of bein' crazy, Pollard."

"It's probably the chloroform. You're not going crazy."

Crump forced himself to draw several long deep breaths. "Times like these make a man wonder."

# CHAPTER TEN

Three days before Christmas, Letha sat in her quarters and wrote reminder notes to herself. A month ago, she had initiated her plan for the Christmas dinner. There were no funds available from the Confederate government for anything resembling an extravagance, with a Christmas dinner certainly falling in that category. Letha devised a plan whereby old but serviceable comforts and blankets were collected and sold by Richmonders she had come to know over the course of the war, with the funds donated toward the "boys'" Christmas dinner. Along with a few outright cash donations from other citizens, and with the considerable influence of Dr. McCaw, the dinner fund had grown large enough to provide for a sumptuous feast. Ten turkeys awaited roasting, with vegetables still being in fair supply and not a problem. Ingredients for over twenty gallons of eggnog were also on hand, and to her delight, enough sugar and flour had been obtained to provide each man a small individual cake. Dr. McCaw had miraculously procured two gallons of oysters for each of the wards, making the feast complete.

A growing mound of gifts covered the floor of nearly a quarter of her room, some of which were already wrapped and others that had been sent in all sorts of containers. Most of the containers Letha deemed unsuitable had been cast away, and only a few remained to be wrapped. She walked to the edge of the clutter and picked up a small, rickety crate that appeared to have been tacked together by someone with little skill. Letha smiled ruefully; that the crate had arrived at its proper destination was clear evidence of Providence. Little remained of the shaky penciled lettering scrawled on top:

*TO M ST R LYL HOU ND PAT ERS N AT CHI BE RO S HAS P TL IN RIC OM D VIR G I NY*

Letha gently rotated the box in several directions, her curiosity growing with each new position. Lyle Patterson was easily the most colorful character who had ever graced the halls of Chimborazo, and there was scant doubt in her mind that the gift sender from the mountains of North Carolina was any less colorful. With a final gentle shake of the container, Letha resigned herself to the mystery of the contents and made a mental note to keep an eye on Lyle at the gift opening.

She located the roll of coarse green paper and began to open it, visually calculating the amount needed. It was when she picked up the scissors that the thought ricocheted through her brain—a missile of unknown origin—and slowly clanked about until it came to rest squarely between her eyes. Granville Pollard would receive no Christmas gift. Cast into oblivion by his own family in the North and dismissed as unfit by his would-be family in the South, he was clearly and painfully a man adrift in a country torn asunder. Letha rested the scissors on the table, drew the chair under her. Since the awful day of the letter, she had striven to immerse herself in her work, redoubling her already considerable efforts at serving the men of her ward, save for Pollard himself. It was as if she had stored her feelings for him in a place as secure and inaccessible as a bank box—requiring a matching key and an attendant for even so much as a peek inside. She had no misgivings about her feelings; they remained as strong as they ever were, perhaps stronger. From a distance, she had observed the change in him, no doubt brought about by the rough but genuine comradeship of Rector Crump and the wide-eyed affection of Nathan Fisher. And the humble, uncomplaining mute, Cloyd Anderson, who had quickly endeared himself to everyone, requiring no more than scribbled notes and animated pantomimes in the process.

Letha rested her forehead in her hands, massaged her temples with her thumbs. The sudden rush of it all was disconcerting, almost maddening, and she did not know whether to praise or curse the thought that had penetrated her brain and reminded her of the secure lock box. Be it deserving of curse or praise, it did not matter; Granville Pollard would receive a Christmas gift. To ignore his plight, or that of any man in a similar situation, would be unthinkable. Now secure in the decision, Letha became aware of another thought, this one lurking in a shadowy place, and she decided to confront it rather than flee. The risk of further rejection was a distinct possibility, perhaps a certainty. Oh, he would be cordial and act the gentleman, to be sure. But would he, would all of them, pity her? Would she be seen as a woman so girlishly smitten that her common sense and pride had evaporated altogether?

She lifted her head, rested her chin on interlaced fingers. The light from her lamp cast an orange glow about the small room that served as both bedroom and parlor. From several cracks in the walls, she could feel the cold draft as the wind found its way around the corner of the frail building. She hunched her shoulders closer to her neck, lowered her neck into the folds of her shawl. In this fashion, Letha sat until the chill caused her to think of bed and a thick layer of quilts over her body, and soon she hurriedly changed into her night clothing and extinguished the lamp.

She burrowed her way beneath the quilts and waited for the warmth to caress her. When it descended, marvelous and heavy, the strong desire to empty her mind of all things meaningful came also. She clamped her eyelids together like gates, pretended that the final intruding thought was approaching from outside of her head, and for a time the gates held fast. But in the end, the ruse failed and the gates gave way. Letha wondered if she would ever be able to accept his friendship instead of his love.

On the morning of Christmas Eve, Granville Pollard put the finishing touches on the melody he had written in honor of the man whose fingers he held as he burned alive in the battle of the Wilderness. The musical score was begun as a gift for Lucy Penders, but had lain untouched after the arrival of the letter. Only within the last week had Pollard decided to resurrect the work and complete it. Now it would be a gift to Letha—a token he fervently hoped would somehow serve to initiate a mending process. Exactly where the process might lead, Pollard was uncertain, but he was certain that he longed for her company. There were things he must to say to her, and though fearful that the words would not convey his sentiments—whatever they truly were—he was compelled to make the attempt.

Pollard listened for a moment to the labored breathing of Rector Crump, then turned his head toward the sound. The surgery, no matter how skillfully performed, had taken a terrible toll on the man. Save for his untamed black beard, Crump appeared to have shrunk since the amputation. The very architecture of his face had undergone a profound transformation. The bone structure of his forehead and eye sockets was now prominent, and Pollard was certain that the alteration was a result of far more insidious forces than weight loss. Gone was the vitality that had filled the wide chest and drew others to it. Even his great crab-like hands had shed their aura of power—hands with thick fingers, once driven as if by powerful pistons in his forearms. They too were dormant, and rested now on his stomach. Pollard stared at them, despised the arranged, funereal look of them. He turned his head from the sight, felt a bit of his own energy escape.

Pollard himself, without having looked in a mirror since his arrival at Chimborazo, knew that his own appearance would no doubt surprise, if not actually shock him, were he to look at his own image. Yes, it was much more than the loss of cells that stored muscle and fat, much more than anything to do with the flesh. The urge to drag himself from his bed and go to Crump's side came at him in a rush. Perhaps if he could grasp the sad hands, arouse them from their frightful repose, it would serve as a catalyst, and Rector Crump would sit up and again growl happily at his friends. But soon the urge subsided, gave way to the knowledge that such an act would be little more than an aggravation, a hindrance to recovery. So Pollard again took up his musical score, began to hum the tune inside his head. He would not allow himself to look at Crump until he awoke.

From her vantage point just outside the kitchen door, the Christmas dawn appeared to Letha atop the peak of the neighboring ward building instead of the horizon, and she quickly dismissed the thought that she had been swindled out of a proper scene. Through her nostrils she inhaled the sharp air, allowed it to penetrate and cleanse her, prepare her for the coming day. The sense of foreboding had crept into her quarters long before the gray light, and she had quickly dressed and sought the solace of cold silence apart from the building. But the frangible walls could not confine the omen, and now it caught up with her in the dawn, refused to be ignored. There could be little doubt that its genesis was the strange admixture of anticipation and dread about the coming meeting with Pollard. It would be, simply and yet profoundly, an unpredictable encounter, and all things unpredictable had long been a bane to Letha. Only through structure and order had she been able to cope with the past thousand days and the demands they had placed upon her.

*And yet . . .*

Letha folded her arms snugly against her bosom and looked above the rooftop. She wished that she could peer into the realm beyond Earth, wished that she could make bold inquiries and receive clear, concise answers. If it were possible, she would ask about the stealthy harbinger who had gained unwanted entry into the privacy of her room and clouded her vision, and she would form defenses and make sound plans for the order of battle. *Battle?* She scoffed at herself as the word tiptoed through her brain. *Come now, Letha, let's not overdo. It is not like you.*

She waited until the chill bored deeper, near her bones, then she turned and walked quickly into the building.

The feast was ready for serving by four in the afternoon, and Letha could think of no credible reason to postpone the meal until the supper hour. The aroma of the roasting turkeys had permeated the entire building, and for the last two hours, every time Letha had glanced into the ward, her gaze was met by dozens of pairs of inquisitive eyes. She turned now from the doorway to the ward and walked into her quarters, untying the stained apron as she approached her chest of clothing. From the neatly folded stacks, she selected a fresh white apron, trimmed in a dark green that would match the color of her dress. She positioned her face over the small mirror mounted inside the open lid. She then unfastened the tight bun of hair behind her head and shook it loose, running her fingers through the thick strands in preparation for the brush. Within two minutes she produced the desired fullness, along with a sheen that highlighted the dark locks. She was tempted to leave it free altogether and risk appearing immodest, but she waited until practicality poked a stern finger in front of her face—as she knew it would—and compromised with a loose gathering held in place by two pins.

She stepped back, allowed more of her image to appear in the rectangle, until her head and shoulders were perfectly centered, and she imagined that she was sitting for a portrait to be painted by a finicky artist whose face she could not see. He reached out and delicately placed a finger on her chin, moved it ever so slightly to the right so that the light caressed her cheek. Then he muttered approvingly before his hand faded away.

Letha reached up and smoothed the flat collar of her dress, disapproved of the redness of her hands. They had become instruments, these hands that were once smooth-skinned and white, with filed nails and well-tended cuticles. They were once ornaments that dangled beyond the ruffled long sleeves of ballroom gowns and dazzled onlookers and accepted the kisses of gentlemen. But no more. The sight of them chided her, reminded her that there was precious little to be gained from forays into a past that seemed a lifetime away rather than a few years. She removed her hands from the portrait, stole a final peek at her hair, then walked into the kitchen.

For over an hour, Letha, Brady Ayden, and two kitchen helpers carted food to the men. The excited chatter at the beginning of the feast soon gave way to quiet exclamations of satisfaction, and Letha heard several of the men hum contentedly, the way children sometimes did when given their favorite foods. The very sick and badly wounded were spoon-fed by Letha and her crew until other men nearby had finished their meals and volunteered in aiding their comrades. Throughout the process, Letha had taken special notice of the small cluster of men gathered around Crump's bed. Pollard's bed was pushed close to Crump's, and Nathan and Cloyd Anderson sat near the end, food plates resting on their legs. With the exception of Crump's, the plates were now empty and sat aside, and as Letha walked down the aisle toward them, she saw that Crump held fast to a large drumstick.

As she drew near, Crump smiled weakly and waved the half-eaten drumstick at her. "It's somethin' of a shame, ma'am, that I ain't able to tear into this thing like a man."

"You appear to have done some damage, Sergeant," she said, returning his smile.

Nathan said, "We got some taters and a little cake down him too, Miz Bartlett."

"Good, Nathan. Good for you."

Crump laid the turkey leg down on his plate. "Sure wished there was some way to keep this till I was feelin' perky again."

In the silence that followed, the impossibility of Crump's wish hovered over all of them, reminded them that the Herculean efforts required to produce the Christmas dinner would not be repeated. Over the course of the last two days of preparation, Letha had on several occasions shoved the intrusive thought away: after the passing of the magical day, back they would go to pitiful strips of bacon and little squares of cornbread and limp greens. It was nearly odious—the ephemeral nature of a feast for the poor.

Letha nodded, lied with words shaded in white. "Ah, Sergeant, but we never know when the tide might turn a little in our favor. The last supply train was better than the one before it. I have not lost hope, and neither should you."

With a forefinger, Crump tapped the drumstick. "Reckon you're right," he said, but it was only a polite reply and he regretted having voiced his wish in the first place.

"Ain't it about time for the presents?" Nathan asked.

"That it is, young sir," Letha replied. "We'll get some of these plates cleared away and proceed with the festivities."

Before she turned to leave, Letha smiled at each man in turn, saving Pollard for last. Her glance surprised him, for he was busy studying the way her hair cascaded onto her back, and she was gone before he could return her gesture.

Three weeks before, when he first gave consideration to the coming of Christmas, Granville Pollard resigned himself to the surety that he would receive no gift. He had cast aside the initial pangs of regret as childish, and thought no more of it—until now. Laid before him on his bed were three neatly wrapped packages and a note from Cloyd Anderson that read:

## I WILL PLAY A TUNE OF YUR LIKEN WHEN YOU WANT

Pollard turned to Cloyd, who sat on the end of Crump's bed, held up the piece of paper. "Thank you, Cloyd, it is a fine gift. I will choose the time carefully."

Crump held against his chest the new quilt his wife had sent, his hands stroking it as if it were alive and able to appreciate his tenderness. He said, "Open mine next, Pollard. It's from me and the wife."

Pollard picked up the package and loosened the wrappings, pulled out a pair of woolen gloves. He tried them on for size and held them up with a nod of approval toward Crump. "Very nice, Crump. These are much appreciated. Pass my thanks on to your wife."

"They'll do you some good soon. You ain't gonna spend the rest of your days all cooped up in the likes of this place."

"Thank you so much, my friend."

From the corner of his eye, Pollard saw Letha slip across the aisle and take a position near the end of his bed. Nathan Fisher reached down and tapped one of the two remaining gifts. "This one's from me and Ma."

Pollard lifted the small package from his bed and pulled away the wrapping paper. In perfectly formed green letters he saw his initials at the corner of a white handkerchief. Under the first lay two more, one with red initials sewn in and the last with dark blue. Pollard laid them in the palm of his hand, touched his fingertip to the lettering, looked up into the grinning face of Nathan Fisher.

"These are beautiful, Nathan. Your mother is greatly skilled. Thank you, and her. Please, in your next letter . . ." He paused, shook his head at himself in admonishment. "No. I shall thank her myself." He glanced at Crump. "And your wife also, Crump. Both of you, write down your addresses, please." He shook his head again, but not at himself. "This is all so very thoughtful of you fellows."

Letha stepped forward, a brightly wrapped gift materializing in her hand. "And ladies, I might add."

Pollard was speechless, felt the warm blood rise to his face. Slowly, he reached up and accepted the gift as he forced air into his lungs and struggled to unbind his tongue. He placed the gift in his lap and then leaned onto one elbow as he located the three sheets of paper on his nightstand. "I, uh, at least in this happy instance, have a gift in return."

He extended the papers to Letha. "In truth, you will see that it is only half a gift, a melody without words. Quite backward, I realize. The words usually come first. I was in hopes that you would help me with the lyrics."

Letha opened the folded top sheet. It read:

> For the Angel of Chimborazo, from your friend, Granville Pollard

Letha's world suddenly became very small, bound by two beds and four men, and the eyes of the men, though innocent in intent, were aimed beacons that held the intensity of compressed suns. At first, as the seconds began to mount, Letha nearly succumbed to the urge to flee far from the building, to seek some cold and windy refuge where she could oil the grinding emotions that now made noises in her head. But Nathan Fisher rescued her; rescued all of them from the embarrassment.

His eyes were no longer intense beacons when he said to her: "You can do it, can't you, ma'am?" It was more statement than question.

She looked down at the notes—neat and black, almost as if typeset—and silently hummed the first few to herself. "Yes, Nathan. I think I can be of help to Mr. Pollard." She looked at Pollard. "After I learn more about the soldier he wishes to honor with this melody."

Pollard nodded. "I will see to that."

"Open yours now, Mr. Pollard," Nathan said.

Pollard quickly ran his finger along the paper seam of Letha's gift to him, uncovered the wound leather belt. It was nearly two inches in width and very well made, with raised oak leaves alongside the polished brass buckle. He unwound it, stretched it to its full length, studied the craftsmanship and detail. Where she had acquired such a belt in war-torn Richmond, he could not imagine.

"It is a magnificent belt," he said. "The workmanship, the brass work . . ."

"Wear it in good health, sir," Letha said.

Crump extended his right hand, said, "Lemme see that, Pollard." Pollard handed him the belt. "Mighty fine work, that it is."

Hound Patterson's howl of excitement pierced the air, closely followed by cackles of glee. In unison, Letha and all four men looked to the source of the commotion. Hound had just opened the package from home, the crate resting between his knees as he sat propped against his pillow. He held aloft what appeared to be a necklace of sorts, about a foot in length, but only Crump recognized the objects that had been strung together.

Crump said, "I'll swear, Hound, it looks like somebody back home is keepin' your dogs busy."

Hound yelped happily as he counted the raccoon ears. "Nine pair! Right you are, Crump. My mammy can run them hills and hollers with the best of 'em. Better'n Pa, even." He sighed longingly. "Ah, my beauties are strong and healthy, just a-waitin' for me, I'll swanny. I'd trade a couple years off'n the end of my life if I could scratch their necks right now."

Nathan looked at Crump and said quietly, "Are those coon ears?"

Crump nodded, growled a little laugh. "Say, Hound, what else you get sent in that big ol' box?"

Hound draped the raccoon ear necklace over his shoulder and began to poke around in the box. He pulled out several pairs of socks, a flannel shirt, and a tightly rolled pair of homespun trousers. Then, with a low moan of satisfaction, he dug out two large glass jars packed with pickled pig's feet. "Lord God a Abraham, boys! It's gonna try me somewhat to pass these around and not gobble 'em all myself." He reached back in the box and retrieved a loose handful of cornbread, stuffed it into his mouth. "Don't look like the pones tolerated the trip too good," he said, after swallowing several times.

Crump pushed himself up on one elbow. "Help me with my crutches will you, Cloyd? I'm a mind to see the world upright for a bit and make sure he don't make hisself sick on them pig's feet."

Nathan had already made his way across the aisle to inspect the various contents of Hound's box. Letha and Cloyd helped Crump, and soon they had him up on his crutches. With Letha and Cloyd on either side, the weakened man made his wobbly way across the aisle and, with a weary sigh, sat down at the end of Hound's bed. After Letha assured herself that he would be all right, she returned to Pollard's bed, sat down on the end.

She smiled. "One of our more colorful soldiers."

"It's a close contest between him and Crump."

"I have yet to thank you for your gift."

"Half gift."

"Yes, of course." The softness of his voice sounded familiar again; there was life in it, despite the weariness. It was as if the gap between their last bedside conversation and the present had been bridged, if somewhat unsteadily.

"Perhaps later tonight, when things have settled down, you might allow me to tell you of the man behind the melody."

"I would like that."

Pollard looked down, pursed his lips. "It is not a happy tale, but neither is it haunting any longer."

They sat quietly, listened to the laughter arising behind them, both hoping that it would not soon end. They turned their heads and watched as Cloyd dashed to his nightstand and stuffed his harmonica into his shirt pocket. He located a scrap of paper and his pencil, quickly writing his note. He walked to Letha and Pollard, held the note out for them to see.

## A TIME TO DANC

He grinned, waited for their reply.

"Yes, Mr. Anderson," Letha said, "I think it is just that."

Cloyd darted across the aisle to Nathan and held out the note, who made the announcement to the others. "Cloyd says it's a time to dance, boys. What you say?"

Hound bounced from the side of his bed. "It is, by Gawd! Cloyd, get to mouthin' on that harp. Come on, boys!"

Cloyd began to play "Dixie," snappy and loud, as Hound danced a one-sided jig that favored his tender foot. Two other men soon clomped down the aisle and joined them. Crump tapped his hand on one knee and motioned to Nathan, urging him to join in. Cloyd saw Crump's gesture and made his way to Nathan's side. With his left hand guiding the harmonica, he circled his right arm around the boy's back. Nathan glanced back over his shoulder at Letha, as if to say, "Look at me!" and tossed one of his crutches aside.

Letha felt a twinge of apprehension pass through her as Cloyd and Nathan danced their way up the aisle, and for a fleeting moment she feared that the omen might linger and spoil the beautiful sight. But the music and laughter of the men filled her ears, chased away the remnants of the thought. It was a time to dance.

# CHAPTER ELEVEN

At evening's end, Pollard watched Letha glide down the aisle toward him, backlit by the amber glow cast from the low-burning lamps. One by one, the men around him had drifted off into sleep, and now the only sounds in the ward were those of the netherworld that he now embraced as a friend. Letha still wore the beautiful Christmas dress, sans the apron. She sat down on the edge of his bed, near his waist, and he could see that her hair was free of the pins as it touched the points of her shoulders. The scent of lilacs filled his nostrils, suddenly a lovely complication of her nearness, and for the first time, Pollard desired to touch her hand, but he did not.

"So you have come to listen to my story," he said.

"I have."

Pollard looked directly at her face, but his vision extended far beyond her and the scent of lilacs was replaced with the choking odor of thick smoke. "I will tell it quickly, for I do not wish to stay there for long. It is the memory of the man that should live, not the memory of his death."

"You do not have to go back there at all," said Letha. "I am content to begin with his memory alone."

Pollard blinked her features back into focus. "For reasons that I do not exactly understand, I feel compelled to tell you the hurtful part."

"As you wish."

"You know of the Battle of the Wilderness?"

"I have heard tales. Some strain belief, others have the ring of truth."

Pollard smelled again the smoke, tinged with wood and leaves and flesh. "They all could well have been true."

A tiny shudder passed through Letha, as if someone had sneaked behind her and touched her bare neck with cold metal.

Pollard continued. "To this day, I have no idea how I survived it. In many ways, it was far stranger than even the day I was wounded." He looked beyond her again, into the smoke. "Once the undergrowth began to burn, there was no stopping it. The forest has a floor, you know—a soft blanket laid down by many autumns, leaves and grass and twigs—and when it catches fire it becomes a smoldering thing that cannot soon be extinguished. It was not long before the men of my unit could communicate only by shouting, and then even that became useless, and suddenly we were at one with the Union side, all tangled up with men and brambles and smoke. It was like a nightmare, and at one point I was certain that I would wake and the smoke would be gone, only the silence of the forest remaining."

Pollard paused, aware of the thudding of his heart, the shortness of his breath. "But it was real. We fought our way up a little knoll, and when we reached the top, I began to hear the screams of the burning men; voices from the fires of Hell they were. And I wanted to run away from them, for their cries were more frightening than gunfire. And I did run blindly through the smoke and brush, until I thought I caught my foot in a tangle, but it was . . . his hand that clamped onto my ankle, like a steel vice, and I kicked at him but he would not release me. I fell to the ground, twisted toward him.

"The smoke parted and I saw that he was Union. My musket was not charged, and I raised the bayonet to lance his face, but he said, 'No, sir; no, sir . . . I mean you no harm. I am near dead.' The fight had drifted away from us, down the slope of the knoll, and his voice was clear, devoid of pain. Almost peaceful."

Pollard was no longer aware of the sound of his own voice; it was as if someone else spoke from inside his head. "Most of the clothing was burned from his lower body and he was charred, like the leavings of an old campfire. I could see the bottom of his ribcage, and the bones of his legs were white. And I smelled him, putrid and sweet. There was a great lump on the side of his head, very little blood. He finally released my ankle and spoke quietly as he touched his head. 'Must've been a rifle butt. When I came too, I was on fire . . . drug myself over here.' He looked down at his side and legs. He said, 'It does not pain me, and I am thankful for that.' Then the sound of his breathing changed, like the sound of someone slowly tearing a piece of cloth. He reached out his hand, sought mine. I took it, held it fast. Then he spoke his final words. 'Won't be but minute or two longer. I thank you, sir . . . and I am sorry for the bother.'"

Pollard felt Letha's fingers warm against his own, for an instant mistook them for those of the burning man's ghost. She locked her fingers with his, tugged him away from the dark reverie. "You are a good man, Granville Pollard."

Pollard shook his head. "A good man would have said something to comfort him. I spoke not a single word."

Letha gently squeezed his hand, felt the tender pressure of his fingers as they responded to her touch. "He did not require your words, Granville, only your hand. It was the only comfort he sought."

"I do so hope that."

"It was."

Pollard lowered his head, looked at the two intertwined hands. "I wish to give him words now, with the melody."

"We shall." She looked down, drew in a careful breath. "Strange, is it not, how men who were trying to kill each other minutes before suddenly become brothers?"

He looked up, waited for her to raise her head. "I don't think it strange. It is the great riddle of this war—men in blue, men in gray—all whirling about in blood and fire and smoke, and most with no firm grasp as to why. And then, in an instant, some like him are taken, others like me maimed. I suppose that the great mystery is solved for him. I know that for me it remains."

"No firm grasp why?" Letha said. "But men on both sides speak with such assurance on the question. The North—your people—claim the eradication of slavery as their just cause, do they not?"

He tilted his head, but did not shake it. "For men like my father, it is far more than that, even as abhorrent as slavery is. It is about the severance of a nation, and although I cannot know for certain, I believe that for Lincoln, that is the greater cause."

"And your cause, Granville. What is your cause?"

"Was, Letha. Was. It was perhaps the shaking loose of my father's iron hand, and perhaps what I thought was love of someone I now know to be unworthy. It may never be fully sorted out in my mind."

Letha felt the warm flush rise past her neck and touch her cheeks. "I doubt that anything meaningful in this life is ever fully sorted out."

"I would not argue with that."

Nathan Fisher's single cry of anguish pierced the ward just as Letha tugged her blankets tightly under her chin, and for a moment she wondered if sleep had somehow already overtaken her and plunged her into an instant nightmare. But the cry arose again, louder, and carried her name.

"Miz Bartlett!"

*Nathan!* With a kick of her legs against the covers, Letha bounded from the bed and grabbed a robe in a single motion. As she passed into the ward, she hammered a fist into the chest of Brady Ayden, who awoke with a start, eyes wild and face covered as against an unknown foe.

"Wake up!" She held his face between both of her hands, made him focus on her. "Go find Major Crawford, now!" She pointed with her left hand, made sure Brady saw the direction. "Two buildings that way. Scream his name when you get inside the door! Scream it! Go!"

As she ran down the aisle she could see a man hovering over a lamp, walking unsteadily toward the calamity, and when she reached Nathan's bed the horrific scene was illuminated. Nathan's features were a mask of terror, his eyes white and round, as he stared at the rhythmic spurts of blood arching from his bare upper thigh. Letha dropped to her knees and clamped two fingers over the source of the blood, probing until she located a pressure point that stanched the flow. Only then did she dare look up into Nathan's face. His fear had subsided with the stoppage of the blood flow and now Letha saw in the boy absolute incredulity.

"I—I just woke up wet down there. I didn't feel nothin', I swear . . ."

"It's all right now, Nathan," Letha said. "The surgeon is on the way. Please stay as calm as you can. Lie back against your pillow. Calm now. Easy does it."

The shadow of two men fell across Nathan's body, and she looked up at Cloyd and Hound Patterson. "What happened?" Hound asked, his voice a hoarse whisper.

"I don't know," Letha said, looking away. "Please give us room. The surgeon will be here soon."

She heard the sound of other men stirring around her, and the light from more lamps rose like faraway fires. Nathan lay quietly now, his hands clutched into fists at his sides. Letha looked across the aisle at Pollard, who sat bolt upright at the end of his bed, his face grim in the dusk. Beside him, Crump stirred awake and rubbed a knuckle into the corners of his eyes, then blinked at the surreal scene across the aisle.

"Good God, pup. What's wrong with him, Pollard?"

"I don't know. The surgeon is on the way."

Crump then saw the blood-soaked blanket, the dark stains covering Letha's hands and forearms, and a wave of nausea passed over him, brought the bile to his throat, and he swallowed against it. "Oh, good God," he said softly.

Letha heard the clump of heavy footfalls behind her, and she twisted to watch Avery Crawford rush toward her, black bag in hand. His uniform coat was unbuttoned and flapped with each long stride. His bushy eyebrows were knotted into a single crooked row at the bridge of his nose. He knelt on one knee beside Letha, fixed his eyes on her bloody fingers, and knew immediately, beyond all doubt, what had happened. His shoulders slumped forward with the knowledge, the familiar invisible burden laid once again across his shoulders. The woman's eyes bored at the side of his head.

Her voice was controlled, but barely able to mask the panic. "*Do something, sir. What must we do now? A tourniquet?*"

Crawford considered rendering the sad verdict with quiet, well-chosen words—the way McCaw would do it if the duty were his. *I am grieved to tell you that a bone fragment has worked its way loose and nicked the femoral artery. The wound is so deeply encased in scar tissue that any attempt at surgical remedy would only succeed in causing useless suffering. There is absolutely nothing that may be done. We must give him over to the hand of God.* Crawford heard the words in his head, but he did not trust himself to utter them. He would do the deed with his eyes only, perhaps a shake of his head at most. He was not McCaw.

Letha hissed his name through clenched teeth. "Major Crawford."

Crawford turned his head slowly, the weariness filling his being like molten lead. He met the fiery darts of her eyes, did not avert his gaze.

With the passing of each second, the dread mounted in Letha's breast—a living, breathing, disgusting gargoyle of hideous proportions—and with the realization that it would surely devour Nathan Fisher, she suppressed the scream that rang inside her head. Her eyes filled with tears and they spilled from the inside corners, trickled to her lips.

"Dr. M—McCaw; go find—"

Crawford shook his head. "He is the finest surgeon I have ever known, madam, but he is not God."

"If there is any way—*any* way—I will get him through the pain."

Crawford said nothing, finally looked down, ran his long hand through the wisps of hair. Letha jerked her head away from Crawford, wished that his sour whiskey breath and downcast face would disappear.

Her loathing drifted to him like a foul smell, but he understood, thought no less of her for releasing it. He stood, looked at the frightened boy's face, knew that he must relieve the woman of the one duty she would not be able to perform.

He shuffled a step to Nathan's side, reached down, and placed his right hand on the boy's forearm. "I am so very sorry, son."

Nathan did not look at him. He said, "How long can I live?"

"As long as someone presses against that artery."

Crawford patted his arm a final time, then picked up his bag and walked away.

Crump watched in disbelief as the tall, slump-shouldered frame passed through the open doorway. The groan escaped him before he could suppress it, and to Pollard it was the horribly inarticulate utterance of a man wounded in battle. He turned toward Crump in time to see him slump onto his side in the bed. Then Cloyd passed behind Crump's bed, his arms outstretched toward the ceiling, like a man being pushed along at gunpoint, and he did not stop until he reached the wall and rapped his hands against it, allowed his forehead to rest on the cold wood.

Pollard's mind reeled, tilted strangely against the compressed agony that surrounded him. The sight of Letha was at once awesome and pitiful—the Angel of Chimborazo defiant, unflinching, and yet doomed in her efforts against the Angel of Death. Pollard willed his brain to a jerky halt, promised her silently that he would be there with her through the long night to come.

Low mutterings rippled up the rows of beds as news of the unfolding tragedy spread, but they faded quickly; none of the men were strangers to the dark whimsy of death. The surgeon had walked away; the die was cast. The believers whispered prayers for the soon dead, the haters cursed the Yankees, and a few simply wished that someone would turn the lamps back down so that they might again sleep.

Within minutes, only the lamp nearest Nathan's bed burned brightly, and the low voices faded into the shadows beyond its light. The silence descended—heavy and burdensome—a presence that could not be ignored, and soon it took on a voice and shrieked into the ears of those who did not sleep. Pollard felt the cold rising from the floor to join forces with the awful silence, yet to his surprise he was bound to admit that there was a certain majesty that came with the union. It did not arise from himself, or Crump, or Cloyd—they were but minor players on the incredible stage, a stage with only one actor and one actress, and a bloody bed in the center. Pollard no longer minded the shriek of the silence, the callous touch of the cold; he was witnessing something so powerful that it transcended even the sorrow he felt for Nathan Fisher and Letha. It was knowledge that he doubted he would ever share with anyone, least of all Letha, for he was not certain that he fully understood it himself. He only knew that it would follow him to his grave. Perhaps beyond. So Pollard watched and waited, mesmerized by the unmoving actor and actress across the aisle.

# CHAPTER TWELVE

It was Nathan who broke the silence, and the sound of his voice, though low and calm, startled everyone save for Letha. "Mr. Pollard, would you get some paper and a pencil?"

Pollard felt his body tense as the request registered in his brain. "Yes, Nathan." He scrambled back to his nightstand and fumbled for a clean sheet of paper and his pencil. He picked up the thin slat of wood that served as a portable table and scooted back to the foot of his bed. "I have them, Nathan."

"I want you to write down some things for my ma. You're the smartest feller I ever met, so I feel some lucky that you're here now. I don't want you to write down exactly every word . . . just for now write down some main things. When—when it's over with, I want you to make a fine letter out of it, if you would?"

"Anything you want, Nathan."

"Good. You ready then?"

"I am."

"First off, tell her that it don't hurt a'tall. That'll help her some. And that I ain't sure if'n I ever really killed a Yank. Always bothered her that I could kill somebody . . . and that even when I shot at 'em, it wasn't with a lick a hate in my heart. I'se mostly just scared. But tell her that I ain't scared now. That's what matters." He paused and Pollard listened as he drew a long breath, released it through his mouth.

"Tell her that I believe in the blessed Jesus, and that I ain't mad at God. I'll leave this world mad at Pa, but I don't want her to know that. That's between me and him. Goes without sayin' that I love her powerful and I'm dependin' that you can figure a way to say that proper. I know it's a hard thing to lay on you, Mr. Pollard . . . hope you don't consider it as bein' too forward, though I wouldn't blame you if you did. And for pity's sake, tell her about you all—my very good friends—and how lucky I was to meet you. I've already wrote her some, but not near enough. And figure a way to tell about how Miz Bartlett made my brace. I tried, but don't know if I made it clear to her. And how Miz Bartlett treated me like . . . a son. Ma won't be jealous a that, I know; she'll just be beholdin'. And tell her to scratch Skunk behind the ears onc't in a while. That's my dog marked black and white danged near like a skunk . . . wish't you could see him. And that's all I want to say."

Pollard looked back over the hastily written notes, made sure that he could read every word. Nathan knew what he was doing and waited patiently until he looked up from the paper. "Got all that?"

"Yes, I do."

"Make a pretty letter for me then . . . in a day or so."

Pollard nodded, could not speak.

"Cloyd? Bring your mouth organ and some paper and pencil."

Startled by the sound of his name, Cloyd jerked up his head, waited a moment for the request to register in his brain. Nervous fingers groped for paper and pencil, and with his other hand he tapped his shirt pocket to ensure that the harmonica was there. Nathan patted his hand on the bed, indicating the place that he wished Cloyd to take.

Nathan held his right hand, palm up. "I always wanted to try that thing."

Cloyd laid the harmonica in his hand. Nathan brought it to his lips and blew lightly, tooted a few experimental notes. He returned it to Cloyd. "Harder than it looks, ain't it?"

Cloyd shuffled two steps backward, stopped and looked at Nathan, then walked to his bed and sat down.

"Sergeant Crump," said Nathan. "Ain't no need to bother with tryin' to get over here. We can hear each other."

Crump did not move at first. His eyes were closed tightly, and three different times within the last few minutes, he nearly made himself believe that the dread scene was nothing more than a nightmare. But the sound of the boy's voice was clear and from only a few feet distant, and it was not a voice from a dream. He pushed up on an elbow, looked across at Pollard, hoping that the man of great intelligence could somehow be supportive, but Pollard was lost in his own thoughts, did not raise his head. Crump said, "Too far, pup? I'm comin' over."

Cloyd stood and walked to Crump's side, placed the crutches under his arms, and then helped him to Nathan's bedside. With a deep sigh, Crump lowered his bulk onto the bed, but could not bring himself to look at Nathan.

"You're gonna get well, Sergeant Crump, and go home to Alabama and your wife and younguns and have a good life, I just know it. You sure have been a good friend to me here . . . and I wisht we coulda knowed each other longer." Nathan held out his hand, felt Crump's settle into it. "Goodbye, sir."

Crump clenched his jaw muscles, touched his tongue to his lips, knew that he could not trust his voice for more than a few words. "Pup . . . by God but you're a good'n, I'll swear. Cain't figure why you'd get took 'fore so many sorry'uns."

"Mr. Pollard, I want to thank you again for doin' the letter. Means an awful lot to me, and it will to Ma, too."

"It will be my honor, Nathan."

He raised his right hand, offered it to Pollard, who grasped it firmly. "Keep singin', Mr. Pollard. It'd be somethin' of a sin if'n you didn't. Like throwin' away a gift."

Pollard looked at his face now, the boy's thin, rueful smile a thing of great beauty, and Pollard could not imagine the features limp in death.

Nathan said, "Goodbye, sir."

Pollard could manage only the slightest transformation of his own features, uncertain if they appeared grim or, as he hoped, affirming. Had the boy been consumed by dread—wailing and pleading in the manner of a child—the past several minutes would have been indelibly stamped into Pollard's brain as an extension of the nightmare that began with Nathan's initial cry of anguish. But the death pronouncement appeared to have calmed him, caused him to focus on those he would soon leave behind, and Pollard could not sort out his own emotions, could not feel the woeful pangs that should now be rippling through his body. Pollard himself had been uplifted, the would-be comforter, comforted. So he clung to the warmth of Nathan's hand, concentrated with all his might on finding a safe compartment in his brain in which to store the touch.

Back in his own bed, Crump lay on his side, his hands and arms tucked under his head, his blanket drawn up to his shoulders. His eyes were closed, but Pollard knew that he did not sleep. Pollard looked back across the aisle at Letha. Throughout the conversations, she had neither moved a muscle nor made the slightest sound. Her bare feet protruded—white and cold—beyond the hem of her gown. The expression on her face was one of defiance, her gaze fixed on the dried blood covering her fingers and hands. They were alone now, the actress and actor—alone on the final stage.

"Miz Bartlett, it's just me and you now," Nathan said.

Letha heard her name float toward her, as if spoken from an adjacent room. The conversations between Nathan and the three men had been lost to her amid the clamor resounding in her brain. She had heard only faraway voices that spoke words that might as well have been a foreign language. But now her name was in the air, directed at her, and she could not ignore it.

"Miz Bartlett, are you listenin'?"

She slowly lifted her head, saw Nathan turn his head to the side and tuck his chin against his shoulder as he sought her eyes. "Yes, Nathan, I am."

"Next to Ma, you're the finest lady I ever come across. There ain't no way to tell you how much I think of you." He touched his fingertips to hers, then spread his hand over the sticky gore. "I lied when I said I ain't scared no more, but there ain't no need for any more of this. I just want it over with." He paused, listened a single time to his own death pronouncement, softly intoned inside his head, then spoke the words aloud.

"Let go now."

He withdrew his hand, placed it over his other hand squarely in the center of his chest, and waited. But after the passing of long, cold minutes, he knew that she could not just let go. The woman could no more let go than if her own life hung in the balance, fingers pressing against the great artery in her own leg. It was too much to ask of her. He knew that he could jerk away from her, physically prevent her from stemming the flow of blood, but the idea was quickly rejected. It was a time for dignity, a time to honor her wishes—futile though they were. Perhaps Crawford would return, firmly grasp her hands, and remove her from the scene. The minutes stretched into a half hour, and then a full hour, but Nathan waited patiently; he could do no less.

Cloyd stood beside Pollard's bed, looked down at him. With the forefinger of his left hand, Cloyd pointed to the fingers of his right, tapped his chest, and then pointed across the aisle to Letha. He spread his fingers and lifted his hand.

Pollard whispered, shook his head. "No, Cloyd. Let her do it." He listened as Cloyd walked noiselessly to his bed and lay down.

Pollard grasped the loose top blanket, pulled it over his shoulders as he curled into a ball at the foot of his bed, and began his vigil. The familiar night sounds of the ward arose from the murky light cast over the rows of beds, but Pollard was as far from slumber as he had ever been. When the Angel of Chimborazo was finally defeated, he would be there for her.

# CHAPTER THIRTEEN

The Angel of Death is patient beyond man's understanding, and to
him, hours are as nothing.

Like a vapor, the chill seeped ever upward from the floor, enveloped
Letha like a damp blanket. An hour before, she registered the initial
shivers that coursed through her body like cold needles flowing with
her bloodstream, and now the trembling was a constant rhythm that
traversed her spine, extending to her extremities. There no longer
remained feeling in her toes, and it was only with the nearly continuous
shifting of her fingers on the wound that feeling was retained. Warm,
fresh blood oozed beneath her fingers each time she sought relief,
purchasing a few more minutes against the numbness. Letha knew
that the trembling was caused as much by fatigue as by cold, and
the whispers in her head that told of the end were becoming more
persistent by the minute. She searched the bank of her memory for
refuge—wondrous places where the breeze was warm in the green oak
leaves overhead and where her little brother gleefully plunked rocks

into the mirror of a pond and where the satisfied laughter of her father wafted over them. And for periods of time that seemed to her far longer than they actually were, Letha removed herself from the battle, shook off the frigid blanket. But with a jolt that caused her to gasp, the agony always returned with an ever-increasing intensity.

With the sound of her last gasp, Pollard flung the blanket away and lowered himself to his hands and knees, crawled across the aisle to her side. Letha turned her head and stared at him with eyes devoid of recognition, her teeth chattering audibly, and when he placed his hand over hers the tremors that racked her body became his own. He left her then, crawled back to his bed, returned with the blanket, and wrapped it around her shoulders. Again, he carefully placed his right hand over hers, followed the curvature of her two fingers as they lead to the pressure point of the wound.

"Letha, I will hold it now. You must rest. Rest."

So pronounced was the movement of her head that Pollard could not determine if she shook it in a negative answer or if the movement represented violent trembling. The sight was too much to bear, the hollow eyes jerking at him as if he were an intruding stranger, intent on doing harm, and he looked away. He muttered a curse at himself; the woman was beyond herself with weariness and pain, not some apparition to cower from. But Pollard would not have another chance. Letha's trembling hand beneath his own became suddenly and frightfully still—like a fragile bird that had perished from the unintended crush of his hand. Simultaneous with the spurt of blood against his fingers, her body flashed before him, brushing his shoulder before it slumped to the floor. Instinctively, with both arms, he reached for her, lifted her head from the floor, cradled it to his chest. It was then that the tiny, awful sound filled his ears. It was a sound like rainwater, leaking through a faulty roof onto a cloth surface—steady in supply and rhythm.

With his right arm encircling Letha, Pollard groped wildly with his left hand in search of the fountain of blood, but he would never locate it. Like the strong hand in the Wilderness fire, a band of flesh clamped around his wrist, directed his hand away from the wound. Pollard did not look at the hand.

"It's time now, Mr. Pollard."

He yanked his head toward Crump's bed, and then Cloyd's, seeking someone to help him, but the men slept and appeared as dark lumps in the gloom.

The fingers around his wrist loosened, then were gone. The spurts of blood were faint, as was the voice.

"You take care of her, Mr. Pollard."

Pollard wrapped the blanket tightly around her body, tucked it under her feet, then placed her head against his shoulder and rocked her like a child. He looked over her head at Nathan's body, saw that the hands, so small and bloody, were perfectly crossed and arranged on the chest.

Within the span of five seconds, the vision passed through Letha's brain, although to her it lingered with bright clarity, the scene slowing to a luxurious pace, allowing her to absorb every delightful detail. Dr. McCaw's square, handsome face split with a wide smile of satisfaction as he hovered over Nathan, his powerful hands covering the wound. Letha could detect no instruments in his hands; it was as if by their touch only, the great surgeon had wrought healing. He moved his hands slowly over Nathan's upper thigh and hip, and as he did, the bloodstains disappeared. Then both the surgeon and the boy laughed aloud, throwing back their heads in happiness, and Letha joined in the joyous laughter. They both sprang from the bed and extended a hand to Letha and they all three began to dance in a close circle, but they were no longer in the ward because she could look up and see the white pinpoints of stars.

There were no other buildings around the dancers, and the air was warm and clean in her face. They danced and danced, whirling upward on magical feet until the stars were as large as mansions, each with its own grand portico and windows aflame with white light. And then the door of the mansion nearest them swung open and she felt Nathan's grip loosen, then break free, and he whirled gracefully a final time as he disappeared through the wide doorway. McCaw's hand slipped from hers as the mansions drifted farther and farther into the distance, and soon they appeared again as stars and then vanished altogether.

Letha attempted to reach up with both arms and remain in the realm of the mansions, but her arms were pinned between her and the body of a stranger, and she could not pound her fists against his chest as she wished. A voice inside the chest called to her, and with the sound of her name, Letha realized that she was earthbound, the hard wood floor of Chimborazo beneath her.

"Letha . . . Letha . . ."

She regained consciousness with a stab of terror ripping through her. Both of her hands were touching her body—the body that did not need her, that did not bleed. She struggled to tear herself away from the arms that held her, but the efforts were futile, her own arms drained of all energy. "Letha, it's Granville. Let me hold you. Just let me hold you."

Pollard listened as the awful sound escaped from deep within her body—an inward groan that seemed not to involve her vocal chords—sorrow and anger in equal measure. He held her tighter, hoping to absorb a portion of the grief. Slowly the groan finally faded into their bodies, and Pollard rocked her until she fell into a fitful sleep.

.   .   .

She stirred against Pollard's chest as the first hint of dawn altered the shadows of the ward. She did not look at Pollard's face as she pushed carefully away from his body, allowing the blanket to fall from her shoulders as she stood and walked haltingly up the aisle. She returned within minutes, clad in a plain gray dress with a dark apron tied to its front. Her hair was arranged in the familiar tight bun, her features devoid of expression. In her hands she carried a pail of water and a large roll of tattered bandages. Pollard, who had returned to sit on the end of his bed, watched as she cleaned the dried blood from Nathan's hip and thigh. From a dress pocket she withdrew the threaded darning needle and sewed together the toes of his socks. She traded the needle and thread for a comb and stroked it through his hair, and with a hand on either side of his head, settled it firmly in the center of his pillow. She then wove his fingers together and arranged the hands perfectly. The blanket that had been cast aside in the first moments of the crisis lay on the far side of the bed and she retrieved it, covered the body from head to toe.

Crump rubbed the sleep from his eyes, pushed himself up on an elbow, surveyed the scene in front of him. He exchanged glances with Pollard, who nodded first to him and then past him as Cloyd stirred in his bed. The three men watched and waited as Letha stood motionless beside the head of Nathan's bed. She betrayed no signs of the night of torment just passed—her hands clasped together in front of her apron, her back ramrod straight, as if in the military position of attention. To the puzzlement of the men, she stood in this fashion for more than five minutes, and then turned toward them.

"We are all much less, with his death."

Pollard shuddered inwardly with the sound of her voice. In it was the solemn assurance that her contention was accurate in her own case, and he opened his mouth to speak words that might point her away from the darkness of it all, remind her that they all, though undeniably lessened, still lived. But a suitable thought would not form in his brain, and it was Crump who spoke. He too had discerned the hollowness in her pronouncement.

"Yes'm, there ain't no disputin' that. But I knowed him good as of any of us, and he'd be mighty sad if we was to give up."

Letha spoke as if she had not heard Crump, spoke to no one, and everyone. "I know only this. He will not be buried in the common lot where no one can ever find him."

She turned stiffly and walked away.

Crump looked at Pollard and asked, "How did it end?"

"She held the wound most of the night, finally fainted. I held her for perhaps an hour as she slept. If it could be called that."

"Did he say anything else?"

Pollard rubbed his fingers over his wrist, remembered the grip of steel, and then the boy's final admonishment. Pollard assured himself that it was no business of Crump's. It was no one's business, save for his own. But even as he spoke, the selfishness seeped to the surface, and he answered. "He was resigned to dying, but, yes, he did ask me to take care of Letha."

Crump nodded at this, as though this were a reasonable request. But for Pollard, the thought of taking care of himself, much less anyone else—even less someone as precious as Letha—all of it felt far beyond his capabilities.

"Anyhow," Crump said, "me and the pup were workin' on somethin' for your stumps—stump, really. He told me that he'd heard the surgeons talkin' about one of your stumps bein' sturdier and longer than the other. Is that right?"

Pollard nodded. "Yes, the right is considerably stouter."

"That's what he said, all right, and then he told me he planned to get some card paper and paste and such from Miz Bartlett and fix you somethin' like his brace to fit onto a block of wood, 'bout the size of a foot. That was gonna be my job, the wood block. We figured, no more'n you weigh, if'n you could just put a little weight down on the good stump, then you could crutch along right smart . . . 'thout nobody's help, don't you see?"

Pollard sighed. "Just now, Crump, it doesn't seem to be that important, but if you think it would work, we can try."

Crump looked across the aisle, studied the yellow pattern of the blanket covering Nathan's body. "It is important, and it'll work."

In the adjacent ward building, Letha located a convalescent who claimed to have been a carpenter before the war. He had taken a rifle ball through the right leg, the missile striking flesh only, and he limped slightly as he took the final steps toward her. He wore a ragged brown shirt, buttoned to the neck, with sleeves that stopped several inches short of his bony wrists, from which long hands dangled like idle tools. From behind an unruly beard, he smiled carefully at Letha.

"So you're needin' a carpenter, ma'am."

"Yes, can you help me?"

"Reckon what it is you lookin' to build?"

"A coffin—and not just another coffin. A perfect coffin."

He nodded as the smile faded away. "Got lumber?"

"I can procure all that you need."

"How big is the dead'un?"

"He was sixteen. Not big."

The man searched her features, saw the unmistakable sadness behind the stoic eyes and firm lines of her mouth. He extended his right hand. "Name's John Willis Tillerman, ma'am. At your service."

Letha shook his hand. "I thank you kindly, Mr. Tillerman. As soon as you're ready, meet me behind the ward building next door." She pointed over her left shoulder. "I will have the boards and tools you need."

Letha watched from the small landing leading to the back door as Tillerman nailed together the boards forming the lid. He had proven himself to be an able carpenter and within an hour had fashioned a sturdy coffin. With Crawford's assistance, Letha had arranged for a horse-drawn wagon and a driver, the latter being a hump-shouldered soldier who stood close to the horse, using the animal as a shield from the wind. Tillerman's hands were red from the cold but seemingly unaffected as his fingers nimbly crept around the edges of the lid. Once satisfied with the fit, he poked several nails into the side of his mouth and began to drive them partly into the boards. He laid the hammer on the ground and lifted the lid from the coffin, placed it on top of the remaining lumber scraps.

He arched his back against the stiffness and then looked at Letha, nodded once. "We gonna load him in there or out here, ma'am?"

"Inside. I will get you some help."

She returned with Cloyd close behind and held open the door as the two men lifted the coffin and entered the building. Once inside, Letha moved to the front of the coffin. In her hands she held two small boards, less than a foot in length and an inch thick. When she reached Nathan's bed, she placed the boards on the floor, separated by a distance she judged to be five feet. The men rested the coffin on the boards, and then moved to opposite ends of the bed. Letha stepped between the coffin and the bed and carefully tucked the blanket under the body. From the pocket of her dress she removed three lengths of white ribbon and tied them at spaced intervals around the blanket.

"Carefully, please."

Cloyd and Tillerman gently gathered the body and laid it in the coffin. Letha kneeled and rearranged the blanket and ribbons to her liking, then stood, looked back up the rows of beds. "As most of you know, his name was Nathan Fisher. He was from a farm near Dothan, Alabama. He was but sixteen years of age. He never once complained, and his spirit was winsome." She stood silently for a moment, swept her gaze from wall to wall, listened to the murmurs of agreement. "He will rest in Hollywood Cemetery, with a properly inscribed headboard. Perhaps some of you will visit him later, in quieter times to come. I know I shall."

Pollard studied her profile, concentrated on each syllable she spoke, but he could not solve the growing mystery that threatened to enshroud her. The tone of her voice was somehow different, subtly altered, and Pollard did not like the sound of it. There was something hollow and mechanical about it, almost dutiful, despite the appropriateness of the word selection. She was too strong in this moment. Unnaturally strong. Nathan's death was horribly out of step with the order of things, even in such a place as Chimborazo, and had stunned her to the very core of her being. Yet she had seemingly pulled herself together, returned to her efficient ways—no detail too small, no oversight allowed. She should be weeping now, barely able to eulogize the boy who had so often caused her spirit to soar far beyond the bleak walls. But there were no tears, only an impenetrable stoicism that frightened Pollard.

She turned and looked at Cloyd. "Mr. Anderson, would you accompany me to the cemetery? I do not know if a sexton will be available to dig the grave."

Cloyd nodded, walked quickly to the wall peg, and pulled on his coat and hat. He returned to his place at the head of the coffin, then made a digging motion for Letha to see.

"A shovel is in the wagon, sir."

Tillerman said, "I'd be honored to dig with him, ma'am."

"It is five miles at least to the cemetery, Mr. Tillerman, and it looks like rain out there."

"I've come a sight farther than five miles in the rain, ma'am."

"Very well then. Thank you, sir." She swept her hand over the body. "Let us proceed."

She waited for them to pick up the coffin, then, without looking back, led the way up the aisle. The wagon driver held the harness of the horse as they slid the coffin into place. Tillerman retrieved the hammer and jumped onto the bed. Cloyd handed him the lid and he quickly nailed it down. The two men sat down on either side of the coffin as Letha took her place beside the driver. With a slight motion of her hand, Letha signaled to the driver.

The man slapped the reins easily over the horse's rump. "Get up there, now, let's go."

# CHAPTER FOURTEEN

As they rumbled past the last of the ward buildings, Tillerman looked across the top of the coffin and extended his hand to Cloyd. "John Willis Tillerman, I am."

Cloyd shook his hand, then made the motion of a man shouldering a rifle and shooting it, quickly pointing to one cheek and then the other. He parted his lips and placed the tip of his forefinger in the space once occupied by his tongue, shook his head.

"Sorry-ass piece a luck, warn't it?"

Cloyd nodded, held his hands palms up, shrugged his shoulders.

"Rifle ball, huh?"

Cloyd smiled grimly, held up two fingers.

"Good Gawd! You don't say?"

Cloyd nodded, again poked the two fingers into the air.

"Good Gawd, but that beats all, I'll swar."

They rode in silence for several minutes, paying no attention to the jostling of the wagon bed. Tillerman reached across the coffin and patted Cloyd's shoulder. "Cloyd, warn't it?"

Cloyd turned toward him, mouthed a "yep" in reply.

"I been a thinkin', Cloyd. Considerin' some of the sorry mess I seen in the last three year, it might not be too bad a thing, not havin' to talk any."

Cloyd reached into his coat pocket, pulled out a pencil and a small square of paper. He braced himself against the coffin and used it for a table as he wrote, then shoved the note toward Tillerman.

## ALL CONSIDRD I WOLD LIKE MY TONG BACK

Tillerman pushed the note back toward him. "Yeah, reckon I'd say the same thing." He looked down for a moment, tapped the coffin with his fingers. "Lotsa sorry-ass luck goin' around these days."

On rolled the funeral wagon through the streets of Richmond. Neither pedestrians nor the occupants of other vehicles paid any attention to the wagon. Though Letha seldom turned her head to the side, she could not help but take note of the pockmarked buildings, some freshly marred by the Federal bombardment. Among the citizenry, there appeared to be no great sense of urgency. The city had long been at war and, like the citizens, projected an aura of weariness. It was a weariness far deeper than the scarred buildings and mangled trees, and the low, heavy clouds of winter only drove it deeper into the bones of the people. Had she cared, Letha would have seen it on the faces that passed close by, but her purpose was singular, and she paid no more attention to the inhabitants of the city than they paid to her.

They stopped only twice, the first time to allow Letha to inquire about the location of the cemetery agent's office. After a detour of three blocks, the wagon halted in front of a dingy red brick building. Letha paid for the grave plot and returned to the wagon seat without a word to the men, then signaled for the driver to continue. As if orchestrated by a merciless power, the wind-driven rain began to slice at them as the wagon approached the arched gate of the cemetery. The wagon rumbled slowly past the gate and down the rutted path to the small shelter house where the sexton stood, his wide-brimmed hat tilted against the wind and rain. He waited until the plodding horse was nearly at arm's length before he bothered to look up into Letha's stony face.

"The sexton, I presume," she said, raising her voice over the wind.

The man looked up from under the hat brim, and with one long finger raised it a bit. His beardless face was without expression. "Who else you reckon'd be drownin' out here in this fine weather?"

Letha stared down at him, drew her mouth into a thin line. "You will be pleased to learn that we wish only to borrow a shovel and lowering ropes."

He turned and reached inside the door of the shelter, withdrew a long-handled shovel around which were coiled two lengths of rope, and casually extended it toward the wagon bed. Cloyd took it from him and laid it beside the other shovel near the coffin.

With a flick of her hand, Letha produced the receipt for the plot and said, "The bill is paid." She stuffed it back into her pocket before the sexton could walk to her seat. The wagon groaned forward as the man pulled his hat back down and disappeared into the shelter house.

After they had covered fifty yards, Letha pointed toward a towering oak, great black limbs steady in the wind. "There," she said, "close to that oak. The agent said the plot would be near it."

The driver turned the horse to the left, felt the pull of the wheels on the softer ground as they left the narrow road. Both Cloyd and Tillerman stood leaning forward in the wagon bed, each with a hand on the coffin for balance.

"No use to get closer, ma'am. Too much mud for the wagon," Tillerman said.

Letha raised her hand, halted the driver. She stepped down from the wagon seat and walked a few steps toward the tree. The men picked up the shovels and hopped down from the bed, then walked to a position on either side of Letha. The wagon driver climbed down from his side of the seat and took shelter on the downwind side of the horse.

Letha pointed to the space beside a freshly painted wooden cross. "This is his resting place."

Tillerman surveyed the sodden ground for a moment, then took a few steps forward. With the tip of the shovel, he traced a three-foot by six-foot rectangle and looked up for her approval.

"That will be fine, sir."

Once past the layer of mud, the men dug quickly. They worked side-by-side until the depth of the grave was such that only one man could wield his shovel from inside it, and then they dug in fifteen-minute intervals until finally Cloyd stood chest deep. He looked up at Tillerman, who nodded and stabbed his shovel into the base of the mounded soil. Cloyd popped out of the hole and stuck his shovel into the mound beside the other. They brought the coffin to the edge of the grave, laid it on the two lengths of thick rope that Letha had positioned. With the ends of the ropes in each hand, the men easily lifted the weight and carefully sidestepped to the grave, slowly lowered the coffin into place. Each man released an end of the rope and began to tug on it.

"No," said Letha, "they will stay in place. I do not wish to disturb him."

They released the ropes, the muffled *whumps* carrying up from the grave. The men stepped back, waited. Letha walked to the grave, the toes of her black shoes nearly touching the edge. From her pocket, she took a small New Testament, held it in both hands, looked down at the coffin. The intensity of the rain increased, the cold drops pelting her face, but she did not feel them. After a long minute crept past, Cloyd and Tillerman exchanged puzzled glances. Another minute passed in silence, and then she slowly slipped the small black book into her pocket.

She did not raise her head as she spoke. "My soul is restless, barren. It would be sacrilege if I should offer words from Scripture." She raised her head, tilted her face directly into the cold rain. "God may choose to forgive me, or He may not. Just now it matters not to me what choice He makes . . . if indeed He is there at all." She took three backward steps. "Finish your work."

Cloyd remained motionless as Tillerman grabbed a shovel and began to fill in the grave. Letha's brief and bitter statements had pierced him through, chilled him far worse than the elements. He had been certain that she would offer words of comfort and reassurance, had expected her to sing perhaps a verse or two of an appropriate hymn. But her words had stunned him into a silence so profound that his severed tongue suddenly was of no consequence, and he could not will his body into action.

Letha turned her head toward him, fully aware of the burden she had laid across his shoulders like a heavy yoke. His gaze was vacuous, the scarred and sunken cheeks shrouding his face in an old man's visage. His fingers worked nervously over his trousers, as if his hands were the only parts of his body that obeyed his brain, for she knew that he did not desire to display himself like a helpless figurine. The faint glow came to Letha from a chamber of her soul—now a small accouterment to her being—and she allowed the warmth to grow, but only enough to rescue the sad, mute man before her. He would have his harmonica with him; it would be sufficient.

"Mr. Anderson?"

Her voice had lost some of its edge, and he was able to turn toward her, answer with his eyes.

"Perhaps you would care to play a tune for Nathan before we leave. It might lift us all."

Cloyd felt his head bobbing up and down, and life returned to his limbs with the realization that all was not lost on this sorrowful day. He picked up the other shovel and began to help Tillerman fill in the grave. Soon they tamped with the flat surfaces of their shovels the low mound of sticky soil, carefully shaping it until they were satisfied with its appearance. Cloyd glanced at Letha and then handed his shovel to Tillerman. He reached inside his coat to his shirt pocket and withdrew his harmonica, turning slightly away from the wind. He began to play "Amazing Grace" in long, slow notes, the melody carrying on the wind down a long slope from the tree. Tillerman removed his hat, placed it over his chest, and bowed his head.

The notes floated to Letha's ears, but she would not allow them entry. They were good things, comforting the kind and decent man who played them. She had provided a means for his solace; she had performed her duty, cared to do no more.

From the corner of her eye, she saw two stooped, black-clad figures trudging up the slope toward the gravesite, and she blinked against the rain, focused on them. They were both women, wintry and bent, and now she could see their pinched, white faces, upturned despite the rain. They were being drawn to the music as surely as if tethered to a long rope and reeled up the hill. On they came until they stood twenty paces distant, and then they sank to their knees and bowed their heads in respect to the dead. In synchronized motion, they brushed their fingers over the black cloaks, signing the cross, then folded their hands, wrinkled lips moving steadily in prayer. Letha looked away from them, waited for Cloyd to finish the hymn. After the last note had faded away, the two women held each other's arms as they pushed up from the mud. With a final nod of respect, they again signed the cross over their bosoms, turned and began to walk away.

Cloyd returned the harmonica to his pocket, shuffled his feet, waited for instructions.

Tillerman said, "That was mighty fine, Cloyd."

"Indeed. Thank you, sir," Letha said. She began to walk to the wagon, and the men fell in step behind her.

Tillerman pointed down the hill, said to Cloyd, "Catholics, them two. They do that signin' on theirselves when they're stirred up. Right decent of 'em to come and do that, get all down in the mud and such. Right decent, I'll say."

When they reached the shelter house, the sexton appeared in the doorway. Letha looked straight ahead as he approached the bed of the wagon and took the shovel from Tillerman. He waited, expecting the ropes, but Tillerman sat back down in the wagon, looked away.

The sexton spoke to Letha. "Where's them ropes?"

She did not look at him as she replied. "Where they belong. Buried with the honored dead."

A huff of exasperation escaped the man. "It ain't easy to come by rope like that these days."

"You have my condolences, I'm sure."

The wagon creaked forward a few feet before the sexton's voice chased after her. "He musta not been too honored, huh? You didn't even leave a name for the headboard."

Letha held up her hand, halted the wagon, and turned backward in her seat. "That is a task that I will not entrust to your slovenly ways, Mr. Sexton. I will leave proper instructions with the cemetery agent in town."

She turned back around, motioned for the driver to proceed.

Letha picked her way through the mud. Every few steps, either Cloyd or Tillerman cupped a hand under her elbow and steadied her. The wagon driver had been reluctant to retrace his path to the door of the ward building, and Letha had dismissed him, agreed to walk the final hundred yards. When they reached the building, Letha stepped up on the landing and scraped the sides and soles of her shoes on the edge of the top tread. She removed the soaked blanket from her shoulders and folded it loosely, then opened the door, glanced back to the men.

"Follow me, gentlemen."

Inside the kitchen, she motioned for them to warm near the stove, then said, "Give me a few moments to change, please. Mr. Ayden will find you some hot coffee."

Like a phantom emanating from the corner of the room, Brady appeared, a finger looped through the handles of two cups. He set them down on the stove and filled them from the big metal pot. He stepped back, waited for the men to pick up the cups, and then faded back into the shadows.

Letha returned before they had drunk half of their coffee. In her arms she carried a thick plaid shirt of good quality and a pair of tweed trousers, both items neatly folded. She laid them on the corner of the kitchen table. "You are welcome to stay as long as you wish, Mr. Tillerman, but I know you must want to change and dry out in your own space." She motioned toward the clothing. "I have a fair eye for sizing men. Please keep these and wear them in good health, sir."

"That's kind of you, ma'am, but it ain't necessary."

Letha glanced at the clothes, then Tillerman. "I seem to have a growing collection of unused clothing, Mr. Tillerman. Keep them."

Tillerman looked down, said, "Yes'm. I 'preciate it."

Letha walked to the stove, brought the coffeepot, and refilled both cups. She rested the pot on the edge of the table. "I am in your debt, sir, and I hope that this effort has not aggravated your wound."

"You ain't in no debt to me, ma'am. The leg ain't much of a bother no more. 'Bout ready to go back to my regiment."

For the first time, Letha studied his broad, bony face, the humble smile, the green of his eyes. She had recorded in her brain many such faces—all attached to some piece of life, some moment frozen in time when a few words, or a facial expression, or even the silent bearing of pain indelibly imprinted the image. But she did not wish to record the face of this good man, and was relieved that he would never know of this barren wish.

"Thank you again, sir. I must return to my duties now."

She nodded, picked up the coffeepot and returned it to the stove, then moved to the side of a kitchen assistant. She picked up a knife and began to carve at the opposite end of the bacon slab, cutting the slices as thinly as she could.

Tillerman took a long sip of the coffee, savored the marvelous burn coursing down his throat and into his stomach. "Cloyd, fore I leave for my unit, I'm gonna come get you one day soon so's you can play for the boys over in my ward. That all right?"

Cloyd's head bobbed up and down as he opened the fingers of one hand to say, "Anytime."

"Good." Tillerman set down the cup and picked up the clothing. "I feel like a possum caught out in a thunderstorm, Cloyd. Think I'll go now." He clapped a hand firmly on Cloyd's shoulder, then walked to the door.

Cloyd set his cup on the table, glanced at Letha's back, then began to walk toward the rows of beds.

Pollard jerked his head up the aisle as Cloyd entered the ward. He followed the sodden, bedraggled man as he passed his bed and nodded a hello. Crump turned his head as he followed Cloyd's progress, waited until he reached the wall peg and hung his coat.

"You got dry clothes, Cloyd?" Crump asked.

Cloyd pointed to his shirt and nodded, and then to his trousers as he shook his head.

"Lookee yonder in that crate." Crump pointed to the box near the head of his bed. "Get them britches outta there. I damn sure don't need 'em."

Cloyd nodded in thanks as he pulled the trousers from the box. He took the harmonica from his shirt pocket and laid it on his bed.

He changed into the dry clothing and sat down on the edge of his bed, waited for the questions that were sure to come.

Crump pointed at the harmonica. "You play for him?"

Cloyd nodded.

"She sing?"

He slowly shook his head, ran a hand over his mouth and then down over his chin.

"Hmm. Too broke up, I reckon?"

Cloyd felt Pollard's stare, but did not look at him. He raised both hands to indicate that he was unsure of the reason, but Pollard read his face and suspected that it was something other than grief behind Letha's omission.

Crump said, "It's gonna take a good while 'fore she gets over this." He shook his head. "'Fore I do, too, far as that goes. Cain't hardly stand to look over there."

Pollard said, "No one will get over it completely as long as we are in this place, least of all her."

Crump muttered for a moment, pieces of words full of frustration. "The Almighty is altogether confusin' to me these days. It's like the whole thing was a trick of some sort. The pup lookin' like he was healin' so good, full of life and all, holdin' all of us up . . . damn it all."

Pollard looked past Crump, would not allow Cloyd an avenue of escape. "Did she cry at all?"

Cloyd knew what Pollard really desired to learn, knew that he must tell him the truth. He reached for his paper and pencil, furrowed his brow as he wrote out the note on the top of his nightstand. He took it to Pollard.

*I DONOT NO HOW TO SAY IT RIGHT BUT SHE IS NOT THE SAME*

*YOU WILL NO SOON WHAT I MEAN*

# CHAPTER FIFTEEN

Pollard moved his eyes but not his head toward Letha as she helped Brady Ayden with the newly arrived soldier in the adjacent bed. Three weeks had passed since the terrible night of Nathan Fisher's death, but Pollard could detect no sign that she was shaking off the shroud of detachment that had enwrapped her. She was as efficient as ever—perhaps more so—in the performance of her duties. *Duties*, thought Pollard; that was all they were now. Before Nathan's death it seemed that anything she did for the men, no matter how tedious or unpleasant, was done in a fashion that masked her effort, caused the recipient of the aid to feel as if he were the only man on Earth for those precious moments of tending. But it was no longer so. Conversations had become merely the exchange of necessary words—little tools that made the tasks easier for everyone. Gone were the smiles, gone were the little feminine nuances of expression that heartened the spirits of broken men.

Pollard moved his head to the right, took in the scene around the new soldier. Crawford was with them now, gouging and prodding at the remnants of the man's left ear. Letha had fresh bandages in her hand, would soon expertly bind the raw flesh, then walk swiftly to her next duty without ever turning around to speak to Pollard or Crump. These things Pollard knew with a nagging certainty, and he turned his head so that he would not have to watch her walk away.

On a bleak, windswept morning in the first week of February, Cloyd Anderson raised his head toward the slow drumbeat of boots and saw the tall figure of Avery Crawford's body slouching down the aisle as if pushed by the same cold wind that rattled the building. As was his wont, Crawford did not look ahead to his destination; he would look at the object of his visit only when he was within a pace or two. Despite this fact, when he was halfway down the aisle, Cloyd felt the tug in his gut that assured him of the reason for the surgeon's visit. Cloyd had known that it would be soon, had prepared himself as best he could. It was not fear that came to him and whispered in his head, but it was a close relative. Cloyd suspected that all of the wounded who were ordered back to their units dealt with the same feeling, and he thought no less of any of them, or of himself. It was a simple matter; it was time to go back.

Cloyd stood, glanced first at Pollard and then Crump, waited for Crawford to stop and look at him. Crawford's skeletal white hand swept over his face, pulled thoughtfully at his beard. "Private Anderson, I am releasing you back to your unit. Quite frankly, sir, I would prefer to send you home, but that is not my prerogative. I am not, nor have I ever really been, a military man. But I am told that it is the military matters that must come first . . . always first." He paused, blinked sadly. "They will come for you this afternoon. I wish you well."

Cloyd smiled, nodded in understanding. He pointed to his cheek, slowly mouthed, "Thank you."

Crawford felt the laugh stir deep inside, but when he opened his mouth no sound escaped. He shook his head and said, "It was a good thing, sir, that the maggots found you before we surgeons did."

Cloyd sat back down on his bed as Crawford clomped back up the aisle. Crump pushed up on one elbow, said, "Well, I was expectin' that; 'spect you were too, huh?"

Cloyd nodded, opened his hands, and then returned them to his thighs.

"Everything's a mite desperate these days," Crump said. "Ain't a regiment out there that's really a regiment anymore, I reckon."

Pollard said, "From what I can learn, there is a noose closing around Richmond. It surely is the grand prize for the Union."

"I doubt it's much of a prize anymore."

"It's the capital of the Confederacy. A symbol, no matter if they bombard it to pieces."

Crump shook his head. "It's all about Robert E. Lee now, Pollard. Has been for a long time. Grant knows that he's gotta get Lee to give up the fight. The boys—they'd all die, if'n he asked 'em to."

"Perhaps, but surely they see the capital as the heart of the Confederacy."

"No. The heart of the Confederacy is Lee. The South can live only as long as he holds out, and he cain't hold out much longer." Crump looked at Cloyd. "You're gonna make it all right, Cloyd. Man takes two balls through the head and lives, he's done paid his dues, I'll tell ya. If'n I was goin' back with you, I'd stay stuck to you like a molasses gob."

Cloyd reached for his coat and hat, signed with his hands that he was going outdoors for a walk. Pollard waited until he walked away, then said, "It doesn't seem fitting that they should order a mute back into it. A man should be able to communicate. And besides, he doesn't have enough teeth left to gnaw hardtack."

"They need his body, Pollard—legs to move, and arms and hands to hold a musket, and eyes to aim it. They don't need a private's tongue for much. And he's got a few teeth in back. I asked him once; he held up three fingers. I figure a man gets hungry enough, he could get by with three." He snorted. "Prob'ly none, even. Just gum it a little and choke it right down. Least he wouldn't have to taste it much thataway."

Pollard sank back onto his pillow. "You are a pragmatic man, my friend. I suppose that is why you are a good soldier."

"'Was,' Pollard. Not 'are.'" Crump waited for several seconds, then said, "Well, you gonna tell me what that means—prag . . . whatever— or you gonna just lay there like a closed book?"

Pollard rolled his head toward Crump. "It means that you have a talent for getting to the heart of the matter."

"Cuttin' through the horse crap, huh?"

"Precisely."

A low rumble of understanding arose from Crump's throat as he shifted his body, stared at the ceiling. After a minute of silence, he said, "For a feller who cain't say nary a word, I'm damn sure gonna miss Cloyd."

"Yes. Yes, so will I."

Save for his clothing, all of Cloyd Anderson's possessions fit easily into his haversack and both of his hands. He had written two notes, then straightened his bed coverings, and now he stood at the foot of the bed. Pollard had cut three-dozen small paper squares, punched holes, and bound them tightly with a string so that Cloyd could easily write and distribute his notes. He held this homemade notebook in his right hand along with three stubby pencils. In his left hand he held his harmonica and his pocketknife. He glanced at the three men staring at him— Pollard and Crump from their nearby beds, and Hound Patterson from across the aisle—and then looked down at his hands. With the knuckles of his thumbs, he lifted the coat pocket flaps and poked the items securely into place. He turned back to the upright crate beside his bed and picked up the notes, took one of them to Pollard, stuffed the other in his trouser pocket. He took a step back.

## POLLARD PLESE READ THIS LIKE IT OUGT TO SOND

Pollard smiled inwardly, then quickly scanned ahead, sorted through the jumble of words, and translated them as he imagined Cloyd would like him to.

"I am not talented at extending farewells, my friends, so this will be a brief note. I will take from this place much more than I am able to leave, and that is not usually my nature. Sergeant Crump has written down my address, should someday any of you desire to look me up. I hope that life takes a turn for the better for you boys. You are all very fine boys, and I will miss you greatly. So long, Cloyd."

Pollard lowered the paper behind his thigh and crumpled it into a tight ball. He looked up to Cloyd then and studied his face for a moment, saw the thickening, sunken-cheeked scars that would always make him appear twenty years older than he was, like some half-starved old man. But his eyes were bright and his smile was sturdy, and these features Pollard fixed in his mind.

Cloyd nodded a thank you to Pollard, then moved to Crump's side, extended his right hand. Crump shook his hand, said, "I'm proud to have knowed you, Cloyd Anderson. You listen to me now. You get mixed up in some bad fight out yonder, you find the biggest rock or tree you can, and stay behind it. This here thing's 'bout over, and you've damn sure give enough to the Cause."

Cloyd turned to Pollard, shook hands. Pollard said, "It has been my honor, Cloyd. Perhaps we will make some music together in a happier time."

Cloyd slowly nodded his head, tapped his hand over his heart. He walked to Patterson's bed, shook hands with the wiry little man. Hound said, "Reckon I won't be far behind you, Cloyd. Maybe we can both find us somebody wide as Crump to lead the way, huh?"

Cloyd walked to the doorway, stopped and turned around. He reached into his pocket, pulled out the harmonica, and brought it to his lips. The tune was his own, the notes long and soft, and he played for less than a minute, but to the men, it seemed much longer.

Letha listened as the notes floated into the kitchen. She lifted her head, did not recognize the melody, knew it was Cloyd's creation. She laid down the heavy knife and wiped her hands on her apron, then turned and walked toward the front door. She cracked the door open a few inches, saw the rickety wagon with three men already sitting in the bed, the gray-coated driver waiting patiently. She waited for the tune to end, then opened the door.

Cloyd removed his hat as he approached her and with his other hand retrieved the note from his trouser pocket, held it out for her to read.

## I HAVE PRACTSED THIS OUTSID JUST FOR YOU

He took a deep breath and pursed his lips as he prepared himself for the effort that no one but the wind had ever heard. He held out his right hand, forced the tortured sounds past the stub of his tongue. "Aaaannk ooouh. Ooouh arrr . . . aaa . . . annhel."

As if guided by an unseen hand on her elbow, Letha felt her arm rising, her fingers reaching for Cloyd's hand. Her brain processed the sounds, ordered them. *Thank you. You are an angel.* His hand gently squeezed hers—tentative, almost fearful—seeking just the right amount of pressure to express his admiration. She registered a tiny movement deep within her, as if a small, flat rock had been flipped over, exposing a hiding place. She cared greatly for this man, for all of them, despised the coldness in her heart as the vile intruder it was. But the intruder could not simply be evicted, swept out the door with a broom, and so Letha Bartlett could only calculate with her brain, could only seek a practical way to help this kind man.

She released his hand. "Thank you, Mr. Anderson, but I am no angel. I am just weary of it all. It makes no sense any longer, if it ever did. Go home, sir. Please go home and live a long and happy life."

Cloyd tilted his head, the question in his eyes before he mouthed it. *Home?*

Letha said, "It could be done quite easily." She glanced toward the door, the men waiting outside. "You have suddenly developed a raging fever from your wound, surprised the surgeons. They do not know what to make of it, but have declared you unfit for duty. I will write it now myself, sign Major Crawford's name to it. I'll take it outside, chase them away. Tonight, I will give you food and some money—and another signed note to show anyone who questions you—and you will not stop until you are home."

Cloyd looked down at the floor, dazed by the scenario the steely woman had proposed, but knew that it was workable and would likely succeed. For a moment he allowed the warm wave of relief to flood through his body and stored it as a memory of Letha Bartlett's loving care. But it could not be; he could not live with the shadow of a coward hovering over him for the remainder of his life.

He raised his head, swallowed, and prayed that she would understand. He was relieved that there appeared to be no great hope in her eyes. He grasped her hand and lifted it to his cheek, held it there for only a moment, then quickly turned and walked away.

He was gone, but Letha spoke the words anyway. "So be it, Mr. Anderson. May the rifle balls not find you again."

# CHAPTER SIXTEEN

The woman awoke from her uneasy slumber, the metallic clack of the door bolt sharp in her ears. It was the first time the man had locked the door to the mailroom they occupied.

She blinked against the weariness and felt the return of the ponderous rhythm of the train as it rolled northward. She had ridden one train or another for four days now, and there were still three long hours remaining. She focused on the expansive, roseate face of the mail agent and saw something she did not like in the thick-lipped grin, an unwelcome wordless message. The small, comforting weight of the derringer pistol in her dress pocket rested atop her right thigh. Tied to the same leg, just below her knee, was a bone-handled knife with a six-inch blade in a leather sheath. She had honed the blade to a razor's edge the night before departing.

They had shared the small room since early that morning, when the mail agent had prevailed on the colonel in charge of the train and insisted that arrangements could be made. The Danville depot was congested with soldiers, and boarding troops had caused the colonel to order the few remaining civilians from the train. The woman had forcefully argued her case, explaining that she was on a mission of mercy, but to no avail until the agent interceded. She had given him her heartfelt thanks and promised not to be a bother.

Her clothing was homespun and functional, dark in color, unattractive by design. Like a soft brown rope, a thick braid of hair trailed down her back. Her features were pleasant, though not striking, the lines of her trim body hidden by the dress. Her hands were rough and broad across the knuckles, and she moved her right hand now to the top of the pocket. The agent looked at her again, a second too long, and she nodded curtly at him as he lumbered closer.

"Well, how are we a-doin' now, little missssy?"

She was certain now; the whiskey slur a clear portent. The weariness was gone. She shifted her position slightly, planted both shoes firmly on the floor, and said, "Just fine, thanks."

"Ahhh, that's good . . . good." He pulled a small flask from his coat pocket. "Bit nippy in here, don't you think, missssy? This here ain't the best I ever tasted, but it lights a little fire inside." He chuckled thickly, his shoulders bouncing up and down with the sounds. "Have a little nip with me, won't you now?"

"Don't care for any. Thanks just the same."

His mouth straightened into a firm line, then downward at the corners. "For a gal who's been done a mighty big favor, you ain't a'tall sociable."

"I thanked you proper, and I meant it. We've talked some, you've done your mail sortin', I've done my ridin'. The trip is about over now."

He took two gulps from the flask. "Not for three hours or so, it ain't." He pocketed the flask, reached behind him, and dragged his chair forward. He sat down with a long sigh, his knees within a foot of her dress.

She locked her gaze with his, moved her hand slowly into the dress pocket, and said, "Surely we can stay mannerly toward each other for three more hours."

The tip of his tongue darted from the corner of his mouth, swept slowly between his lips. "I'se hopin' that you had sense enough to see that I'm tryin' to be reeeal mannerly, missssy. Your soldier man's been gone a long time, ain't he?" He raised the forefinger of his right hand, extended it across the space between them, touched the tip to her knee. "Way I see it, you can stop feelin' lonely right now with me here. Sort of a warm up for your man, don't you see?"

"Move your finger back, Mister."

He spread his fingers, clamped them over her knee. She could see the sweat beads glistening from the fleshy hollows below his eyes, felt the fingers begin to creep above her knee. In a blur of movement, she drew the derringer from her pocket and aimed it squarely at the bridge of his nose. The hammer cocked with a firm *snick*, the gun steady in her hand.

"Wellll. Fiesty'un, ain't you now." He slid his fingers from her knee. "Trouble for you is that ain't much of a pistol."

"It might not kill you, true enough. But it'll hurt you long enough for me to pull my knife, and then, Mr. Mail Agent, I will gut you like the hog you're actin' like and watch your insides dribble over your boots."

He looked at the small black hole, the steadfast hand, the flinty eyes. He slowly straightened his back and with a great wheezing breath, stood, backed away from her. "This here is gov'ment property. If I'se to go get the colonel and tell him you had a gun in here, he'd throw your sorry ass off this train. Might even lock you up."

"Go ahead. Take your stinkin' whiskey breath and blow it all over your colonel and see if he comes to check on me. And even if he does, this little pistol will be in a place where a gentleman officer would never look, and then after he leaves, it'll be back in my hand before you can get near me."

The agent snorted through his nose, narrowed his eyes for a moment as he shook his head as if to clear it of some implausible vision. He dragged the chair back to his desk and plopped down on it, his passion now nothing more than a cloudy memory. He looked at her, held up a meaty paw, waved it like a flag of surrender. "Put the pistol up, will you? Some of them triggers are a little flinchy."

She pointed the derringer at the ceiling, eased the hammer down, slid the weapon into her pocket. "Do we have an understandin', then?"

He nodded. "We do."

He turned away from her, began to poke at the pieces of mail strewn over his desk. The great rattle and hum of the rails filled the room, calmed the raw nerves of both the man and the woman. The agent glanced at her first, was relieved to see both of her hands in her lap, then he looked at her face.

"The whiskey . . . it, uh, sometimes clouds my thinkin' a little." He mouthed a raspy little laugh at himself.

"I'd say more than a little. It right near cost you your life."

"Anyways—no hard feelin's, huh?"

"I'd as soon put it behind us."

Another puff of air pushed through his lips as he raised his hand, flopped it down on the desk. "Where'd you say he was, your man?"

"Hospital in Richmond. A place called Chimborazo."

"Leg, you say, huh?"

"Right leg. Cannon ball to the knee, then knife and saw to the thigh."

He looked down at his desktop, did not see the envelopes. "Never did catch your name."

"Never said it."

"I'd like to know it, if you don't mind."

"It's Nelda. Nelda Crump."

"Well. Goddamn, but I do hope you'uns make it back to home, Nelda Crump."

. . .

The insistent knocking on the back door came to Letha as an irritation. Brady Ayden would be near the stove, as he always seemed to be; surely he would answer the door. She waited for several more knocks, then pushed away from the little table in her quarters, slapped the pen down on top of the sheet of paper. It was past eleven o'clock and the only people who came late and knocked on the door were visitors, or worse yet, relatives. She shook her head as she made her way to the door, glanced at the familiar, vacant face of Brady Ayden as he stood motionless beside the stove. "Must you wait on me to tell you every single thing to do?"

She opened the door a few inches, spoke into the crack without looking. "Yes. What do you want?"

The woman's voice was soft and even. "Sorry for the bother, but are you the matron named Bartlett?"

"One and the same. What is your business here?"

"My name is Nelda Crump, and I've come to take Rector home."

Letha swung open the door and watched the lamplight illuminate the floppy hat, the wide eyes under it. "You are Rector Crump's wife? From Alabama?"

"Been four days a-comin', and I aim to take him back with me."

"Well, I, uh—please, please, come in. I'm sorry."

Nelda stepped into the kitchen, looked down at her shoes. "I tried to scrape 'em off, but . . ."

"Ah." Letha waved her hand. "It doesn't matter."

Nelda looked around the room, the steady movement of her head stopping at the sight of the raggedly dressed soldier standing beside the stove. She acknowledged him with a polite nod of her head, but he did not respond, looked through her with one dispirited eye, the other aiming away from her. She turned away from him, looked toward the yellow glow escaping from the open door to the ward. "He in there?"

"Yes." Letha touched Nelda's forearm. "I'll take you to him."

. . .

Pollard turned his head toward the two approaching figures, watched closely as they changed from shadows to women with each quiet step. He did not recognize the woman who trailed closely behind Letha. When they were ten paces away, the stranger looked past Pollard, put her hand to her mouth, and he knew who she was. Pollard pushed himself straight against his pillow, heard the soft snoring beside him, stared unabashedly at the woman.

Letha stopped and Nelda nearly bumped into her. Letha turned, whispered. "It might be better if I woke him, prepared him?"

Nelda nodded, answered through her fingers. "All right." Letha took a step toward the bed, stopped as Nelda's hand touched her elbow. "Wait, please."

Letha turned toward her. "What is it?"

"I need . . . I need to see it." She paused, swallowed. "Before he sees me see it."

"I understand. Certainly."

Letha leaned down, carefully gathered the bottom of the blanket, and slowly lifted it until the stump was visible. She waited and did not look back, heard the breath hiss past the woman's teeth, the tiny sob.

Pollard had not moved, could not move. The Angel of Chimborazo, fractured heart and all, was very near, and with her she had brought another angel.

Nelda moved forward, touched Letha's shoulder, said, "I'm all right now. You can wake him."

Letha repositioned the blanket, placed her hand on Crump's shoulder, shook gently. "Sergeant Crump. Sergeant Crump, wake up."

Crump stirred, the familiar voice coming to him from afar, then closer, and he could feel her hand on his shoulder—firm and insistent. He twisted his head against the pillow. "Wha . . . what's wrong?"

"There is nothing wrong, sir. Nothing at all. In fact, something is very right. Your wife is here. She has come to take you home."

Crump clamped a hand over his forehead, dragged it down over his face. Letha's words echoed in his head: *wife . . . here . . . take you home.* He was suddenly acutely aware of his heartbeat—a fist tapping against the back of his sternum in unison with the soft whooshing in his ears. He rolled onto his shoulder, then the flat of his back, stared wide-eyed at Letha.

She took a step backward, allowed Nelda to rush past her with outstretched arms. Without a word, she curled into the space beside his chest, wrapped her arms around his neck. "Good God a'mighty, woman," he whispered. "God a'mighty. How—how?"

"It doesn't matter how, Rector. I'm here."

Pollard looked up at Letha, hoped that the soft light would make it easier for her to meet his eyes, hoped that the tender scene unfolding so close at hand would restore some small part of her, prove to be a beginning. Seconds passed, the silence broken only by a cough from far up the row. At first, only her eyes moved toward Pollard, and then, very slowly, her head followed. Pollard wanted desperately to reach out, draw her close, told himself to be thankful for the meager energy emitting from her look. Her expression changed, nearly imperceptibly—the tilting of a painting in faint light—and Pollard was uncertain of the cause, feared that it could be pity. First Nathan in death, then Cloyd reclaimed by the war, Hound Patterson soon to follow, and now Crump, to be taken home. The inner circle was being broken, a chunk at a time. The man without a country would soon be a man without close friends. Yes, the energy could be pity, nothing more.

Pollard smiled, said, "Something right indeed, Letha." He turned his head toward the reunited couple.

Crump turned his head toward Letha, his voice a hoarse whisper. "I ain't lettin' her go tonight."

"Nor should you, sir. Whenever she wishes, Mrs. Crump may join me in my quarters. I will fix a place for her." With a final expressionless glance at Pollard, Letha turned and walked up the aisle.

Nelda sat up on the side of the bed, removed her hat, and placed it beside her. Crump rolled to his side, propped himself with an elbow. "Pollard, this is my wife, Nelda."

She stood, stepped across the space between the beds, and extended her hand. "I am proud to know you, Mr. Pollard."

He took her hand, felt the strength in it. "Likewise, Mrs. Crump. The honor is mine."

"Just Nelda."

He smiled. "Just Granville."

She moved back to the side of Crump's bed, snuggled close to his waist. "So you're the music man Rector writes me about."

"After a fashion, I suppose."

"That's not what I'm told."

"Your husband is kind with his remarks."

"Her husband is heavier on the truth than kindness, Pollard," Crump said.

Nelda thought of her husband's letters describing the time Pollard and the matron had sung the hymn, saw again the heavy scrawl on the paper, remembered the struggle to convey to her the awesome day. Now she had heard them speak softly, barely more than whispers, but the message in the letter was much clearer. Crump had described more than the bond of music in the letters, had in his direct, mannish way told of another bond, something Crump and all the rest hoped would grow between this man and their beloved matron.

The time was short. "He tells me that Miz Bartlett sings fine too."

"Yes, she has a marvelous voice."

"I surely hope that I can hear you two sing before we head out."

Pollard peered through the weak light, saw the shape of a smile on her lips. "I would be willing, but I speak only for myself."

The smile grew wider now, and she laced her fingers with Crump's. "Well, Granville, you stay ready."

. . .

Nelda lay curled against Crump's chest, felt the slow rise and fall, the steady thump of his heart. They had not spoken for an hour, had been perfectly content with each other's touch. The ward was quiet now, as close to silence as it ever became. Pollard was asleep, his breathing deep and rhythmic.

Crump whispered, his breath warm on the nape of her neck. "Why didn't you write and tell me first?"

"I was afraid you'd tell me not to."

"The boys with your sister?"

"Yes, they'll be fine. You know that."

He inhaled the aroma of her skin—the faint reminder of fragrance now mingled with the odors of the world—loved her, kissed her neck. "You ain't said nothin' about the leg."

"It doesn't matter, Rector. We'll be fine."

"It's a mighty big chunk of me gone."

"I'd rather have what's left of you than the whole of any other man."

"I swear by God on high, woman. I won't ever whine, won't give you reason to pity me."

She reached back, stroked his head. "I know."

"Did you have any trouble . . . gettin' here?"

"Not really. I knew the trains would be a problem. Just some rudeness along the way."

He laughed softly. "You never been much for toleratin' rudeness."

"That's not changed."

Long, easy minutes passed in silence before he felt her head move, heard her ask, "Where did the boy lay?"

"Across the aisle from Pollard."

"Our boys are never gonna get messed up in somethin' like this, Rector, even if I have to hide 'em in a cave."

"No need to worry. This thing's 'bout finished."

"But what if it's not settled? This thing has drug on for four years. Who's to say it couldn't last for years to come?"

Crump shook his forehead against her neck. "No. It'll be settled. For good."

His words had the ring of truth about them; he had been a part of it, would always be a part of it. Surely he knew the truth. She tucked his words into a secure place, alongside their boys, trusted him. She thought of Pollard now, remembered the awkwardness of her husband's description of the man forsaken by his family, the man without a country. How would it be settled for him?

The silence came again, but only for a moment. The scratching began under the floor, moved closer to their bed until it was directly under it.

"Rats?"

"Yep," Crump replied. "I reckon quite a bunch live down there."

She tilted her head backward in a question. "I'm surprised you haven't shot holes in the floor."

"Thought about it, back at first." He paused. "They don't seem to be much of a bother anymore, considerin' the things that take place around here."

# CHAPTER SEVENTEEN

Letha awoke early, rubbed her eyes, and looked across the room at the empty bed she had made up for Nelda Crump. She dressed quickly, combed her hair, and arranged it into the tight bun. She opened the door to the kitchen, saw Nelda asleep in a chair at the kitchen table, her head resting on her forearms. She laid her hand on the woman's shoulder and shook her gently. Nelda opened her eyes, blinked twice, and raised her head toward Letha.

"For goodness sake, Mrs. Crump. I intended for you to join me in my quarters. I have a bed made up for you."

"Yes ma'am, I appreciate that. But it was only a couple of hours ago that I left him, and I didn't want to wake you. I know you need what little rest you get."

"That is very thoughtful, but next time, don't hesitate. I am very adept at falling back to sleep. Why don't you go to bed and rest for a time now?"

"No thanks. I don't require much sleep. I intend to help you with whatever you want me to do until you think he's ready to leave."

"It's not really up to me, Mrs. Crump. I—"

"Just Nelda."

"Yes, certainly. Nelda. And I don't think I ever told you my first name." She smiled. "Just Letha. As I was saying, it's up to the surgeon, really." She thought of the tottering Crawford, declining with the passing of each day. "But I can assure you that he won't be a hindrance, not at all."

"Well then, I'll rely on you to say when it's all right."

Letha looked down into the trusting green eyes and was glad that there was no true responsibility to exercise. *Take him, Nelda Crump. Take him now to his home and feed him and tend him and love him. Take him far from this place where death lurks like spiders in shadowy corners.* "The sooner, the better, Nelda. Home is where he needs to be. But what you might not realize is that you are the one who should store up your energy for at least several days. I imagine it was difficult enough for you to make this journey, but, now, with him . . . it will be a daunting task."

"We'll manage."

"I am certain that you will, but rest for a while, please. He is not the same man who left home so long ago. The journey will be a great burden for the both of you."

Nelda looked down at the table, rubbed her hands together, then slowly nodded her head. "I reckon you're right. A couple of days might do me good at that."

"I promise it will. Now go to bed and sleep for as long as you want. I'll see that no one disturbs you. There will be plenty you can help me with when you wake."

"I'll take a little nap; that'll fix me good as new."

"Good, that's what I want to hear."

Nelda pushed away from the table, stood and stretched her back, then walked to the bedroom doorway. She placed her hand on the jamb, turned back toward Letha. "Rector wrote me about your singin'. Claims it's far above the ordinary."

"Your husband is very kind."

"Says Granville Pollard is awful good too."

Letha's hands came together, and she looked down as if surprised by their union, quickly separated them. "Yes, he is quite good, actually."

Nelda smiled. "I'm not much good at it myself, but I sure do like to hear it done right." She saw Letha's hands begin to move together again, then stop abruptly as she pressed them flat against her dress. "Well, I won't be long in the bed. You'll find me to be strong help."

By midafternoon, Nelda Crump had fallen easily into the routine of the ward. The main chores were familiar to her. Cooking, washing pots and pans, laundering, cleaning up messes—these things had always been a part of her daily routine, and she worked her way through all of them efficiently and with a smile on her face. Letha had shown her the basics of wound dressing, and though at first hesitant, Nelda had soon gained the trust of even the most grievously wounded. Crump had urged her to walk among "the boys," as Letha did when she had time, and ask if she could write letters for them. To her delight, she had been asked to write three, and the smiles she received when the men looked at the well-formed script were gifts that she would treasure, valuables to be locked away in her mind.

The second day passed even more swiftly than the first, and despite Letha's warnings to herself against doing so, she had come to depend on the tireless woman. Crump was invigorated by her presence and made it a point to crutch his way up and down the aisle several times both days in order to gain strength for the long journey. But by the end of the second day he realized that there was only so much strength to be built with so little food, and had decided to heed both Letha's and his wife's admonishments. He sat beside Nelda now on the edge of his bed, her arm wrapped around his back.

Pollard sat upright against his pillow, his covers reaching to his waist. In his lap were scattered several sheets of paper scored with lines and musical notes. Most of the lamps in the ward had been turned low, and only a few quiet voices could be heard from the long rows of beds.

Nelda shook her head, said softly, "I might be able to make some sense out of it, but I'm afraid it would take a long time."

"Not as long as you might think," Pollard replied. "Look." He held the sheet so that she could lean forward and follow his fingertip. He hummed the three notes as his finger tapped the paper. "Humm . . . hummm . . . hummmm. It's just like reading, only the notes are sounds, or words, or parts of words." He tapped the notes again as he sang softly, "*You . . . can . . . sing.*"

The three words in beautiful tenor hung in the air, and she could hear them clearly even after they should have faded away. Then, like a slow ripple, dozens of voices—first in whispers, then aloud—arose as the name "Pollard, Pollard, Pollard" became a soft drumbeat in the ward.

"Oh my," she said, her arm tightening around Crump's back.

"Told you so," Crump said.

Pollard made her look at him and said, "With me now, the same words. Don't be shy."

"Oh, I couldn't. I—"

Pollard placed his forefinger over his lips. "Shh. Let's sing 'we'— 'we can sing.' With me. Trust me. *Weeee*"—he held the first note until she joined in and they finished in unison—"*caaan . . . siiing.*"

Nelda giggled and felt a warm blush on her cheeks. Pollard said, "I knew it! I can always tell. You have a lovely voice, Nelda. You must not be afraid of it. You are not afraid of the sound of your voice when you speak, are you?" She shook her head. "Of course not, because you're used to it. After you've sung for a time, you will become used to that sound also, begin to trust it, like it."

"I don't know. I imagine a frog would sound all right if it mixed with you."

The men joined in her laughter, the sounds building in their chests.

Crump said, "That felt mighty damn good. It's been a while, ain't it, Pollard?"

"That it has, my friend. A while indeed." He looked at Nelda, said with a flourish, "See what our duet hath wrought, madam?"

Nelda hugged Crump, rested her head on his shoulder. "Laughter is music, isn't it, Granville?"

The question came at him like an invisible force, pushed against his body like a strong breeze. The musical laughter of his mother sailed on the breeze, passed through the middle of his head, then faded away. He did not pursue the memory, waited on the silence. "Oh, yes. Yes it is. Music in its highest form."

Nelda kissed Crump on the cheek—a quick, happy peck.

They both saw the emptiness in Pollard's features now, the enchanting energy of the moment suddenly sucked away, but did not understand the cause. Pollard looked down at the sheets of paper, began to shuffle them aimlessly as the smile on his lips thinned, then disappeared. The silence grew steadily into a presence, discomforting and probing, and both Crump and Nelda struggled to find words that would bind the mysterious wound. Without warning, the simple little word began to echo in Crump's brain, and the mystery was solved: *Home.* They were going home, Pollard was not. Could not, for he had no home.

Crump knew that no suitable words would come to him. The thing had happened too quickly, too powerfully. He said, "Nelda, get me my coat and hat and let's take a walk. I need to get used to the outside air again."

They stood on the back porch, Crump leaning forward on the crutches, Nelda tucked against him. The night wind was listless, without an edge, and Crump turned his face into it, waited for the question.

"What happened in there?" she asked.

"I think it struck him that we're gonna leave soon . . . for home."

He felt the tension pass through her body, felt her head turn to the side, heard her say, "Oh, Lord, Rector, I never thought—"

"Hush, hush. You didn't do nothin' wrong, woman. Nothin' a'tall. It was real nice. He'd tell you so hisself right now."

She turned her head against the wide chest. "Rector, what will become of him? What can he do with two stubs?"

"He's got one sorta peg they rigged for him on the best stump. If he makes a life for hisself, it'll be with that voice somehow, back up North, in the big cities. Won't nobody have any money in the South to splurge on payin' a man to sing, even good as he is. But I figure them Yankees'll have right smart a-spendin' money left, be wantin' to do fine things and forget the war. They might pay for his singin'."

"Even if they know he fought against them?"

"He can turn that around, spin a yarn or two about it all when anybody asks him. Won't nobody doubt him, both feet gone and all. He's mighty smart. He'll manage that." He paused, savored the clean air in his face.

"It pains me to think there's nothing we can do to help him."

"It's been gnawin' at me for a long time. He needs connectin' up with city folks in the North and we're dirt farmers in the whipped South. That's a mighty sorry connection, ain't it?"

"Pretty sorry."

Crump made a little noise, a rumble that quickly changed into words. "Ah, it's got to happen. It's the only way."

"What? What is the only way?"

"He needs Letha Bartlett. And what's more, she needs him. Before the boy died, she felt more'n a spark for Pollard, I'll tell you that for sure."

"I remember what you wrote, Rector. But, you're not exactly—"

"An expert on such matters?" He raised his hand from the crutch handle, drew her closer. "I was expert enough to snag you, warn't I?"

"Yes, yes you were. And I'm glad."

"There was somethin' strong with them. And then . . ." She felt his beard move side to side as he shook his head. "Oh, he was a fine one, that pup. I'll swear I never heard him whine one time. Had a smile that lit up the whole damn room. I know she thought the same thing all of us did, that he'd be spared. Just one fine boy that would make it through, keep us happy till the end of these dark times." The rumble again arose from his chest. "She believed it. We all believed it."

"It just wasn't meant to be, Rector. Some things just aren't meant to be."

"Don't see why that one warn't."

She shook her head, said, "Broodin' over what's done won't help anything. I'm not gonna do that. She needs to find her way back to Granville, is all. With the singing, maybe. I've already planted a seed there, told her how much I would like to hear them together."

"Well, it's a start."

"I'm willing to stay here for a while longer if that's what it takes. The boys will do fine with Sis."

"We'll see. But we cain't risk stayin' long enough for the Yanks to take the city. I'm not sure what would happen then."

"Surely you don't think that's about to happen?"

"All I can tell you is that, for the South, nothin' very good can happen. This city is starvin'. This place is starvin'. Half the moanin' that goes on around here is from empty bellies. Letha, McCaw—the head surgeon—they do wonders with what they can get their hands on, but there's no decent meat to be had. You've seen it already for yourself, ain't you?"

"Yes, I have."

"What I'm sayin' is that nothin' would surprise me anymore. Nothin'. And I damn sure don't mean for us to be around here when the Yanks come struttin' in."

"Well then, it's time to get busy."

# CHAPTER EIGHTEEN

The heart has strange abysses of gloom, and often yearns
for just one word of love to help.

Lucy C. Smith

Avery Crawford entered the kitchen pursued by a frosty blast of early
morning air, his open gray coat flapping like a pair of broken wings as
he strode toward the stove. He had no way of knowing that, along with
Letha Bartlett, he was about to condemn a man to death. He nodded at
Letha, said, "Might I have a cup of coffee, Mrs. Bartlett? The morning
has a bit of chill to it."

"Certainly, Major, please help yourself."

He looped his finger through the handle of a tin cup, poured it half
full. He waited, knowing that Letha would extend her usual courtesy
and pretend not to notice his next destination. She stepped away, said
something to the kitchen helper working on the opposite side of the
room. With a casual glance, Crawford moved quickly to the whiskey
closet and filled the balance of his cup. He walked back to the kitchen

table, sat down heavily. Letha approached the table, a small square of cornbread in the palm of her hand.

He looked up, shook his head. "No, thank you, let the boys have it. I prefer my coffee."

"As you wish, Major."

She began to turn away but he raised his hand, said, "A moment please."

"Yes?"

"Unless you have an objection, I intend to assign Brady Ayden back to duty with his unit."

Letha looked toward the ward, did not have to see Brady to know what he was doing. "I am sure he's in there right now, standing like a small tree, waiting for someone to give him direction."

"His head wound was basically superficial, admittedly with some disfiguration. But on the whole, he *should* be fit for duty."

"Should?"

"I haven't had the opportunity—if one may charitably call it that—to spend a great deal of time with him, but his mental state seems almost unstable at times." Crawford took a long sip from the cup, looked at Letha from under the bushy eyebrows.

She said, "Are you asking me to assess his mental state, Major?"

"At this point, I trust your judgment more than my own, madam."

Letha felt the weight of the silence descend on her, an unwelcome burden that she did not wish to deal with. The unwanted power was in her hands now, could not be ignored. She assured herself that she had tried, done her best to pump life into the withdrawn man, could not think of a single thing she had not done that could have made a difference. She felt the cold tug in her gut, acknowledged the truth: Brady Ayden had become an irritation to her, and she did not wish to look at him any longer.

"I think he just . . . doesn't care anymore. Doesn't want to put forth any effort for any reason."

Crawford took another sip, swallowed slowly, felt the wonderful burn caress his throat. "That's what I suspected. I cannot very well withhold a man from duty simply because he does not care, can I?"

Letha shrugged her shoulders. "I suppose not."

"I would imagine they will come for him this afternoon, given the need in the field these days."

"I should mention to you that Sergeant Crump's wife has arrived and intends to take him home very soon."

"Where is home?"

"Northern Alabama."

Crawford nodded, looked into his cup. "I hope that she is a strong woman."

"She is."

He sniffed, rubbed the end of his nose with a knuckle, and pushed away from the table. "Well then, I'll take my leave and come back in a while for rounds." He tilted back his head and drained the cup. "Thanks for the coffee. And the advice."

Letha carried the square of cornbread back to the pan, then turned toward the ward, stepped just inside of the doorway. She found Brady precisely where she knew she would, standing halfway down the aisle, his arms hanging loosely at his sides as he stared at the low ceiling. Letha walked directly to him, waited for him to notice her. Several seconds passed before he slowly turned his head toward her.

"You need to get your things organized. Major Crawford and I have discussed your condition and decided that you may return to your unit in the field. They will probably come for you this afternoon."

He trained his good eye on Letha and cocked his head slightly so that the wandering eye tilted strangely upward, causing her to look away from his face. "Don't wanna go."

The quiet words surprised her and she forced herself to look at him. "Well, no, I suppose many of the boys don't wish to return to duty, but that doesn't change what they must do."

"I done everythin' you told me to do, didn't I?"

"Yes, you did, but that doesn't have anything to do with your return to duty. You are . . . well now. Well enough to go back."

She recognized it now, had seen it before in other men—the haunted expression, as if they had looked into the future and spied their own ghosts. He said, "I ain't well enough."

"I'm sorry, it is out of my hands. The decision rests with the military authorities."

He looked away, shook his head slowly, said, "No, it don't."

Letha opened her mouth to speak, but closed it. There was nothing to say; she possessed no will to attempt to crack the peculiar veneer that covered the man. She spun away and left him standing in the aisle, staring at the same spot on the ceiling.

The wagon came for Brady Ayden in the cold shadows of late afternoon. Letha heard its rumbling approach and then the snort of the horse as it stopped near the low porch. She spoke to the kitchen helpers as she wiped her hands on her apron, then walked to the door and opened it. She had seen the driver before—the dirty bowler hat jammed down over wild locks of filthy yellow hair. Beside him sat a young soldier who appeared to be no more than a teenager, his forage cap pulled low over his brow, the tatters of his coat sleeves flapping gently in the wind. His hands were wrapped around a short-barreled carbine, the butt planted between his shoes. He turned his head tiredly toward the door and said, "They say you got one goin' back. Send him out."

Letha heard footsteps behind her, the familiar slow shuffle on the wood floor. She turned, glanced uncomfortably at Brady, whose hands were empty, then stepped away from the door. He moved to the opening and stood motionless for several seconds as he peered into the yard. A smile formed on his lips as he looked at Letha, and suddenly he appeared to her much younger, the lines of his face soft, save for the jagged path of scar tissue that had replaced his eyebrows. It was a perfectly winsome smile, and it dazed Letha, piercing her through.

Slowly, the upturned corners of the smile straightened, then turned downward. He said, "Don't recollect ever seein' you smile at me."

She attempted to stop the churning in her brain, but the thoughts were like balls bouncing off the inside of her skull, and she could not control them. He slipped past her through the doorway without closing it behind him. Letha unleashed a quick torrent of words at his back. "I, uh, I wish you well, Brady Ayden."

He did not look back. He walked directly to the soldier sitting beside the driver and slammed his right fist against the man's jaw, the soldier's head snapping backward as he crumpled into the driver, the weapon clattering to the floorboard. Brady calmly picked up the carbine and turned to face Letha. He cocked the hammer and grasped the barrel with his left hand, thrust his right thumb into the trigger guard, and placed the muzzle under his chin.

The scene played out before Letha's eyes in a lazy horror, the scream that she could not utter building in her throat. From a distant place, she felt her hand slide down the rough wood doorway, felt the jolt of her knees striking the hard floor. The report of the gun was a thunderclap, the fountain of blood and bone and brain tissue spewing upward to a height of twenty feet, then falling delicately in a fine pink mist. Like a thick rope being released, the lifeless body coiled into the mud.

For a long moment, an eerie calm settled about the yard, and her vision grew dim, as if someone had draped a fine linen cloth over her eyes. Then voices erupted all around her, and she could feel the pounding of footfalls on the porch as men swept past her, could see dark shapes of men jumping down from the wagon seat. The voices were a discordant babble, just remotely human, and Letha clamped her hands over her ears, seeking only silence. But the clamor oozed under her hands, an icy liquid that she could not hold at bay, and then hands touched her arms, her shoulders, and she twisted away from it. It was only when Nelda Crump's cheek touched hers that the mad whirl slowed, and she lowered her hands, listened to the whisper in her ear.

"Letha. Letha, I'm with you now, and I won't let anyone else bother you. Let me help you. Come with me . . . come on now."

They had been alone for a half hour, the closed door to the tiny bedroom separating them from the death that seemed to surround them. Letha lay in the bed, facing the wall, her body curled into a protective ball. Nelda sat beside her and patted her arm, hoped that Letha would speak first, provide some clue that would direct her effort to help. With a childlike whimper, Letha began to weep, the sobs shaking her body in an uneven cadence. At first, Nelda believed it would prove to be a cleansing; tears were often a necessary thing, and so she waited patiently. But soon the weeping took on a worrisome tone—dark and foreboding—and Nelda knew that it was hurtful, something to be silenced quickly.

"Letha, for mercy's sake, get hold of yourself now. That's not the first man to do himself in. There was nothin' you or anyone could have done. These are strange times. Hush now."

But she would not hush, the anguish deepening with each strident note of her weeping, and Nelda doubted that she had heard the words just spoken. Nelda stood, looked down and shook her head, then pulled the cover up and over her legs. When she opened the door, the worried faces of Crump and Pollard met her, asked silent questions. Hound Patterson braced Pollard, who leaned precariously on his left crutch.

Crump said, "That boy warn't right. She ought'n to blame herself."

"I told her as much," Nelda replied, closing the door behind her. "Or at least I tried. I don't even think she heard me talkin'."

Pollard listened to the pitiful wails seeping from the closed door. He despised the sound and lowered his head. "Somebody must find Dr. McCaw. He is the only one she might listen to." The wailing rose in pitch. "For God's sake—somebody please go find him."

"Where should I look?" Nelda asked.

"The main surgery unit. I'm not sure where it is. Just ask in one of the other wards. You might find Crawford or somebody . . . anybody."

She looked quickly at her husband, said, "I'll be back soon. Just leave her be."

The orderly pointed down the long hallway toward a tall man walking slowly toward the front door of the building. "That'd be him, ma'am."

Nelda hurried down the corridor, her shoes tapping out a crisp cadence on the wood floor. The man opened the door and paused, hearing the familiar urgency in the feet that often sought him. He closed the door, turned to face his pursuer. Nelda slowed her approach, stopped at a respectful distance. The quiet energy of the man radiated from his handsome features—eyes deep-set and wide, with a strong nose set over a grand moustache that was gray in the middle and dark at the corners. The moustache hid most of his mouth, but there was a softness that could not be hidden. His hair—flecked with gray—was worn short, functional, trimmed to the top of his ears and well above the white collar of his shirt.

It was with no apprehension that Nelda addressed the chief surgeon of the entire hospital. "Dr. McCaw, I hope?"

He smiled easily. His voice was soft, yet masculine. "Yes, ma'am, for better or worse, your hope is answered."

"I'm Nelda Crump, wife of a soldier I've come to take home. He stays down in Letha Bartlett's ward. That's where the trouble took place."

McCaw's brow furrowed. "Trouble? What kind of trouble?"

"A man, headed back for his regiment . . . he shot himself in front of her. She's blamin' herself for some reason. She's holed up in her room and bad off. Me and some of the men are awful worried about her; we hoped that you would come and try to help her."

"Surely."

Pollard and Crump jerked their heads toward the sound of footsteps on the porch. Nelda walked through the doorway, closely followed by McCaw. Nelda walked to her husband's side, said, "Rector, Mr. Pollard, this is Dr. McCaw."

McCaw reached out a hand, touched it first to Crump's hand as it rested on the crutch handle, then tapped Pollard's hand in similar fashion. "Gentlemen," he said with a slight nod. He looked directly at Crump. "Your husband and I have met, Mrs. Crump. Unfortunately, it was on a professional basis. You appear to be doing well, sir. The thought of home, perhaps?"

"Yes, sir. Havin' this woman here and thinkin' 'bout home is strong medicine."

McCaw glanced toward the closed door. "The soldier who committed suicide—had Mrs. Bartlett made him one of her special projects?"

Crump said, "Sorta tried when he first came, but I'll tell you that boy warn't ever right, no sirree. I think that ball passed too close to his brain pan."

McCaw looked at Pollard. "Your impressions, sir?"

"He would not allow her or anyone to penetrate his shell, I suppose one could say. She made efforts early on, but they were rejected, as far as I could tell." Pollard paused. He looked down for a moment, then back at McCaw. "You may have heard about the young soldier named

Nathan Fisher, the manner of his death. That incident . . . that night took something from her. And now this." He shook his head.

"Well," said McCaw, "this is one of the strongest women I have had the honor of serving with. Now, so close to the end, I have no intention of seeing her broken."

He moved to the door, knocked softly. There were no sounds coming from the room, only a silence that for Pollard and Crump had been worse than the weeping. McCaw opened the door and stepped inside, quietly closed the door behind him.

He pulled the chair from under the little table, placed it beside the bed, and sat down. Letha remained drawn into a tight ball, her head tucked down, shoulders hunched up near her cheeks. McCaw drew a long breath, released it slowly through his nostrils. His gaze wandered the barren walls of the room that now reminded him of a wooden cell. He had no wish to be reminded of the Spartan existence to which Letha Bartlett—at his urging—had subjected herself. But the thought formed too quickly, piercing his flimsy defenses. *You have asked too much of her, McCaw. Perhaps even more than you have asked of yourself.*

"My dear Mrs. Bartlett, please forgive my intrusion. You may cast me away with the flick of your hand, as perhaps you should."

He paused, studied for a moment the motionless form, seeking any sign of acknowledgement or response, but there was none. He leaned forward, drew the web of his thumb and forefinger over the bushy moustache. "I realize that this appears somewhat presumptuous of me to come in here and even attempt to be of aid, however meager. But be assured that I do not see myself as some great healer, able to hover over you for a few moments and relieve your burdens. The burdens are too great . . . for all of us. I have come mainly to grieve with you. This war has taken slivers of our souls that may never regenerate." He hesitated. "They should not regenerate, but rather remain here to be buried solemnly with the fallen soldiers. But no matter what you may feel now—and believe me when I tell you that I know something of the depth of your sorrow—the greater part of your soul will survive."

McCaw heard the faint rustle of her clothing on the mattress, saw her body uncoil ever so slightly. He waited for a minute to creep past, then another, before he spoke. "We have seen so many die that by now we should be immune to grief. But neither you nor I have been granted that luxury. We must bear the weight of it somehow, without allowing it to break us. We are too near the end, my dear, to allow that to happen now. The bloodletting will soon be past and we will bind our own wounds, you and I, and live on."

Letha's arm slid from her side as she slowly rolled onto her back, looked at McCaw from beneath puffy red eyelids. She spoke in a raspy whisper. "I have become so weary of it all that I have forgotten how to give them hope. And that is unforgivable." She lifted a hand, pointed toward the porch. "Out there today. I could have prevented that with no more than a smile."

"I doubt that it would have been that simple."

She shook her head. "No. It was that simple." She turned her head back to the wall.

McCaw considered probing further, attempting to learn more about the relationship between Letha and the suicide victim. Armed with more information, he might at least be able to begin the process of dissuading her of the unreasonable notion that she could have saved the man. He looked at her, heard the hollow echo of her voice, and decided that this was not the time for probing.

"Well, we will put that to rest for now." He straightened his back against the chair, lightly clapped his hand to his thigh. "I do have an offer of help for you, and I must insist that you accept it. You need rest away from the hospital. My wife Hannah and I would be most honored if you would come spend a few days with us." He sighed at himself in self-admonishment. "With her, mostly, given the demands on my time, but that is to your benefit. You might recall that you met her briefly, at the start of all this. You will find her to be a most gracious hostess, but that is the least of her many attributes. She has the God-given ability to listen, truly listen, to others—a gift that, in my view, is a hundred times more valuable than talking to others. You will see that she can help. All right?"

Letha asked, "And what of my duties here? I will not simply walk away from them."

"Mrs. Crump has offered to stay on for as long as you require, and I will find her some help. I have had the pleasure of knowing her for only a few minutes, but I am impressed by her demeanor and her strength. It was not an empty offer, and it was made wholly out of respect and concern for you."

"She and her husband need to go home now, to tend to each other and their children."

"She assures me that her children are in capable hands. A few days delay will be of no consequence."

"Unless the Yankees overrun this city."

"It has not come to that yet."

"But it will."

"Yes. It will, but not for a time."

The room grew silent, and for McCaw the walls had mysteriously crept closer, the wooden stare of the boards suddenly intolerable. He stood. "Mrs. Bartlett, the time has come for others to help you. You have given so very much of yourself that I feel justifiably guilty—as if I have usurped a portion of your soul—and I have no wish to retain that feeling. I will return with my carriage in a half hour, and in the meantime I will ask Mrs. Crump to come help you gather some of your things."

He paused for a moment, then said, "I trust that you will do Mrs. McCaw and myself this honor."

Letha nodded her head against the pillow, said nothing.

"Good. I will see you shortly."

. . .

Letha walked unsteadily past Pollard with Dr. McCaw's left arm wrapped behind her back. In his right hand he carried her small piece of luggage. The clarity of the scene caused Pollard to groan under his breath, the incredible reversal now complete. Letha Bartlett no longer walked, steadfast and able, as the comforter of the wounded, but rather shuffled along as one of their number. Pollard looked down at the floor, would not watch her leave the building.

He felt the touch of Nelda's hand on his, heard her say, "She's gonna be all right, Granville. And so are you."

# CHAPTER NINETEEN

From her kitchen, Hannah McCaw heard the familiar clomp and rattle of the buggy as it halted near the house. She was mildly surprised when the front door of the house opened instead of the back door; this was not her husband's practice when alone. She walked into the parlor, and with a discreet glance into Dr. McCaw's eyes and a pleasant nod toward Letha, grasped the reason for the unannounced guest.

"Hannah, my dear," McCaw said, "you will no doubt remember Letha Bartlett, the fine matron of one of our wards."

Hannah stepped forward, took both of Letha's hands in her own, and said, "Most certainly, Dr. McCaw, and I have since heard you speak of her with near reverence on more than one occasion." She extended her arm toward the couch. "Come, please, sit down. Welcome to our home."

McCaw guided Letha to the couch. "The time has come for some well-deserved rest away from the hospital, Hannah. Need I say more?" McCaw said.

Hannah smiled. "You need not, sir."

"Then if you ladies would excuse me, I will disappear for a bit and steal a few moments' rest myself."

Hannah nodded and waited for him to leave the room. She looked at the bony white knot of Letha's hands as they sat on her knees, saw the wearied curvature of her shoulders. The woman's expression was unreadable, mostly a portrait in stone, and Hannah knew that for the evening to come, the gift of listening would be useless. "May I call you Letha?"

Letha nodded slowly. "Yes, certainly."

"Hannah for me, all right? It is not a time for formality."

Letha shook her head, as if to clear it. "I—I am sorry. My manners . . ."

"Hush, my dear, no need for that." Hannah reached out and laid her hand atop Letha's clenched fingers. "Do you like birds, Letha?"

Letha's head inched a turn toward the unexpected question. "I do, I suppose."

"I have great affection for them myself, but I confess that before the war, I did not. My change of heart has to do with their ability to spread their wings and soar above the horror of all this. Sometimes I imagine myself able to soar with them, glide on the wind, above it all, free for a time from the failings of humanity."

Hannah lifted her hands above her lap, spread her fingers. "Let your hands be a bird with mine, Letha. Humor my silly little request. I will ask nothing more of you during your stay."

Letha was suddenly aware of her hands, felt the tension in her fingers, extending to her forearms like strands of wire. She relaxed her fingers, slid them apart, looked at Hannah's uplifted hands. Carefully, she began to raise her hands and accepted the tiny bit of freedom.

Hannah sighed softly. "Ah, that was a wonderful first flight. Thank you."

Both women returned their hands to their laps, and Hannah saw that Letha's fingers did not wind back together. "Now," said Hannah, "from birds to soup, and then off to bed for you, young lady. The finest rendering of a split pea recipe that you will ever taste, I must boast."

Hannah touched her hand to Letha's back. "Come now, I think I hear the frightening sounds of Dr. McCaw rambling around in my kitchen."

With heavy quilts drawn up under her chin, Letha lay on her back looking at the moonlit windowpanes. The second-floor bedroom was scarcely larger than her hospital quarters, but in it she sensed a security she had not known for over three years. It was the same feeling she had as a child, tucked safely away in a quiet corner of her house, the muffled voices of her parents drifting upward—lovely reminders of caring and concern. She wondered if James and Hannah McCaw had raised children, wondered if they were quietly discussing the grown woman in the guest bedroom who now required their attentions in the manner of a child. Womblike, the weight of the quilts pressed down on her body, gently forbidding her to move. But she did not desire movement. She felt gratefully incapable of producing the slightest twitch of muscle fiber. The moonlight grew dim as her eyelids descended, and when the pale glow was gone it was replaced by a clean blue sky, and in her ears was the sound of rushing wind as she soared, looked down on Earth.

Pollard threw off his blankets and swung his legs over the side of the bed.

Crump opened his eyes, peered through the murky light, asked, "What's wrong?"

Pollard moved his head slowly to face Crump. "Nearly everything I can think of."

"Must seem like that, I reckon."

"There's no 'seem' to it, Crump. It's just the way it is."

"She needed to get away from here for a while. Ain't nobody I'd rather have her with than McCaw, and it ain't likely that he married a dunce for a wife neither. I figure the two of 'em will surely do her mighty good." Crump rolled onto his back and waited for Pollard to speak, but a long minute of silence passed.

At last, Pollard said, "I have to get out of here for a while, Crump. I feel like an animal trapped in a box. A wretched animal with both feet chopped off, waiting for I don't know what."

Crump tossed his blankets back, started to rise. "I'll go with you."

"No. Thank you, but no." He looked at Crump, shook his head. "No, just me. One day soon I will have to leave this building and get on with life, and it just occurred to me that I will have to learn to do for myself or be pitied for the remainder of my days. I consider death a better bargain."

He reached down for his brace and slid it over the stump of his right leg. He retrieved his crutches and hobbled to the clothes pegs on the wall, bracing himself against it until he was able to drape his shirt and trousers over his shoulder. He made his way back to the bed, dressed, and with a tiny groan of pain, again hoisted himself up. He teetered for a moment, found his balance on the flat surface of the brace, and began to move toward the aisle.

Pollard labored over the uneven ground for a quarter of an hour before he was satisfied with the distance between himself and the nearest ward building. The night sky was star-studded, the moon a white ball that appeared to hover only a few feet above the sleeping city that lay below. He had not known that Chimborazo was perched atop a great hill at the edge of Richmond, and the surprising revelation caused a tiny spurt of hope—perhaps the height itself was a sign that he should not feel so lowly—but he was distrustful of the feeling and did not allow it to grow.

He moved to a lone tree, shiny and black, at the edge of the hill, and leaned his shoulder against the cold bark. He stared downward.

Save for a smattering of lights, the city was dark, but his eyes were well adjusted, and Richmond revealed itself in blocky Cimmerian shapes, as if randomly shoved together by the hands of a giant. Pollard shook his head. He recognized Richmond as a city with the bleakest of futures for many years to come. He had heard—and in fact believed—that the remaining inhabitants would torch the city if the Yankees ever positioned their forces to take it. It was not a question of ever; of this Pollard was certain. It was simply a question of when. Another month or two, maybe three? It did not matter. The city was doomed, and he was inextricably linked to it. And then what? A prisoner of war camp, perhaps, or would the victors cast condescending looks at the footless man and leave him to fend for himself?

The chill crept back into his bones and with it the vision. He looked at the deep black crease in the earth that snaked away from the tips of his crutches. The winter rains had carved it from the soft ground, and it lay before him like a trough leading to a pit with no end. He could see his body floating over the ravine and then slamming, doll-like, ever farther down the slope, until it disappeared into the blackness, became another bit of rubbish at the edge of Richmond. One swift thrust of his arms would make the vision a reality, would solve the great mystery that lay beyond the walls of life. He had always believed that they were phantom walls, that this life joined with the other life, stretched into infinity. But now, joined with the dying city below, Pollard was not certain. Perhaps there was a great black void beyond the stars that swallowed cities and men. Perhaps the void was preferable to the city, preferable to his future.

The wind shifted, pushed up the long hill toward him, and on it there were musical notes, barely discernable. Pollard turned his head to the side, sought to capture with his ears the notes that he was certain were being played on a piano. He could not identify the tune. The sounds were like tiny chimes carried on the wind; the notes sounded neither joyous nor sad. Suddenly, the wind swirled again and they were gone, sucked back into the dark city. He heard the rasp of rough bark against the sleeve of his coat, felt his body slide down until his hip touched the dank earth. And then he wept.

She had followed him quietly and carefully, at one with the edges of the deep shadows of night, and when he reached the tree, Nelda Crump had crept to within ten yards. A peculiar admixture of sadness and relief flooded her as she watched and listened to the soft sobs. Only moments before, she had sensed a nebulous evil hovering about the man as he raised his head to the sky, and she nearly rushed to him. But it passed quickly and now only the sorrow remained. She pulled the shawl tightly around her shoulders and retreated into the shadows. There she would maintain her vigil until Pollard gathered himself and began his return to the ward.

Four days passed with Letha doing little more than coming down from her room for meals and then quickly returning. The strange heaviness of body that she had experienced the first night in the McCaw house lingered, and she did not wrestle against it, did not grit her teeth and attempt to ignore it. For here, in the sanctity of her little room, there was simply no reason for making such an effort. The war was all around her, encircling the city with an ever-tightening noose, yet it might as well have been on another continent. The foul bandages of the ward had been replaced by clean quilts and things made of lace and spotless window curtains. The groans and midnight mutterings of wounded men had been replaced by the clean *whoosh* of wind around the corner of the house. When she sat in the high-backed chair or reclined on the softness of the bed, Letha imagined that she was surrounded by unassailable fortress walls, marvelous barriers that no Union general would dare assault.

She sat now, in midafternoon of the fifth day, on the cushioned seat of the chair in the corner of the room. Through the windowpanes she watched patches of clean white clouds sweep past from west to east, toward the ocean and the alien lands across the waves. Letha wondered if the winds would swirl to the south and speed toward the namesake of Chimborazo Hospital. Thousands of miles the winds would have to fly in order to reach Ecuador and the dormant volcano called Chimborazo. Letha smiled ruefully at the pitiful comparison. The might of a volcano measured against what was, in reality, little more than a cluster of wooden huts barely sheltering men who were in large measure helpless. A worthless sentinel, unable to watch over the doomed city below.

Letha turned her head toward the sound of soft knocking on the door. She stood, walked to the door, opened it to see the pleasant face of Hannah McCaw. For the first time, Letha framed the portrait, saw the black hair drawn into a tidy bun, the high cheekbones touched ever so delicately with rouge. Hannah had mischievous eyes for a woman in her late forties, and Letha could not help but smile at them.

"I'm sorry for the bother," Hannah said, "I thought perhaps you might care for some company."

Letha nodded. "Yes, certainly. Please come in." She laughed dryly. "It is your home."

"Ah, my dear, but it is your room, for as long as you desire." Hannah walked to the other chair in the room, turned it toward Letha's, and sat down. She waited for Letha to sit down before speaking again. "Your color is much better, Letha. The rest has helped no doubt, but I attribute it mainly to my cooking." She laughed, left a place for Letha to join in.

Letha looked down at her lap, smoothed the fabric of her dress, then nodded. "It is marvelous—your cooking. I wish I had the appetite to do it justice."

"It will come back." Hannah waited for Letha to look up at her, then said, "Many things will come back, my dear. Many things."

Letha looked away toward the window, felt the weight of Hannah's contention settle on her. The resentment came like a tiny twinge of pain, quickly followed by an equal measure of guilt. Clearly, Hannah McCaw was anything but a busybody. She had taken her in like a child, offered solace, relief. It was a statement she had the right to make, even though it probed deeply.

Hannah registered the small, fleeting energy from the resentment, had expected it. It was a necessary hurt to be dealt with—the same as when Dr. McCaw wielded the scalpel or the lance—pain traded for healing. Too many days had passed; the wound continued to fester. But it would fester no longer.

Hannah said, "I have heard of your singing ability. It might help if you allowed it to come back. Dr. McCaw and I are in hopes that we may hear you while we have you captured here."

"Whatever you might have heard is exaggerated."

"I think not."

Letha shook her head, looked down again. Hannah McCaw was untying the mooring ropes of Letha's snug little boat as it bobbed peacefully in the harbor. Soon it would drift out to sea and the waves would batter it and cause her to cling to the railing. Letha was powerless in her efforts to stop the motion, was not certain that she had even tried. The shoreline was already receding.

Letha stood, walked to the window. "My voice is not solo quality. I sang with someone else."

"A patient?"

"Yes. A man whose talent is extraordinary."

"Ah, I see. It is not unusual to find wounded soldiers who are fine musicians. What is his name?"

"Pollard. Granville Pollard."

"What is the nature of his wound?"

"Wounds. He has lost both feet."

Hannah nodded solemnly. "It is the way of this war, to remove limbs. But his spirit, it seems that it remains intact?"

Letha lifted her head, clasped her hands at her waist. *His spirit, she asks. Who may testify to the condition of anyone's spirit, even one's own?* "He . . . has made progress."

"No doubt with your help."

"I tried to lift all of their spirits as best I could."

The past tense of the verb jabbed at Hannah's ears, resounded with a weary resolution. Dr. McCaw had provided the details of the suicide outside the door of Letha's ward, and she also knew of the long night when Letha Bartlett had held at bay the Angel of Death. What Hannah had not known was the toll exacted by the two deaths, but there was now no doubt in her mind that somehow the past tense of the verb symbolized the surrender of Letha's will.

"That will come back, too. The desire to lift their spirits, and in the doing, yours will be lifted."

"Of that I am not certain."

Hannah stood, walked slowly to Letha's side. "You are something of a legend around Chimborazo, Letha. Everyone knows of the night you tried to save the doomed young man." Letha's head turned slightly toward her. "Tell me of him, the man whose life you extended."

*Why are you doing this? Why do you push me out into the roiling sea?* The silent questions flashed hot and red in her brain, but she confined them there. Letha said instead, "In age, he was more child than man."

"But in heart?"

"He had the finest heart of any person I have ever known."

"Share him with me, Letha. I want to know him too."

Letha peered through the top panes of window glass. "His name was Nathan Fisher. He came from rural Alabama. We considered him to be our walking miracle. By all rights, he should have lost a leg to the saw, but he did not. It was a long road to recovery . . . or what we thought was recovery. I remember in the beginning, his face white with fright and pain, yet he somehow managed to smile at me. At the surgeons, even. I can recall not a single occasion on which he complained, ever. He was unfailingly polite, cheery; he had the gift of steering the boys' thoughts away from their own wounds, their sadness. I was convinced that he was God's own gift to us all, some flesh-and-blood reminder that all was not lost, that some things were redeemable, even in the midst of this abomination."

Letha paused, the bitterness oozing from her even before she spoke. "And then, as if God had only teased us, the great fountain of blood. I have only flashes of memory about the remainder of the night: the feel of the drying blood on my fingers, of the cold seeping up from the floor, of being held. Often they come back, the memories, usually unwanted. But they come anyway."

"You said, 'of being held'?"

Letha nodded, looked at Hannah through puffy red eyes. "Granville Pollard held me."

Hannah saw it then—the love—a flame reduced to the smallest of embers, but clearly love. She knew that there was no justification to cross this boundary, that it was a line beyond which harm could be done, yet Letha herself had opened the door. Hannah ignored the whispering voice of caution in her head, plunged forward. "I think that Mr. Pollard may be extraordinary in a manner beyond his music."

Letha stood statue-like for several long moments, her features devoid of emotion. The clouds raced too swiftly along above the treetops, and Letha felt the urge to somehow reach up and slow them down. Life was like the clouds—fast-paced and flimsy, too much at the mercy of capricious winds. "My father I loved greatly, and he died too soon of fragile health. My husband I loved greatly, and his constitution also proved unsuitable for this life. Nathan Fisher I loved as a son, and he was taken by this war that I can no longer fathom." She paused, looked at Hannah. "And Granville Pollard I am now afraid to love, not because of his wounds, but because of the vicissitudes of life . . . or is it the whims of God?"

"Ah, Providence. The indefinable, the unknowable. I don't waste much energy with all that. I choose to focus on people." Hannah paused and reached out and tapped the windowpane. "People are as real as this glass. Providence I cannot touch."

They stood in silence, though not uncomfortably, as the wind moaned around the corner of the house. A long sigh escaped Letha. "It seems as though I have loved only broken men."

"They are all broken, Letha, in their own way. We have only broken men to love, but love them we must."

Letha felt Hannah's shoulder touch hers, could smell the fragrance of her perfume, heard her say, "And love them we will."

# CHAPTER TWENTY

"I'm gonna ask him if'n he'll come home with us. Just for a time, you understand." Rector Crump intended for the statement to be part question, but once the words began to tumble over his tongue, he knew that he would have to add more. Nelda sat across the table from him, her hands folded neatly, her eyes registering mild surprise. "It'd be all right, don't you think? Just for a time."

Nelda unfolded her hands, touched the tips of her fingers together. "How long is 'a time,' Rector?"

"Well, I, uh, reckon it'd be for . . . well, it'd have to be till the war stopped and things settled down some." He looked away from her for a moment. "I know it's a burdensome thing to ask—not but one damn leg between two men and all—but you know me well enough. I ain't gonna let this slow me down long. A good farrier needs mostly his arms, and Andrew, I 'spect he's strong as a post by now, so he'll be a part of it, and—"

Nelda silenced him with the straightening of her fingers. "Rector, I'm not gonna throw a fit if you want to do this; there's no need for all this bold talk. But it won't be as easy as you think."

"I know that, woman, but I cain't stand the thought of him not havin' a place to go, endin' up at the mercy of the Union. Nobody can tell me that they won't be mighty spiteful for a long time to come."

Nelda shook her head. "I don't think any of this talk matters much anyway, Rector. You've forgot one thing in all this."

"And what would that be?"

"That he'd even want to. Or even if he did, that his pride would let him."

"He don't seem like the prideful sort to me."

"All men have pride, no matter how many body parts they've lost."

Crump scrunched up his mouth, rubbed a hand over his beard. "Tarnation, woman, I know that, but this would be the sensible thing for him to do. He ain't a man starin' at a whole lot of choices."

"Rector, you go ahead and ask him—with my blessing—and if he wants to come, we'll make do. We always have."

Crump nodded. "Well, that's good to know, and I 'preciate you standin' with me on this."

She smiled, reached across the table and clamped her hands over his. "When haven't I stood by you, Rector Crump?"

He placed his hands over hers, squeezed them gently. The late-night weariness filled him, as it had for what now seemed to be a great portion of his life—the portion measured in Chimborazo time. It always came from the inside out, a living thing that grew from the core of his body and then radiated outward until even his beard felt limp.

"I ain't asked you yet, but, what are we goin' back to, woman?"

Nelda held his gaze silently, pictured the little farm in her mind, saw the house and the sheds and the land, all without the touch of a man's hand for so long. Saw the countryside for miles around the homestead stripped as if by hordes of locust. Armies were hungry things—gigantic, hungry things. "Less than before, Rector." She smiled grimly. "Less than before."

He looked away. He had no will to learn more, at least for tonight. He pushed away from the table, reached for his crutches. "I'm gonna ask him now. He don't ever seem to be asleep. Just as well do it now."

"Yes, you had. He won't have long to make up his mind. Letha's comin' back day after tomorrow, and I want to start on home, Rector. We have a family to tend to."

"When did you hear that?"

"This afternoon."

"Why didn't you tell me?"

"Meant to, but I got caught up in the work." She looked at him slyly. "You remember seeing me sitting around any today, Rector, chewing the fat with the ladies' club?"

Crump grunted a low laugh. "No, I reckon not." He stood and gained his balance. "You need to come too, so's he'll not think it's just me."

Pollard heard the soft clumping of crutches coming down the aisle and opened his eyes. He was surprised to see Nelda with Crump; evening visits had become very infrequent since she had been pressed into service. He followed them with his eyes until they were within a few steps of Crump's bed, and then he closed his eyes, offered the couple what little privacy he could. But the sounds that came to him were only those of two people sitting down side by side, and Pollard sensed that very soon Crump's hoarse, low voice would fill the silence.

"Pollard, you ain't asleep, are you?"

Pollard opened his eyes. "No."

"Good. Didn't figure you'd be." Crump cleared his throat. "Me and the wife, uh, we got somethin' to say to you, Pollard. We've been thinkin' some—a lot, really—here lately 'bout where you're gonna go till the dust settles and you can do somethin' with your music. And we think, that is, we hope, that you would come to Alabama with us for a time. Till you get your bearins'." Crump poked a hand in the air, waved it at Pollard. "Now don't say nothin' right now, without thinkin' on it some. At least sleep on it tonight, all right?"

"This has my blessing too, Granville," Nelda said. "You'd be as welcome as you could be."

Like a balloon inflating his chest, Pollard felt the emotion well up and swallowed against it. "This is . . . overwhelming. I, uh, don't know what—"

"Now like I say, don't say nothin' at all for now, Pollard. Just sleep on it. Besides, I'm whipped as a coon been run by hounds all night, and I don't want to argue in such a condition, you understand?"

Pollard raised a hand as if he wanted to say something, but Crump dismissed him with a wave and flopped back onto the bed. "We all need some rest around here and I ain't gonna spout nary another word tonight."

He jerked at the covers and then rolled away from Pollard. Nelda leaned down and arranged the blankets for a moment, then patted her husband on the shoulder. She moved to the foot of Pollard's bed, said, "Letha is coming back day after tomorrow, Granville. Word is that she's better."

Pollard skirted the edges of sleep for most of the night, his thoughts drifting between dreams and reality. He had not wrestled with the decision of whether or not to accept Crump's offer; in truth, there had never been a choice. Crump and his family were about to embark on a phase of their lives that would demand all that they had to give, perhaps more, and the insertion of Pollard's circumstances into the situation was not an option he could live with. But the restless night had a theme, a singular vacuum around which his thoughts and dreams whirled, drawing ever closer to the black hole at the center—the black hole that had consumed Nathan Fisher in death, and Cloyd Anderson in war, and Letha Bartlett in spirit. The black hole that would now consume Crump and send him to a war-ravaged homeland that would scarcely resemble the one he had left so long ago.

Pollard watched the gray light of dawn color the ceiling until he could distinguish one plank from another. He waited for Crump to stir, to see the dawn with him.

To his surprise, Crump did not stir, but spoke in a low voice that seemed to come from a distance far greater than the few feet separating them. "Didn't sleep too good."

"Nor I."

"I was thinkin' on how we could rig the bed of a wagon, once't we leave the train, so's me and you could ride the last part of the way home without bangin' around so. And I figure that—"

"Crump."

"What?"

"I am unable to convey in words just what your offer means to me, but I cannot accept it, my friend."

Crump raised his hand and said in a louder voice, "Now listen—"

Pollard held up his hand in a matching gesture, shook his head. "No, we will not argue over this. There are difficult times ahead for all of us. And all of us—you and your family included—have very limited resources. To know that you and Nelda are willing to share yours with me—and to risk adding my burden to your own—well, as I said, words fail me." Pollard laughed softly. "And you would agree that this is not usually the case."

Crump lowered his hand to his side, looked up at the ceiling. "Well, dammit, that's about what I figured you'd say, but—"

"No 'buts,' Crump."

Crump shook his head against the pillow. "You must have a sight more faith in the goodheartedness of the Yanks than me, Pollard. They're gonna own this ground real soon."

"You forget that I am one myself."

"You ain't either, Pollard, you was just unlucky enough to be born up there. You ain't no Yank in the heart of it all."

"I am no longer certain just what I am in the heart of it all. I got caught up in something bigger than myself, swept along on a current that I could not resist. Did not want to resist. And now the swift river has about run its course and will soon deposit me into the ocean, but I deserve that."

"That 'somethin' bigger' you got caught up in was freedom, Pollard. Pure and simple."

"Ah, freedom. A concept many in the Union say that we have denied an entire race of our fellow man. That, they say, is why we slaughter and maim each other."

Crump spat dryly in disgust. "Slaves my ass. I never had nary a single slave, don't have a single friend down home who had one neither. Of all the men in my regiment, I cain't recall but a handful ever claimed to have one of their own, and they was prob'ly blowin' hot air. And what's more, Pollard, I hear tell that General Bobby Lee hisself turned his'n loose . . . and that Grant hadn't." He snorted. "Hell no. The lot of 'em's crazy as bed bugs if'n they think we're fightin' to hang onto slaves we don't even have." He lapsed into a brief, stony silence. "Pollard, I'll tell you true—if'n I was to see a man lay a whip on another human chained to a post—includin' a man black as two feet up a horse's ass—I'd take the whip and use it on the whipper."

"But it is more than just the whipping posts, Crump. It has become a way of life down here—part of the economic engine—and slaves are required."

"Well they ain't for me or mine, and won't ever be. I stand with ol' Bobby Lee. Turn 'em loose."

"Why, then, Crump? Why did you go to war, leave your family, sacrifice a leg?"

Crump furrowed his brow, relaxed himself with a slow breath. He looked away for a moment, allowed his thoughts to churn. He did not know if he could offer an explanation that would be adequate to the likes of Pollard. Then it struck him—the simple statement echoed softly inside his head—and Crump knew that it said more than a thousand fancy-sounding words.

"Cause they came down here."

Pollard said nothing, nodded slowly, examined the statement. "Yes. Perhaps that is much of it. But you and the men that you know are ordinary farmers and tradesmen. What about the land owners whose plantations it would take you an hour to walk across?"

"But you came down here to fight on the rich folks' side, Pollard. You're squeezin' my poor mind here. You ain't some ignorant farrier or dirt farmer. Your eyes were open, seems to me."

"I didn't come down here to fight for them."

"But by God you did, like it or not."

A great sigh leaked from Pollard as he slumped forward. "And that burden is mine to bear to my grave, Crump—maybe beyond."

Crump was irritated that the conversation had veered hurtfully off course. He waved his hand and made a deep sound in his chest. He said, "That ocean you talked about heading for runs deep, Pollard. You need a good boat. Me and the wife could be your boat."

Pollard shifted his body to face Crump. "I hope to find passage in another boat, and for a much longer journey."

Crump smiled, let the silence gather for a moment. "I know you do. And that's what me and Nelda want for you too, but who can say about that? Letha Bartlett may never be the same. We figured that we'd work out some way to give you both a chance after the war."

"I do not claim to know what is in her heart now, much less how she feels about me. But I am not willing to risk a long separation now, Crump. The only opportunity I have is now, don't you see?"

Crump sighed tiredly. "Yes, Pollard. I reckon I see." He paused. "I don't know what made me ever think I could win an argument with you."

"We have not had an argument."

"Yes, we have. We just didn't say all the words."

"Well, let's not start now, all right?"

"I figure me and the wife will leave the day after Letha comes back."

"You should. It's time for you to go home, Crump."

Letha returned to the ward on Sunday, after the evening meal had been served and the men had settled in for the night. From the matron's quarters, Nelda heard the wagon wheels, first as they creaked to a halt and then, a half minute later, as they jerked back into motion. She walked quickly to the kitchen door, heard the light footfalls on the wooden porch. Nelda opened the door as Letha was reaching for the handle.

"Welcome back, Letha."

"Thank you," she answered softly as she stepped into the kitchen. Letha glanced around the room, saw the order, the cleanliness. "You seem to have managed quite well without me, Nelda. I greatly appreciate your efforts."

"Oh, I have managed to scrub and cook and wash and the like, but I'm afraid that I'm not as soothing with the men as you. I've answered a hundred questions about when you were comin' back." Nelda smiled, gave her a sturdy hug, and then stepped back. "There is only one Letha to them."

Letha looked down, touched the tip of her tongue to the inside of her cheek. "That is kind of you, but I think you overestimate my importance."

Nelda extended her hand toward Letha's traveling case. "Let me put that in your room. You go show your face in the ward and we'll see who's right."

Letha allowed Nelda to take the case, then took a tentative step toward the ward doorway before stopping.

"Go on, Letha. Those boys will sleep much better tonight if you let them know you're all right." She paused, smiled. "And one man more than all the others."

Letha walked slowly to the open doorway and stood in the shadows cast by the lamps. Within seconds a voice rang out. "Lookee here, boys! She's back! She's come back!"

Like dark waves in a choppy sea, the forms of men bobbed up from beds, pushed higher on hands and elbows, some swinging their legs over the sides of their beds. And with the motions came the growing murmur of voices and some called out: "Praise be . . . I told you it wouldn't be long . . . well, Jerusalem, now . . . Miz Bartlett . . . Lord have mercy . . . I'll declare, boys, if it ain't so!"

The man who first announced the good news extended his hand into the aisle, fingers wiggling for her touch. Letha reached out and clasped his hand, released it and took hold of another as she began to move down the aisle, from one side to another. The sound of hands clapping rose behind her and then rippled past her, and she felt the gooseflesh rise on the nape of her neck, the flush come to her face. She moved slowly, the eager hands clinging and patting, the words and phrases rising up to her ears as a wondrous liturgy. The tears were warm on her cheeks, and she swallowed against the fullness in her throat. She looked ahead to the end of the aisle and saw Crump perched on his crutches, his hands clapping together in a steady rhythm. Beside him, Pollard struggled to gain his balance, then stood shoulder to shoulder with the bigger man, found her eyes. Quickly, she looked down at the man nearest her, nodded her thanks.

She scarcely noticed the touch of the last few hands as she mouthed words of appreciation through smiling lips. Suddenly she stood in front of Crump and Pollard, the latter's eyes still seeking hers, his features set in a resolute smile. She heard the growl of Crump's voice, turned toward him.

"Ah, the Angel of Chimborazo, done come home now." He smiled broadly, bowed his head in deference.

She heard her own voice, weak and faraway. "Sergeant Crump. How kind of you, sir."

Pollard balanced himself on the bulky prosthesis and held out his right hand. "Welcome back, Letha. We have—I have—missed you greatly."

She placed her hand in his and he lifted it to his lips, kissed it gently. Behind them, the voices grew louder, some cheering, and one rose over the others. "A song for the boys! The two of you, a song for the boys!" The chant began, grew to a crescendo. *"A song, a song, a song!"*

Pollard still held her hand, saw the emotion roll over her, nearly overwhelm her, and he gripped her hand tighter, drew her a step closer. "Are you up to it?"

"I am a bit taken aback by all this. I am afraid that I am as weak as my voice just now."

Pollard glanced at Crump and made a wordless request. Crump raised a hand to shoulder height, waved it for a moment until the voices died away. "Let's give her a day or so to get her feet back on the ground, boys."

The chant began to rise again, but Crump again waved them into silence. He glanced at Letha, then quickly to Pollard. "Tell you what, boys. Me and the wife are headin' for home day after tomorrow, and I'll do my best to get a song out of 'em as a goin'-away present."

The men clapped and murmured their approval, and slowly the shadowy forms melted into the beds. The evening silence again claimed the long room, and soon only low voices could be heard.

Crump looked past Letha, saw Nelda standing in the doorway, her arms folded comfortably at her waist. "Well, me and the wife got some talkin' to do. I'm headed to the kitchen."

Pollard waited for Crump to make his way up the aisle and then said to Letha, "Sit with me a moment, please." He extended his hand toward the end of his bed as he sat down near the pillow. "The time away has served you well, Letha."

She nodded slightly, the hint of an apology in the gesture. "I have rested, gained some perspective, I suppose."

"Mrs. McCaw, is she as remarkable as her husband?"

"Yes, quite so, in her own way. Without her support, I do not believe that he could be the rock that he is around here."

"I'm certain that you are correct."

Letha looked down into her lap, began to rub the tips of her fingers together as the silence gathered. She felt Pollard shift his weight, heard him inhale deeply. He said, "You have been gone for only days, and yet it seems a very long time."

Letha looked up now. "Yes, it seems longer than days." She pressed her fingers flat on her dress, smoothed wrinkles that were not there, then placed her hands at her sides and began to push up from the bed.

Pollard raised a hand. "Wait. Please." The thoughts ricocheted inside his head like rifle balls against boulders, and he could only wait until they lost their energy, slowly bounded to a halt, became knowable. Did he dare allow her to go, to sleep for a night and then again become a part of the morning routine, lost in the needs of the men? The time was very short; Crump and Nelda would be gone in hours, no longer able to perform their subtle maneuvers on their behalf. His heart thumped against his ribs, the voice clear now in his head. *She is here now, close enough to touch.* It was a very dangerous place to go, was in fact the tragedy that almost broke her. And yet it was the only place he could go if she was to know his heart.

"I must tell you this one thing, Letha. Please trust me when I say that I do not tread this old ground lightly, but that night with Nathan . . ." He looked away, suddenly fearful that what he was doing was selfish beyond measure. The words caught in his throat, hung there like the acrid smoke from a battlefield. "I—"

Her voice was soft, wistful. "It's all right, Granville. The boy will always be a part of us. It's all right to go back there."

Pollard felt the weight rise from his shoulders, wanted to gather her in his arms and hold her. "When I held you that night—I hesitate to do so, but must confess to you that it was wondrous for me. And I do not in any way demean the memory of Nathan Fisher. We know that he was better than all of us—simply, profoundly better than any of us. And his death was a tragedy. But to hold you, to be of some small comfort . . ." He shook his head, swallowed. "I have never felt more whole in my life."

Letha lowered her head very slowly, linked her fingers like slender white vines. Pollard waited, unable to draw the deep breath that his body demanded. She looked up, cocked her head slightly to one side, her mouth set in a line that Pollard hoped was a smile. "Life and death, so inextricably linked, Granville. It is a mystery that I cannot sort out. Made you whole, but emptied me. And now, if you are saying what I think you are . . . I am bewildered."

"Letha, I had great feelings toward you before that night, believe me. Attribute my stupid silence to mental and physical weakness, selfishness, male stubbornness, whatever you wish, but I cannot undo all of that. I know that you must have taken it as rejection, but it was not. I was weak, pitifully weak. I am sorry."

She reached out with one hand, touched his hand with the tips of her fingers. "I do not know what to say to you just now, Granville. I once was strong—or so I thought—and now I too feel very weak. I seem unable to order my thoughts about anything."

"Then do not attempt to order them, Letha, but do this one thing with me tomorrow. Sing with me for Crump and Nelda, help me give them a wonderful farewell. Then let come what will, and I will live with it."

Letha stood and looked down. Pollard saw the line of her lips form an unmistakable smile, though rueful and without energy. She turned, walked away, and Pollard could not hear the sound of her shoes.

# CHAPTER TWENTY-ONE

They arose to sing just after breakfast. Pollard balanced his weight on his crutches and the prosthesis as he stood near the foot of his bed. Letha, her hands folded at her waist, stood close enough to blend her voice with Pollard's, but she carefully maintained the arm's length separating them. Someone had pulled a chair into the middle of the aisle and beckoned Crump to sit as the guest of honor. Nelda stood behind him, her right hand placed on his shoulder, and to Pollard, they appeared as a couple posing formally for a photograph or a painting. Two dozen other men—some standing, others lining the edges of beds—formed the audience for the singers.

Pollard glanced at Letha for a moment, then looked at Crump. "I have not spoken to Letha about my selection, but I know she is familiar with the melody. I heard her hum it once, several weeks ago. It is called 'When This Cruel War is Over.'" He looked at Crump and Nelda. "For you, my friends, a journey home, and then these words will ring true for you and your children."

Pollard drew a full breath as he looked at Letha, waited for her small nod. Then they began to sing.

Dearest love, do you remember, when we last did
meet,
how you told me that you loved me, kneeling at my
feet?
Oh! How proud you stood before me, in your suit of
gray,
when you vow'd to me and country to be true
throughout the fray.

Pollard was careful to restrain his powerful tenor voice, and soon Letha's voice rose so that the harmonic strains were heard as one. Crump, Nelda, and the men surrounding them became fixtures in stone, as if afraid that the tiniest movement might somehow break the wondrous spell that the music had spread over them.

Weeping, sad and lonely, hopes and fears how vain!
When this cruel war is over, praying that we meet
again.

When the summer breeze is sighing mournfully along,
or when autumn leaves are falling, sadly breathes the
song.
Oft in dreams I see thee lying on the battle plain,
lonely, wounded, even dying, calling but in vain.

If amid the din of battle, nobly you should fall,
far away from those who love you, none to hear you
call—
who would whisper words of comfort, who would
soothe your pain?
Ah! The many cruel fancies, ever in my brain.

They sang the remaining verse, following it with the chorus. When the last note faded into the still air of the room, Letha realized that her shoulder was touching Pollard's upper shirtsleeve, yet she had no recollection of having moved, knew only that she had been drawn to his side. With a nearly imperceptible motion, she withdrew to her original position, lowered her head slightly. She felt the emotion begin to leak from her. She was not certain if she desired to cling to it or simply allow it to fade with the song.

The room was hushed, but everyone in it could still hear the voices as the seconds slipped away. It was Crump who first brought his hands together, and immediately everyone joined in the clapping. It was a subdued ovation, reverential, and only a few voices murmured words of appreciation.

Crump shifted his weight on the chair, then slowly stood as Nelda helped him set his crutches. He clumped forward and stopped in front of Pollard and Nelda. He blinked hard, swallowed carefully. "Well, you two . . ." He shook his head, swallowed again. "I said onc't that it'd be damn near worth dyin' to be sung over like that, and here you've gone and done it over me livin'."

He looked behind him, motioned for Nelda to come to his side. She took the crutch from beside his leg, replacing it with her arm. "Sung over us both, you did; sung us toward home." Crump shook his head again. "It's a high honor in my chest just now. That's the onliest thing I can think to say."

Nelda said softly, "It was the most beautiful thing I ever heard. I thank you."

Pollard smiled and extended his hand to Crump. The big man hopped forward on his leg, grasped Pollard's hand, then quickly drew him close. He spoke softly and only Pollard and the women heard what he said.

"If'n it ain't to be that we meet again in this life, I hope we'll meet in the sweet bye and bye, Pollard."

Pollard nodded, said, "Perhaps so, my friend, in the bye and bye."

Crump released his hand and turned to Letha. "Ain't no proper way to thank somebody like you. Reckon I'd be a fool to try." He made a half turn toward the men. "Boys, wherever you scatter to when this thing's over, you tell the story of the Angel of Chimborazo wherever you go. Hear me?"

The men nodded, pledged their vows quietly as Crump swung his dark-eyed gaze over them. He turned his head back toward Pollard and Letha, but spoke to Nelda. "I 'spect we'd better go on quick, woman. I don't want to get to blubberin'."

Letha spoke for a moment with the wagon driver before returning to the passenger side and looking up at the man and the woman. Crump wore his gray uniform coat, which now hung loosely on his shoulders, his forage cap tugged tightly over his forehead. His right trouser leg was neatly cropped near his hip and sewn shut with a heavy black thread. He was perched on two tattered blankets, folded so that he was cushioned from the hard seat. Nelda sat on the outside, her boots firmly planted against the slanted floorboard. The morning breeze was mild, the portent of spring palpable in the air. Nelda wore the same clothing she had arrived in, though freshly laundered, and her wide-brimmed hat sat at an angle similar to her husband's cap.

Letha reached behind them and patted the cloth sack. "I surely wish there were more provisions to send you off with."

Crump raised a hand, shook his head, said, "No ma'am, don't say no more or I'll leave it yet. Feel a mite guilty as it is. We'll find a bite or two along the way. Don't worry 'bout us none."

Nelda said, "It is thoughtful of you, Letha, but—"

"The sack leaves with you," Letha said, her mouth set in a firm smile. She reached forward and took Nelda's right hand in both of hers. "You have done all of us, and especially me, a great service, Nelda Crump. I shall always be indebted to you."

Nelda looked toward the porch, where Pollard stood in the open doorway, then back down at Letha. "You can clear your debt with me right now by promising to look after yourself as well as all of the men, and by following your heart when this is over."

Letha felt Nelda's grip tighten for a moment, then slid her fingers from the woman's hand. She nodded. "I shall try, as best I am able."

She felt Crump's gaze. She met the dark eyes and said to him, "Sergeant Crump, it has been my distinct honor to have known you, sir."

He shook his head slowly, touched the bill of his cap with two fingers. "The honor was all mine. All mine." Crump looked past her now, saw Pollard's gaunt figure draped against the doorway. Pollard was smiling, the morning sunlight tinting his hair, and the memory of his voice in song passed through Crump's brain with a clarity that overwhelmed him. That a man who could make such heavenly sounds could ever take up arms suddenly struck Crump as an unsolvable mystery. Pollard raised his hand in farewell, and Crump again touched the bill of his cap, said, "Keep singin', the both of you'uns." He glanced down at Letha for a moment then turned away, set his shoulders squarely to the front, said to the man holding the reins, "Drive on."

The wagon creaked along toward Fredericksburg Station, the dying city passing before Crump's eyes in surreal fashion. They had traveled no more than a mile before he decided to fix his vision to the front, just over the horse's knifelike brown ears. It was of some comfort—though Crump despised the admission—that Richmond had never been a part of his heart, a part of the Cause to which he had given his leg. He had fought for forty acres of Alabama soil, and the pines and hickories jutting proudly from it, and the little creek with the grassy banks that ran deep and cool in the spring, and the square solid house where his boys had been born. These things were worth a man's leg, and far more. No, he did not wish to see Richmond any longer, and he knew that even if he were departing from a city victorious, he would still be looking over the horse's ears, thinking of home.

When the train station came into view, Crump spoke quietly to Nelda, though he did not turn his head toward her. "Gonna be a little crazy around these trains, I reckon."

"Yes, Rector, it will, but we'll make it all right."

"How long, all told?"

"Four days, maybe five, with the switchin' and all. It's a mess at Knoxville, then one long last stretch to Huntsville."

Crump's thoughts raced ahead, blocked out the tortuous train ride to come, latched onto the road that ran south out of Huntsville—the beautiful, winding road that they would follow for twelve miles until it reached the grove of hickories and the lane to the left. Then one final mile with the smell of late winter giving way to spring filling his nostrils, leading him home. The wagon wheels clattered through a rut in the road, sending a jolt of pain into his stub, and he caught his breath, waited for a moment before he spoke.

"How'd you get up to the depot?"

"Walked," Nelda answered. She read his thoughts, did not allow him to ask the next question. "We'll get us a horse and wagon in town."

"With what? I hear money ain't worth much nowadays."

"I have some things that'll serve for money." She felt the small bulge of the pocket sewn into the inside waist of her dress, tried not to think of the silver locket with the fancy scrollwork and the gold ring nestled beside it.

Deep furrows creased Crump's brow, and he moved his plug of tobacco to the other side of his cheek. "What things?"

"What does it matter, Rector? All that matters is getting you home."

"No, woman, it ain't the onliest thing that matters. I can hop like a damn jack rabbit for a dozen mile if'n I have to, 'fore I let you—"

"Hush, Rector, I know more about how you'll feel after this train ride than you do, and you'll do well to be sittin' upright time we get to Huntsville. So don't be tellin' me what I can and can't do with things."

He turned his head only far enough to glance at her eyes, then huffed under his breath as he looked back over the horse's ears.

The train rumbled southwest into the Virginia countryside. The slanting rays of the setting sun filtered through the cracked window glass of the car and cast a lovely spectrum that Crump watched with half-closed eyes. The deep lassitude had already crept into his body, wrapped itself around his bones, but he accepted it, recognized the necessary price to be exacted by the long journey home. Nelda sat with her hands folded together over the provision sack, her body rocking comfortably with the steel rhythm of the rails. They had talked little, eaten sparingly from the sack at midday.

The band of colors danced in the window glass and then faded away as the tracks curved gently and led the train into thick shadows. Crump shifted his weight, looked away from the window. "Reckon I won't hardly know Andrew or Ethan either one."

Nelda smiled, said, "Oh, you'll know them, Rector, but the best part of four years has put some changes on them. Andrew is gonna be a big man, like you. His shoulders are wide and sloped already and he can carry most anything I ask him to." She laughed quietly, shook her head. "Now our Ethan—he's more likely to find a way around work than into it, though he's gonna be nearly as big as his brother."

Crump chuckled. "Ah, that's that Sanders blood showin' up, like that shiftless brother of you'rn."

"Truman Sanders was doing just fine for himself before the war, and he'll do just fine after it's over as well."

"It's just that nobody can figure out how he does it."

"He's just got a nose for business, and what's more, it'd suit me fine if Ethan took after him on that." She raised her eyebrows and cocked her head at Crump. "Not every man feels the need to sweat from dawn to sunset, Rector."

Crump looked at the crack in the window, hoped to see again the tiny rainbow, but the sun had passed low into the hills and shadows. "Good God a'mighty, I miss them boys."

"Well, it won't be long now."

They rode in silence for a mile, the murmurs of the other passengers mingling with the rumble of the car. Crump said, "I reckon the best part of four years has changed me even more than them."

Nelda turned toward him, saw the edge of fear in his eyes. "Those are good boys, Rector, and we've already talked it out, your losin' your leg. It's already behind them."

He shook his head. "I know they're good boys, woman, but it won't be that easy." He pushed a jet of air past his lips. "If'n I coulda just kept the damn knee stump, that woulda helped a lot. Just the damn long stump." He shook his head again, his beard touching his chest. "I feel like a sawed log."

"It wasn't meant to be, Rector. Let it go." She turned and reached behind him, pulled his coat up over his shoulders. "There's a window broken out up near the front and I doubt there's any wood for the stove. It'll chill down quick now."

Two days later, on a cool, windy afternoon, the train chugged into the Knoxville station and lumbered to a halt. Nelda sat tilted toward her husband so that he could rest his head on her shoulder. He had slept fitfully for the past two hours, and Nelda was thankful for the opportunity to get up and move about for a while. It would be a long night, and there would be one more beyond, she was told, before they reached Huntsville. She gently braced his head as she slid her shoulder clear and then patted him on the cheek.

"Rector. Rector, wake up now. We're in Knoxville depot." She waited for his eyes to open and watched as he blinked into the present. He cleared his throat and dragged his fingers through his beard. "I'm going to get off for a while and walk around," she said. "Need to fill the canteen too. You all right?"

He nodded, mouthed a "yes," but made no sound. He swallowed, sniffed, then said, "Yeah, I'm all right. You go on. Me a-layin' all over you like some sack a 'taters. You must be wore plumb out."

"I won't be long." She stepped past him, nodded pleasantly toward the old woman sitting on the opposite side of the aisle.

Crump rocked his head back toward the window, studied the activity in the rail yard. Twenty feet distant on parallel tracks sat two boxcars, and Crump saw ragged blue-clad men being herded up a wooden ramp by two soldiers with carbines carried across their chests. *Yanks*. He had not meant to make a sound but the words slipped from his lips. He noticed movement across the aisle and turned to see the old woman lean forward, her knitting project now forgotten in her lap. She wore a dark brown homespun bonnet, and when she strained to see past Crump and through the window, her bent wire-rimmed spectacles tilted downward on a pale cheek.

"Who is them ar soldiers, and where is they a-goin' to?"

Crump said, "Yankee prisoners, goin' off to a pen, I 'magin."

The woman's thin hand knifed upward and jabbed at the top of her bonnet as she leaned far out into the aisle. Her voice was a low keen, the loathing palpable in the close air of the car. "What'd we ever do to them that they should come down here a-killin' our brothers and sons? They ought to set that ar boxcar afire and give 'em a head start to Hades."

Crump was startled by the vehemence spewing from an old woman, who for the last hundred miles had seemed to pass the time with little more on her mind than the socks she was knitting for Confederate soldiers. But the sight of the hated enemy, scrawny and unarmed though they were, had seared her soul. She glanced down to the revolver holstered on Crump's side, then pointed with a bony finger at the flap of material covering his stump.

"By rights you ought to shove that winder up and commence to shootin' 'em, soldier, seein' as how they've gone and chopped you near in half."

Crump shook his head wearily, said, "No, ma'am. I've lost my taste for killin'. I just want to go home now."

She eyed him warily for a moment, squinting through the corners of her spectacles, lowered her gaze again to the revolver, then snorted dryly. "Well I'll declare, then, soldier, if you was to lend me that pistol, I'd go to work myself."

Crump stared at her now, his mouth half open, and he did not know if he should be amused or alarmed. She scrunched up her cheek in an effort to raise the low side of her spectacles, then said, "I'm a sorry shot with a pistol, but I could shoot among 'em and mark several, I reckon. Might even get lucky and kill a brace or so."

Without realizing it, Crump slid his hand protectively down over his holster, felt the cold steel of the hammer touch his palm.

"Well, whatcha' say, soldier?"

Crump shook his head. "I believe you would, wouldn't you?"

"You're damn right I would."

"You wouldn't if'n you'd seen some things I seen."

"Well, sir, I ain't been in the fray, but I seen some sorry things down Chatt'nooga way, I have."

Crump closed his eyes, let his lungs fill with air. In the silence, he heard the rustle of her dress as she sat back in her seat. Quietly, and as much to himself as to the woman, he said, "I seen a crick run red with blood onct'. Some from our boys, some from they'rn. And I seen enough blood leak from me to fill a whiskey jug 'fore I stopped it. And now as I think back, I'm evermore sure I don't want to see no more of it." He sighed, turned his head away from her. "The thing is over."

A man lumbered slowly down the aisle, separating Crump and the woman for a few seconds, and then he heard her say, "Won't be over for me till there's good Tennessee dirt over my coffin box."

# CHAPTER TWENTY-TWO

Vash Mimms waited patiently in front of Huntsville Station, watching for the train. He stood under the short roof extending from the front of the depot, from time to time sliding a half step backward when the breeze carried the cold drizzle too close for comfort, then returning to his original position. Though thirty-eight years of age, his round face bore only the wisp of a beard along his jawline, his small mouth pouty and childlike, and any of the people lining the platform would have judged him little more than half his age had they observed him, though none would know him.

His long coat was worn but serviceable, dark brown in color and matching the wide-brimmed hat pulled low over his forehead. His left arm hung with a slight crook, the result of a rifle ball that shrieked past the corner of the Dunker church at Antietam and nicked the tendon near his elbow. When Vash Mimms's wanderings took him close to his relatives and acquaintances near Decatur, the crook of his arm was much more pronounced and elicited warm sympathies from those who did not know him well. The townsfolk who did know him well doubted that the wound was as serious as he let on, but none would ever challenge him, given his nature, which belied the boyish innocence of his features. That he had been crafty enough to deceive a half-drunken surgeon into discharging him was now a comfortable memory and caused Mimms not the slightest twinge of guilt. Nor did the fact that in his right coat pocket he carried a very reliable short-barreled British Tranter revolver.

The wind shifted, pecked his face with cold rain, and he retreated to the edge of the sparse gathering, became another formless figure in the gray morning light, peering at the oncoming locomotive as it puffed down the tracks toward the platform.

As the train crept alongside the platform, Nelda gently shook her husband's shoulder, said to him, "We're here, Rector, wake up now." She waited as he shook off the fitful slumber and blinked owl-like at her. "It's over, Rector; we're a dozen miles from home."

He blinked again, sniffed as if to test the air for the redolence of Alabama. "Huntsville? We're here?"

"Yes." She reached over and took his coat, which he had used as a blanket during the night. "Lean up and let's get this on you. The weather looks heavy out there."

He shivered involuntarily. "The weather ain't been so good in here neither."

"We'll build a good fire when we get home, sip hot coffee. That sound all right?"

"No. It sounds like Heaven."

She smiled. "Little short of that, but it does sound fine, I'll admit."

They waited until the other passengers shuffled down the aisle before Nelda got up and organized Crump's crutches, then helped him onto his leg. He swayed for a moment, leaning a shoulder into hers. "I'm weaker'n a one-legged piss ant."

"You'll feel better in a bit. I'm gonna find you a sitting place in the depot and a bite to eat while I ask around about a horse and wagon."

"First thing you need to do is point me toward the outhouse. My teeth are floatin'."

"There'll be a line."

He made a noise in his throat, said, "There won't be one behind it."

They made their way into the aisle, and Crump glanced at the seat that the old woman had occupied. He had told Nelda of the incident involving the Union prisoners, and she had discreetly accused him of exaggeration. Until she disembarked near Chattanooga, the woman had kept to herself and worked steadily, appearing to Nelda as the portrait of an elderly dignified Southern lady dutifully knitting socks for the soldier boys. He said, "Reckon ol' Tennessee Granny is happy on her home dirt now."

"The poor old thing, I hope so."

Crump shook his head. "Still don't believe me, huh?"

"Surely she was just spoutin' off, Rector, for pity's sake."

He pushed out a single syllable of laughter, shook his head again, patted the handle of his revolver. "If I'd a give her this piece, them Yanks would'a been as good as back on the battlefield, I'll tell you."

She looked at him and wrinkled her nose. "Who can say? These are strange times. Let's go."

When they were a step from the end of the doorway, Crump stopped and looked back over his shoulder. He said softly, "Speakin' of weaponry, what are you totin'?"

She touched her right hand to her dress pocket. "The derringer is in this pocket."

"And?"

"One of your best knives is sheathed low on my right leg."

He nodded, turned back to the doorway, and clumped out into the wind.

Vash Mimms eyed the passenger car as a single crutch poked from the opening, quickly followed by another, then tapped their way forward as the bearded man swung his weight over them. Then a woman's hand appeared on the man's shoulder, guiding him down the two steps. Mimms slowly turned back toward the car, lowered the brim of his hat, and took several steps forward. He hesitated, waited until an elderly couple shuffled off in the same direction, then moved forward again with them, toward the depot.

Crump waited until the dark eyes peering from underneath the wooly eyebrows settled on him, then said to the horse trader, "Folks say you're the man to see about buyin' a horse and wagon."

A gnarled finger slowly rose and pushed up the hat brim a couple of inches. The man took three strides toward Crump and Nelda. Behind him loomed the battered gray wood of his livery stable. "Folks'd be right." He paused, stroked one end of a drooping moustache. "Course, I ain't pretendin' the choices is real good. Best'ns went off to war."

Crump nodded. "Suspected that."

"What you got to be buyin' with?"

Crump pulled several crumpled Confederate bills from his coat pocket and began to straighten them out as he counted, but the man shook his head, waving a hand in unison with his hat brim. "Nah, nah. Ain't interested in no paper."

Crump glanced at Nelda and slowly stuffed the bills back into his pocket. Nelda said, "We got other things."

"Like what?"

Crump said, "Hold on, now. We're a little ahead of ourselves. Let's see what you got 'fore we talk further."

The man turned and led the way into the stable, with Crump and Nelda close behind. No one paid any attention to the man with the slightly crooked left arm who stood twenty feet distant, near the corner of the building.

Crump began his appraisal of the two horses as he crutched steadily toward the stall. He stopped, leaned his shoulder against the top rail. With little more than a glance, he dismissed one of the animals. She was a little chestnut mare, clearly mutton-withered, and she would have a short, choppy stride that would make for a poor wagon ride. Beyond these faults, her pasterns appeared weak, as did her forearms. Crump turned his attention toward the larger mare. She was a dappled gray three hands taller than her stall mate, and the look of her back was steady with only the slightest bit of sway. Her quarters should have been stronger, and the gaskins hinted at weakness, but she would do for the ride and perhaps a good deal more on the farm. He liked the look of her ears, which stood at a forty-five degree angle with the axis of her head.

Crump cocked his head at the larger animal. "The gray, how old is she?"

"About nine, I 'spect, though I ain't had her long." He moved to the mare, grabbed a handful of mane, and brought her to Crump. "Look for yourself."

Crump pulled the horse's lips away from her incisors. "Here, girl, let's have us a look at them choppers, all right? Easy now, easy." He pried open her mouth, saw the markings which he judged had been burned into the center of the teeth in an effort to deceive the unwary. The center marks disappeared around the ninth year, and Crump had known more than one horse trader in his time who had attempted to move the clock backwards. But the center teeth were showing the telltale triangular shapes of age and told Crump the truth. He figured the animal at twelve years, maybe thirteen, but he was uncertain about calling the trader's hand; it might do more harm than good in the bargaining process. He glanced at Nelda, thought of the little pocket inside of her dress and the things it held, decided that they could not be traded with a half-hearted effort.

Crump shook his head as he patted the horse's muzzle. "I'm afraid somebody's tinkered with this horse's teeth. Them markin's looked burned in to me, and the center teeth are already startin' to triangle."

The man sniffed and passed a hand over his moustache. "Know horses, do ya?"

"Some."

The dark eyes clouded as he sniffed again, then said, "Mister, I don't take lightly to somebody callin' me—"

"Whoa now, whoa," Crump said. "I said 'somebody' tinkered with 'em, didn't say you did. It's a good job they did, coulda' fooled most anybody. I ain't blamin' you. No offense intended."

The man shifted his shoulders as if moving an unseen weight, swallowed, then said, "Well, whatever this here mare's age, it's a solid animal and I ain't keen to part with her lightly."

"I understand, but I was hopin' to get some good years outta her on the farm. Ain't just lookin' for a ride home."

"Well, you seen what I got. Now let's see what you'uns got."

"I ain't seen any wagon yet."

The man motioned to the opposite side of the stable. "I got three of 'em—all serviceable—and the tack you need to hook her up and be on your way."

Crump nodded. "Let me and the wife go over here and talk a minute or so."

They turned away from the man and his horses, made their way toward the doorway and the other man who they could not see—the man with the crooked arm, who now stood just beyond the opening, listening, and watching through an inch-wide crack in the wall.

Nelda slid her hand between two buttons of her dress and nimbly unfastened the little wire hooks she had sewn at the mouth of the hidden pocket. She withdrew her hand, fingers cupped over the ring. "He'll take the ring, Rector. I think he'll take the ring."

"Hope so." He held out his hand.

"No. Let me try. Maybe he'll be a little softer with a woman."

"I doubt it, but you can try." Nelda started to turn around, but Crump placed a hand on her arm. "Listen to me, now. Whatever you do, don't let on about the locket. Just let him think this is all we have."

She nodded, turned around, and walked at Crump's pace back to the horse trader. She looked into the hooded eyes, held them for a moment, then slowly opened the fingers of her right hand. The thick gold ring covered the center of her palm and she moved her hand so that the light from the doorway touched it. "It was passed down from my granddaddy to my daddy and now me. Nobody's sure where Granddad came up with it. Some say a far land, but nobody knows for sure. You'll never see another like it, sir."

A dirty finger and thumb smoothed the long moustache, and Crump saw the man draw a quick unwanted breath, but he steadied himself instantly. He leaned his head closer. "Lemme see."

Nelda allowed him to take the ring. He rolled it slowly in his fingertips, pretended to judge it with knowing eyes. He made a sideways motion with his head, casually pursed his lips. "Well, it's a big ring all right, but who's to say it's solid gold?"

Nelda took back the ring, clutched it to her bosom. "Sir, we are to say. We're Rector and Nelda Crump, and we live twelve miles south of town and lots of folks know us. We're not hard to locate, should you ever find us out to be liars."

He thought for several seconds, listened as the voices of reason and greed argued inside his head, and in the end, the voice of greed was the loudest. "Well, I'll tell you. It might do for the mare, but not for the wagon too. I 'spect you got other things to trade, don't you?"

Nelda stole a glance at Crump, was afraid of what she saw in his eyes, spoke quickly. "It's a fair offer, this ring. And what's more, you're dealing with a man who gave a lot to the Cause, and he just wants to go home now. We're not beggars—and I'm not beggin' now—I promise you. But I am askin' that you consider all this in your price."

"Lots of boys give a lot to the Cause, lady. I'm a businessman in a hard time that's about to get harder, and I got to get more'n that ring in this trade."

Nelda opened her mouth to speak, but the sight of the crutch darting up silenced her. Crump held it at arm's length, parallel with the ground, pointed it at the trader's chest. The old fire rose in his belly. It was the insanely glorious power that had sustained him in a dozen engagements when the rifle balls were angry hornets in his ears, when wet, red pieces of men flashed before his eyes. It was almost good to feel it again, but he suppressed it, knew that he could not make war with this weasel of a man over a horse and wagon.

Crump's voice was steady, a low rumble from his chest. "We're through here now, and I'd warn you not to work your tongue again till we're outta earshot, 'cause I wouldn't take your old mare and wagon now if you was to lower the price to a bucketful a piss." He paused, dared the man to speak, but the droopy moustache only twitched from side to side. "And if you was to work your tongue again, I'll show you what a big one-legged man can do to a little two-legged man."

The point of the crutch was two feet from the trader's face, and it hung there like a weapon for five long seconds before Crump lowered it to the ground. He positioned it in his armpit and swung his body away from the man. He said to Nelda, "Put the ring away."

Crump listened as he and Nelda made their way to the door, and he was certain that the trader did not move.

As she passed the edge of the doorway, Nelda nearly bumped into the man wearing the long dark coat and wide-brimmed hat. He touched the hat brim with two fingers and nodded deferentially as he spoke. "A word, if I might, folks."

The voice carried the familiar Alabama lilt, and it smoothed the sharp edge of surprise for Crump and Nelda, who jerked their heads in unison at the stranger. They halted in step, eyed him for a second, then Crump said, "A word about what?"

"Name's Vash Mimms, folks." He nodded again at Nelda and extended his right hand to Crump, who hesitated for a moment before returning the handshake.

"Crump. Rector Crump, and this here is my wife, Nelda."

Mimms said, "I was headed in here myself and stood back to wait my turn when . . . well, I don't want you to think strange of me—I ain't no eavesdropper—but I just couldn't help but hear some of what was goin' on in there."

He paused, raised his crooked left arm away from his body, then gestured toward the space where Crump's leg should have been. "I left a piece of this arm up at Antietam, and it ain't much good to me now, so I know a little about what you're dealin' with." He yanked his head back toward the livery stable. "And when I hear such as that"—he paused again, grimaced and shook his head—"makes me sick to my stomach, it does."

"We'll figure somethin' else out," Crump said.

The hint of a smile appeared on Mimms's face, the sincerity etched into his round features. "Well, folks, that very thing is why I stopped you." He looked at Nelda. "Ma'am, I believe I heard you say you was headed south a short piece. And, well, I'm homebound to the south myself. Up here seein' a sister, I been, and I'm headed home this very day." It was no longer a hint, the smile widening and pushing his full cheeks upward. "It'd be a fair honor to carry you home. The very least I could do for a soldier and his family."

Crump looked at Mimms closely, held his gaze, searched behind the soft brown pupils for signs of rot. Crump had recognized rot behind the eyes of men before, and sooner or later, they had proved him accurate. Mimms did not avert his gaze, held his smile with true affection, and in the man's eyes, Crump saw no rot.

"That's more'n kind of you, Mr. Mimms—" Crump began.

Mimms interrupted gently. "Just plain Vash will do, folks. I ain't hard to get to know."

Crump continued, "Well then, Vash, it is a kind offer, to be sure. I take it you got a wagon?"

"No, sir, I ain't. But I got a fine dun gelding that don't pay no more attention to two riders than one. He's gentle as a lamb, and besides, I'll be leadin' him afoot."

"Aw, no, that's too much to ask a man."

Nelda took her husband's arm, squeezed gently as she said, "Mr. Mimms—Vash, I would only feel right if I took my turn walking."

"How far is it, did you say?" Mimms said.

"About twelve miles," Nelda replied.

"Pshaw! I could trot that far in this cool weather. We'll be there by midafternoon." He noted the sergeant's stripes on Crump's uniform. "You just steady Sergeant Crump in the saddle, and let me do this thing for you. Please." He reached out, clamped a firm hand on Crump's forearm. "This'll be something to brag to my young'uns about one day."

# CHAPTER TWENTY-THREE

Crump rode in the saddle for a mile before he began to feel at ease. Nelda rode behind the saddle, her arms encircling Crump's waist. He sat nearly straight now, no longer feeling the need to tilt his torso to one side in an effort to counterbalance the absence of his leg. His wife's body felt small and warm and wonderful behind him, and Crump was thankful that he could shield her from the wind-driven mist that persisted. In a hotel lobby back in Huntsville, she had pulled the old farm trousers from her bag, and now wore them under her dress. For the first time since departing, Crump wondered idly if she still wore his good knife low on her leg, under the baggy trousers, or if she had stowed it in the bag. But it was an unnecessary thought, and it quickly passed into the wind. He concentrated on further solving the rhythm of the tall dun gelding.

Crump rested his left hand on the sturdy horn of the fine double-rigged Texan saddle. He had complimented Mimms on its quality, not to mention the beautiful mount, and the man had quietly and humbly replied that the acquisition of both was due mainly to a streak of wild luck, the like of which he never expected again. Crump reached forward and touched the thick black mane, combed it with his fingers and then patted the muscular withers. Yes, what a fine animal indeed, and with an owner who possessed the good sense to know what he had and care for it properly. There were few things in life that Crump appreciated more than the proper bond between a man and a horse.

He looked beyond the horse's alert ears and studied the man walking steadily with the reins in his right hand. He seemed oblivious to the irritating elements, his gait attuned to that of his horse, his boots flipping up little clods of damp soil that would soon be mud. The fire that had risen in Crump during the confrontation with the horse trader had completely died away, and he could no longer smell even a hint of its smoldering. The transition from the sorry horse trader to the fellow soldier intent on aiding them was nearly dizzying, and Crump had taken longer to adjust than had Nelda. When Crump had wondered aloud if such good fortune could actually be descending on them, Nelda had whispered of Providence and things meant to be. She had whispered that Crump had suffered and sacrificed enough, and that Vash Mimms appearing in their path was not accidental.

Crump shook his head now at the strange ways of life, marveled at the goodness in some men and the sorriness in others. It was a great mystification, and Crump did not wrestle with the fact that lowly men would never sort it out. He looked up, saw a ragged opening in the sodden gray sky, felt the wind freshen and rush past his face. He passed a hand over his mouth and beard, pressed the water down onto his coat, then smiled. The rain would soon pass and the wind would die down, and then perhaps he could converse with this good man who was leading him home.

They covered another mile before Crump realized that the irritation to his stump could become a problem if he did not rest it from time to time. He shifted his weight, rubbed his stump gingerly with his hand, then called down to Mimms, who had not missed a long stride since departing Huntsville.

"Vash, reckon we could rest a spell? This dadblamed stump is actin' up a little."

Mimms slowed and then halted, turned back and stroked the horse's jaw. "Yes, sir, you bet. I should've asked before now. I'm sorry."

Crump threw up a hand. "Not a'tall, no need for sorry. I'm the bother in this caravan."

Nelda and Mimms helped Crump down, then Mimms began to untie the crutches from the saddle. Crump said, "No, just leave 'em, Vash. I'd just enjoy to stand here and lean on this fine animal for a spell. Get my blood runnin' in a different direction." He nodded toward the shards of sunlight falling on thick woods in a low valley that was rimmed by a half mile of the road they had just traveled. "Gonna be more like travelin' weather from here on, I 'spect. How far you got to go past our place?"

Mimms pulled a red handkerchief from behind his shirt collar, wiped the moisture from his face. "Oh, quite a ways. Near twenty-five mile, I reckon."

Nelda said, "Besides your sister, are all your people down that way?"

He looked down the road for a moment, then said, "Not many left. One way or another, the war thinned us out a lot." He looked at Nelda, then quickly at Crump, and neither could discern whether the change in his countenance tended toward sadness or anger. "And what of us warn't took was changed."

Nelda looked away, embarrassed that she had asked the question that had taken him to the dark place. Crump began to fidget with the cinch ring of the saddle, moved his hand over the damp leather, said, "You got her oiled good and deep, Vash. Rain don't much matter to a saddle like this." He patted the horse's neck. "Nor to a horse like this'n. What do you call him?"

"Smoke."

The horse twitched its ears, swung its great head back toward the sound. "Yeah, I called your name, boy," Mimms said softly.

"Ahhh," Crump sighed approvingly. "That's perfect."

Nelda removed the top of the canteen, offered it to Mimms, who shook his head. She then offered it to Crump, who took it and gulped down two long swallows, handed it back. She pilfered a look at Mimms, who stood in profile, peering down into the sunlit valley. The round lines of his face, so youthful when he smiled, were longer now, his eyes harder. She silently scolded herself for asking the question, though it was certainly innocent enough. Chimborazo had taught her that some of these men who went off to war stayed in faraway places even when they were removed from the fray, and were not predictable. Perhaps Vash Mimms was such a man. Rector Crump was as wonderfully predictable as sunrise and sunset, set in his ways and words and mannerisms. She thought no less of her husband as he functioned in his ordered world, in fact, cherished him all the more. His world had a solid foundation, and they had built a life and a home on it, and would never grow weary of one another. These things she knew and cherished as one with her man.

She would leave Vash Mimms to himself for the remainder of the trip, would not dare probe into seemingly innocent places that might cause his eyes to harden again. She would thank him from her heart for the kindness passed on to them, and then say good-bye, and remember only his round smile and his soft eyes.

They stood in silence for another minute, Mimms remaining motionless, looking not at the valley but at the empty road behind them. Crump broke the silence. "Well, I'm ready to move on. Let's heave my carcass back on the saddle."

. . .

Vash Mimms moved forward in his mind, covered the two miles to the long straight stretch of the road where he would kill the man and woman and take the things in her secret dress pocket. He would be able to see ahead for a good half mile, and at the pace he was keeping, it was a near certainty that he could maintain the empty road behind them. These thoughts produced no guilt, no sorrow, no feelings of any weight. He saw himself as a survivor, a being that now roamed a senseless Earth in search of things that would sustain him, make the remainder of his stay more pleasurable. And if his roamings caused people to die from time to time, so be it. Everyone had to die of something.

Vash Mimms had never been a good man, even before the war and the Dunker church at Antietam, but never would he have considered cold-blooded murder for a ring and whatever other little thing was in the woman's pocket. But on that soft September day, only eighteen months past, whatever spark of decency remaining inside him perished alongside the thousands whose blood soaked the fields and woods. Mimms went there now, knew he would again find justification for his deadly roaming, even though justification had long since ceased to be a requirement for his actions. He went back now simply to pass some time on the road.

As Mimms stood behind a stout oak in the woods that hovered over the little building, he thought he was looking at a schoolhouse until the grizzled old man they called Larney croaked from behind a nearby tree. "It's a Dunker church, it is, boys. Them knot-headed Germans dunk their folks in the water just like ol' John the Baptister in the good book, hee hee haw! This here church is 'bout to see some infernal dunkin' in blood, it is, hee hee haw!"

There was no steeple atop the square, whitewashed building, and from his vantage point, Mimms saw the south end of the structure with the single door and two large windows. To Mimms the two smaller windows at attic height appeared as eyes, as if the Dunker God's eyes watched the woods, waiting to see what Mimms and his fellow Rebs would do when Joe Hooker's boys made their first charge. In truth, Mimms remembered only vaguely what the Dunker God's eyes saw after the first rifle balls whined into the trees. The Yanks came across the field like a mass of fast-moving blue ants, puffs of rifle smoke popping all up and down the line. And then, much sooner than Mimms had anticipated, the blue ants were men at the edge of the woods, and the world became a whirl of muzzle blasts and groans and screams and curses. And Vash Mimms was certain that he was spending his final moments on Earth.

Suddenly his shoulder was against the church building, God's square eyes looking down on him, and his left arm flew violently away from his body. The initial pain was in his shoulder socket, and he was surprised to look down and see torn cloth and flesh at his elbow. The nausea rose upward from the pit of his stomach, and he swallowed against it as he dropped his musket and slid his back down the white wall of the church. He placed his head on his knees, let the wounded arm dangle at his side. The wild noises seemed to encircle the church like a whirlwind and just when he thought he could stand the wind no more, it slowed to a low whoosh and then ceased, and all he could hear were the pleas and groans of the wounded. A hand pushed up his head and the stench of rotten teeth and wet tobacco filled his nostrils. Larney, the old man who had identified the Dunker church, looked at him with dark, beady eyes. Mimms felt a rough hand on his arm, heard the raspy voice.

"They'll likely whack the sumbitch off'n you, but you're homebound, boy. Come on 'fore Hell comes back to this here church. Hee hee haw!"

Mimms struggled to his feet and allowed the cackling man to tug him along into the tree line until they reached a deadfall tree. Mimms pulled his good arm from the clamp of the man and shook his head, sat down on the scaly bark. He craned his head and peered back through the mass of leafy branches until he spied the square eyes, still looking at him.

"Come on, boy," Larney said. "This here little fight ain't over by a damn sight. This ain't no place for the shot-up."

Mimms ignored the man, drew a long breath, realized that the nausea had subsided. He risked another look at his wound. The angry flesh had been plowed up as a red furrow and from its bottom he could see the white of a tendon peeking back at him. There was only a trickle of blood. Mimms tested the arm for function, found the motion suitable, and was pleased that the testing did not increase the pain. He knew then that it was a perfectly lovely wound, one that would, with some careful conniving, free him from this insanity. His head was clear now, and he believed that he saw all things with the clarity of God's square eyes—eyes that did not weep at the carnage in the fields and the woods, eyes that simply saw and did not care; eyes that were perhaps amused with the goings on of men.

The old man's stench was full in his face again, the beady eyes quizzical. "Nothin' hit you in the head, did it, boy? You're a little gone away."

Mimms turned his head, pushed up from the tree with his right arm. It was all so wonderfully clear now, this path he must follow. He said the words without looking at Larney. "Leave me be. I'll make it on my own." Then Vash Mimms began to walk steadily up a grassy hill, picking his way around the wounded, ignoring their pleas with a majesty equal to that of the Dunkers' square-eyed God.

Nelda saw the end of the long bend in the road, beckoning two hundred yards ahead, remembered that a lengthy straight stretch would follow, the stately pines lining the corridor like tall green-clad soldiers. Soon the wild azaleas would peek from the ground cover amid the tree trunks, their curled fingers of white and pink and red swaying in the soft breezes of spring. She looked to the southwest, flew as the crow flies over the fifteen miles that separated her and her man from the Tennessee River that ran wild and free toward the Cumberland Mountains. She thought of the late spring day four years before when they took the boys to see the great river, and listened again as Rector told them that he must go north and fight for a cause. Listened as he told them that the land was like a person, with a heart and soul and blood, and that the rivers were to the land as blood vessels were to the people. She listened and did not weep, looked ahead to the day now at hand with the river running close by and the mountains only a cloudbank away, and with her man warm in her arms. She laid her cheek high on his back, and they moved as one with the puissant flow of the horse as she saw more of the great pines pass before her eyes.

The first hint of evil came with the slowing of the horse, though in years to come, when the woman thought back to the horrific moment, Nelda Crump would not be able to say precisely from where the evil came. It might have been in the air, spewed from the fouled soul of Vash Mimms, or upward from the earth on which he trod, transferred through the hooves and sinews of the horse. Wherever it came from, Nelda would remember it as the most profound fragment of knowledge that her brain had ever absorbed. And she would regret to her dying day the fact that she could not snatch her husband's revolver, only inches from her right hand, and fire at Vash Mimms even before she looked past Rector's shoulder.

In one smooth motion, Mimms regripped the reins with his left hand, very near the horse's muzzle, and pulled from his coat pocket the revolver. He whirled around and raised the weapon as he took a long stride alongside the horse. From the center of Crump's body arose a short guttural sound, and when he reached for his own revolver his hand collided with Nelda's, her fingers already wrapped around its handle. The crack of Mimms's weapon was muffled, the man having placed the muzzle against Crump's left side as he pulled the trigger. The force of the blast lifted Crump from the saddle and threw him from the horse along with Nelda, whose hand still struggled with her husband's for control of the sidearm. Even before her body slammed into the ground, Nelda disentangled her right hand and plunged it into her dress pocket in search of the derringer. She heard the horse whinny and caught a glimpse of Mimms jerking on the reins as the animal reared.

In the seconds that followed, she glanced wildly about for a glimpse of Crump's big revolver, but it was nowhere in sight. Reflexively, she thumbed back the hammer of the derringer, prepared to fire the only shot that might stop Mimms. Then came the sound of quick footfalls on the soft ground as she looked up into his expressionless face, saw cold eyes of death, then the revolver muzzle as Mimms took careful aim. Her hand moved in a blur, and she heard the high-pitched bark of the derringer and saw blood splatter from his thumb, saw the weapon spin to the ground. Nelda sprang from her knees at the gun and clamped both hands over it as Mimms fell on her, his hands covering hers. His wrist was against her cheek and she twisted her head and sank her teeth into the white flesh until bone stopped her progress. Mimms screamed, jerked the wounded arm away but held fast with the left. The rage energized him and with his head, he butted Nelda high on the cheekbone. Strange patterns of whirling colors floated through her head as her grip on the revolver begin to weaken. Suddenly, she felt frantic fingers clawing upward, past her ankle, toward the knife.

She opened her eyes and blinked against the stinging tears, looked past Mimms's shoulder. The shadow fell over them both and she heard Crump's cry of fury. He held the knife handle in both hands, high over his head, and then fell full force on Mimms. The long blade took him through the back, piercing his left lung, and a long groan passed from him as did the hiss of air from his lung. Crump's hands fell away from the handle, his energy spent, and Nelda snatched Mimms's revolver from his trembling fingers and cocked the hammer. As if powered by a mechanical gear in his neck, his head slowly ratcheted toward her beneath her husband's weight and Nelda pushed the muzzle squarely between his eyes and pulled the trigger. The head snapped backward, then rebounded facedown into the loose earth, and after a final tremor rippled through the corpse, it was motionless.

For an unearthly moment the echo of the gunshot hung in the air, then a silence descended. So deep was the void that it produced a sound of its own as it hovered over the road, blanketing the living and the dead. It was only when the dun gelding complained with a loud snort that Nelda released her white-knuckled grip on the handgun and shook it from her fingers. She carefully rolled Crump from atop the corpse, listened to the faint wheezing sounds of his breathing. She saw blood trickling from two jagged, pea-sized holes below her husband's right eye. She looked closely, brushed over them with a thumb, and saw the dirty white fragments of Mimms's skull shallowly embedded, blown there by the lead ball.

Nelda found her voice, hoped that Crump would not hear the fear in it. "Rector, can you hear me?"

The thick black beard moved up and down and he opened his eyes. His voice was weak but steadfast. "Look at it . . . tell me."

Nelda opened his coat, pulled away the blood-soaked shirt and underclothing. The entry wound was at the bottom of his ribcage, two fingers in width, with black burn streaks extending in starlike fashion. When she saw the exit wound, near his navel, a spark of hope flickered wildly. The ball had not traversed the core of his torso.

"It doesn't look so bad, Rector. It went in low in your ribs and came out by your belly button. There's not a lot of blood now."

He heard the hope in her voice, regretted it. "I managed to turn a little 'fore the bastard pulled the trigger, but . . . my breathin' ain't good. Must've nicked the lung."

She did not reply, reached quickly to the knife jutting up from the corpse, wrenched it four times from side to side before pulling it free. She swiped the blade across Mimms's coat then cut two wide squares and one long strip from her dress. The squares folded, she pressed them over the wounds. "Hold these while I tie 'em up." Her hands moved expertly over his body. "The horse isn't spooked bad, Rector. I think I can calm him down, and then we're gonna get back to town and find you a—"

"No!" He waited for his breath to return. "I'm either gonna bleed out inside or I ain't. There's no ball in me. Doctor don't matter none."

"But, Rector . . ."

He clamped a hand on her arm, locked on her eyes. "Listen to me, woman. I want to see the boys." He swallowed, passed the tip of his tongue over his lips. "I think I can get up now. Catch the horse. Easy, though. Don't run up at him. Talk low to him." He drew another careful breath. "Then get us up on him . . . tie me on if'n you have to. Ride straight to your sister's place."

Nelda stood on weak legs, steadied herself for a moment, glanced at Mimms's body.

Crump said, "He was a fooler, that one, warn't he?"

The woman did not reply, moved slowly away toward the horse.

# CHAPTER TWENTY-FOUR

The big horse trotted easily along the road, his hooves drumming an even beat in the shadow world of Crump's mind. Nelda's arms encircled his shoulders, her hands holding the reins in front of his slumped body, his hands clasping the saddle horn with a waning strength. He made no sound. The strip of leather Nelda had cut for his mouth was wet and mangled, and had served its purpose; the pain was fading. Everything was fading. He opened his mouth and let the strip fall away. It was a good thing and a bad thing, this fading of the pain, Crump thought. The relief was sweet and coursed through his veins, though he knew it was a false friend. Only when the pain was great did he have a chance to see the boys. The ride had jostled his wounds and he knew that he bled both from the inside and the outside. He could feel blood in the bottom of his boot, and for a blissful moment he retreated from the scene, allowed himself to be the age of his boys and walk barefoot through a summer mud puddle, feel the cool wetness on the soles of his feet. But he quickly traded the old muddy water for the blood of the present; there was a decision to be made, and very soon.

He held out for another quarter mile, then reached back with his right hand and grabbed a handful of Nelda's dress. He felt her rein in the horse, waited for the drumbeat of hooves to cease. He shook his head. "Get down, come close."

She slid off of the horse, picked up the loose reins and held them tightly with one hand as she slipped the other between Crump's hands. His head rested on the horse's mane and Nelda laid her head beside his, closed her eyes, knew what he would say.

"It ain't gonna work out," he whispered.

"Oh, Rector, we're so close. No more than two miles."

"Don't matter . . . it's too near done." He focused on her face, watched as her jaws clenched tightly, saw the tears seep from her closed eyes. "No time for that now, my woman Nelda. Listen. Tell the boys they's Crumps, and never to lose their honor. It's all I'm fixin' to take with me now. And tell 'em I'll see 'em in the sweet bye and bye."

She nodded. "I will."

"One prideful thing, I know, but you take me home and fix me 'fore the boys see me . . . 'thout my leg and all. Don't want 'em 'memberin' just half of me."

"I'll see to it."

He fought for breath, waited for the last of his strength to accumulate. He tried to smile, did not know if his lips obeyed his will. "I've wondered some. Would it've mattered to you, my gone leg . . . when we laid together?"

"Oh, Rector. My Rector, no. I would have loved you as I loved you before, in every way."

He nodded. "Figured that. But it's good to hear it."

Nelda listened for the sound of his breathing, clung to it with the same tenacity with which she would hold onto his hands over the edge of a high cliff and tug for his life. But it was a battle that could not be won, and she would soon have to loosen her grip and let him go.

"I'm gonna try . . . to hear Pollard . . . and Letha a'singin' to me."

The breeze kicked up, whispered through the high boughs of the pines. With a long rattling sigh, he died. She pressed her cheek against his, stroked the back of his head, and wept softly.

She pulled back on the reins, guided the horse off of the narrow path and into the deep shadows cast by the pines. Her sister's house and barn loomed a hundred yards down the path, curls of smoke rising from the stone chimney. Nelda looked back at her husband's body, tied securely with his own killer's rope. The minutes oozed by, became a half hour, and the horse grew restless. The woman dismounted, held the reins taut and stroked his muzzle, whispered low to him, trusted him. She let the reins fall and the animal began to graze on the sparse grass.

Nelda suppressed a great sob when the front door swung open and her sister walked out onto the porch. She carried a pan, and when she reached the edge of the porch she tipped it to the side, drained the contents. Nelda attempted to peer inside the doorway, sought movement, wondered if her sons were inside. It was doubtful in midafternoon; they were more likely near the barn or out in the field with John. Her sister sat the pan down beside her on the top step and began to watch a yellow kitten pounce on imaginary prey beside the porch. She was a tall woman, taking the height from their father's side of the family, and her face was longer than Nelda's, though the resemblance easily identified them as sisters.

Nelda retrieved the reins, began to walk carefully in the shadows, ever watchful for a glimpse of her boys. When she had halved the distance, Nelda lashed the reins to a tree trunk, then continued for several paces before stepping out into the open. She placed a forefinger vertically over her lips, waited for the other woman to notice her. The kitten tired of its game, padded away from the porch, and it was then that Cleo Barnes looked up with a start, sprang to her feet. Before she could call out, Nelda shook her head, tapped her forefinger against her lips, then with her other hand motioned for her sister to come quickly.

When Cleo drew near she held out her arms, saw the anguish in Nelda's eyes, the angry welt high on her cheek. They embraced warmly, their arms encircling one another, then Cleo gently pushed Nelda to arm's length. "Little sister! My God, what has happened?"

"We were so close, Sis. So close . . ." Nelda lowered her head, squeezed the tears from her eyes with a long blink.

"What do you mean? Where's Rector?"

Nelda held onto her sister's arm as she led her back toward the horse. As Cleo stepped around the trunks of two great pines, she caught her breath and her free hand flew up to cover her mouth. She spoke through her fingers, her voice incredulous. "Oh no. Dear Lord Jesus . . . no."

The horse grumbled, shifted his front hooves, and Nelda placed her hand on his neck, ran it over the thick hide. "A couple of miles back," said Nelda.

"Who—who did this?"

"He said his name was Mimms, and it's probably the truth, since he meant to do us both in." She paused, clenched her jaw. "He's dead. This was his horse. The varmints can have him now."

Cleo stepped forward to Crump's body, roped to the saddle. She placed her hand lovingly on the long black hair, cupped her palm over the bristly cheek. "Oh, Rector, Rector. We all figured you'd make it back somehow."

"He did, from the war. Only to be took by one of his own."

Cleo shook her head, said, "I can't understand what, how . . ."

"In time, Sis. In time, I'll tell it all. But not now."

She nodded. "I'm sorry, Nelda, I didn't—"

"Shhh. It's all right. Just hold me again for a minute." Nelda laid her head on her sister's shoulder, sucked in a jagged breath. "Where are the boys?"

"With John, out back, choppin' wood."

"That's good. Rector . . . we had a few minutes there at the end, and he wants to be fixed proper before the boys see him. I want you to go call John away from the boys, tell him what happened and that you're goin' to our place with me to wash and fix him."

Cleo looked at her sister, asked the question with her eyes.

"Oh, Sis, it's awful to put this on you, but I don't know any other way. If I go to them now, I won't be able to keep Andrew away from him, and Ethan, oh . . ."

"Hush now, shhh. We'll break it to them, and we'll do it right. Trust me."

"I do. I do so trust you, Sis, that's the only way I could ask this of you." She paused, breathed deeply, stopped the slow gyration of her brain. "Then you can ride back and let John come help me with the coffin. I want it just right. And then he can go back and get you and the boys. And then we'll sit a spell and remember him."

Nelda and her sons were alone with the body now. John had fashioned a fine coffin with a lid divided in two sections. The lower section was already nailed in place. He had departed to make arrangements with the preacher for the burial the next morning. Cleo was in the kitchen, fussing about in an effort to prepare some food she had brought with her. The boys were dressed in the clothes they would wear to the burial—clean white shirts with good collars, adorned with black ties in neat bows. Their trousers were of good homespun brown cloth, the cuffs falling loosely on brogans wiped clean. In ten days, Andrew Crump would mark his thirteenth birthday; his younger brother, Ethan, was three months past his tenth. Nelda stood between them, an arm around each set of shoulders. Andrew had the swarthy look of his father, his black hair clean and combed, and he stood within an inch of his mother's height. He had said little during the family wake, biting his lip from time to time at the mention of his father's name, but he had shed no tears. Ethan, with his mother's round, expressive face, had wept unashamedly several times, and his face was streaked with the paths of tears. His head rested against Nelda's side, the ordeal having exacted a heavy toll.

Nelda was satisfied with Rector Crump's portrait in death. She and Cleo had, on several occasions, either been present or actually assisted in the preparation of bodies. They first watched in teenage awe as their grandmother, alongside their own mother, worked with long lean fingers and bony forearms on the body of a relative. When she was finished, she stepped back from her work, nodded first to herself, then to her granddaughters, and spoke the words that had drifted back to Nelda as she washed her dead husband's face. *There's a certain pinchedness of the face that can't be took away, children. This is all's can be done in the matter.* And so it was in this matter. They had done what they could; Rector Crump would return to dust from the imperfect handiwork of loving fingers. Nelda pushed the thought of decay from her mind, believed that the grand spirit of her husband was in a far land, a place of wondrous mystery.

She moved her hands over the shoulders of her sons, drew them closer, said, "Remember now, the both of you, what you see here is the body that carried your pa through this life, and it's a proper thing to do him honor here like this, but the long life's yet to come." She paused, looked in turn at both of them, then back to the coffin. "You boys are gonna hang onto that with me, aren't you? I can depend on you, can't I?"

They both nodded silently. Ethan rubbed his head into her side, sobbed quietly. Nelda said, "You're worn down, aren't you, little man?"

"Yes'm."

"Well, it's about time to get you tucked in. Go let Aunt Cleo get you started, all right? Lay your clothes out nice. I'll be in directly to tuck you in." She kissed the top of his head then released him. She slipped her arm down from Andrew's shoulder to his waist, said, "Let's me and you take in some night air, all right?"

The breeze on the porch was cool and fresh on their faces, a welcome change from the close air of the house. Andrew wrapped his fingers around the porch rail and tilted his head toward the sky. Nelda raised her head, studied the heavens with her son. Aloft, swift clouds raced with the winds, and the starlight cast down was intermittent, unpredictable. They stood silently for a minute before she heard him sniffle, and then again. He raised his arm to wipe his nose on his shirtsleeve, but his mother gently intercepted it, placed a handkerchief in his hand.

"I want to know what happened back there on the road, Ma. I want to know."

Nelda slipped an arm around his waist, sucked at the clean air. "All right, Andrew." She paused, prepared herself for the replaying of the bloody scenes. "A man, a very bad man, fooled me and your pa into believing he was tryin' to help us. He offered a ride on that fine gelding you saw. But he meant to rob us. I'm sure he heard us talking with a horse trader, maybe even saw that I had some things to trade—he just popped from the doorway as we were leavin'. He was a nice-soundin' man, an Alabama man. We believed him."

She shifted her weight toward her son, would need the sturdiness of his body now. "Then, a few miles back up the road, he just pulled a pistol and turned and shot your pa before we could do anything. Knocked us off the horse. I was carryin' the derringer and managed to get off a quick shot as he came to me, and I think the ball must've hit him in the gun hand, 'cause the pistol spun away. We fought for it. I had both hands on it, but he was too strong. And just when I knew he was gonna take it away from me, I felt your pa pull the knife I had on my leg, and he stood up, how, I don't know . . . and fell on the man's back. Drove it in the middle of him, and then I shot him."

Six hours—a quarter of a day—was all that separated Nelda from the scene that already seemed to her oddly and yet profoundly a part of her past. A man saved his wife from certain death, died with honor, became one with the wind in the sky and the white starlight, became a part of the family history that would be retold for generations to come. A twinge of guilt jabbed at her, but only for a moment, and it was quickly replaced with the fullness of pride deep in her chest. Even with his body not yet cold in the ground, with no proper marker over it, Nelda Crump had begun the honored task of telling and storing and safekeeping, and in the doing of it took strength that she would infuse in her sons.

Andrew clamped the handkerchief over his nose, then wadded the cloth into his fist. "If'n the Yankees had been the ones done it . . . it'd be easier to take."

"Yes, Son, it would. But it wasn't, and the last thing your pa would want you to do is to waste time hatin' a dead man. The man was evil, and he paid in the end. We'll let it rest there. Have to."

"And Pa . . ." said Andrew, the bitterness coating his words, "he's just as dead as the bad man, and he was a good man."

"Andrew, your pa is honored dead, the other man is shameful dead. That's how we can live with it."

They accepted the silence again for a time. Then Nelda said, "Your pa said to tell you that he'd see you again in the sweet bye and bye."

"I remember. He would never say 'Heaven,' always that."

"It was just one of his ways, Andrew. He had his ways."

Another minute passed and then the boy turned his head, looked directly into his mother's eyes. "I've heard Aunt Cleo and Uncle John talkin'. They say times are gonna get harder yet. Are you scared now, without Pa?"

She took both of his hands in hers, felt their square strength, said, "No, Son, I'm not gonna live scared." She held only his right hand, touched a finger to one of the veins behind the knuckles. "There's

Crump and Sanders blood in there, Son, and those bloodlines don't carry fear, no matter what." She pulled his head to her shoulder, whispered the question into his ear. "Are you gonna be scared, Andrew Crump?"

She felt his head move from side to side. "I'm tryin' not to be, Ma."

# CHAPTER TWENTY-FIVE

The letter arrived at Chimborazo just after noon on the first Wednesday in March. Letha cradled the envelope in her hands, and with a faint smile, stared at the sturdy penmanship of Nelda Crump.

Miss Letha Bartlett and Mr. Granville Pollard

The lettering was neat, with a touch of femininity in the loops, but for the most part it was the hand of a farm woman who did not write often, and then only for a good reason. Letha had not expected to hear from the Crumps so soon. She made a rough calculation of their journey home as well as the laborious pace of the mail routes; there was no doubt, the letter had been written only a few days after their arrival in Alabama. The tinny clank of the dinner trays being washed in the kitchen now sounded like tiny alarm bells in her brain as the smile faded from her lips. She walked quickly to her quarters and laid the envelope on her dresser, took two steps toward the door, and then turned back and picked it up. A plaintive voice—youthful and familiar—carried to her from the ward, called her by name, and she was thankful for the plea. She whirled away from the dresser and made her way toward the voice.

Only Pollard's lamp remained aflame in the ward, its low light casting his shadow across the sleeping man in the adjacent bed. The yellow light barely reached into the central aisle, and it came as a surprise when Letha broke the radius of light; Pollard had not heard a sound. He quickly arranged the papers on his lap and set them aside, looked up at her face then down to the white envelope pinched in her fingers. He motioned toward the edge of his bed, and she sat down.

Letha ran her fingertips across the lettering. "We have news from the Crumps of Alabama." She attempted a smile, but could not hold it.

"So soon?"

With the question, the gnawing in the center of her body began afresh. She thrust the envelope toward him. "It is addressed to the both of us. I would prefer that you read it first."

Pollard took the envelope, cocked his head for a moment in silent query, and registered his first twinge of apprehension.

Letha stiffened, clenched her jaw, then pushed up from the bed. "I will be on the porch."

Pollard watched her leave the circle of light, then reached for a pocketknife on the nightstand and slit open the envelope. There were two small sheets of unlined paper, slightly frayed along the edges, and Pollard knew that the words he was about to read were drawn from the writer's soul. He scanned the first page, did not allow himself to see words, only the strong, looping hand of a woman. Then he began to read.

Dear Letha and Granville,

I have very sad news about Rector and know no other way to say it but strait out. We were turned on by a highwayman who tricked us into thinking he was helping us home. He shot Rector through the middle but he lived long enough to save me. I do not know how he did it but Rector got hold of my knife and fell on him as we fought over the pistol. Then I shot the bastrd in the head. We were only a few miles from home and Rector tried so hard to hang on till he could see the boys but could not make it. We had some time for a few words and I am thankful for that at lest. He was not bitter at the end. He had things to say to me and for the boys and did it very well. I have always been proud of him and surely was ther at the end. Did we ever tell you that we have knowed each other since we were little ones? It is strange that he made it thru the war and canon balls and knifes and saws only to be killed by one of his own. But strange are the ways of the world. Is it not so? The boys are doing alright. I will be strong for them and in time they will be for me. Later on when the hurt is not so sharp I will write more. But just now I feel it getting worse and will stop. But not before telling you of his last words. He said he was fixng to hear you two sing to him and somehow I think he did.

From your friend Nelda Crump

Pollard had not taken a breath since beginning the letter, and he gulped for air as he sagged back against the straw-filled pillow. He turned his head to the side and stared at the dark, quilt-covered mass that now occupied Crump's former bed. The beginnings of rage stirred within him. Crump dead. He could not imagine such a thing. Weakened, sawed in half, the soldier in him relieved of duty—these great changes in Crump's life, Pollard could accept. But dead, fallen and cold, and now low in the grave? The tobacco-edged smile gone forever? The gravelly voice that came up from the wide chest, stilled forever? Gone. Gone with Nathan Fisher, into the black sky above Chimborazo. Swallowed up like all of the others who left in smoke and fire from the Wilderness and Cold Harbor and Spotsylvania and Petersburg and—

*Stop! Let them all go. They are not yours to hold onto. Not Nathan nor Crump nor the nameless burned man whose hand you held in the Wilderness. Let them all go.*

Pollard's chin slumped to his chest, and he began the process of gathering himself for what was now a dreaded rendezvous with Letha. At least she had a premonition, or so it had seemed; perhaps the blow would glance obliquely off of her spirit. A spirit that had recently shown signs of healing, albeit modest progress. Pollard swung his legs over the side of the bed, set the prosthesis and the crutches. He worked his way to the peg on the wall and grabbed a coat, tossed it over his shoulders.

She waited at the edge of the porch, facing away from the building, a shawl pulled over her shoulders, her hands clamped together over her bosom. Pollard swung the crutches softly over the boards, stopped when his upper arm touched hers. He sucked in the cool night air through his mouth, knew that every moment of silence would speak louder than words, and that enough silence would render the pronouncement unnecessary. But she would not allow the silence to lengthen.

"And in the silence, there is grim news."

Pollard closed his eyes for a moment, matched the blackness inside his eyelids with that of the sky. "Yes, Letha. Your fears have proven true."

"He is dead?"

"Yes, tragically."

"How could it be otherwise, Granville? Sergeant Crump was not an old man." She turned to face Pollard, clutched his shirt with both hands. Her voice was heavy with weariness. "Will anyone live through this evil thing? To be old, to look *back* on it instead of *at* it?"

"It cannot kill us all, Letha, unless we allow it to."

"I am sick to the core of my being of death. It has made me old in spirit." She released his shirt, spat out a cruel laugh. "Yes. I will be allowed to become old. I am so already."

She stepped to the edge of the porch, sat down, gathered her dress about her legs, and rested her chin on her knees. Pollard sat down beside her, placed both crutches on the wood planks.

"How?"

"A highwayman. He managed to deceive them into believing he was helping them home. He shot Crump without warning, and there was a struggle. She provided few details, but somehow Crump pulled a knife and got it in him as she and the man fought over his gun. She shot him dead."

Letha raised her head, peered off into the impenetrable sky. "Even reduced to a shadow of himself, he was more man than most will ever be."

"Yes, he was."

"Their sons, did she write of them?"

"Yes, they are bearing up well. They are his sons—Nelda's sons. I would expect no less."

"Strange, so strange. For what seems an eternity, I've tended the soon dead, prepared more bodies than I can count. At times actually accepted death as routine. I carried part of this man's body from the surgery table to the waste pit. Watched him fairly cling to life. And yet . . ."

"And yet," said Pollard, "you can scarcely imagine him dead, can you?"

Letha turned her head to Pollard, sought the faint white spots that were his eyes. "No. No I cannot."

"Nor I. I believed him to be a survivor."

The night wind freshened, rushed past, touching them with cool, clean fingers. They lowered their heads, accepted the chill, the silence.

Pollard took the letter from his coat pocket, offered it to Letha. "You must read it yourself."

She made no move to accept it. "I have no wish to read it."

"You should, Letha. He spoke of us at the end. We were of comfort to him, according to Nelda."

She glanced at him, then away. "You tell me what he said, Granville. It would pain me to read the letter."

He slid the letter back into his pocket. "Very well. He said that he was going to hear us sing to him."

She looked back up at the sky. "I hope that he did."

"And I."

The wind shifted, blew directly into their faces, and for Letha it was a wind of confusion—equal parts doubt, fear, weariness, and, somehow, even now, hopefulness. Without the hopefulness, there would be no confusion about life after Chimborazo. She would urge Granville to return to the North, make a life with his music in what would certainly be a land of opportunity. She would simply go her own way, make herself useful to someone somehow. It did not matter how. But the flicker of hope was in her brain, could not be extinguished, and in the diminutive flame lived the delicate memory of a love for Granville Pollard that existed such a short time ago—a love so vibrant that it had forced her to risk the humiliation of rejection. She pressed her fingertips to her temples, wished that Pollard was a thousand miles away, wished that he would hold her in his arms. *Is it love or the memory of love? Are the two the same, Letha?*

A groan arose from inside of one the nearby wards, the note of pain plaintive and clear as the peal of a bell. She remembered Pollard's declaration, thought, *No, Granville, it will not kill us all, but it will make us suffer, and if we suffer enough, would death not be a bargain?*

Letha turned toward him. "Our time here grows very short, Granville."

"Yes, Letha. I suspect that within a few months—"

"No. Weeks at most, more likely days."

Pollard was stunned by the tone of finality in her voice. "How can you be so sure? The tides of battle sometimes move strangely."

"The tide of battle is now a blue tidal wave. I was told in confidence by Dr. McCaw that plans are laid for the evacuation of Richmond."

"I can scarcely believe . . ." Pollard shook his head. "When?"

"He thinks by the end of the month, or perhaps early April."

Pollard clenched his teeth. He was thankful for the veil of darkness that hid his face. He replayed the sound of her voice, searched it for the slightest hint of emotion, found none. His fingertips wandered aimlessly over the cold rough wood of the porch floor, instruments suddenly rendered as helpless as the brain that could not locate words of assurance for the woman he cherished.

The rustle of cloth filled his ears and before he could look sideways, Letha was on her feet and walking toward the door. Pollard groped for his crutches, struggled to position the prosthesis so that he could stand. Letha faced the door and did not turn around until he began to move toward her.

"This general, this Grant, sheds the blood of his men in wanton fashion, from what I hear." She paused, tilted her head as if to listen to the night wind. "When he comes, will he come to spill your blood as well?"

*No!* The word resounded inside Pollard's head, but when he opened his mouth to release it there was only silence, and seconds passed before he said it softly. "No. No, Letha, I do not believe him to be an evil man. He is a driven man, as is Lincoln, as is Davis. All of them, both sides, driven men."

She lowered her head. "As are we all."

# CHAPTER TWENTY-SIX

*Sunday, April 2, 1865*

Letha sensed the man's presence even before she looked up from the hot pan of cornbread that she had just placed atop the stove. Dr. James McCaw fixed dark, steady eyes on her and nodded slightly. With the cupped fingers of his right hand he motioned for her to follow, and then walked quickly to the corner of the kitchen.

He turned to face Letha, who walked to within a stride of his position, then said, "Yes, sir, is something amiss?"

McCaw nodded slowly, made no attempt to conceal the dolor that cloaked him. "Grant has broken through. The evacuation of the city has already begun."

The fear came as a single icy claw, traced a jagged line along the pit of her stomach. "Dear God. So soon? Broken through now?"

"It was inevitable; only the sheer will of President Davis delayed it this long."

"What are we to do? I don't know just what . . ."

"My dear woman, you have already done what you can."

"But the men, the wounded. What will become of them?"

"Once we inform everyone, I imagine that the scene will remind us of the miracles of the New Testament. The halt, the lame, the blind. Anyone who can crawl will rise up and flee."

"And those who are unable to crawl?"

McCaw shook his head, closed his eyes for a moment. "Soon Union surgeons of high rank will come here and seek me out, and they will dictate everything. I should think that they will require much, if not all, of Chimborazo's wards for their own wounded. Ours will be moved, perhaps to Camp Jackson, or some location even more meager. I suppose it is possible that . . ."

McCaw allowed his voice to fade, seeing that the woman before him, looking directly at him—*no, through him*—no longer heard anything. McCaw reached out and touched her forearm. "Mrs. Bartlett? Are you all right?"

Even before her eyes began to regain their focus, the peculiar smile touched her lips, as if a scene was unfolding in her brain that elicited confusing emotions. McCaw cringed inwardly at the sight of it. It appeared to convey nothing, and everything. Letha blinked twice, and McCaw saw that she had framed him in her vision. "Are you all right, madam?"

The smile vanished, her eyes narrowed. The soliloquy was delivered calmly and precisely. "I should not have been so finicky about the cooking of the rat on my stove. Nathan might have partaken with Mr. Patterson, might have ingested the creature's resistance to death. There is no resistance to death in the slaughter hog or the corn it consumes."

She spun away from McCaw, walked stiffly back to the stove. McCaw glanced into the ward room, saw some of the men looking quizzically in his direction. He walked toward them, the pronouncement he was about to make resting on a handy shelf in his mind, but he thought only of Letha Bartlett, hoped that he had not glimpsed the shadow of madness.

McCaw made his way past the eyes staring from the beds until he was halfway down the long aisle, and then he sidestepped between two beds and turned around, faced the men, his back to the wall. He stood ramrod straight, waited until the low murmur of anticipation subsided into absolute silence. With his right thumb and forefinger, he smoothed the black and gray moustache.

"Gentlemen, as some of you know, I am James McCaw, chief surgeon of Chimborazo. I have grave, but not unexpected, news. My assistant surgeons are delivering this message even now in the other wards. Earlier today, Grant's forces broke through the defenses of our city, and we are now in a state of evacuation."

The sound of quiet desperation spread at once among the men, racing in both directions like a wind-driven grass fire. McCaw raised his hand to restore order, but before he could speak again, the long arm of the man nearest him jutted from under the red and green quilt that covered him, his hand clenched into a shaking fist. His fingers opened, claw-like, clutched the edge of the quilt, and threw it from his body. His voice was filled with pain and rage.

"I'll be dammed by Gawd a'mighty 'fore I run like a coward." He swung his legs over the side of the bed and jumped to his feet, only to be instantly seized by a racking cough that rattled from the bottom of his lungs. He choked back the wet sounds, unable to speak another word, then flailed his arms violently as McCaw stepped forward and wrapped both of his arms around the man. McCaw held him closely, smelled the sweat of agony that permeated the thin rags covering his shoulders, the foul odor that wafted from diseased lung tissue, but the surgeon was not repelled. He held the man until the struggle ceased, the coughs soon giving way to great sobs. Tenderly, McCaw lowered the man back into his bed, pulled the quilt up under his chin. From his coat pocket he took a clean white handkerchief and gently mopped the man's feverish brow as he spoke so only the soldier could hear him.

"It is my great honor to tend you, sir. Rest easy now; your duty is complete."

McCaw stepped back to his original position, waited again for the sound of silence. "The time for valor is past. It is time to go home. I am arranging with all dispatch as much transportation to the train station as I am able to muster. There will be great confusion, great turmoil, but I do not believe that the occupying forces will seek to do any of us harm." He swept his arm toward the city below. "They will have the object of their desire, the capital of the Confederacy."

He paused, looked for a moment at the ceiling, then back down at the men. "I pray Godspeed for those of you who choose to leave now. For those of you who are not well enough to travel, I pledge to do everything within my power to secure for you the best treatment possible. I am of the firm belief that I will be able to communicate on your behalf with other men of medicine—no matter the color of their uniforms."

He drew in a deep breath, expelled it slowly. A delicate splotch of yellow intruded into his peripheral vision; he turned his head slightly and located Letha half hidden behind the doorway. "You men, we surgeons,"—he lifted his hand toward Letha—"your dedicated matron . . . all of us. We have done what we can. And now it is finished."

Some of the men were coiled like taut springs, ready to clutch a few belongings and flee, but they waited, their respect for McCaw a thing greater than fear. They waited until the steady clump of his footfalls was no longer in their ears.

Pollard sat calmly on the edge of his bed, ignored the urgent din that grew within seconds and enveloped him. Men ripped quilts and blankets into the spaces between beds, and those able jumped to their feet, groped for crutches and articles of clothing. For the more seriously sick and wounded the process was tedious, labored, and soon some of them flopped back onto their beds, exhausted, slack-jawed, and resigned to fates unknown. It was over within five minutes. Pollard surveyed the ward, counted nine occupied beds in addition to his own.

He pulled his crutches from under the bed and made his way to the kitchen. Letha stood alone at the long stove, absently fingering the brown top of a pan of cornbread. One of the Negro kitchen assistants had vanished, leaving two large skillets of bacon angrily hissing and popping on the stove. Bess had stayed, though, and now she noticed the skillets and muttered to herself as she pushed them to the back of the stove. Pollard glanced at Letha's face, suddenly aware that she had ignored the skillets.

"Letha, come sit with me, please."

He led her to the kitchen table, pulled out a chair for her, and then one for himself. She folded her hands neatly on the table, looked straight ahead down the near-empty ward. Pollard touched her hands. "Letha, I am staying with you. I will help with the men who could not leave."

She continued to stare into the ward. "How many remain?"

"There are nine."

"Three are near the end. This will hasten their demise. Within days, there will be only six. Dr. McCaw and most of his assistant surgeons will remain, Granville, and Bess wishes to stay for now. So there is no need for you to remain." She looked at him now, a wan smile curving her lips. "At least not on that account."

Pollard covered her hands with both of his, squeezed gently. "It is not only on that account that I choose to remain. You know that, don't you, Letha?"

She nodded. "Yes."

"You offered your love once—not so long ago—and I was a fool not to accept it. I can only beg you give me a second chance, though I am undeserving."

Slowly, she lowered her head to his hands and closed her eyes, and to Pollard, she appeared as a weary child, succumbing to nightfall. "I am not the same woman, Granville. Chambers have formed in my mind that did not exist then, chambers that I am afraid to enter, and their doors stand open."

"It is the accumulation of four years of sacrifice that no one could make without feeling strange just now. It is temporary; we will close the doors together."

"And with what shall we put our lives back together, Granville? Silver or gold have I none, nor you. Where shall we go? My home is no doubt in ruins; yours forbidden in a foreign land. We are the conquered, the vanquished."

"I do not know exactly how we will make it work out—just that we will, if you cast your lot with me."

She raised her head. "I can give you no answer just now, Granville. I only know that there are nine men in the ward who need to be fed and cared for. Just now, that is all I am able to deal with." She pushed away from the table and stood. "At least, there will be ample food for the meal today."

The conflagration that would consume Richmond began just before midnight. Letha rested on an empty bed nearest a dying man, her eyes half closed, waiting for the end of his piteous struggle. Pollard sat on the floor, a pan of water beside him. He dipped a cloth into the tepid water, rung it out, then dabbed it over the brow and cheeks of the man. At first, Pollard believed the new discordant sounds to be a part of the death rattle rising from the man's chest, but they were soon distinguishable, distant, and he recognized them as the mournful mutter of battle.

He peered over the top of the man, asked Letha, "Do you hear that to the east?"

"Yes. The sound of cannon."

"Not from the east, near the water. There can be no fight there."

The explosions grew louder, more frequent, and mingled with the excited voices of men running alongside the building. Pollard reached for his prosthesis and crutch, but before he could gain his feet, heavy footfalls thumped over the kitchen floor and the form of a man filled the dimly lit doorway to the ward.

"They've fired the *Patrick Henry* down to the wharf at Rocketts! The magazine's a-goin' off, by Gawd!" The man laughed crazily, held both hands over his head. With a final roar of laughter, he departed as quickly as he had arrived.

Letha sat bolt upright on the edge of the bed as Pollard came to her side, sat down beside her. "It is to be expected, Letha. The final ugly sounds. They will pass in the night."

She nodded silently, lay back down on her side, hands folded under her cheek, and continued the deathwatch.

A half hour crept by, then suddenly the airborne clamor took on a new and more ominous tone. The hiss of artillery shells was clearly discernible to Pollard, and he knew at once that the munitions armory was ablaze. The great shells now arched lazily and randomly through the sky above the city. He maneuvered his way to the partly opened window on the east wall, peered outside. Other buildings blocked most of his view, but above the rooftops a yellow luminescence was rising, and every few moments the white trail of a shell marked the sky. He heard the faint rustle of clothing behind him, turned to see Letha walking up the aisle toward the door.

He caught up with her beyond the easternmost line of buildings, at a point only fifty yards from the edge of the long slope that stretched downward to the city. Seemingly oblivious to the damp ground, Letha sat with her legs curled tightly, one hand firmly planted for support, the other covering her ankles. She appeared as a woman who lounged on a picnic blanket covering the warm verdant grass of June, perhaps watching the flow of water as it gurgled over rocks in a small rill. She did not have the look of a woman who was witnessing the burning of a city. He studied her features, painted with the distant light, was relieved that the beauty of her face was not tainted with an umbra that revealed anguish.

Pollard sat down beside her, could think of nothing to say to her. He turned his head toward the mesmerizing spectacle below. It was as if the invisible hand of a giant was striking matches along Main Street, so rapidly were the new fires popping up, driven by a steady breeze from the southwest. The halo of light widened over the center of the city, stretching toward the heavens, and every few seconds it was pierced by the graceful curve of an artillery shell.

Letha raised her chin, shifted her weight slightly. "Dante's inferno is spread below us just now. I wish that I could remember his lines, those powerful three-line stanzas. It is strange that I cannot remember them, given the sight before me."

"It is a terrible and awesome sight indeed."

"On the morrow they will come—our conquerors—but they will find their prize very meager."

He nodded. "They did not come for the city proper, but for its spirit of resistance. They will not care about the ash heaps."

"Nor the people."

"Some of them will not, but most will. Lincoln will. He will care greatly." He paused and could not wipe away the thought, or the profound desire to express it. "They are but men, like any of us. Like me, Letha. I could have been one of them, if circumstances had dictated. And I would have cared about the people."

"The vagaries of this life are unfathomable, aren't they?"

"Mostly."

She lifted her hand from her ankles, swept it grandly over the scene. "Does the hand of God preside over this inferno?"

"I want to believe that the inferno is man's creation alone."

"You *want* to, Granville, but do you?"

"I cannot say."

"I myself was once evermore certain of your wish. But no longer. I see a Hades down there too large to have been created only by the hand of man." Letha stared with flat eyes at the city aflame before her.

The fire was audible now, a growing wail of the banshee. With a high smoky arc, a shell streaked above the fiery glow, then descended with a thunderous crash.

"Don't forget where Dante ended his journey," Pollard said.

Letha sighed, lowered her hand. "Yes, yes. I remember the beautiful Beatrice, Granville, and the earthly paradise atop Mount Purgatory, and the throne of God, and angels, and all of the grand story." She moved to his side, touched her head to his shoulder, felt the encircling embrace of his arm. "But it was only a lovely story, Granville. Only a story." She reached up with an open palm, caressed his cheek. "You held me through the night of blood. Would you hold me now through the night of fire, if I asked you?"

"Only my death could keep me from it."

"But I cannot ask you. We must return to the men."

As the early morning sunlight blended with the firelight, two black carriages, each drawn by a single horse, clattered through the smoke along Main Street. Ensconced within the ornate carriages were the mayor of Richmond and five of his most trusted city officials. They wore dark frock coats, stiff white collars encircling their necks, short stovepipe hats sitting squarely atop their heads. Each man also wore a stony visage, his eyes directed precisely forward. They passed below Chimborazo at a measured, funereal pace, and though none of the men dared voice it, each believed that he was riding toward the Union Army to bury the city for all time. The mayor, who had not wept during the four years of war, clenched his teeth with a grim resolve, swore silently over the image of his father's grave that he would not blubber in the face of the victors. He would give them the keys to the city, but his soul would remain locked away in a place that they could never touch.

He relaxed his jaw muscles and spoke evenly. "Proceed apace, driver. I wish for this to be finished."

Pollard shook his head, looked up in disbelief at Letha, whose hand rested on the quilt-covered shoulder of the man who had clung to life through the night. "It seems nearly impossible that he still lives."

"I have long ago ceased to be amazed by the resiliency of some of these men."

From outside the building, a voice pierced the morning. "They're a-comin'! The Yanks are a-comin'!"

Pollard and Letha hurried to the edge of the hill, looked down on the transcendent scene. A compact body of immaculately uniformed Federal cavalrymen rode down the street, their mounts handsome and well-fed, hooves clattering on the hard-packed earth. The formation of men and horses was a precise moving rectangle, as if the riders knew that they were being judged.

The advance party disappeared into the smoke of Main Street, but the sound of thousands of footfalls soon replaced the rhythm of horses' hooves, and with it came the first strains of "The Star-Spangled Banner" as the infantry came phantomlike from the smoke. It was a blue sea of soldiers, well accoutered and robust. The wind freshened and parted the dark billows. Regiment after regiment, the irresistible sea rolled forward.

Letha looked on in awe at the antithesis of the ragged, often shoeless mass of the Confederacy. "My God, how could we have ever believed that we could defeat that?"

Pollard sighed, remembered the might that radiated from the tall masonry walls of his father's foundry back in Pittsburgh, thought of the tons of armaments that had belched from one end of the complex. "Davis and Lee—and thousands of others—must have thought that the will of their soldiers could overcome anything."

"And you?"

"A blinded fool."

The band music faded into the distance, but still the troops filed down the street. Finally, the rearmost ranks came into view and marched with jaunty strides over the footsteps of their comrades.

Pollard shifted his weight over his prosthesis, adjusted the pinch of the crutches in his armpits. "Well, the city has new owners. It can only be a matter of days before the entire Confederate Army capitulates."

He felt the warmth of Letha's hand on his own, the touch of her cheek to his shoulder. She took his right crutch from him and let it fall to the ground, then wrapped her arms around his waist, snuggled the side of her face into the folds of his shirt. She began to hum the chorus of "When This Cruel War is Over" and he joined in, comforted by the familiar resonance growing in his throat and chest.

They finished the final note, held it in the air as long as breath sustained it. She did not move her head, tightened her hold around his body. "Oh, sing for me, Granville, please sing for me. Sing the first verse, sing it slowly. Sing for us all."

> Dearest love, do you remember, when we last did meet,
>
> how you told me that you loved me, kneeling at my feet?

Three hundred feet below the crest of Chimborazo Hill, the beautiful tenor notes carried down to the ears of men who longed for homes hundreds of miles north. A wan smile moved the lips of a Union soldier who marched at the end of his rank, nearest the foot of the hill, and he discreetly turned his head and peered upward, but like a mystical sentinel, the unknown soloist was protected by the smoke.

The soldier moved his head back to the front, fixed his gaze on the head of the trooper in front of him. He spoke softly; only the soldier beside him heard the words. "It's a natural fact that some of these Southern boys can sing like angels."

The man first answered with a cock of his head, then pushed out the low rumble of a laugh. "You suppose, do you, Miller, that angels've been shooting at us for four years?"

"Reckon not, Conley, but if that boy up there on the hill is a Rebel, it's enough to make a man wonder."

> Oh! How proud you stood before me, in your suit of gray,
> when you vow'd to me and country to be true throughout the fray.

# CHAPTER TWENTY-SEVEN

Cloyd Anderson had no clear idea of how he had finally located Chimborazo Hill. Three days had passed since the muzzle blast of the cannon deafened his left ear and addled his brain. Sometimes he was able to think clearly, but never for more than a few moments at a time. In his lucid moments, he fashioned mute prayers with the stub of his tongue, asking for the complete return of his mind, and he believed that the clear moments would soon stretch into minutes and then hours. Still, he sought the merciful Angel of Chimborazo and the surgeons whose aid might be required. Cloyd did not consider it a sin to believe that God would possibly need the assistance of human hands and brains to bring him healing. In fact, since he was a child, he had been taught to believe that God helped those who helped themselves. So he stood now, in a crystalline moment, watching from a small copse of saplings the end of the great blue river of men that had just flowed beyond Chimborazo.

He knew that he had finally found the city of Richmond simply by following the firelight at night and the columns of dark smoke by daylight. Even when his mind refused to function properly, the eerie light drew him, a moth to the flame. At times, as he made his way east from Appomattox, he registered twinges of guilt about walking away from his regiment, but he had done it in the light of day, had even bade farewell to his sergeant with a penciled note of apology. The weary sergeant simply nodded his head in approval. He also instructed him to walk east, keeping the bank of the James River on his left-hand side, and that if his mind took a bad spell and he found a river on his right-hand side, it would be the Appomattox River. He would then only have to point his nose north by northeast and he would again run into the river leading to Richmond.

As Cloyd began to walk toward the gray maze of identical buildings, he suddenly remembered that Letha Bartlett's ward was near the edge of the long hill, and he quickened his pace. He smiled, the memory of the winsome face of the matron and the sandy-haired man who sang the heavenly tones limpid in his brain.

Arm in arm, Letha and Pollard stepped up onto the porch of the ward. As Letha reached for the door, Pollard glimpsed a man staring at the adjacent building and he turned his head, focused on the face of the raggedly clad man.

"Wait," Pollard said. "Look next door."

Letha turned her head, drew in a quick breath. "Is it . . . yes, it is Cloyd Anderson."

She helped Pollard secure the other crutch, then walked directly toward Cloyd, waving her hand as she greeted him. "Mr. Anderson! Over here, sir!"

Cloyd did not hear her, but the green of her dress flashed into his vision and he spun to his left, blinked her into focus. He held out his right hand as he closed the distance separating them.

Letha grasped his hand with both of hers, said, "My word, Mr. Anderson. What a surprise." She made a cursory appraisal of his condition, judged that nothing was amiss with his limbs. He wore a forage cap, a gray waistcoat streaked with dried mud, and serviceable trousers of brown homespun. The handle and cylinder of a Navy revolver protruded above his belt. The outside two toes of both feet were visible through the tops of tattered brogans. She searched his face, could discern no change in the ropy scars that were his cheeks. It was the look of his eyes that gave her pause, caused her to ask the question.

"Are you . . . well, sir? Do you hear me clearly?"

He narrowed his eyes for an instant, then opened them widely as he pulled his right hand free. He dug his fingers into his coat pocket, pulled out the stub of a pencil and several scraps of paper. After sorting through them for the least used, he poked the others back, indicated that he wished to write.

"Yes, certainly, but let's join Mr. Pollard over there. He is most anxious to see you, I'm sure."

Even before Cloyd had stepped onto the porch, he extended his right hand to Pollard, who shook his hand and said, "Cloyd, it is good to see you." Pollard glanced at Letha before addressing Cloyd. "Are you all right, sir?"

"Let's go inside," Letha said.

They sat at the kitchen table, and Cloyd pursed his lips and labored over the paper. He finished the note, looked up. He turned his head to the right, exposing the left side of his face, pointed to his ear. Pollard and Letha both noticed the black powder burns that pockmarked his cheekbone and upper neck. Cloyd made a fist, then popped it open near his ear, his fingers propelled outward.

Pollard nodded. "A shell?" Cloyd shook his head, extended his arm straight from his body, again made the mock explosion with his hand. "A cannon blast? Was it a cannon blast, Cloyd?"

Cloyd nodded vigorously as he shoved the paper across the table. Pollard picked it up, held it so that Letha could also read it.

*IT MIXD ME UP SOME TO. I COME AND GO SOME TIMS IN MY HED.*

"I think it will get better over time, Mr. Anderson. I will get a surgeon to tend you soon, but I think that you just need to rest a while. We have ample food now, at least for a time."

Cloyd nodded his understanding, walked his fingers over the table like a stick man, then pointed toward the road below Chimborazo Hill.

"You saw them come?" Letha asked.

He nodded, opened his eyes wide, slowly stretched his arms to their full length.

"Yes, they were many."

Cloyd bent again over his paper and pinched the pencil in his fingers, but the pencil did not move and within a few seconds his hand began to tremble. The pencil fell free on the table and he calmly folded his arms, laid his head on them.

Letha stood, moved to his side, saw his open eyes. "Mr. Anderson, can you hear me?"

She looked at Pollard, shook her head. "I have seen this before, or something like it. But the others came around slowly, always forward, with little regression. And he seemed recovered at first, and now he has relapsed. It is strange."

"Indeed. Perhaps thoughts, or words, trigger something in his mind, make him go back. Who can say?"

The thought coursed through Pollard's brain like a frigid wind. Sooner or later, Cloyd Anderson would likely inquire about Rector Crump, would ask if he had written since his arrival back home. Pollard knew it was selfish, but he hoped that Cloyd would never ask the question, would simply assume that all was well. The unvarnished truth was that the desire sprung from the fear that revisiting Crump's death could prove unhealthy for Letha. The woman's love for him had clearly been rekindled—at least to some degree—and Pollard feared anything that threatened to extinguish the fragile flame, feared it more than the weighty burden of guilt.

Had he known of the fate that would befall the gentle Cloyd Anderson before the dawning of another day, Pollard would have wept.

The Union major opened the door to the building and swept into the kitchen. Trailing in his wake was a young lieutenant, his cheeks still flushed with the events of the grand day of victory. Golden locks fell over the lieutenant's uniform collar, the wispy moustache and goatee adorning his face, little more than the yearning for maturity. The heady days just past had swelled his chest, now prideful and full, and he could scarcely sleep at night; the composition of orations that he would deliver to admiring townsfolk back in Ohio filled his brain, and a thing as trivial as sleep was of no import. The lieutenant's name was Chauncy Cooke, and he would attain his twenty-second birthday in ten days.

The major stood six feet tall, and with the added height of his hat, presented an imposing sight as Letha peered into the kitchen through the open doorway to the ward. She looked over her shoulder at Pollard, who stared, motionless, at the visitors. Letha registered a twinge of apprehension at the proximity of the officers to Cloyd Anderson. Pollard had convinced her to leave him at the kitchen table, where he had apparently slept for the last five hours. She studied Cloyd for signs of awakening as she walked toward the kitchen, but he remained absolutely still, his forage cap resting beside his head.

When she entered the kitchen, both officers removed their hats, and the major bowed slightly from the waist. "Madam, I am Major John Sadler and this is my aide, Lieutenant Cooke."

Letha steadied herself with a deliberate breath. "I am the matron of this ward, under the direction of Dr. James McCaw, chief surgeon. What is it you wish of me?"

"I am merely taking stock of the situation, as are other officers about the complex." He nodded his head deferentially, said, "It is a vast complex. Your labors here, and those of others like you, must have been magnificent."

Letha ignored the compliment, her features set in stone. She waited until the silence took on a sound of its own, saw the major stiffen. "I ask again," she said. "What is it you wish of me?"

"How many patients remain?"

"Ten."

"Ambulatory?"

"Five at most. Do you intend to move them?"

"Most likely within the next several days. We have our own wounded and sick to place."

"And where will you place ours?"

"That is yet to be decided. My superiors are in consultation with Dr. McCaw. We will give you as much notice as possible."

"How generous."

Sadler looked past her into the ward. "I have a detail outside that will soon come around and take up any weapons the patients have."

Letha smiled crookedly. "These men have no fight left in them, Major."

"Yes, well, just the same, I have my orders. We want no surprises, you understand. Certainly, we expect no . . ."

Sadler hesitated, distracted by the sight of Cloyd Anderson pushing slowly up from the table. From his position, Sadler could not see below the top of the table, but Lieutenant Cooke could, and he spied the revolver jutting above Cloyd's belt. Cooke looked quickly at the face of the awakening man, was stunned by the skeleton-shaped face with the sunken, scarred cheeks and the cloudy eyes. Cooke saw, too, the man's long, thick fingers creep over the table and curl around its edge.

"S—sir, this one has a sidearm in his belt."

Sadler took a sudden step toward the table, pointed at Cloyd's waist. "Slowly, and with two fingers only, place that weapon on the table."

Letha took a step toward Cloyd, but Sadler quickly raised his arm in front of her. "For God's sake, major," Letha said. "This man is deaf in one ear and mute. He's confused. Let me—"

For reasons no one would ever know, Cloyd sprang up from his chair and it clattered to the floor. Cooke took a step backward and with one smooth motion drew his own revolver, trained it squarely at Cloyd's chest.

"Dear God! You fool!" Letha shouted at Cooke.

She again attempted to reach Cloyd, but Sadler's arm was a solid barrier, and when Cloyd saw the woman bounce off of the long blue arm, the cause for all the alarm became clear to him. *They just want your gun, Cloyd. Lay down the gun.* He groped for the handle, closed his right hand around it, but the muzzle did not clear his belt.

The unearthly roar of Cooke's revolver rolled down the aisle. Pollard staggered onto his crutches, raced to the kitchen. Cooke stood, mouth agape, the muzzle of his revolver leaking a thin column of smoke as it rested at his thigh. He spoke in a squeaky whisper. "I—I—he was going for . . . I didn't know if . . ."

Sadler silenced him with a look, then said, "Holster your weapon, Lieutenant, and close your mouth."

Pollard let his crutches fall to the floor, knelt beside Letha, who had ripped open Cloyd's shirt. The hole in his chest was near the top of his ribcage, where it curved toward the sternum, and Letha's hands methodically swept away the blood—one hand quickly followed by the other—as if the useless mopping could somehow cause the wound to disappear. Other than the rapid movement of her hands, Pollard could discern no sign of despair. It was when he placed his hands over hers, stopping their movement, that he first heard the discordant, tuneless humming rising from her throat.

"Letha! Letha, listen to me," said Pollard. "It is no use. Turn away . . . please." He grasped her by the shoulders, gently pushed her body away from the scene.

Pollard leaned his head close to Cloyd's mouth, heard the wet sounds of impending doom. "Cloyd, can you hear me?"

He moved his head a fraction of an inch, rolled his eyes toward Pollard. His mouth opened, but he could make no sound. The fingers of his right hand crept over his chest, past the wound, and dug into the wadded cloth of his shirt.

Pollard groaned inwardly, reasoned that the dying man wanted to write a note, but there would not be time. He smoothed the cloth, located the shirt pocket, felt the harmonica and a single scrap of paper, one edge moist and crimson. He pulled it free and saw the block printing of Cloyd's hand. Cloyd's head moved up and down twice, and then he released the final wheeze of breath, his eyes set in death. With a thumb and forefinger, Pollard closed the eyelids. He looked down at the note.

*WHOSOMEVER FINDS THIS PAPER NOS THAT I HAVE CROSD OVER TO THE OTHUR SIDE OF THE RIVIR. THAT IS ALLRITE. I HAVE NO BAD FEELINS TOWRD ANY MAN. EVN YANKES OR EVN GOD. THES ARE THE LAST WORDS OF CLOYD ANDERSON.*

With the harmonica and the note clenched in his right hand, Pollard reached for his crutches, grasped the handles, and settled his weight over the prosthesis. Sadler took a step forward to offer assistance, but Pollard shook his head, struggled alone until he stood. He shuffled into a position directly facing the officers, looked past Sadler's shoulder at Cooke, but the young man could not meet his eyes.

Within the last minute, Pollard had sketched the outline of a withering tirade that he intended to sear into the brain of the lieutenant. But with the passing of each second, the words on the note pushed aside the hateful intentions, and he spoke without rancor. The unadorned truth would mete out abundant punishment.

"What is your name?"

"Ch . . . Chauncy Cooke."

"Well, Lieutenant Cooke, I should like for you to know something of this good man whose life you have just taken. Were it not for his spirit—which infuses me just now—I would do my utmost to darken the remainder of your days on Earth in such a manner that would cause you to despise yourself. But he would want me to do no such thing. He came here for the first time with his tongue and teeth shot out, but still tried to smile. And even with no tongue, he tried to play this instrument." Pollard raised his hand, turned the harmonica slowly for a moment. "But we shall hear it no more. We shall see the smile no more." He sucked in a quick breath, steadied himself, looked down at the bloodstained paper. "He communicated with little notes, like this one. It will perhaps become for you a keepsake of the war. Something to balance your victorious pride. " He paused. "You found the courage to shoot him. Can you find the courage to read this?"

Pollard extended his hand, held the note in his fingertips. Sadler turned his head slightly, nodded toward Cooke. The lieutenant took a halting step forward, then two more, finally raising his hand to accept the note. His chest rose and fell quickly, as if he had just run the length of the long building. He lowered his head, read the words, then spun on his heel to face the wall.

Pollard said, "Major, I would ask two small favors of you. First, send for Dr. McCaw, whose assistance I require in tending our matron. Secondly, after I have had the honor of mopping this man's blood and cleaning him properly, a burial detail would be most appreciated. I would perform the duty myself, but as you may note, my condition is ill-suited for grave-digging."

"By all means, sir." He removed his hat, shook his head. "This is most regrettable. I—"

"It is not necessary to say anything more, Major. Only the two favors, if you please."

. . .

McCaw strode into the room, followed by a Federal surgeon and two aides. Pollard had managed to draw water and locate rags with which he had cleaned Cloyd's body and cleared most of the blood from the floor. Cloyd's shoes were bound together with a thin strip of cloth and his hands were arranged over his chest. Pollard sat beside Letha, an arm around her shoulder, her head resting against the wall. She no longer hummed, only stared at the body stretched before her.

McCaw looked at Pollard, remembered the first time they had met, regretted that he did not recall his name. "Ah, so we meet again, sir. Forgive me for not holding onto your name."

"Granville Pollard, Dr. McCaw."

McCaw knelt down, touched his hand to Letha's, then placed it on her cheek. "My poor Mrs. Bartlett, do you hear me, my dear?"

Letha made no response, began to hum in unrecognizable notes. Her fingers were clenched whitely in her lap. McCaw stood, turned to the Federal surgeon. "Colonel, please have your aides assist me in taking this lady to her quarters."

Pollard followed them into Letha's bedroom, watched as they settled her on the bed. The blue-clad surgeon motioned for the aides to depart, then he raised his hands, shook his head. "A most unfortunate incident, Doctor. I regret this deeply."

"Thank you, sir. We will make do. Hardship is no stranger to this place."

The officer nodded curtly, turned, and walked from the room.

McCaw studied Pollard for a moment, thoughtfully stroked his moustache. "Did you witness what happened?"

"No. I rushed to the kitchen after the shot was fired."

"Without doubt, she was close."

"It could not have been more than a few feet."

"The deceased, did she think highly of him?"

SING FOR US

"Very, as did we all. He was a remarkable man who could communicate more affection without a tongue than we who speak."

A faint rumble grew in McCaw's throat as he nodded. "Yes. Yes, I remember the case. Major Crawford told me of it. The surgery of the maggots."

"The same."

McCaw closed his eyes for several seconds as he tapped his thumbs together. He gathered the quilt at the foot of Letha's bed and drew it up to her shoulders. He approached Pollard, said, "You are the singer Mrs. Bartlett told my wife about."

"Yes, sir."

"Did you manage to get her to sing after the suicide incident several weeks ago?"

Pollard sensed a change in McCaw's tone. It was unthreatening, but somehow disconcerting—a thin cloud that filtered the sunlight. "Yes, as a matter of fact I did."

McCaw nodded slightly. "This good woman's war is finished, Mr. Pollard. We must make her well again and send her home."

A silence grew, the thin clouds shielding the sun thickened. "What if she has no home to return to?"

"In that case, Mrs. McCaw and I will ensure her safety and well-being, for as long as necessary. I have asked far too much of her, and now it is my honorable duty to restore her, to the best of my abilities." He looked down at her again, then said, "And where is home to you, sir?"

Pollard balanced a lie on his tongue, weighed the consequences, swallowed the unclean taste of it. A man such as McCaw could be dealt with only with truth. "Pennsylvania."

McCaw looked directly at him now, unblinking. "Most unusual."

"Indeed, sir. I came to the South to study music, fell in love—with a woman and the Cause."

"And that woman?"

279

"She informed me in a letter that . . . a man in full was required."

McCaw nodded, pursed his lips, asked quietly, "And this woman?"

*There can be no turning back now, Pollard. The die is cast.* "I am a man somewhat undone physically, Dr. McCaw, but my mind has always been my greatest asset. I could have found a way to the trains and departed with the others, had I desired."

"None of the trains were pointed at Pennsylvania. Is that why you stayed?"

Pollard's head moved slowly from side to side. "If my wealthy father, who has disowned me, took a miraculous change of heart, and dispatched private transportation to fetch me home to become owner of his foundry, I would refuse it. Unless Letha Bartlett came with me."

"And were she able, would she go with you?"

"My heart answers 'yes,' but only she could say."

McCaw turned slowly, walked back to the bedside for a moment, arranged the quilt around Letha's body, though it was unnecessary for purposes of her comfort. He required a minute of reflection, a brief interlude outside the zone of intensity that radiated from Granville Pollard. He returned to Pollard.

"Well, Mr. Pollard, I can only say to you now that this lady's health is paramount, wouldn't you agree?"

"Most assuredly, sir."

"I am certain that Mrs. McCaw will come at once to attend her. Hopefully, this darkness will pass, as did the initial episode, and then she may make whatever lucid decisions she chooses." He cocked his head slightly, pushed up his moustache with his upper lip. "But if it does not pass quickly, we will take her to our home and make whatever decisions we deem in her best interest."

"I understand what you are saying, Dr. McCaw, and I understand what you are not saying as well."

McCaw eyed him silently, displayed no emotion. "Good, Mr. Pollard." He motioned toward the ward. "Mrs. McCaw will assist you with the patients who remain. I doubt that it will be a problem for more than a few days. They will be sent to Camp Jackson. As will you, sir, when the Federals decide to claim this place."

Pollard knew that he would never go to Camp Jackson—it meant a greater distance between him and Letha—but he did not allow the knowledge to surface, said only, "I appreciate all of your assistance, Dr. McCaw." McCaw nodded curtly and walked away.

Letha opened her eyes, stared at the naked planks of the wall. She had heard the conversation between the two men, had desired to hear it, felt no remorse from what was, in truth, a deceitful silence. She listened as Pollard shifted uneasily on his crutches, knew that he was watching her. The image of the bullet hole in Cloyd Anderson's chest—the awful, leaking, dark red cavity that could not be sealed—flickered over the gray boards, but she would not again close her eyes to the harshness of the world. A good man's troth was extended to her, as surely as if a precious stone set in a ring lay in his palm. She raised her hand and extended it behind her, fingers open and seeking, knowing that Pollard's would quickly find them.

He hurried to the bedside, laced his fingers with hers as he knelt on the floor, pulled her toward him. "Letha. Thank God you are all right. I thought . . . oh, God."

Letha placed her other hand around the back of his neck, buried her face in his chest. "How much of the inferno must we endure, Granville? Will we ever see the view from atop Mount Purgatory?"

"Yes. The day will come."

"You will take me there?"

"Somehow, I swear it."

Letha hid the mournful smile on her lips, loved him for the gallant vow; despite the fact that he was without means to fulfill it, the vow was no less real. She held him tightly, allowed their world to shrink within the confines of the small room, knowing that in the room his pledge could not be put to the test.

"Hold me again, Granville. Hold me tightly."

He lifted her head, tenderly framing her face in his hands, kissed her eyelids, tasted the salty tears. His lips brushed her cheeks, then quickly found her mouth, and she did not resist. The passion rose within them—the gentle fire of a first kiss—and it replaced the spilled blood of friends and the looming unknown. And for Letha, with the kiss came surrender, the ardor causing a certain rearranging of possessions loved and stored within her. A husband long dead, and Nathan Fisher, and Crump, and Cloyd Anderson—their memories could no longer be allowed to claim the places in her soul where passion deserved to live. It was the sweet abdication of her soul that filled her now, the mysterious exchange of death for life.

Pollard moved his lips to her ear, whispered, "With all of my soul, I do love you so."

"And I you, Granville Pollard."

"Enough to marry me, such as I am?"

"Yes, such as we both are."

# CHAPTER TWENTY-EIGHT

Catherine Pollard peered from her bedroom window at the juncture where the waters of the two broad rivers churned together as one and became the Ohio River. As was her penchant in times of contemplation, the young woman's fingers twirled slowly through the thick ringlets of wheat-colored hair that lay upon her right shoulder. Her vantage point on the second floor of the stately brick mansion afforded her the view of a queen looking down on her domain, and though even queens could not claim to possess wild rivers, they could possess cities, and the girl imagined that she ruled over Pittsburgh as it lay nestled between the brawny arms of the Allegheny and Monongahela. She was eighteen years old—older than some of the queens who had ruled in far lands— and who had, with the mere flick of a finger, decided if subjects lived or died. *Cath-er-ine*. She whispered her name, weighed the three syllables, wondered if her father had considered them regal when he named her.

If Catherine were queen, she would bring Granville home.

The sun was low in the cloudless sky and the rivers clung greedily to the light, the scant leavings unable to penetrate the city beyond the first row of buildings. Her gaze drifted, as it always did, eastward down the north bank of the Monongahela, and locked onto the dark walls of her father's foundry, and Catherine knew that a king ruled.

Catherine turned from the window, walked to the dresser, and looked down at the two letters that lay side by side. She picked up the single-paged letter that she had read two dozen times since its arrival weeks before. The envelope was addressed to her, not to the king, and she knew that her brother had done this to ensure that the letter would be read and not tossed into the fireplace. It contained not a single note of self-pity, was bluntly informative in describing the one-sided contest between flesh and metal projectiles, and made no mention of Lucy Penders. It was this omission that had caused Catherine to write Lucy and delicately remind her that Granville would need her now more than ever, and that thanks to God were in order for the fact that he had survived, had not changed in his sum and substance.

Catherine returned Granville's letter to the dresser, touched her fingertips to the three-page letter from Lucy Penders, knowing that she would not again read it. One reading had proven sufficient, and Catherine was uncertain why she had not already destroyed it. The letter was, from a literary standpoint, quite remarkable—structured with a thorny beauty—and she surmised that its haunting connection to her brother had stayed her hand. But the destruction would soon take place, literary quality be damned. In the end, it amounted to nothing more than the cold rejection of her beloved, wounded brother.

Catherine had of course shared with her parents the sad news contained within both letters—had, in fact, no choice, since it was her mother who always received the mail. On both of the fateful days, the stoic wife of the king had inquired soon after Catherine had retired to her room to read the letters. Catherine had simply handed her the letters and watched as her mother sat in the high-backed chair near the window. After reading Granville's letter, she wept silently—having long ago acquired and cultivated this most useful skill—and when she stood and placed the letter on the seat she had just vacated,

Catherine noticed only the slightest quiver of her chin. Weeks later, at the reading of Lucy's letter, Catherine thought that she detected the crooked lines of anger around the woman's mouth, but one could never be certain about such things. Her father's reaction to the news, if any, remained unknown to Catherine, and she knew of the possibility only because she had confirmed with her mother that the passing on of the information had taken place.

Catherine returned to the window, looked again across the rivers at the city, then the foundry. It would be a high time in the city for days and weeks to come. Richmond had fallen, the word having arrived only hours ago. Her father, all full of himself and euphoric, had just proclaimed it upon his arrival home from his duties at the foundry. The despicable Rebels—the trash who would render the nation asunder and enslave men—had been at last squashed into submission. The fact that his only son had been mutilated in the process had no apparent effect on the righteous vibrancy of his voice.

The supper hour had arrived, and Catherine steeled herself in preparation for the conversation that would ensue around the dining table, then chided herself as she realized that it would not be a conversation, but rather the required attendance at the king's court. She walked to the dresser and picked up Lucy's letter, carried it to the fireplace, and tore it into three neat strips. She reached down and laid the paper on the iron grate. Tonight, after supper, she would instruct the butler to build a small fire just before bedtime.

On the morning of the wedding, Hannah McCaw walked to the azaleas that grew on a sunny upslope fifty yards from her back door. The first offerings of spring were white and pink in hue, though not yet robust in their growth, and Hannah regretted that the wedding was not a week hence. But the floral arrangement that would adorn the table in her parlor would have to suffice. Given the pace of events swirling through the former capital of the Confederacy, a week was a very long time. With a small pair of scissors, she snipped the flowers and placed them in her basket, then turned and hurried toward the house to complete the preparations.

The grandfather clock in the foyer chimed the three-quarter-hour notes preceding eleven. Hannah poked at the azaleas a final time and then straightened the large family Bible positioned beside the flowers. In fifteen minutes, the Reverend Elias Burnett—now stuffed into his Sunday clothes and talking in muffled tones to Dr. McCaw—would read from the good book and intone the words that would create the legal and improbable union of Letha Bartlett and Granville Pollard.

It was with considerable reluctance that Dr. McCaw had agreed to allow the ceremony to take place in his residence. His admiration and respect for Letha could not have been greater, yet his doubts about the worthiness of Pollard were of equal weight. The discussion between Dr. and Mrs. McCaw had been lively, though, as always, within the bounds of proper decorum. Hannah had prevailed, but by the slimmest of margins. Letha was obviously of sound mind, Hannah had reminded Dr. McCaw, and her spirit seemingly restored in large measure, albeit subdued—more peaceful than joyful. But that was to be expected; on the whole, the times were less than joyful for Southerners in the city of Richmond in early April of 1865.

For all his initial bluster, Dr. McCaw, once convinced that the marriage would take place with or without his blessing, had decided to wield the weight of his position to substantial advantage. The Federal officers with whom he now worked had shown him, and the remaining patients, the utmost respect and consideration. The horrific incident resulting in the death of Cloyd Anderson was simply one of the war's grotesque aberrations. Dr. McCaw's request that Letha's ward be left unchanged as long as possible had been granted, largely as an attempt to remove the cloud hovering from Cloyd Anderson's unseemly killing.

The living arrangements for her and her husband-to-be were accepted without so much as the raising of an eyebrow. It was understood that the couple would continue to care for the few remaining Confederate patients until such time as the new owners made a decision regarding the ward's further use. McCaw was informed that this occurrence was likely to take place within perhaps two or three weeks.

The bride and groom stood now, facing each other, hand in hand. Hannah McCaw's eyes focused with a will of their own on Pollard's crutches, then down to the crude prosthesis, and she released a small sigh of disappointment. He was a handsome man with fine features and possessed a voice said to be nearly angelic. He was well educated, articulate, and his love for and commitment to Letha were beyond question. Hannah herself had lent encouragement to the relationship during Letha's first convalescence in the McCaw home. And yet . . .

Hannah looked back toward the table with the azaleas and the Bible, but despite the enchanting sight, the thought pierced her—Granville Pollard was a footless man without a country. And he was about to wed a woman whose soul had been shredded by dealing with the results of four years of abject slaughter, a woman whose own home had been stripped as if by a plague of locusts. And although Letha appeared stronger now, seemingly of sound mind, the previous breakdowns might well portend even more dreadful agonies of the psyche.

It was with great effort that Hannah stuffed the troubling introspection into a compartment of her brain and fixed a smile on her face. She walked toward the bride and groom to ask them to proceed to their places in front of the new azaleas and the good book.

The countenance of the king was not altogether kingly, and for this fact Catherine Pollard was thankful; it represented one fewer obstacle to be overcome in the saving of her brother from the dread unknown. Her father stood now, quartered toward Catherine, one hand resting on the wrought iron railing of the balcony, the other cupped precisely around of the bowl of his pipe. The cool evening breeze whisked eastward the little clouds of gray smoke, toward the juncture of the rivers and the city beyond, and Catherine knew that his thoughts were on the far bank and that she could safely study him from the living room as she summoned her courage. Three days had passed since the glorious word had arrived from the tiny crossroads in Virginia named Appomattox. The war was won.

Sterling Pollard's features were distinguished, though in Catherine's mind, not molded in the fashion of men who ruled foundries and swayed the course of wars. His hair was trimmed precisely around the curvature of his ears and allowed to fall only to the top of his coat collar. His nose was straight, nearly delicate, his lips thin, chin more rounded than square. He was clean-shaven, but years before, when Catherine was a child, had sprouted a moustache for a short time, only to appear at supper one evening without it. She vaguely remembered having made a giggly comment about the appearance of his upper lip, but she distinctly remembered the withering sidelong glance from her mother, and her father's appearance was never again the subject of conversation.

Sterling Pollard carried himself in the manner of a man much taller and heavier, somehow able to infuse his physical body with the invisible powers he possessed over men and things of iron, though it was only during the final year of the war that Catherine had gained this insight. Influential men had visited the Pollard mansion—men with imperious visages and broad shoulders and voices that were better suited to commanding than requesting—and Catherine had watched, unseen, from the safe shadows of the house as her father, in no more than a conversational tone, had caused their metamorphoses into obeisant men.

And yet, despite the respectful distance she always accorded her father, a bond existed between father and daughter, albeit more spiritual than physical. That they were much alike in spirit had only recently been revealed to Catherine. A week before, surrounded by three male acquaintances, who in turn had made thinly veiled references to Granville, she suddenly felt the blood of the king coursing through her veins. It was like flexing a powerful muscle that had never been tested. Speaking precisely, and in the conversational tone favored by her father, Catherine asked them just how it came to be that they had been granted godlike powers of discernment and knowledge about her brother. The question—or more likely, the unexpectedly cool, cutting manner with which it was posed—had a rapier-like effect, and as if shoved backward a step by unseen hands, her would-be tormentors babbled apologies until she decided to sheath her weapon. It was marvelously heady— yet frightening—this power of the tongue, and bewildering beyond measure as she later pondered it in the solace of her room. The same endowment that had allowed her to gallantly defend her brother was bestowed by the father who had used it to excise from the family his only son. It was an unknowable riddle, a secondary aggravation that for now did not matter. What mattered now was the knowledge that Catherine, daughter of the king, possessed at least a bit of his efficacy, was not wholly defenseless.

Sterling Pollard released twin streams of pipe smoke from his nostrils as he turned his head toward his daughter's approach. "I feel as if I am posing for a portrait, and in poor light, no less." He smiled thinly, made a motion with his pipe hand. "Join me."

Catherine walked to his side, placed her hands on the railing. "I'm sorry, Father, I did not mean to be rude."

"Not at all." He drew on the pipe. "You are in a contemplative mood?"

She nodded, drew in the familiar aroma of smoke and cologne, and said, "Yes, I am that."

"I suppose that I am also." He pointed toward the dark ribbons of water and the city beyond. "It is a time of fulfillment, Catherine, a time of victory for our city, our nation, and yet for me there is something of a void in it all."

Her heart fluttered. *A void! Oh, God, let the void be Granville, please.* "How so, Father?"

"I have been a part of a four-year effort to save this nation, and four years is a very long time. And now, it is suddenly and irrevocably finished. The final word of the most historic chapter of the Pollard family has been written."

Catherine felt the rush of hope leak from her and chastised herself for giving life to the fairy-tale wish. She gathered her wits. "Yes, it will be different, Father, but will not the foundry—and our family—carry on as before? You will simply make things other than cannonballs and tools of war, as it was before."

"Of course, of course, the business will carry on quite well, no doubt." He raised his head, drew on the pipe, pushed out the smoke with a soft whoosh. "But it can never matter as much as it just did, and in that fact lies a worthy lament."

"I understand about the business, and the war effort that is now past, but . . ."

"But?"

Catherine felt her fingers tighten around the cool iron railing, sensed that the balcony was soon to become a boat in a storm-tossed sea. For a moment she floated above the calm sea, looked down on herself and the king who awaited her reply, sought a way to lessen the coming tempest, found none.

"The family, Father—it is the family that I so wish could be made whole again."

The silence thickened for long moments, became one with the gloaming. "Do not raise that subject, Catherine."

"I must. He is part of our family."

"He was, but is no longer." He paused, stiffened. "You know full well that it is a forbidden subject."

"Grant me this, Father. Grant me one conversation and I will speak to you of him no more."

"It is a waste of your time."

"But you will grant it."

He turned toward her and met her gaze, respected her courage, saw himself in her eyes. "Speak your piece, Daughter, and in the doing, be rid of him."

"He fell in love, Father, in a land to which you sent him. A land to which he did not wish to go. He was charmed by a beautiful woman and a beautiful city, and he was such a young man."

"He was old enough to make decisions about right and wrong."

"'Right' and 'wrong,' you say, but how can you hold a young man in love to such a strict standard? In 'rights' there are some 'wrongs' and in 'wrongs' there are some 'rights.' He was swept away by something immense, Father, as big as love itself, and by a cause that the woman he loved whispered about in his ear."

"So you wish to speak of causes. Let me educate you about causes—right and wrong. It is, and always will be, something of a thorn in my flesh that I did not personally take up arms against this insurrection. It was by the highest authority that I was finally convinced that I could be of more service here than on the battlefield, and I must admit that I see the wisdom in that now. The point being that I would have gladly shed my blood, blood that might have been spilled by him. Him, and his cause that would rend asunder our nation. Him, and his cause that would shackle human beings and tie them to the whipping post."

"I cannot believe that he—"

Her father silenced her with a withering glance. "Whether or not he took up arms with those specifics in mind is irrelevant. He stood shoulder to shoulder with men who *did*, with all their hearts, believe in those dark causes, and he fired hellish missiles at men such as I, and no doubt maimed and killed some of them." He paused, rapped his pipe on the railing three times, the meeting of wood and iron a drumbeat in the dusk. "Those, Catherine, are the cruel facts about causes. The only facts that matter."

She felt the heat of his eyes but did not avert her gaze, knew that if she did all would be lost. She wondered if her mother stood below them, listening and praying in the shadows. "Were his sins committed against you, Father, or God?"

He recoiled inwardly from the sting of the question. "You tread perilously close to blasphemy, Daughter."

"So be it. Will you answer my question?"

"I believe that you have already made up your mind about the answer."

"I too am hurt by what he has done, Father, and I know that my hurt is but a trace of what you must feel. But Granville has not sinned against me or you, despite your great pain."

"How wise you must feel yourself, to make such a statement."

"I claim no great wisdom."

"That is good to know."

"How can you forget the price he has paid, Father? His wounds are terrible. Can you not allow for that to be at least something of a penalty for his wrongs?"

"His mutilation represents nothing more than the manifestation of his 'wrongs,' as you say."

Catherine lowered her head, the futility closing around her throat like a strong pair of hands. It was time to play the final card. "I have been reading my Bible daily, father."

"I would expect no less of you."

"I have read the same story every night for the last week."

The heat in his eyes abated, and she knew at once that he had seen her card. He said, "Ah, yes, the great old story of the prodigal son. I am intimately familiar with it."

"Then I ask you to do what the father in the story did."

"The son in the story did not even steal anything; he only asked for his inheritance before he should have. My son stole honor. My son has caused a chorus of whispers behind my back and a hundred sidelong glances, and he has caused the Pollard name to be denigrated. No, it is not the same." He looked away. "Were it only money, I would gladly forgive the debt. But it was honor, and honor once stolen may not be repaid."

Catherine blinked at the tears welling up in her eyes, could not distinguish anger from sadness, feared that they would always be the same. She clenched her teeth. She would not allow him to see her weep.

The king spoke softly now, as softly as she had ever heard him speak. She ignored the touch of his hand on her arm. "I am truly sorry for your sake, Daughter, but that is my final word on the matter."

He turned quietly and walked away. Below her, Catherine heard the soft rustle of a dress, the careful closing of a door.

# CHAPTER TWENTY-NINE

Granville Pollard opened his eyes from a light and dreamless slumber, the hint of dawn probing the borders of the ragged curtains covering the window in Letha's quarters. She slept, molded to him under the quilts, her skin a velvet garment. He breathed shallowly, lest the wondrous spell of the night just past be broken. The aroma of their bodies was full and earthy and Pollard drank it in as a nepenthe, marveled at the mysterious essence of the flesh that was infinitely superior to the bouquets of expensive perfumes or colognes registered in his memory. He clamped down his eyelids, refused to allow the world outside of the room to take shape. The ubiquitous blue-clad army that slept contentedly in the city was now the army of the entire nation, had been so for six days. *Ap-po-mat-tox*. Pollard silently rolled the lyrical syllables over his tongue, knew that they would ring for centuries to come as reminders of both the rebirth of a nation and the death of a would-be nation, doubted that the minds of men would ever be capable of sorting out the complexity of it all. Now, and only for precious moments, would the army and the future that it represented remain formless and unthreatening, and Pollard touched his lips to his wife's forehead, dared not stir. The gray light seeped into the room, and with it, riding on the sweep of the breeze up Chimborazo Hill, came the distant bugler's clear notes of reveille.

"Are you awake?" she whispered.

"Yes."

Letha moved her head slightly. "I hear the bugle call."

"Did it wake you?"

She rolled her forehead against his chest. "I'm not sure. And you?"

"No, I was awake, lost in your touch."

She made a noise in her throat, pressed her body closer, kissed his chest. "And I in yours, in dreams."

Pollard sighed, traced his fingertips across her back. Outside, the bugler's notes were replaced with the voices of men, the wooden rattle of a wagon, and the world rushed past the thin frame walls. "If we could but remain in dreams, Letha."

"But we may not."

He sensed a tone of worry in her reply and quickly said, "It was just a frivolous thought. We will be able to make dreams of our own someday, beyond all this."

"'Beyond all this' will come very soon, Granville. The days are passing too swiftly. We have little time to decide on where we shall go."

"Beyond all this will be music, my love. I will build us a life—so help me—with my music. I have plans, admittedly modest, given the present times, but plans nonetheless."

He paused to give her a chance to respond, but in the silence her doubt was made known. "Letha, I understand your doubts, but music survives all—even wars—and now there is no more South and North, only one nation," he said. "And this nation will have music at its heart and will have new life breathed into it, and somehow I will force myself into that dynamic and build us a life."

Letha rolled onto her back, gathered the quilts under her chin. "I have great faith in your abilities, and you know that well, but we down here are the defeated. The vanquished. To the victors go the spoils,

Granville, and they are the victors. And this man Lincoln—the power is in his hands now, and I fear him."

Pollard pushed up on his elbow, looked down at her, and shook his head. "I do not fear him."

"How can you not?"

"His dream is unity—one nation. It is not in his interest to keep the South underfoot and downtrodden. He cannot have his nation whole with half of it dysfunctional—from an economic standpoint alone, not to mention the spirit of the people."

She shook her head. "It will take a very long time to heal, even if what you say is true. Especially the spirit of the people."

"Yes, I know, but what I say is true, Letha." She looked directly into his eyes now, but only for a moment, quickly looking back at the ceiling. Pollard continued. "This man is not a bloodthirsty monster. There will be—there must be—a rebuilding of the South."

She looked at him again, her smile rueful. "You seem to know him well."

"My father has been a devoted supporter since the speech at Cooper Union."

"Cooper Union?"

"In New York City, a year before the outbreak of the war. It had a profound effect on my father and many other prominent Easterners like him."

"A single speech had such an impact?"

Pollard relaxed his elbow, released his body into the mattress, and picked out his own focal point on the ceiling. "Actually, it was a single line. The last. It was burned into my brain during my last visit home to Pittsburgh. The rumblings of war were growing even then, and I think that my father sent me back with some reservations, though certainly not about my loyalty. It was simply a matter of my safety. Not in his worst nightmare could he have conceived of my defection."

"Surely your engagement to a Southern girl would have concerned him."

"That had not yet taken place; he considered it no more than a silly infatuation; something that would pass. Then, the night before my departure, he tapped his finger on a newspaper article about the speech and declared that it was the greatest address in the nation's history. He recited the final sentence, and then insisted that I repeat the sentence, hoping, no doubt, that I would be as taken with the sentiment as was he."

"And we know the rest of the story."

"Yes."

A silent minute passed, then Letha said, "The sentence—what was it?"

"He said, 'Let us have faith that right makes might, and in that faith let us to the end dare to do our duty as we understand it.'"

She lay motionless, sifted the words in her brain. "And what of Crump and Cloyd Anderson and the four men remaining in the ward and thousands of others like them? Did they not do their duty as they understood it?"

"Yes, they did."

"And you, Granville?"

"I will never be able to give you—or myself—a satisfactory answer, any more than I could explain the placement of the planets. It was all a great whirl of emotion—a young woman whom I intended to marry, her family, her mother especially forceful, a mansion, a city, the shaking away of my father's iron hand, passionate songs sung in the glow of firelight, a thousand things." He exhaled forcefully. "And, in truth, a selfishness that now seems boundless and shameful." He wrapped his arm around her waist. "My duty now is to you—to us. That is all that I am sure of."

It was enough, the only explanation that she would ever require. Letha, as if watching chalk lines disappear under a rag, eradicated all but the last sentence of her husband's answer. She nestled against him, trusted him.

He brushed his lips over her hair, kissed her ear. "We wandered away from my plans."

"Tell them to me."

"There are still the old singing schools in the rural South—admittedly modest, to be sure, but there must be some that remain and are in need of headmasters. I have asked Dr. and Mrs. McCaw to make inquiries on our behalf. I know that they do not altogether approve of me, but they will do their utmost for your sake—and I feel no guilt at this. All I ask is a chance, however slight, and I will make the most of it. And the skills you have acquired here, along with a letter of recommendation from Dr. McCaw, would help in the beginning. These schools are mostly in small communities, but there is always a country surgeon in need of help." He opened his mouth to say more, but suddenly the spurt of energy waned, and the fragility of the future he offered appeared before him as badly cracked glass—holding together, but susceptible to the next gust of wind.

In the silence she sensed the energy escaping from him, as palpable as the lowering of his head, the slight turning from her. She drew him closer, said, "Oh, Granville, you are enough for me, whatever comes to pass. Don't doubt my faith in you. I only ask that we leave Richmond, at least for a time. I do not wish to deal with the ghosts that linger here."

"Nor I."

# CHAPTER THIRTY

My Captain does not answer, his lips are pale and still;
My father does not feel my arm, he has no pulse nor
will;
The ship has anchor'd safe and sound, its voyage
closed and done;
From the fearful trip the victor ship comes in with
object won;
    Exult O shores, and ring O bells!
    But I with mournful tread,
     Walk the deck my Captain lies,
     Fallen cold and dead.

Walt Whitman

*A half hour before midnight, April 15, 1865*

Sterling Pollard was possessed of the firm belief that the rules of
authentic manhood did not provide for the public shedding of tears,
and that on the few occasions when this marginal activity of weeping

was warranted, the man so affected remain cloistered until the weakness passed. He sat in his favorite high-backed chair, settled in the corner of his snug windowless library, the yellowish light of a low-burning lamp painting the side of his face as a single tear traced its path across his cheek. He was impeccably dressed in a stiff-collared white shirt, silk vest, and a black woolen suit. It was as if he were in attendance at a formal event, even though his next destination was his bedroom. Sterling Pollard removed his silver timepiece from his vest, flicked open the cover and glanced down at the hands. Abraham Lincoln had been dead for sixteen hours. He closed the cover and returned the watch to the vest pocket, raised his head, features set in gloomy meditation.

In the bedroom above her father's library, Catherine sat on her bed, her back molded into the two large pillows leaning against the headboard, covers drawn to her waist. An hour before, she had listened as the opening and closing of the library door signaled the return home of her father and his entry into his sanctum. The day just passed had been one of dreadful silence, her father pacing back and forth in the living room awaiting word from his men stationed at the telegraph office in the city. Catherine and her mother had sat on the divan, hands in laps, stunned and powerless as the tortured man marched with his hands clasped behind his back, muttering under his breath. Catherine had felt no remorse at the cool flood of relief that finally came when her father's men arrived at the front door and spoke quietly and respectfully. He had then simply turned, taken three paces toward his wife and daughter, and announced, "Our president is dead. I have matters to attend to." And with that, he had vanished into the night with the men.

Catherine picked through the string of memories that centered on the great man called Lincoln. That he was cold and dead was somehow a fact altogether unacceptable, preposterous beyond measure, much as the fact that her brother was, in her father's reckoning, the equal of cold and dead. She had seen Lincoln once, a few years before, as she tiptoed beside her father in a crowd as the tall man intoned words that caused the listeners to nod and whisper approval. She had no memory of what he had said, but she remembered what he looked like. It was like remembering a portrait of sorrow. Dark hollow eyes peered from under bushy, hooded brows, and knifelike lines extended from his long nose to the beginnings of the beard that covered his chin, but it was his mouth that defined the sorrow. For it appeared to Catherine that even when he smiled, the other features of his face resented the effort, like fleshy buttresses determined to nullify even the hint of anything other than sorrow.

She conjured up the long face now, wondered if the undertakers could defy the buttresses, or if they should even bother with the attempt. The morbid image was indistinct, and soon Catherine was struck with the realization that another image was superimposed on the gaunt, dead face. She closed her eyes, pulled the clean, youthful lines of Granville's face from the dead man's, framed it in her mind's eye.

"Damn! Damn!" Catherine slammed her fists into the mattress, felt the blood rise in her temples. Below her, a staircase and a few steps away, was a father who had the power to restore life to the son he considered dead, and yet he sat, silent and unmoving, mourning the death of someone else not of his flesh and blood. That the fallen man was president of the United States mattered not a whit. That man had been swept away into the other world, the world where no mortal could wield power, the world to which no mortal could cry out and be certain that his voice was heard. "Damn!" Sterling Pollard, master of vast regions below the heavens, would not lift a finger to succor his only son.

With both hands, she flung the covers from her, swung her legs across the bed, and bounded to the floor. It was when her hand touched the doorknob that Catherine Pollard experienced an image that she would always believe to be divine, even though it was the image of a dead child. Her fingers slid from the doorknob, and she raised her other hand to brace herself against the door. *"My poor boy . . . my poor boy."* The words of the great Lincoln came to Catherine in bold black typeset, as they had appeared below the photograph in the newspaper after the President's youngest child had died three years before. Poor little Willie lay in his tiny coffin, appearing for all to see as a sleeping child who should in the morning rise up and call his beloved papa to his side. She recalled the rumors that had swirled out of Washington—tales of a grieving Lincoln returning to the crypt and having Willie's coffin opened so that he could see the boy yet again. Some claimed that the rumors were just pitiful rantings of the morbidly curious, yet other voices, her father's among them, declared that the trips to the cemetery were absolute fact, evidence of the man's compassion. In her heart, Catherine had always held the stories as truth, and for her there was nothing aberrant in the sad visits, only evidence of a love so deep that it sought to tear down the phantom walls separating this life from the next.

Catherine walked softly back to her bedside, sat down, slowed her breathing. She had nearly made an irreconcilable mistake. It was clear now, this gift from the dead father and son. She would sit for a time, gather her thoughts, then speak to the king with the controlled voice of true power. She would speak to him of lost sons and powers of life below the heavens.

Sterling Pollard heard the soft knock on the library door. A low current of anger, tingly and warm, registered under his skin for an instant before he realized that the intruder could only be his daughter.

He waited for the thing to pass, then said, "Come in."

Catherine padded across the cold floor, stopped at his shoulder, placed her hand on the back of the chair. "I cannot sleep, Father. There is too much amiss about this night."

"Indeed, Daughter, it is a black night. Indeed."

"I will understand if you wish to remain alone."

He raised his right hand, aimed his fingers at the chair beyond the low table in front of him. "As you wish." As Catherine walked to the chair, he discreetly guided a thumb and forefinger over his cheeks, erasing the tracks of his tears.

Catherine curled her legs over the satiny fabric of the chair and arranged her gown. She waited, hoped that he would speak, guide her to a safe beginning, but he did not. She said, "The vice president, Mr. Johnson, is he not a good man, Father?"

"Andrew Johnson is a good man, but he is no Lincoln. The president is not replaceable."

"I believe no person to be replaceable."

He looked at her for a moment, then back at the wall. "I would take issue with that, had I the will to debate."

"I'm sorry, I did not come to debate, only to be with you."

He nodded, made a tent with his fingers, rested it against the bridge of his nose. Outside, a gust of wind wrapped around the corner of the house, then whined away through the barren tree limbs.

Catherine said, "I remember his face from the time I stood with you at the speech. It seems so long ago now, but I remember much about his face. It was the face of sorrow."

"He dealt with more than his share."

"Yes, the burden of the war must have been immense."

"Certainly that . . ." His voice trailed off, as if he had more to say, but held it in a safe place.

A quick spurt shot through the middle of Catherine's chest, rushed to her head, but she calmed herself just before the words tore past her lips. *Willie, little Willie! Oh, let him be the one to go there first. It must be Father that leads us there. Give me words!* She slowly drew in a breath through her nostrils, careful to disguise the filling of her lungs. "I cannot imagine sorrows greater than the war."

He tapped his fingertips together, lifted his head, then placed one hand over the other in his lap. "Those were aggregate sorrows, I suppose one might say."

"As opposed to individual sorrows?"

He nodded. "Yes. Personal sadness. Loss, actually."

*One more step, just one.* Catherine nodded pensively, framed her features in a manner indicating the deep concentration of one sorting through scattered pieces of a complex puzzle. She cocked her head to the side, made him look at her, waited. He said, "I never ceased to be amazed at his management of the army, even after the loss of a young child."

Catherine put her hand to her throat, felt as if her body rocked visibly with each thud of her heart, said softly, "Oh my, yes. Little Willie. I remember reading of the tragedy, hearing the strange stories coming out of Washington. Yes, yes . . ."

Her father had stiffened ever so slightly, and Catherine pretended not to notice. He said, "Strange stories? The visits to the crypt, you mean?"

"Yes, that rushed to mind. The very thought is heartbreaking."

"Why do you consider the accounts strange?"

She shook her head apologetically. "I . . . well, there are those who claim that it was all wild rumor."

The granite that was his face did not change, the modulation in his voice did. "I believe it beyond all doubt. The naysayers only wish to paint his portrait as one-dimensional, devoid of compassion, and he was not that."

*It must be now. There will be no second chance.* She gathered herself, trusted the mettle that had passed from father to daughter, felt it course through her veins. "I'm certain you are correct, Father. Great men—all truly great men—must possess a great element of compassion."

Sterling Pollard moved only his lips, formed the semblance of a grim smile, joyless and insubstantial. The die was cast. She could only wait as the seconds oozed past like long drips of water sliding from the point of a leaf.

He sighed audibly, leaned slightly forward in his chair. "It would hold, then, that you do not consider me a great man."

Catherine felt her legs uncoil, guided by impulses she did not command, and she slid from her chair, walked quickly to him, kneeled in front of him. She placed her hands over his, laid her head on his right knee. "That is not so, Father. I know that you are a great man."

He moved his fingers over hers and patted them. "I fear that I am lacking an element of greatness."

She rocked her head back and forth on his knee. "You lack nothing, Father. Nothing."

He lifted a hand, held it over her head for a moment, then stroked the silky strands of hair covering her shoulder. "Leave me be for a time, Catherine. Go to bed. Just leave me be for a time."

Catherine sat in a chair in the corner of her bedroom, feet tucked under her body, two thick quilts gathered to her chin. She had drifted in and out of sleep, somewhere in the netherworld between dreams and substance, and the stiffness that had settled into her back and shoulders told her that several hours had passed. At first, she thought the soft knocking on her door was at the edge of a dream, but it grew more distinct, took on the waking sound of knuckles on wood.

She sucked in a quick breath as she opened her eyes and blinked in the candlelight. "Come in," she said.

Sterling Pollard opened the door and stepped into the room. "I have come to the conclusion that I do not consider myself a great man, but, in deference to you and your mother, I will attempt to make some arrangements concerning your brother."

"Oh, Father! Father! You'll never know how much this—oh, thank you!" She tossed the quilts aside, started to leave the chair, but he lifted a hand as he shook his head.

"Do not thank me, Daughter. I confess that my heart remains hollow, and I make no predictions about when it might change. I am unable to muster an apology for that to anyone ever." He paused, made it clear that what he had just said was set aside, finished. "I shall contact my friend, George Peabody, of Baltimore, to whose fund for the building of the Peabody Institute I have contributed substantially. Now with the war concluded, his institute, and the academy of music within it, will be completed in short order. I am certain that he would be receptive to finding a low-level position for your brother, despite his disgrace. In the morning I shall contact the military and dispatch my men to find him. They will give him a letter of safe passage and money to provide for his needs in the beginning. They will direct him to living quarters in Baltimore. Then I will have done my part."

Catherine wept silently, waited for his final words. He stepped back into the doorway, said, "I only wish that I could grant the whole of your desires, Catherine, but as I said, I am not a truly great man. Such a man perished a few hours ago."

# CHAPTER THIRTY-ONE

"Snowden." Letha said the name softly, turned it over on her tongue. "It has a peaceful sound to it."

It was the name of the town to which Letha and Pollard would journey. Tucked into the extreme northeastern corner of North Carolina, the tiny community said to have been spared the ravages of war, to have felt only the hot edges of the thing as it roared both south and north of the town and up and down the Atlantic seaboard.

From his chair beside the little table in Letha's quarters, Pollard smiled, nodded in agreement. "Yes, it does. Quiet and peaceful."

Letha closed the top of the storage trunk and fastened the leather strap that held it in place. In the morning, when they departed Richmond, the trunk would contain every earthly possession they owned. The horse and carriage into which it would be loaded belonged to Dr. and Mrs. McCaw, although the means of transportation was arguably a gift, since the doctor and his wife had made it clear that they were unconcerned about when the horse and carriage were returned. Pollard suspected—and Letha was certain—that the McCaws would have declared the transportation an outright gift if not for the matter of protecting Pollard's self-esteem. So they had not spoken of it.

"We shall never be able to repay Dr. and Mrs. McCaw. The width and breadth of their contacts and influence is amazing," Pollard said.

"I don't think repayment is an issue with them, Granville. They wish us to have a new beginning, an opportunity."

"But I shall repay them for everything it's possible for me to repay—the horse, the carriage, provisions. All of it."

Letha walked to the table, sat down across from him. "In time, perhaps." She took his hands into hers, saw the great foundationless hope in his eyes, knew that she would always have to be the realist. "In the beginning, about all that we will have is each other, Granville, and that is quite enough for me. But I do not want to see you disappointed when we arrive. Dr. McCaw took great pains not to paint an unrealistic picture of the school or its resources."

"Yes, I know. But it is a beginning, however modest."

*For richer or poorer, in sickness or in health.* She nodded, smiled. "Yes, my love, it is that."

She pushed away from the table, walked out of the room and through the kitchen to the door leading to the ward and pulled it open. Behind her, she heard Pollard's crutches tap the floor, then felt his body close behind her. Before them lay the aisle separating the empty beds, the fragile light of late evening bleeding through the makeshift window curtains.

Letha said, "It looks so small without the boys. So very small."

"Indeed it does," Pollard said.

They stood silently, and with the silence came remembrance of the living and the dead—Henry the nurse, shambling down the aisle with a handful of bloody rags, and Avery Crawford, bent like a six-foot sapling in the wind, and Hound Patterson cackling at the sight of the rat surgery that saved his foot, and all the others who lived. And hovering over them, the ghosts of the dead—Crump, his gravelly voice booming up the aisle, and gentle Cloyd, his fingers furiously scratching out a note on a scrap of paper, and Brady Ayden, adrift in the wilderness of his mind, and above them all lingered the pure spirit of Nathan Fisher.

Letha framed the drab room as a photograph in her brain, would always recall the room as it appeared now—colorless in the fading light. She worried that it was not a place suitable for the safekeeping of spirits. The fact that she was about to close the ward door forever weighed heavily on her, caused her to feel as if she were about to commit a betrayal of sorts, or even a sin of omission, unable to adequately honor the living and the dead.

Pollard saw her head bow, her eyes close. He said, "We will not leave them here, Letha, but take them with us always."

"Would that it be so."

"It will be so." Pollard looked past her shoulder, fixed his gaze on a particular bed, then another across the aisle. "Nathan and Crump will see to it."

The road between Richmond and Petersburg was well patrolled by Federal troops, and within the past two hours Pollard had been required to produce the letter from Dr. McCaw and, more importantly, the letter of passage from General Weitzel, who commanded Richmond. The midmorning sun beamed warm and full on the left side of Pollard's face, and as he drove the carriage south he reached up and tipped his hat brim down, his shirt collar up. It had been a long time since the sun had shone too warmly on his face. Letha rode beside him, despite his urgings to take a more comfortable place on the quilts in the body of the carriage.

The distant clatter of fast-approaching hooves on the road mingled with the sound of their carriage horse's hooves. Pollard and Letha looked at one another, assuming that they would again be challenged for their papers. "I don't suppose that they have much else to do these days," Pollard said.

He turned, looked back down the road at the two approaching horsemen, and when he saw that they were not in uniform, a cold hole opened in his gut. He thought of Crump and Nelda, bloodied on another road. "They are not soldiers," he said evenly as he reached down to the floorboard and gripped the revolver. He placed it on the seat between them and said to Letha, "Lay the folds of your dress over it, and lift them quickly if there is trouble. At the same time, fall forward in front of the seat."

She rearranged her skirts. "Surely if they intended harm they would not make such a long and bold approach."

"Agreed. But . . ." He shook his head and began the process of halting the horse.

Pollard glanced back again and saw two riders on beautiful mounts, the men well dressed. It was the sight of the taller man that caused Pollard to suck in a hurried breath. The man was wearing a black bowler hat.

"What? What is wrong?" Letha asked.

"The tall one, in the bowler. He reminds me of someone."

The riders had slowed their horses to a walk, were now only ten yards behind the carriage. "Who?" Letha whispered.

Pollard shook his head and could only say, "A man . . . works . . . for Father."

The lathered horses drew even with the carriage, and Pollard smelled the sweat and the pungent tack. Then a gruff voice that he had not heard in six years broke through the steady rhythm of hoof beats. "Master Granville Pollard, I believe."

Pollard looked into the steely eyes of Issher Rohrback. The goatee and moustache were flecked with white, the long face cast in the mold of one habituated to the feel of power. Broad shoulders held his body ramrod straight in the saddle, his right hand resting easily on the pommel and the reins. A duteous step behind him sat a younger man whom Pollard did not recognize.

"Mr. Rohrback."

Rohrback touched two fingers to the brim of his hat, looked at Letha.

Pollard said, "May I introduce my wife, Letha."

Both Rohrback and the man behind him nodded deferentially, but did not speak. Rohrback pointed toward the folds of Letha's dress and said to Pollard, "There is no need for that. I have been sent as a peaceful emissary."

Pollard said, "I find that difficult to believe, Mr. Rohrback, especially given the assassination of Abraham Lincoln. I would imagine that my father is in a vengeful mood."

Rohrback looked down at Pollard's prosthesis and the trouser flap at the bottom of his other leg. "Much of life is difficult to believe, wouldn't you agree?"

Ignoring the remark, Pollard said, "Deliver his message if you must, Mr. Rohrback. My wife and I wish to be on our way."

The man looked down the road for a moment, then back at Pollard. "Perhaps you are traveling in the wrong direction."

Pollard swallowed and felt a giddy little ripple pass through his head. He could not speak, asked the question with his eyes. "Your father sends much more than messages," Rohrback said.

"I . . . I do not understand."

"No, you do not." He reached behind him and loosened the saddlebags, swung them easily to Pollard, who caught and held them in his lap. "There are important things you will find in there—and there are important things that you will not. The things you will find include a large sum of money—United States currency. And a letter of safe passage from the general who commands even Weitzel. And in case you encounter scoundrels, two fine revolvers that I myself have inspected for proper function. In there you will also find directions to quarters in Baltimore, where the Peabody Institute—including an academy of music—is under construction. Mr. Peabody is to Baltimore whom your father is to Pittsburgh. Upon your arrival, his people will assess your skills and find a position for you."

Pollard looked down, with blurred vision saw Letha's hand on his forearm, the touch weightless and airy. He shook his head from side to side, as if attempting to awaken from a dream.

Rohrback spoke again, did not change the tone of his voice. "Now for the things you will not find. In there is neither forgiveness nor respect. In there is no attempt to understand what you did—only the knowledge that you did it." He paused, made Pollard look at him. He then raised his left arm and placed on the pommel the shiny steel prosthesis that functioned as his hand, looked down at it. "A memento from a little engagement near Gettysburg. You might have heard of it." Rohrback looked back up. "This word is from me. Had your father not dispatched me, it would have been my wish to enter my grave before laying eyes on you again. But now that I have, I would be disinclined to spit up your ass if your entrails were on fire."

The two men turned their horses, but before they could spur them, Pollard shouted, "Why? Why did he do this?"

Rohrback twisted his body in the saddle and shot a final glance at Pollard. "Your guardian angel—Miss Catherine."

The two men nudged the flanks of their horses and rode away at a trot.

Pollard and Letha sat in dazed silence. They felt as if they had just been visited by phantom riders, now returned to the unseen world from which they had swooped. But resting heavily on his thighs was stark evidence of the visitation, and Granville Pollard began to move the tips of his fingers over the leather, closed his eyes against the kaleidoscope of images that crowded every crevice of his brain.

With his right hand he reached for Letha, searched for her fingers, waited for them to lace with his own. He said, "I do not know if we have just been saved or damned."

She fixed her gaze on the road stretching before them, followed it for a quarter mile before it gently curved and was swallowed by a dense copse of spruce and red cedar. "It could be neither. If you choose, you may simply toss the bags in the brush, and it will be as if the men were ghosts. As if . . . he . . . were a ghost."

Pollard raised his head and opened his eyes. He looked down the road and smiled. "Catherine, a child no longer. I have no fear that we shall find one another someday." The smile faded. "As for Father, if only I did wish that he were a ghost . . ." His voice trailed away.

"But you do not."

He shook his head. "No."

"In that case, my love, we must turn the carriage around."

# EPILOGUE

*May, 1880—Baltimore, Maryland*

The solitary man stood in front of the Biltmore Suites Hotel. He wore a fine linen suit and a vest to match, and in the fingers of his right hand he cupped the bowl of a well-seasoned pipe. From the adamantine surface of the street, the slow-paced evening clatter of horse and carriage rolled gently toward him, and on the sidewalk the steady rap of shoes and boots rose and fell in a quiet cadence. The man fussed with his pipe, tamping needlessly at the perfectly packed bed of tobacco, though not in the manner of an unpracticed smoker. He only resorted to the activity on the rare occasions when his brain allowed for disquietude, and even now, he was certain that none of the strangers could possibly know of the tight fist that lay hidden in his stomach.

The man with the pipe paid little attention to the descent from the hotel steps behind him of an elderly couple. He clamped the pipe stem in his teeth and flipped open the folded note on which the desk clerk had written directions. The elderly gentleman spied the note as he passed, and saw him raise his head and look down the street, then back again to the piece of paper.

"I beg your pardon, sir," rasped the old man.

The man jerked his head toward the sound, pulled the pipe from his mouth. Thinking that he perhaps had blocked the path of the couple, he said, "Certainly. Uh, excuse me," and took a step to the side.

The old man's mouth opened—a fleshy gap in the cumbrous face of a bon vivant—as he shook his head vigorously. "No, sir, not at all. I was merely going to ask if I could be of assistance in directing you somewhere. We know Baltimore quite well."

"Yes. Well, that is kind of you, sir, but my directions seem clear enough."

The old man wore his short stovepipe hat cocked at a jaunty angle, and he tilted his head in the opposite direction as if to obtain a proper balance. He said, "Oh, but one can never be certain in the city. I would be happy to make sure." He smiled again, waited.

The fist tightened in the man's stomach, and with it came the prickle of irritation at the nape of his neck. "Well, if you insist. I am attending the performance at the Conservatory of Music . . . very near here, I understand."

The old man's eyes opened wide in delight and his wife broke her silence with a birdlike twitter from behind the black veil hanging from her garish hat. He said, "Oh my, sir, but you are in for a treat! We attended last evening and would return tonight had we been able to procure seats." The old man and his wife exchanged glances, nodded in unison as if they shared a secret too wondrous to explain. He said, "Granville Pollard is the finest tenor we have ever heard, and we have heard many."

From behind the veil spilled the energetic chirp of the woman's voice. "And such a gentleman too, oh, I tell you. He always mingles afterwards with the audience, never in a rush to leave, and—"

"And his lovely wife," the man chimed in. "Such a dark-haired beauty she is. Ah, and the lad looked to be about twelve , wouldn't you say, dear?"

"Yes, dear, and such a rosy young chap, oh—"

He cut her off again. "Oh, we rattle on, sir, but it is with the best of inten—"

With a quick spin to his right, the man with the pipe abruptly walked away.

The old man stared after him, his features frozen for a moment in a crinkled maze, and then he cocked his head, said to his wife, "Well now. He didn't even give us a chance to approve his directions."

"He didn't seem the sort who needs much help, dear."

"True enough." He watched intently as the man strode briskly away, small clouds of pipe smoke marking his departure. "At least he started in the right direction."

# ABOUT THE AUTHOR

Photo © 2014 Stacee Clawson

Born in California, Missouri, Steven Wise lived in North Carolina from 1971 to 1983, where he met his wife, Cathy. Together they have two children and five grandchildren. They currently live in Columbia, Missouri, where Steven owns the commercial real estate appraisal firm of Cannon, Blaylock & Wise. Steven is the author of three previous novels: *Midnight, Chambers,* and *Long Train Passing*.